Who Was Chief of Sexual Sadism at Austin Flint Medical Center?

When a beautiful woman was found butchered in bed at a renowned big-city hospital, it became apparent that something very evil was going on. But it was something that went beyond ordinary concepts of medical malpractice and sexual immorality . . . something as shadowy as a mad person's mind and as deadly as a surgeon's scalpel. . . .

Dr. Paul Richardson, fighting to prove his innocence, and struggling to keep his love for a woman whose secret shame was laid bare to him, had to unmask that evil, no matter who among his respected colleagues it hurt. He must let nothing stop him—no matter what it revealed about a once-respected institution built to serve and heal people, and now perverted to manipulate and destroy them. . . .

INFORMED CONSENT

INFORMED CONSENT

by
Harold L. Klawans

A SIGNET BOOK

NEW AMERICAN LIBRARY

PUBLISHER'S NOTE

This novel is a work of fiction. Names, characters, places, and incidents either are the product of the author's imagination or are used fictitiously, and any resemblance to actual persons, living or dead, events, or locales is entirely coincidental.

Copyright © 1986 by Dr. Harold L. Klawans

SIGNET TRADEMARK REG. U.S. PAT. OFF. AND FOREIGN COUNTRIES
REGISTERED TRADEMARK—MARCA REGISTRADA
HECHO EN CHICAGO. U.S.A.

SIGNET, SIGNET CLASSIC, MENTOR, ONYX, PLUME, MERIDIAN AND NAL BOOKS are published by New American Library, 1633 Broadway, New York, New York 10019

First Printing, October, 1986

1 2 3 4 5 6 7 8 9

PRINTED IN THE UNITED STATES OF AMERICA

──Prologue──

leven, twelve, thirteen. Every member of the jury was present and accounted for. Paul Richardson studied each of them individually as they came out of the jury room, then scanned the mismatched group as a whole. His best guess placed the jury somewhere between 350 and 400 pounds overweight, but that was probably a conservative estimate. He always was conservative in assessing just how overweight people were, especially himself.

Paul had been careful to apportion a smile to each of the jurors as they filed in. He was feeling pretty confident despite the prickly discomfort of his gray worsted testifying suit. Up until a year ago, Paul had consistently made good on his vow to wear suits only to funerals. But when the lawyers insisted that the jurors wouldn't believe an expert witness if he weren't "properly attired," ultimately taking their argument, and Paul, out shopping, their reluctant witness could only agree to wear the suit they picked out for him and paid for. Paul looked down at his feet. He had worn the appropriate shoes and his socks matched both his tie and each other.

The twelve jurors were now seated in the jury box. They watched Paul as he stood in the witness stand. The one alternate sat alone just outside of the box inspecting her fingernails. She was the youngest, no more than twenty-three or -four and not at all bad-looking. Though she was about fifteen pounds too heavy and wearing clothes that were more than just a bit too tight, Paul had to admire the intriguing distribution of her excess weight.

5

He had impressed them yesterday. His testimony had gone well. He had taken his time and looked at each of them, first one and then another, as he had given his expert opinions. It was an old trick but to a real pro that kind of technique came instinctively. Talking to a jury was not that much different from giving a good lecture. To be effective you had to talk to each listener as an individual and to the group as a whole at the same time.

The black foreman had liked him. So had the old lady in the back row. He was always a hit with the old ladies. Then again, he was probably the only witness who had paid any attention at all to her. Strange, how it all became a contest. He was an expert witness for a woman whose life had been ruined by a hack surgeon. As an expert he should only be interested in the truth, but since he was also concerned with justice he did care who won the case. The three-piece suit, the eye contact, and even the old lady in the back row all were by-products of Paul's absolute certainty that Courtney was a butcher who had damn near killed Mrs. Martin by out-and-out malpractice.

"Order in the court." The bailiff's announcement broke the spell. "Circuit Court of Illinois. Martin versus Courtney *et al*. Judge Frank O. Mancuso presiding." As soon as the judge entered the courtroom the high-pitched voice once again boomed out its message. "You may be seated."

Paul sat down.

"Dr. Richardson."

"Yes, Judge."

"You understand that you are still under oath."

"Yes, your honor."

With that the judge turned to one of the defense attorneys and said, "You may begin your cross-examination."

For the first time that morning, Paul took a good look at his adversary. He looked to be in his middle forties. Just about Paul's age. Average height, average weight. With a good head of hair graying tastefully at the temples like an ad for Grecian Formula. Paul knew without checking that his socks matched his tie and obviously each other. Paul was sure that he made a good impression on the jury. A nice, solid, hardworking guy. Nothing flashy. Just trying to do an honest job for his misunderstood client.

Paul had been through this all before, more than once. Despite the competition, he was sure that the jury was still with him. They were as overweight as he was.

The attorney advanced very slowly until he stood about six feet in front of the witness stand. He slowly looked at each member of the jury and finally let his gaze rest on Paul Richardson. Very effective use of the silence. Paul hoped he'd get a chance to use that ploy himself sometime soon.

"Dr. Richardson."

"Yes, sir." Always be polite.

"My name is Henry Arft. I represent the neurosurgeon in this matter, Dr. Charles Courtney. By the way, do you happen to know Dr. Courtney?" As he asked this question, Mr. Arft stepped to the side and nodded ever so gently toward his client. Dr. Courtney was seated at the defense table. He was tall, well over six feet in height, with a full head of wavy gray hair. The perfect picture of a quiet, confident surgeon whom every patient could trust implicitly. No Grecian Formula for him. There was only one minor flaw in the image: he had already been thrown off the staff of half a dozen hospitals for a list of medical misdemeanors that would choke a horse.

"Personally? No, sir," Paul replied.

"Do you know any of the defendants in this case?"

"No."

"Dr. Garver?"

"No."

"Dr. Kokos?"

"No."

"Nurse Moss?"

"No."

"Are you familiar with the Marion Memorial Hospital?"

"Not really."

"Fine. Now, Dr. Richardson, I am not quite sure that I understand your criticism of my client, Dr. Charles Courtney, in this case. You have, of course, read all of Mrs. Martin's records, and as far as I can tell, you think Dr. Courtney did only one thing that was a deviation from the accepted level of practice."

"Yes, sir, as far as I am concerned as a neurologist.

Whether or not his surgical technique was within the acceptable standard of care—''

"I know that this is an issue here," Arft interrupted him. "But, Dr. Richardson, you are not an expert on neurosurgical techniques."

"No," Paul admitted. You didn't have to be an expert to know that Courtney was a butcher. He had all the finesse of a left-footed elephant.

"Then you have no criticism of the surgical procedure itself."

"That is outside my area of expertise, so I have no opinion." Legal opinion, that is.

"You have no criticism of the need for the operation?"

"I would not have advised it."

"But advising it was not something that was truly negligent?"

"No."

"Then what, pray tell, is your criticism?"

"Dr. Courtney failed to obtain informed consent from Mrs. Martin."

"And that's all?"

"Yes, sir."

"And how did that harm Mrs. Martin?"

"The failure to adequately explain the possible risks as well as the potential benefits of the surgery deprived Mrs. Martin of the information she needed to judge whether or not she should agree to the procedure—''

"How did that—"

"May I finish my answer please?"

"I'm sorry. I thought you had finished. Go on," Arft conceded. One point for the good guys.

"The failure to inform the patient of the exact risks inherent in the operation led Mrs. Martin to agree to the procedure. Had she known all the facts, she would not have been willing to undergo the operation. As I understand, she herself testified to that. And so did her husband. Had she not undergone the operation, it is obvious that the mistake that took place in the operating room—''

"Dr. Richardson! Judge!" Arft interrupted forcefully. "This witness is not a witness on surgical technique. I move that his last statement be stricken from the record and that the jury be instructed to disregard it."

"I will do so, Mr. Arft." Judge Mancuso gave the appropriate instructions to both the jury and the court reporter, then warned Dr. Richardson to limit his testimony to his own areas of expertise. But Paul had managed to express his honest opinion and the jury had heard it. Another point for the good guys.

"What is informed consent, Dr. Richardson?" Mr. Arft asked.

"Whenever you are going to do any procedure to a patient that has any significant risk, any chance of causing harm, he or she must be informed of all the risks and must agree or consent. Hence, informed consent."

"Is it necessary for all surgical procedures?"

"Absolutely," Paul said.

"Why?"

"Because all such procedures involve some sort of risk."

"What makes you such an expert on informed consent? After all, you are not a surgeon."

"Several things. My training as a physician. My role as a medical educator. But mostly my experience in doing clinical studies on patients. In such studies we are very careful to ensure that their rights are protected."

"Clinical studies. Doesn't that mean experiments carried out on people?" The concept apparently left a bad taste in Arft's mouth.

"Yes," Paul admitted.

"I am sure we would all agree that in such experiments, experiments performed on seriously ill patients suffering from terrible diseases, every step must be taken to protect their rights, in fact, their very lives. That is something we all accept. But such human experimentation using patients as guinea pigs is very different from a routine surgical procedure, isn't it?"

"No, not really."

"How can that be?"

"The absolute rights of the patient must be fully protected in both instances." One more for their side.

Henry Arft had clearly lost this round. Paul could see it in the eyes of the jury. They had heard what he had said. They understood the issue very clearly. Courtney had never explained the risks. Mrs. Martin didn't know that anything could go wrong. She was sure the operation was as safe as having a tooth pulled. That's why she agreed to it. But during that surgery something had gone very wrong, indeed. Mrs. Martin, now paralyzed from the neck down, was living proof of that. Whether Dr. Courtney had made a mistake in surgical technique was only a secondary issue. His failure to obtain informed consent was enough to nail him.

Mr. Arft had a few more questions to ask.

"You know the role Ms. Leslie Moss played in this matter?"

"Yes, she was the nurse in charge of Mrs. Martin."

"Was it her job to inform Mrs. Martin of all the possible risks including paralysis?"

"No, not at all. The surgeon must do that."

"Then what mistake did she make?"

"She allowed Mrs. Martin to go to surgery without a signed consent form on the record."

"And Dr. Kokos, the anesthesiologist?"

"He put the patient to sleep without checking for an informed consent on the chart."

"And Dr. Garver?"

"Same problem. He assisted in surgery on his own patient without—"

"An informed consent." Mr. Arft finished Paul's answer as a prelude to his next question: "And is the hospital negligent also?"

"Yes."

"Why? No, let me guess. For allowing a patient to be operated upon without informed consent."

"That is absolutely correct."

Paul did not understand Henry Arft's change in tactics. He seemed to have changed sides. It was as if he were making the case for the plaintiff, not the defense. And very successfully, too.

"You think informed consent is very important."

"Yes," Paul agreed.

"And that the failure to obtain it is a serious mistake?"

"Yes," Paul again agreed.

"A woefully negligent act?"

"Yes."

"Bordering on the criminal?"

Why was he asking that? Paul wondered as he answered with yet another "Yes."

"I have nothing more, Judge," Mr. Arft said.

"We will take a twenty-minute break," the judge announced. "The witness is excused unless Mr. Cooper has anything to ask in redirect."

"No questions, your honor."

The judge hit the gavel on the desk once and disappeared through the back door of the courtroom. The jury stood up and filed out across the platform toward the jury room.

Paul got to his feet, more than ready to make an escape. He looked toward the plaintiff's desk.

"Great job, Paul."

"Thanks, Mort. Good luck."

With that Paul turned to leave the courtroom, but found his path unexpectedly blocked by Henry Arft.

"Dr. Richardson."

"Yes."

"I have something for you." With that he handed Paul a folded set of papers.

Paul slowly opened them and read the title: McCormick versus Richardson, Lenhardt, Austin Flint Medical Center *et al*. "What the hell is this?"

"Just what it says. You're being sued by Mr. Frank McCormick."

"Frank McCormick?" Paul repeated. "What for?"

"Malpractice. Professional negligence."

"What?"

"The surgery you advised him to undergo has made him worse."

"I'm not really convinced that that is true," Paul said. "And besides, it was an experimental procedure and he knew it."

"Are you sure he knew that?"

"Of course. I obtained the informed consent myself."

"Are you certain?"

"Definitely."

"That's peculiar. There's no informed consent on the chart. In fact, Dr. Richardson, your failure to obtain informed consent is one of the major issues in the case." Henry Arft was smiling.

Paul now understood the change in tactics. Arft had been trying the next case and had used Paul as an expert witness, an expert witness against himself.

"That's a bogus issue. Informed consent was obtained. I even remember who witnessed it."

"Who?"

"Jackie Baumer?"

"Nurse Baumer?"

"Yes."

"I'm afraid that won't help your case very much."

"Why not?"

"She was killed this morning."

"Killed?"

"Yes. It was the news this morning."

"I never listen to the news in the morning," Paul said softly, shaking his head in disbelief. "Killed?"

"Stabbed, I believe. Several times."

"Where did it happen?"

"In her apartment, right across the street from Austin Flint."

"Why?"

"Who knows?"

The recess was almost over. As Paul walked out of the courtroom, Henry Arft gave him one last parting shot. "See you in court, Dr. Richardson."

1

"I was walking down a street. It was very dark. The streetlights were on, but they were very dim and flickered a lot. They didn't give off very much light.

"Suddenly I heard these screams. They were terrifying—absolutely horrible. They didn't even sound human.

"I looked up at the buildings. They were all very old. Somehow I could tell exactly which one the screams were coming from. I'm sure I'd never seen that building before, but it seemed strangely familiar to me.

"Then the screams stopped. It was dead silent." Frank stopped and was also silent, as if his own behavior both emphasized and gave deeper meaning to the brief interruption of action that had occurred in his dream.

Geraldine Scala said nothing. She had been Frank's therapist too long to be that easily manipulated by him. She just sat quietly at her desk and waited patiently for him to resume his story, trying not to let her mind wander during his dramatic pause. Sometimes, like today, that was particularly difficult. She wondered how Paul's testimony was going. Probably just as well as he'd predicted it would. Too bad Frank McCormick's progress wasn't matching up to Paul's original prediction.

The operation had really been Paul's idea all along. One of his brilliant hypotheses. One that, unfortunately, hadn't worked out very well. It wasn't entirely clear why Frank hadn't improved. He had been the perfect candidate: bright, young, articulate, well-read. Probably too well-read. His withdrawal into a world of books had, in retrospect, been one of the first signs of his schizophrenia. In the first six months or so following the operation, Frank had shown a marked improvement, but now he was much less in touch with reality than he had been before the surgery and far more paranoid. She might have to put him on a major tranquilizer. Haldol or perhaps Thorazine. She'd have to discuss it at one of their weekly research meetings.

"Aagg!" Frank's outburst startled her. "It was a terrible scream. I can still hear it. It came from the fourth floor. I went into the building. It was cold and damp. I raced up all four flights of stairs as fast as I could.

"The screams had stopped.

"The silence was as terrible as the screams had been.

"I took an ax." Where had he found an ax? she wondered. "And smashed in the door.

"The apartment was a shambles. The furniture was broken and scattered all over. There was just one bed and the mattress had been thrown into the middle of the room. On a chair I saw an old fashioned straight razor. It was smeared with blood—fresh blood. Bright red blood. I touched it. And I tasted it.

"On the far wall was a fireplace. There was no fire in it.

"But there I saw some patches of hair. Long blond hair. The strands were hanging straight down into the hearth, dripping blood."

Dr. Scala stopped fingering her own long blond hair. Frank McCormick was not looking at her. He was lying on the small couch staring at the ceiling.

"I looked in the chimney.

"There was a body inside it. A woman's body. It had been shoved up the chimney, head hanging down. Blood was oozing from her neck. I pulled and the head came off in my hands."

He stopped again.

Once again Dr. Scala waited.

Frank kept looking at the ceiling. She kept waiting.

"That's all there was, Dr. Scala," he announced.

"Did you recognize the woman?" she asked.

"Yes."

This was quite different from the free associations she did

with most analytic patients. With Frank she had to be directive if they were ever going to get anywhere. "Who was it?"

She waited. He would tell her, but she would have to be patient. Was he consciously aware of the obvious sexual connotation of the chimney? A female sexual organ he wanted to enter, to enter for the first time—hence, the blood.

She had waited long enough. "Who was it, Frank?"

"You."

"Are you sure?"

"No. I thought it was you. But when the head came off, it wasn't you any longer, it was . . ." He stopped.

The hour was almost over but she knew it would be better not to force the issue.

Still she waited.

"My mother," he said softly.

Gerri realized all too well that it would not be safe to pursue the sexual nature of the dream any further. Not with Frank. This dream was just too violent. Too blatantly destructive. He was not stable enough to go into it any deeper.

"I tasted the blood."

"From the razor?"

"Yes." He paused. "And from her neck."

It was 11:30. Their session was over.

Frank got up quickly, as if it had been just another session, and said good-bye. He would be back again to see her on Friday.

Gerri began to write out her notes on the session, when the phone rang. It was Detective Ward from the Chicago police department. He wanted to talk to her about the murder of Jackie Baumer.

"Are you sure you want to talk to me?"

"Yes."

"But I hardly knew her."

"That may well be," the detective replied. "But it's important that I talk to you today, if at all possible."

"I'm very busy."

"It will only take a few minutes," he insisted.

"I have a meeting at twelve, but I am free until then."

"I can be in your office in three minutes."

"Look, Detective Ward—are you sure you want me? There's a Dr. Scala in Pathology. I often get his mail."

"Yes."

"Why me?"

"We found a picture of you in Baumer's apartment. Torn in half and covered with blood."

She hung up the phone and hurried to complete her notes.

There had been blood on the razor and on the torn photograph.

Had he tasted it?

What a horrible thought. Frank had hardly known Jackie. There was no real connection between the two of them.

It had only been a dream.

Only a dream. A peculiar phrase for someone trained in analysis. There was no chimney in Jackie's apartment and she was far from being virginal. That was one fact with which Gerri was all too familiar.

She shuddered. Whether she liked it or not, Frank McCormick was getting crazier. That too was a hell of a term for a psychiatrist to use, but it was accurate. He was getting crazier.

The courthouse was less than two and a half miles from the Austin Flint Medical Center but the noontime traffic was at a standstill. It was that way whenever it rained and today it was raining for the eleventh day in succession. And it was not a light warm mist, but a cold, driving downpour. Like so many other Chicagoans, Paul took a perverse pride in such days, as if Chicago had a unique claim on such intolerable weather. The Windy City had just breezed through its mildest winter on record. That it was followed by the coldest, wettest spring in over four decades seemed all too appropriate.

Umbrellas clogged every intersection. It was a lousy day for a ballgame. Luckily the Sox were on the road. If this had been a home stand they'd probably have been scheduled to play at night. By then it might actually clear up, but the outfield would be a swamp. Paul finally managed to get a cab. The ride took forever.

Jackie Baumer dead. Killed. Murdered. He remembered the first time they had made love. And the last time. That had been only a few months ago. Some acting-out on his part, and as always, she had been willing and available. Now she was dead.

Frank McCormick. That crazy kid. Of course that was why

they had operated on him. For schizophrenia. A brain implant. And it had been his idea. Now that McCormick was worse, maybe he had a right to sue. But Paul had warned him and his father that something could go wrong. Hell, he was sure he had a copy of that informed consent in his office. Or at least pretty sure.

It was five after twelve when the battered Yellow Cab without any shocks let him off in front of the medical center. He was already late for the research meeting. What a juxtaposition. One minute he was being sued for negligence in human experimentation and the next he would be running a meeting set up in part so that he could oversee the proper protection of patients' rights and safety in neurological and neurosurgical research. It was a crazy world, full of crazy people. Not all of whom were patients, he reminded himself.

As soon as he walked into the office, Chris, his secretary, greeted him with a message: "Dean Willis wants to talk to you. He says it's urgent."

"With him it's always urgent."

"It's about some lawsuit."

"Bad news travels fast. Is everyone in the office for the meeting?"

"Bud's making rounds."

Paul nodded. He didn't expect Bud Chiari to make the meetings when he was in charge of the clinical service. "How about the others?"

"Everyone's here but Dr. Scala."

"She's always late."

"She's a psychiatrist," Chris explained.

"That's no excuse. We'll have to start without her. I'll call the dean afterward." He hesitated. "They all know about Jackie. I mean about her . . ."

"Yes."

That had been an unnecessary question. Of course they all knew about it. Every hospital in every city Paul had ever known functioned as a small town within a town. From the coffee shop to Recovery, information spread as if by osmosis.

Paul really didn't feel up to discussing Frank McCormick and other research projects today, but he had to. Science had to march on.

While the rest of the group exchanged greetings, Richardson settled at his desk. Everyone had some coffee and there was his usual large glass of orange juice waiting on his desk. Paul tried to drink two full glasses of juice each day. Not for the vitamin C. He just loved orange juice. He took a couple of swallows and turned to Don Lenhardt, the chairman of Neurosurgery and second in command on the clinical-research team.

"What's on the agenda today, Don?"

"Three things, Paul. First the final protocol for the brain implants in Parkinson's disease. Then we have a new patient to discuss, a man who has just been admitted for the experimental epilepsy surgery. And we have a follow-up of sorts."

"Let's start with the protocol," Paul said, turning to Floyd Baker.

For someone who had been fairly close to Jackie Baumer, Floyd Baker seemed unperturbed. Correction: Baumer and Baker were rumored to have been fairly close. Paul had no firsthand knowledge of the nature of their relationship, nor did he know whether they truly ever established one at all. Sexual activity alone, as he well knew, did not a relationship make.

Floyd presented the final draft of the protocol. It was straightforward enough. The subjects would all be Parkinson patients who were severely disabled and no longer responded to either standard or experimental medications. The procedure would be an implant of tissue from an adrenal gland, which Don Lenhardt would place inside the patient's brain. The risks were the usual surgical ones and they seemed to be fairly minimal. It was unlikely that the patient's Parkinson's disease would get worse.

They had done the same sort of procedure on McCormick—an adrenal implant—though the indication was very different. Because he had schizophrenia and not Parkinson's disease, the surgical team implanted the tissue into an entirely different region of the brain, but all in all it was pretty much the same concept. And Frank McCormick had certainly not gotten any better.

As Floyd outlined each step in the surgery and the care and evaluation of the patients, Gerri Scala tried to slip quietly into the room. She couldn't. It was too crowded and the only empty chair was all the way across the room so that she had to walk right in front of Floyd Baker and in front of Paul's desk. And besides, as Paul reminded himself, she was too damned good-looking to sneak into a room full of men. That long blond hair was just too long to ever be inconspicuous.

Floyd finished.

"Any questions or criticisms? If not, we will send the protocol on to Human Investigation for their approval." There were not questions. "Okay? What's next?"

"Dr. Richardson?" A hesitant question. From someone he did not know. A girl. A woman, rather. A big woman. Big-boned, tall, full-figured, but not at all unattractive. Renoir would have approved of her well-rounded figure. Paul must have been very preoccupied to have missed her.

"Yes?"

It was not the girl but Bill Goodman, his senior resident, who answered. "This is Edie Robinson. She's a senior student doing a three-month rotation with the research group."

Then Paul remembered. "You are interested in going into neurosurgery."

"Yes. Dr. Lenhardt suggested I might do this to get more of a taste of both neurosurgery and neurology."

"Very good. What was your question?"

"I didn't understand why you want to do an adrenal transplant in the first place."

Paul looked at his watch. She was right. They had raced through the protocol. That was okay for him and Floyd Baker and Bill Goodman and maybe even Don Lenhardt, but the others were not neurologists. This was the first time they had discussed the project fully. Edie was not the only one who deserved a better presentation. The neurosurgery resident, Marvin Rickert, and his own lab technician, Herb Adams, and even John Corrigan would profit from it.

"Edie, what's wrong in the brain of a patient with Parkinson's disease?"

"There's no dopamine."

"None at all?"

"No. Not none at all."

"Try to be more specific. What's the basic problem in the brain in parkinsonism?"

"The cells which make dopamine—" she started.

"Which ones?"

"The ones in the substantia nigra."

"Right."

"Those cells die and so they don't make any more dopamine."

"Correct," Paul told her, and then asked her another question. "Now, where does that dopamine act in the brain?"

She thought for a minute and shook her head.

"You did very well. Bill."

"The striatum."

"Precisely. So, in Parkinson's disease we have a lack of dopamine in a specific part of the brain, the striatum. Now, Herb . . ."

"Yes, sir."

"I think you can answer this one. It's a chemical question, not a clinical one."

"I'll try."

"Dopamine is related to what other chemicals made in the body?"

"That's easy. Adrenaline and noradrenaline."

"Since that was so easy, let's try another. Where is adrenaline made?"

"In the adrenal glands."

"That's right. So . . ."

"I get it," Edie spoke out.

"What's that?" Paul asked her.

"The whole protocol. You're going to transplant adrenal-gland tissue onto that part of the brain that has lost its dopamine and hope that the cells will grow and produce adrenaline or something else related to it that will replace the dopamine."

"That's it. In a nutshell."

"Will it work?"

"Of course," answered Don Lenhardt.

"I'm not that absolutely confident," Paul added. "It works in some animals. Whether it will in patients remains unanswered. That's why its called human experimentation."

Seeing that the first item on their agenda was completed, Bill Goodman brought up their newest problem. "Mr. Rogovin died."

"What happened?" Paul was surprised, but no one else seemed to be.

"He turned sour about ten o'clock or so last night," the resident began. "Dr. Lenhardt came in. So did Dr. Baker. We were going to do a spinal tap and a CAT scan to see if he had bled again from his vascular malformation. But he arrested before we could do anything, and we couldn't resuscitate him."

"When did he have his surgery?" Paul asked.

It was Don Lenhardt who answered this question. "Last Wednesday."

"Six days post-op," Paul observed.

"Yes."

Paul began to think out loud. "I guess we have two major possibilities. He could have bled because our procedure didn't completely eliminate his malformation. Or maybe he reacted to the agent we injected, the JNF-2."

"We've been through that, Paul," John Corrigan said. "A dozen times. More. How many animals have we studied, Herb?"

"Over four hundred," the chief technician answered.

"Paul, none of them reacted to our agent."

"I know, but guinea pigs aren't people," Paul said.

"We even did monkeys."

"Yes, but we never studied animals who had bled recently. Like Mr. Rogovin."

"That shouldn't make any difference," John replied.

"Shouldn't. Who knows?"

"Human Investigation approved the protocol as safe. So did the FDA."

"Still, I think we should do some more experiments."

"Come on, Paul." This time it was Don Lenhardt. "We can't stop everything now and go back to the lab. We have patients who need this procedure. People we have nothing else to offer."

"True. Still . . ."

"Be reasonable!"

"Okay. We'll do a few more experiments in the lab, but . . . we won't stop our present work. Fair enough?"

Everyone agreed. John was still not convinced the lab work was necessary. He believed that JNF-2 was safe enough for human use. But he did not object, and Paul's plan was agreed upon unanimously.

"Did we get an autopsy?" Paul asked.

"Yes," Bill said.

"Well, we'll see what happened at brain cutting, then."

In the last few minutes they talked briefly about the new patient. Paul and the team would see him later in the afternoon.

It was one o'clock. Everyone had somewhere else to go. Even Gerri Scala hurried out without saying anything to him.

When they all were gone, Paul closed the door and flicked on his FM radio. WFMT was giving the news. He didn't want that. WNIB was playing music. The Schumann "Spring" Symphony. In honor of the season, Paul assumed. They should be playing some Te Deum or other. Despite himself he began to hum the melody as he stared out the window at the el tracks standing silently outside his window.

Schumann had been a manic-depressive. So had Jackie. She was almost always a bit on the hypomanic side with limited judgment. But he had liked her. No, that wasn't true. He hadn't liked her. He had in some strange way been fascinated by her. He half-wished he hadn't given up cigars. He could use one now. Maybe there were still some in one of the recesses of his desk.

His search was interrupted by the phone. "It's Dean Willis," Chris announced.

"Did he call again?"

"No, I called him."

"Why?"

"You told me you wanted to talk to him after the meeting."

"That's a pretty flimsy reason. Put him on."

After three separate clicks he heard that familiar voice in all its matter-of-fact self-importance.

"Paul."

"Yes."

"Dean Willis."

Hell, I know that. I called you. Paul wished he'd actually said it.

"Yes."

"Corrigan is quite worried."

"He didn't say anything to me in our meeting."

"Well, he is very concerned. So is his whole company. They have sunk a lot of money into this place."

"I know."

"And they would be distressed if it all backfired. You talked them into that study."

"I know."

"And the bad publicity won't help them or us."

"No, I guess it won't. But look, we're clean."

"You sure?"

"Absolutely. I obtained the informed consent myself."

"But it's not on the chart," the dean objected.

"I have a copy. I was going to send it to Human Investigation. I never got around to it," he admitted.

"We know that."

"Don't worry. I do have it."

"Wonderful. Where is it?"

"In my office here somewhere."

"Find it and get us off the hook before we get burned too badly."

It was a direct order. "I will."

"Fine."

That was it. That was all the dean wanted. But it wasn't all Paul wanted. "What about Jackie Baumer?"

"A tragedy."

"What happened exactly?"

"She was beaten up and stabbed. Probably raped too."

Paul said nothing. He had wanted more than just a bare outline.

"Do me a favor, Paul."

"If I can."

"Stay out of this one."

"Okay." If I can.

The "Spring" Symphony was over. Replaced by Vivaldi. *The Four Seasons*. That was pushing it a bit too much. Especially for Paul, to whom music began with the "Jupiter" Symphony. Back to WFMT. The news was over. It had been replaced by a series of madrigals. Vivaldi was better than that.

There was a knock on the door and Arnold Chiari came in. Paul was glad to see him. They had been friends now for a dozen years, since Bud had been a first-year medical student, and right now Paul needed a friend.

"Vivaldi. My, my, your taste has improved."

"Not really. FMT is doing a madrigal festival or something. Bud. I need to talk to you."

The younger neurologist sat down across from Paul's desk but Paul continued to stand by the window.

"Something's going on here that I don't understand."

"What's that?"

"Jackie Baumer was killed . . ."

"What's to understand? She was murdered. I know you liked her."

"I'm not sure I liked her."

"All right, were intrigued by her."

"Perhaps."

"Made love to her."

"A few times. And that was some time ago."

"I never understood that, Paul. I try not to criticize you," Bud said, "but she was . . ." He paused, obviously struggling to find the nicest way to say it without losing the truth. ". . . strange. Heaven knows how many guys she'd slept with."

"Bud."

"It's the truth, Paul."

Paul wasn't so sure he wanted to hear this truth.

"She'd pick up guys in singles' bars. So this time it backfired. Maybe she just did it once too often."

"I wish it were that simple."

Bud was puzzled until Paul told him about the lawsuit and the missing signed consent form.

"It must just be a coincidence, Paul."

"She gets killed on the morning the papers were served. That's some coincidence." Paul changed the subject. "What could have gone wrong with that surgery on McCormick?"

"We've gone over this before."

"Let's go over it again," Paul suggested.

"First of all, your theory could be wrong."

"I'll be the first to admit that that's more than just possible. It could all be my error. The problem may not have been a decrease in function of adrenalinelike cells. It was my idea, and if the opposite was true—"

"Which some scientists do believe."

"Yes. If the opposite is true, then putting in the adrenal cells would have made him worse. So it could be my fault."

"The surgeon could have put the cells in the wrong place."

"Lenhardt's a good surgeon."

"But the area you wanted him to hit is pretty darn small," Bud reminded him.

"Surgical error. Don Lenhardt's mistake."

"Then there's the chemical we used to ensure that the cells were able to grow inside the brain."

Paul nodded. "Dillinger 307, an experimental drug developed by Corrigan and his coworkers at Dillinger Chemicals."

"It is possible that it caused some damage," Bud said.

"It looked safe in the animals, but guinea pigs are guinea pigs. Humans are something else. So it could be John Corrigan's problem."

"And of course something could have gone wrong in the tissue culture in the lab."

"My fault."

"Not really. You don't do the lab work yourself."

"Okay, Floyd Baker and John again, and Herb Adams."

"Mostly Herb Adams."

"True."

"There is one other possibility, Paul."

"What's that?"

"Maybe nothing went wrong."

Paul said nothing.

"McCormick's schizophrenic. Schizophrenics tend to get worse. Maybe his disease just got worse all by itself without any help from us. He was getting worse before surgery. That's why we had to do something for him."

"That may be. But I can't just assume that."

"I know," Bud agreed.

Paul could still hear the FM.

More Vivaldi. A different season. Winter. But still Vivaldi.

"Paul, if you want to say that everything between you and Jackie was over long ago, that's okay with me. In fact, it's probably better that way."

"You know about that one night three months ago?"

"Yes."

"How?"

"You sometimes forget my wife works part-time as a nurse on Neurology. Jackie was not exactly the most discreet person in the world, not even when it involved you."

"Do you think Gerri knows?" Paul asked.

"Probably not."

As Bud Chiari left, Paul remembered where he had last seen the stack of signed informed-consent forms. They had been in a cigar box on his desk. He hadn't seen that cigar box in ages. He hoped it hadn't been tossed out with the ones that had still had cigars in them. There had been some important papers in there too. The one by Sharf on the neurological complications of pregnancy, and one by Refsum on his own disease.

Vivaldi was over. Some violin sonata was on. Beethoven, he guessed. Played much too lushly for his taste. It sounded like Francescatti or Elman. It would probably turn out to be some young fiddler he had never heard of. He'd never know. He couldn't stay and listen. He had to make rounds.

Edie Robinson and Bill Goodman were waiting at the nursing station for Paul Richardson, and as soon as they saw him coming down the hall, Bill picked up the patient's chart and they both walked down the hall to meet him at the conference room. Paul was so used to teaching a room full of students that the room with only three of them in it was a reminder of Comiskey Park in the days of his youth, a White Sox–Brownie game with a thousand fans or less in the entire ballpark. The good old days, before '51, when no one came to opening day and attendance dwindled progressively as the season wore on.

Edie told him about the patient. His name was Mike Kreevich. He was thirty-nine years old. He had had seizures for about seven years. They began a year after a severe head injury.

"Tell me about the injury," Dr. Richardson said.

"He was driving a motorcycle and lost control and smashed into a concrete siding. He was brought into the hospital unconscious."

"How long was he unconscious?"

"I'm not sure," she answered.

"I have his old record here," Bill Goodman said. "Let me look." He read through part of the records. "About two hours."

"Not too bad. Edie, do you know what retrograde amnesia is?"

"Yes. When someone gets knocked out, retrograde amnesia is a loss of memory beginning at the instant of the injury and then going backward from that time. Things that happened right before the injury can't be remembered, while those that took place further in the past can."

"Very good. Now, what is the significance of retrograde amnesia?"

"I'm not sure."

Following his usual practice, once the student didn't know an answer, Paul asked the resident the same question.

"Bill?"

"It's one of the best ways to estimate the severity of a head injury. The longer the period of retrograde amnesia, the more likely there is to be some degree of permanent neurological damage."

"So once he woke up, how much retrograde amnesia did Mr. Kreevich have?"

"We don't know." It was Bill Goodman who answered, even though the question had been aimed at Edie Robinson.

"Why not? Didn't they evaluate it?"

"They couldn't."

"Couldn't. Why was that?"

"He had a major speech problem. He was aphasic."

"Edie, what's aphasia?"

"Loss of ability to speak correctly because of a brain injury."

"Right. This kind of loss in the use of language is due to a lesion where?"

"The left side of the brain, unless the patient is left-handed."

"Is Mr. Kreevich left-handed?"

"No, he's right-handed."

"So in Mr. Kreevich . . . ?"

"The injury had to be to his left hemisphere," she replied, answering the unfinished question. Paul was impressed. She was good. Tough in appearance, too tough for Renoir, but good nonetheless.

"This may be harder. How was his left hemisphere injured?"

"He had a depressed skull fracture," she said.

"Meaning?"

"Part of his skull was crushed in and was pushing on his brain."

"What part of his brain?"

"Left frontal lobe."

"Where exactly?"

She hesitated. "It's hard to describe."

"Show me."

She reached up with her left hand. Her hair was dark and curled down to her shoulders. She ran her fingers into her hair and then lifted it up, away from her ear. With her right hand she pointed to an area just above and in front of her left ear. "About here."

Paul smiled. He could not have done better.

"A direct injury to the speech area. What happened?"

She told him about the surgery which had been performed and about Mr. Kreevich's recovery, which had been excellent. His speech had returned to normal. Then about a year later he started having seizures. She described the seizures very carefully. They were all the same. He would be talking and then all of a sudden he couldn't speak anymore. And then he would pass out, and when he woke up, he couldn't talk for an hour or more.

Edie also understood the significance of it all. The seizures were due to a scar in the speech area. When the seizure started, the first thing to be affected and the last to recover was the patient's speech. He was now having five to ten seizures a day. He was completely disabled by them.

His medical care had been excellent all that time. For the first five years Arnold Chairi had been his doctor; for the last year and a half, Floyd Baker. They had tried every drug in the book, and nothing had helped very much. "Mr. Kreevich is here," she announced, "for surgery."

That Paul already knew.

He also knew how dangerous such surgery was. Any surgery on the speech area was likely to cause a permanent loss of speech. Why had he left Lenhardt and Baker talk him into this one? As far as he knew, only one research team had ever successfully done surgery in the speech area of the brain, and nobody at Austin Flint was as experienced in epilepsy as that group.

They went to see Mr. Kreevich.

His physical examination was normal.

Then Paul started to talk to him. He asked him questions. Edie had said that the seizures always started while he was talking.

"Where were you born?"

"St. Louis."

"When?"

"Nineteen-forty-four."

"A great year. In fact a unique year for St. Louis. Do you know why?"

"I guess I don't."

"You a baseball fan?"

"Yes."

"Cardinals?"

"Of course."

"Not the Brownies?"

"No, they left town when I was only a little kid. To go to Baltimore, of all places."

"Now, what happened in forty-four?"

"The World Series." He knew. "The only all St. Louis World Series. The Cards played against the old Browns, and the Cards won."

"And who played for those forty-four Cards?"

Mike Kreevich thought. He read about it so many times as a kid. Slowly the names came back to him.

"Stan Musial.

"And George Muncrief." Then more quickly.

"And Whitey Kur . . ."

". . . owski." Paul Richardson finished the name, but no one heard him.

Mr. Kreevich was motionless.

His face was pale.

His mouth remained half-open as if he still wanted to speak. However, no words came out. His eyes opened wide and looked at them blankly for several very long seconds. His entire head jerked to the right, and the right side of his face jerked and he fell backward unconscious. He stopped breathing.

They waited.

Ten seconds. His face and neck continued jerking rhythmically.

Twenty seconds.

He gasped for air. A single noisy inspiration.

His neck no longer jerked to the right.

He was now breathing with deep rapid movements.

The face had stopped twitching.

They continued to wait.

Ten seconds.

Twenty seconds.

Thirty seconds.

His eyes opened. He was awake. He was breathing normally. He could not talk.

He didn't know who Whitey Kurowski was, or the St. Louis Cardinals. He could not even say his own name.

As they left the room, Bill Goodman said, "I saw one last night. This postseizure phase will last about an hour."

The three of them talked about the seizures. It was obvious that they started in the speech area. The question was what they could do about them. They were going to do a twenty-four-hour brain-wave test to see if all the seizures came out of the same exact location. If they did, it would make the surgery at least possible. No easier, but at least a reasonable alternative.

They were done and Paul had forgotten to tell them about the '44 Browns and their one-armed outfielder. As he was leaving the ward he noticed another medical student, a girl who had taken neurology with him three months earlier and whom Paul recognized, although he could not recall her name. She walked toward him and said, "I was so sorry to hear about Jackie."

Paul began to answer but realized as she walked by him that she was talking to someone else. To Edie Robinson.

Why Edie?

Jackie was a nurse on Neurology, in his department. Why Edie?

On the way back to the office he stopped by his laboratory, two stories above his office. He made it a point to stop by the lab every day, or at least every other day. Not to spy or maintain surveillance but to go over results, answer questions, and most important, make his very presence felt.

The lab was quiet. The bustle that had been a permanent feature in the good old days was gone. Paul missed it. The change was in part due to the switch from studies of animal behavior to tissue culture. There were no longer rows of cages of gnawing rats or jumping guinea pigs. No longer were the medical students and technicians grading animal behavior while using the lab as a second home in the medical center. Instead the lab was now subjected to meticulous sterile technique which virtually eliminated visitors and created a deathly quiet, as if the cells grew better away from both bacteria and noise.

He stopped at the door and put on a surgical gown, a mask, and sterile rubber gloves, and after stepping on the pad which opened the door, went into the lab.

Six feet, two inches of Herb Adams was there hunched over a microscope, his ever-present Walkman in place. Herb reacted to the opening of the door, saw Paul, and nodded. He looked back in the scope for a few seconds, wrote a few words in his lab notebook, and then sat up.

"How are things going?" Paul asked.

"No problems."

"What are you checking?"

"The fetal adrenal cultures. After all, Corrigan tells me we are getting fairly close to trying another implant."

"Probably in a week or two."

"Not in another schizophrenic?" he asked. Paul wondered why he asked. Herb had been at all the lab meetings. He had been one of the opponents of doing any more work on schizophrenia. He knew what had been decided.

"No," Paul admitted. "Not another schizophrenic, a patient with Parkinson's disease. The protocol we discussed today."

Paul sat himself at the microscope and gazed down at the thin regular sheets of small round cells. The cells all appeared to be similar; smooth and spherical.

"They look good," he commented.

"Thank you."

"Clean." Paul continued to look, examining the entire culture. He then lifted off the one culture and replaced it with another. It looked just as nice.

"How many do you lose these days?"

"About one a month. Less than one percent."

"Not bad. In fact damn good." Paul was obviously pleased.

"Better than any other lab I know. That Dillinger 307 does its job very well."

Paul remembered that the cultures had not looked that healthy two years ago but did not bother to ask why once again. Herb didn't know. It was probably their increased experience. The more you did something, the better you got at it, and they now had two years' more experience and they had also changed which antibiotics they used to ward off infection.

Paul went over the inventory of tissue cultures with Herb. They had seven pairs of human adrenal cultures that looked good. The next step would be to see if the function of all the cells was still preserved. After all, once they were put into a patient's brain, what mattered was not whether the cells looked nice but whether they made the right chemicals.

This had been checked once before, some two months earlier. They reviewed the data. Six of the pairs were very active; the seventh was not.

"Should I run all seven?"

"No, pick out the best four or five," Paul decided.

"Now?" That was the key question. If they did it too long before the surgery, the results would not be reliable enough. A tissue could turn off at any time. And each time you bothered the tissue you risked contaminating it. Antibiotics or not.

"Yes. I'm sure we'll do the procedure in the next two weeks."

By the time he got back to his office, it was after five and everyone had gone home for the day. Chris had left the mail and the dictation on his desk. He took off his white coat, turned on the radio, switched the dial back to WFMT, and got to work. There were only three letters which Chris had felt were of sufficient interest to pass on to him. The first was from George Bruyn in Amsterdam. A short note. No news. Just a chess move. Queen to King's three. Paul smiled. When would he tell George? He had thrown out the chessboard and replaced it with a chess program for his office computer. In fact, he didn't even put George's moves onto the computer himself. Chris did it, and then after the computer had chosen its next move, she would type it out for his approval. He read his next move. He'd moved his . . . Nuts, he thought he'd already lost that piece. He signed the letter and put it in his out box.

The second letter was from a Dr. Steven Levy in Los Angeles asking him to see a patient with unusual movements. The patient was willing to travel to Chicago. He wrote "schedule" on the top of the letter and threw it in the out box. The third was from the American Academy of Neurology. It was a survey. He wished he still had his old system, with a box labeled "Ignore immediately." But he didn't. He just put it aside.

It was 5:30. He was going to pick up Gerri in half an hour.

WFMT was playing Dvořák. The Cello Concerto. He hummed along as he called home. Carolyn answered. Joshua would be home around 6:15. He had a ride home. Was Gerri coming for dinner? Yes, he told her. She was glad but she wasn't making a fancy dinner. Just some chicken and vegetables in the wok. She'd make a nicer dinner on Friday. It was all right. Gerri would love it. They would be home around 6:45.

Paul was really going to miss Carolyn when she went to school in the fall. So would Joshua. She had been both a sister and a stand-in mother for him, ever since their mother had died almost a year and a half ago.

There was only one in-house letter of any consequence: a memo from Dean Thomas Browne Willis. There was to be a meeting of all defendants in the case of McCormick versus Richardson, Lenhardt et al. tomorrow in the dean's office at three. Chris had penciled in a note. "I have freed your schedule and will remind you. P.S. Detective Ward will be in to see you at nine."

He signed the dictation without reading it. Six letters and fourteen copies of a memo. He put on his coat, picked up one copy of the memo from the pile of dictation, turned off the radio and lights, and left his office, stopping in front of the department bulletin board. He took down the notice of last week's Grand Rounds, featuring Dr. Ira Shoulson of the Rochester School of Medicine speaking on Huntington's disease. Next year they would invite Anne Young and Jack Penney down from Ann Arbor to discuss their work on Huntington's. In its place he put up the memo. It was his annual reminder:

To: All neurology residents and fellows

From: Paul Richardson, M.D., Chairman, Department of Neurology

This is to remind you that as physicians we are merely the custodians of the medical records which belong to the patients. Records must be readily available at all times. The exact whereabouts of all records must be known to those responsible for them. The records must not be removed at any time from the usual and accepted methods of maintaining and storing them.

Anyone sequestering or otherwise making medical records unavailable is subject to immediate dismissal.

The phone rang.

It was probably Gerri. He didn't answer it. He was on his way.

Down one flight, across the main building, up two flights, down one long hall and then another short hall.

Gerri Scala was seated at her desk. The door was open. She looked aggravated.

He wasn't that late. Besides, he usually had to wait for her. She probably wasn't angry at him, he decided.

"Hi, beautiful," he said gingerly.

"You bastard." She was.

"Did I do something?"

"Did you do something?"

"That's what I asked."

"No, not you. Not the great Paul Richardson. Not the beloved guru of neurology."

"Gerri, stop it. What did I do?"

"To put it crudely, you fucked Jackie Baumer," she said. "I prefer that to 'made love' with her. It makes me feel a little less deceived if you just fucked her."

"I told you."

"Paul, you told me about last year. Not about three months ago."

She was right.

"Why?" she asked.

"Who knows?" It was not exactly an answer.

"Well, if you don't, I sure as hell don't."

"Gerri, you were the one who didn't want to make any commitment."

"I know."

"I asked you."

"I realize that."

"And you said—"

"No."

"So I acted out. It only happened once, and I'm sorry."

"That doesn't do much good."

"No."

"Why didn't you tell me?" She didn't give him a chance to answer. "Why did I have to find out this way? I can't remember the last time I was so humiliated."

"How did you find out?"

"From a detective named Ward. He says he's a friend of yours. Is he?"

"In a way, I guess. We've worked together in the past. We respect each other. We like each other."

"He shows his respect in a strange way. He came in here and all but accused me of killing Jackie Baumer because you were fucking her."

"Gerri—"

"That's what happened."

"How did he know?"

"About you and Jackie?"

"Yes."

"She kept a diary."

"I didn't know that. I suppose I'm in it."

"Yes, you are."

"How did he know about you and me?"

"That's no secret around here. Or are you trying to hide us too?"

"You know I'm not."

"She had a picture of us in her apartment."

"Of us?"

"He showed part of it to me. It was the one Carolyn took of us when we went to see *Nicholas Nickleby* last winter. It used to be in your office. It had been torn in half."

"I didn't give it to her."

"Paul, I'm just going home by myself tonight. Tell Joshua

and Carolyn that I got one of my migraines. I probably will, by the way.''

''If that's what you want.''

''It is.''

''Will you come over Friday? Carolyn has been planning the meal all week.''

''Yes. I told her I'd be there and that I'd teach her how to make hollandaise sauce. Just because you're a bastard doesn't mean she should be disappointed. I love those two kids of yours.''

It was still raining. The drive home took forever. Why was it that in real life spring rain was never as beautiful as it was in poetry? Or as charming? At least not on the clogged expressway leading up to Highland Park.

2

It had been such an easy lie. Easily told and just as easily believed. Gerri had gotten a headache, a migraine. She was sorry, but she would come for dinner on Friday night just as she had promised.

After dinner was over and the dishes were done, the three of them sprawled in the family room half-watching the TV together. Joshua tried to wade through Upton Sinclair's *The Jungle* and Carolyn did some physics. None of them were terribly involved in what they were doing. Carolyn was more intrigued by Tycho Brahe's shiny brass nose than his contributions to astronomy. Joshua simply considered Upton Sinclair to be boring. As boring as Paul had found his assigned reading in high school. Jane Austen. How well he recalled that particular chore. Even the Simenon Paul was reading seemed to go nowhere in particular. It just wandered around the sixteenth arrondissement with glasses filled with chalky solutions of pernod and water. Shades of Hemingway.

He tried to tell Joshua about Upton Sinclair, about muckraking, about other Chicago writers from Dreiser to Brashler, but Joshua wasn't interested. Joshua didn't even care about the onetime Chicago bus driver who later won a Nobel Prize for literature. So instead they talked about the White Sox and colleges. Midwestern colleges close to home for Carolyn. It was the first time all three of them had talked about it together. They reached no conclusions but at least they were starting to think about it.

Paul was still thinking about it when they turned in. He did not go to sleep easily. The book he was reading hadn't helped him any. The murder in the Maigret book had been a particularly messy one. Like Jackie's. He couldn't help thinking about her, associating thoughts with her.

He was still not sure why he had gone to bed with her the first time, much less the last time. She was young and seductive and vibrant, but she had had no—he had trouble finding the right word—no . . . no class. That was it. That's what Bobbie would have said. No class at all. Maybe that was why it had started. She was as unlike Bobbie as possible, and with Bobbie dead it was a natural choice.

It was not Jackie he thought most about as he tossed in his bed; it was Bobbie. The one sudden death reminded him of the other, more painful one, a little more than a year and a half earlier. Bobbie. Gerri had class. But she wasn't Bobbie and that wasn't a fair comparison for him to make.

He also wondered about Jackie Baumer's autopsy. Everything but the dissection of her brain had already been completed. That was yet to come. They had no other choice. The brain had to be fixed in formalin for several days. If they didn't do that, it would be just like cutting thin slices of Jell-O that had not yet set. They put all the brains into ceramic jugs and then collected them and did all the brain cutting at one time. They did it as a teaching exercise each week, with pathologists and neurologists there. If they were on schedule, they would cut Jackie's brain next week.

He would miss that if he possibly could.

Paul got up first, as he always did now, and woke both kids. Unlike Wednesday, Paul listened to the news on the radio as he got dressed, and when he got downstairs to fix breakfast, he read both the sports section and the news section. He should have saved himself the effort. Jackie Baumer had already been reduced to a very short sixth-page follow-up that said nothing, and the Sox had lost, leaving them four games out.

Once he dropped the kids off at high school and promised that he would be home no later than seven, he put on a cassette he had picked out before he left home. The choice had been easy. Something slow and dignified and appropriate for the occasion. Not a true dirge like Mahler's Fifth. Nor as majestic as the Verdi Requiem. After all, it had been Jackie Baumer.

Howard Hanson. His Symphony Number Four, an orchestral requiem in memory of his father.

The kyrie eleison began as he got on the highway. As far as Paul knew, Hanson was the only American composer whose hometown had put up a road sign to honor him. Paul loved that sign. He had seen it only once while driving north from Lincoln, Nebraska. "Welcome to Wahoo, Nebraska, the birthplace of Sam Crawford (first baseman of the Detroit Tigers during the glorious days of Ty Cobb), Darryl Zanuck (famed Hollywood producer), and Howard Hanson."

There he was, playing third banana to Wahoo Sam Crawford. What bothered Paul was not the third billing Hanson had received. What else could a serious American composer expect? But Crawford had been an outfielder. In his twenty-one years in the majors he had played 2,197 games in the outfield and only 150 at first base. First baseman indeed!

Traffic was heavy. When the Lux Aeterna movement ended, he was only halfway to the hospital. We rewound the tape and listened to it again. This time he hummed his way through most of it. Humming along was always a good defense against thinking.

Tom Ward was already waiting in his office. Paul checked his schedule for the day with Chris, poured himself a cup of coffee, dribbled some milk and Sweet 'n' Low into the cup, and after putting on a fresh white coat and realizing that he had nothing more that he could possibly do, he then went into his office and sat at his desk opposite the waiting detective.

"Hi, Doc."

"Hello, Tom."

"It's been a long time."

"Yes it has," Paul agreed without very much enthusiasm.

"About three years, I think," Tom went on, not being dissuaded by the physician's apparent disinterest. "It was that poisoning business. You helped us a lot in that case."

Paul sipped his coffee and said nothing. They both knew what he had done and what he had not done in the past. There seemed to be no reason to engage in reminiscences just then.

"Things have changed quite a bit around here. Your office is much neater than I ever remember it being."

Paul continued to give most of his attention to his cup of coffee.

"I also see that you have taken to wearing ties. And if I'm not mistaken, you've even lost some weight."

"You haven't."

"No, I haven't," Tom admitted. "In fact, I have put on a couple of pounds."

"A couple?"

"Five, maybe six."

"Six? I would have guessed a bit more."

"Maybe it is a little closer to eight."

"I thought so. But you didn't come to see me so that we could test my carnival skills."

"No, Doc, that's not why I stopped by to see you."

"And it wasn't to shoot the breeze about the good old days."

"Right again."

"You came here to talk about Jackie Baumer."

"Yes."

"So tell me."

"Some of it you already know. She was killed the night before last. Sometime between ten-thirty and one-thirty in the morning. Probably before midnight."

"How do you know that?"

Tom reached into his pocket for his notebook but answered without referring to his notes. He knew he had lost the initiative, but that was all right with him. The story would be the same either way. "She was supposed to have worked the late shift. Eleven P.M. to seven-thirty A.M. She called in at ten-thirty to say she might be a bit late. At eleven-thirty they got concerned and called her apartment but got no answer. Finally at one o'clock the supervisor got worried and had Security check her apartment. She lived right over there in the nurses' residence, but you know that." Tom waited for a response. Paul gave none. "On the fifth floor. I'll bet you can see her apartment from your window." Tom started to get up.

"You can," Paul said slowly. "You have to stand to the

right of the window and look up a couple of floors, but you can.''

"And vice versa.''

"What?''

"You can see your office from her bedroom window, if you stand to the right of the window.''

"I'm sure you can,'' Paul conceded.

"Anyway, when Security got there she was dead. First they called the dean.''

"Willis?''

"Yes. Then he called us. By the time we got there it was after two-fifteen and the body was already beginning to get cold. Your pathologist thinks she probably died around midnight,'' Tom concluded.

"How had she been killed?''

"Her hands had been tied to the bed and she had been gagged and beaten up pretty bad and stabbed about half a dozen times. Once in each lung, once in the heart, and a couple of times in the stomach. You want to see the pictures? I've got a set here.''

"I'll pass on that.''

All at once Paul wanted a cigar very badly. But he knew there weren't any in the office. His coffee was cold. He finished it the way it was.

"Doc, how kinky was she?''

"Kinky? What do you mean, kinky?''

"You know what I mean. Was she into bondage?''

"How the hell should . . .'' He stopped himself. "Not as far as I knew,'' he admitted, and then asked, "Had she been raped?''

"Hard to tell. She had had intercourse within a few hours before death. But rape? Who knows?''

"How do you figure it, Tom?''

"A sex crime. She was fairly straight with you.'' It was as much a question as an answer.

"Yes,'' Paul answered.

"But not with everyone else. At least not as far as we can tell. Most likely somebody got carried away. She picked up strange men sometimes, in strange places.'' That was what Bud had told him yesterday. "I guess she made a mistake.''

"How did you know about me?'' Paul asked.

"Two ways, Doc. She kept a diary."

Paul was not surprised. Gerri had already warned him about that as unpleasantly as possible.

"With dates, initials, and then some sort of coded rating system. There was no entry for last night or the night before. From looking at it, it appears she would fill it in a week or so at a time. We found your initials. P.R." This last was said almost as an aside, in a stage whisper.

"I'm not the only P.R. here."

"No, but we also found a picture—"

"I know," Paul interjected, "you showed it to Dr. Scala. Why the hell did you do that? Without coming to me first. Dammit, Tom, I thought we were friends."

"We are."

"Then why?"

"To make sure she was surprised."

"And was she?" Paul asked as sarcastically as he could.

"Yes."

"But why?"

"I had to eliminate her as a suspect. I really found both halves of that picture. That meant that she was a special friend of yours. So I wanted to make sure she wasn't involved in this in any way, so you could work with me on this thing. I don't have to tell you how complicated it could get if someone around here turns out to be involved. This place has as much clout as it ever had. Maybe more. Your dean plays that game damn well. The pressure is already on to keep things as quiet as we can."

Tom did not have to explain it in any greater detail. Paul understood what he was up against. "Okay," Paul said slowly. "Still, I wish you'd talked to me first."

"I couldn't."

Paul understood.

"But," Tom went on, "it was most likely some guy from a singles' bar."

"A Mr. Goodbar."

"What?"

"Nothing." Literary allusions were not Tom's forte.

"Look, if I need your help, can I count on you?"

"Yes," Paul said.

"You going to her funeral?" Tom asked.

"No, I don't think so." He paused. "When is it?"

"Tomorrow at eleven-thirty."

"No," Paul repeated softly. That was one more event he would put on his schedule to miss.

Tom got up to leave. "So long, Doc."

"So long, Tom."

"I'll keep in touch."

"One more thing, Tom. Can I have a look at those pictures?"

"Here, keep them. I have an extra set."

It was only after Tom Ward left his office that Paul took a good look at the photographs. They were worse than he had imagined. He had seen pictures of hundreds of dead bodies in his career. He had participated in scores of autopsies. He had even watched the autopsies of good friends. And he had seen Bobbie after that damn accident. He had identified her body. But this was different. There was blood everywhere. She had probably bled to death. The kitchen knife was still sticking out of her naked chest. Just above her left breast. He tried to remember whether he had seen that knife before in her apartment. But he couldn't. They had never gone to her place to make dinner. They had only gone there to make love. He had only been in the kitchen to get something to drink. It was probably her own knife. There was no reason for anyone to bring his own knife to her apartment. There were probably no fingerprints on it or in the apartment. Fingerprints were only important in grade-B movies. *Charlie Chan* and the other great black-and-white potboilers of the 1930's.

He felt sick to his stomach. Whoever had killed her must have really been sick. And not just sick to his stomach. It couldn't have had anything to do with the missing consent form. It was too brutal to be a premeditated murder done in order to facilitate some other crime. This was an act of passion. Of abnormal passion. Of deviant passion. It had to be a coincidence that the damn form was missing and that she had witnessed it. Coincidences do happen, after all. Every day. . . .

He was certain he had another copy of that form somewhere in his office. It was only a matter of finding it.

He didn't know how long Chris had been standing in his office watching him. She must have come in just after Tom Ward left.

"Can I get you another cup of coffee?" she asked.

"Yes, if you would."

"Dr. Scala called." Always formal and proper.

"And?"

"I didn't want to interrupt you and Detective Ward. Besides, she said that it wasn't that important and that she would see you at the meeting with Dean Willis."

"Did she sound angry?"

"I'm not sure. I don't think so. Mostly she sounded in a hurry."

"I'll call her."

"You can't. She's going to be tied up with patients until the meeting. Dr. Lenhardt called. He specifically asked that you call him back this morning."

"Okay."

"And I was supposed to remind you today that you are scheduled to be the discussant at the clinical-pathology conference next week."

"Oh damn. I'd completely forgotten that."

"That's why I was supposed to remind you. You are free until one. You can get started now."

"I don't even have a copy of the protocol," he protested.

"Yes you do. I put a copy on the top of your bookcase this morning. Right under the bumblebee."

"Ah. The Brancusi File. Where else would one put a CPC?"

"Paul?"

She rarely called him by his first name. "Yes, Chris."

"What happened to Jackie Baumer was terrible."

Paul could still see the pictures of her mutilated torso. They were not just another visual memory encoded in the back of his brain, but a much more vivid, ongoing experience, as if somehow they had etched themselves onto his retina, and his optic nerves were continuing to bombard his brain with the same images. Over and over again. Certainly Tom Ward had had better sense than to show her those same pictures.

She anticipated his question. "Ward didn't show me those pictures."

Paul was glad of that.

"But he did tell me about it. It's a ghastly thing. I'm so sorry that it happened."

Why sorry? he wondered. Why tell him? She knew what he really felt about Jackie. She had been intercepting Jackie's calls for months.

"I . . . I'm worried. We all are."

"All?"

"All the women who work here. There could be some sex maniac wandering around here looking for more victims."

"I doubt that, Chris. And so does Tom Ward. Jackie was a bit . . . um . . ." Bud had said it best. ". . . strange. She did wander around picking up strangers at singles' bars—"

"Among other places."

"That's true," Paul conceded. "But this time it was most likely not someone from around here. And certainly not someone who forced himself into her apartment."

"Are you sure?"

"That's what Tom said."

"Do you believe him?"

He hesitated. "Yes . . . yes, I do. I don't think that this was just a random sex crime."

"He's not just covering up something to make it look better for the hospital?"

"No. I don't think so."

"Some guy she picked up?"

"Yes."

"A Mr. Goodbar?"

He smiled despite himself and the situation. "Yes. Look, I've got to get to work. Call Lenhardt for me."

He found the CPC. It was exactly where Chris had said it was, underneath the Brancusi Bumblebee. It was scheduled for the next Thursday.

For the first time, Paul read it.

CLINICAL-PATHOLOGY CONFERENCE

A forty-one-year-old woman with known systemic lupus erythematosus and a progressive neurologic disorder.

Discussant: Paul Richardson

SLE with a neurologic problem, Paul thought to himself. Where should he start? At the beginning, the very beginning. Who first described SLE? Paul didn't remember. He wasn't sure he had ever actually known that fact. Who first described involvement of the nervous system in SLE? That he was sure he had never known.

He thought for a moment. Lupus erythematosus. A red rash, hence erythematosus. Over the cheeks. Like the face of a wolf. Hence the term "lupus," from the Latin word for "wolf." But who published the first case report of a patient with SLE who had neurologic manifestations? First he looked in Garrison's *History of Neurology*. It wasn't there. It wasn't in Rose and Bynum's *Historical Aspects of the Neurological Sciences*. But he hadn't really expected it to be. Then he looked in Volume 36 of the Vinken and Bruyn *Handbook of Clinical Neurology*. And there it was. The neurologic manifestations of SLE had first been described in a paper published in German by the great Viennese dermatologist Moritz Kaposi in the year 1872. Kaposi. A strange name, an unusual name. What did he know about Kaposi? Nothing. Where was that history of dermatology he had ordered last year and then never read? It was right there in his bookcase staring down at him. It was still in its unopened plastic covering.

He opened it and then sat back to read about Kaposi. He had been the professor of dermatology at the University of Vienna when Vienna was *the* university, at least as far as medicine was concerned. Born in the year 1837 in the little town of Kapsovar. Born Moritz Kohn. Paul had not known that. He wondered how many people did. Kohn of Kapsovar. He was sure there was no roadsign outside of Kapsovar recalling the birth of Moritz Kohn. Perhaps Howard Hanson had not done so badly after all.

The phone rang. It was Don Lenhardt.

"Paul?"

"Yes."

"How the hell could you have gotten us in this mess?"

No formal pleasantries. No beating around the bush. It was one of the few things that Paul sincerely admired about the head of Neurosurgery.

"You know damn well that you are supposed to be in charge of obtaining informed consent on all patients on combined neurology-neurosurgery research protocols."

"That's right."

"I'm not at all sure that it's right. It was your idea originally. I was never too sure of it myself."

"We all agreed. Unanimously."

"Yes, we did. And that made you responsible to explain all the risks of the procedure to Frank McCormick."

"Yep."

"And to obtain a signed informed consent from him."

"Right."

"And you didn't."

"Wrong."

"What do you mean, wrong?"

"Just what I said. To put it into simple English, it means that I did explain the potential risks as well as the possible benefits to Frank and to his father and they both signed the appropriate papers right on the dotted line."

"Then why isn't it on chart?" Lenhardt asked.

"That I don't know. Perhaps it's been misplaced by Medical Records."

"Or perhaps it never existed."

"It did. I—"

"Who witnessed it?" the neurosurgeon asked.

"Jackie Baumer."

"Very convenient."

"What do you mean by that?"

"Not much, but there's no way that a dead witness can contradict you."

Paul worked hard to keep his temper. "Look, Don. Before you operate on anybody, the operative team goes through its own checklist, right?"

"Of course."

"And informed consent is one of the things that has to be checked. If it isn't there, you can't operate unless it's an absolute emergency."

"That's correct. So what?"

"So what?" he echoed. "Since you were allowed to operate, someone must have seen that consent form."

"There's only one problem there."

"What's that?"

"Jackie Baumer did that checklist on all of our experimental patients at that time."

Paul had forgotten.

"All very convenient, Paul."

But for whom? Paul wondered.

"Look, Don. It's not that big a problem."

"Not that big? I don't know about you, but I don't like being sued. I've never been sued before. Malpractice! Negligence! I don't see how—"

"I have a copy of the consent form."

"You do? Why didn't you say that earlier?"

"I tried."

"Bring it to the meeting."

"I'll try."

"Try?"

"I'm not sure where it is at the moment. It's someplace in my office. I'll find it."

"You better."

"I will."

"In that pigsty?"

"Don't worry. I'll find it." With that he hung up.

The phone rang again. This time it was Chris reminding him that he had to stop at Medical Records on his way to make rounds.

Why? He was six behind in signing his charts.

So? After three, his admitting privileges had been suspended.

So? He'd admit his patients under someone else's name.

Whose? Bud's. She then told him that Bud was twelve charts behind. In fact the whole department was behind. He got the message. As chairman, he had to set an example.

Would she call Medical Records? She already had. The charts had already been pulled. They were awaiting his signature.

It took him only five minutes to get from his office to Medical Records. No guinea pig had ever mastered a maze better than Paul had learned all of the intricacies of Austin Flint Medical Center. From his office he went up one floor, then across the enclosed ramp to the Professional Building, down two flights, never waiting for the elevator, through the back door behind the men's washroom, down the old fire escape of the hospital, which was now inside the Professional Building but had to be maintained because of some fire law or other, through the fire-escape door, straight down the main corridor, then halfway down the short hall, up half a flight of stairs to the original research wing, and he was there. Medical Records. The clerk smiled as she recognized him. Somehow to Paul her smile seemed triumphant. His records were waiting for him. All six of them. They were in the second room on the left. Would he like some coffee? No.

He sat down before the small pile of records and got to work.

EDWARD STEWART, 276-465.

Paul remembered him well. He was left-handed and had had a stroke which involved his left side. He had made a good recovery.

EDWARD STEWART. He looked at the list of what he had to do.

Discharge summary: sign. He signed it.

Admission physical: countersign. He countersigned it.

Verbal order: okay it. He okayed it.

Discharge order: write it. He wrote it. He was good at following orders.

DAVID PHILLEY, 353-471.

Another patient he remembered. He'd had multiple problems and been diagnosed as having multiple sclerosis. He checked the list and did what it told him to do.

The third chart stopped him.

AL KOZAR, 992-252.

He didn't remember that patient at all. He mustn't have been in the hospital very long. He certainly had not made much of an impression on Paul. He checked the list.

Discharge summary: sign. He tried but he couldn't find it.

Admission physical: countersign. Again he failed. It had never been signed.

He got up and went to the front desk. He who smiles last smiles best.

"I can't complete this chart."

"Why not, Dr. Richardson?" said the smile.

With that he produced the evidence. "There is no discharge summary. The admission physical was never signed." He gave her the chart. Her smile faded.

"Let me check something." Time for her to marshal her forces. She went back to the master file. She came back with a master card.

AL KOZAR, 992-252.

They read it together.

Discharge summary: W. Goodman.

Admission physical: W. Goodman.

Attending physician: P. Richardson.

Her smile was back. "Dr. Goodman is your resident, isn't he?"

"Yes."

"Would you remind him to complete this record?"

"Yes."

"If he gets too far behind, he won't get paid," she said with a smile.

Paul was sure she wished she had the same control over him. The thought terrified him.

"I'm sure he's well aware of that fact," Paul said.

"There is one peculiar thing here," she said.

"What's that?" Paul asked.

"Dr. Goodman signed out the chart once for two days. See, it's recorded here." She pointed it out to him and he saw. "I wonder why he didn't dictate it then. It's a thin chart. It wouldn't have taken him very long."

"I wonder too . . . about something else."

"What's that?"

"Do you keep a master card on every chart?"

"Of course."

"With a complete record of everyone who has taken the chart to work on it?"

"Certainly."

"Even just to read it?"

"Even just to read it."

From the tone of her answer, Paul could tell that she had found his question to border on insulting. To imagine that they did not keep accurate records of such matters was a form of heresy.

"Could I see one of those?" he asked.

"Any particular one?"

"Yes. Mr. Frank McCormick."

"A neurology patient?"

"Yes."

"Do you have his hospital number with you?" She answered for him. "Of course not. I'll check alphabetically. It will only take a little longer." Another smile.

In two minutes she was back with the card and the chart. Paul took them both and went back to his stack of charts.

FRANK McCORMICK, 299-434.

Attending physician: P. Richardson. He looked at the list of those who had signed out the chart. The list was impressive.

William Goodman.

Don Lenhardt.

Floyd Baker.

Geraldine Scala.

Sam Hairston.

Paul Richardson.

He could explain five out of the six.

William Goodman—to dictate the discharge summary. He checked. It had been dictated.

Don Lenhardt—to sign the operative report. It had been signed.

Floyd Baker—as part of his ongoing research review.

Geraldine Scala—to sign her psychiatric reports. They had been signed. But why had she kept it three weeks?

Paul Richardson—to cosign the discharge summary. He had cosigned it. He didn't recall having done it, but it was his signature.

But who was Sam Hairston?

It didn't take him very long to find out. Hairston had been the general-surgery resident who had scrubbed in with Lenhardt. He had spent all of two weeks on Neurosurgery. Paul had all he could do to remember him. Hairston had taken the chart to dictate his surgical summary. It had been dictated. All six were accounted for.

Then he looked for the consent form. He knew he wouldn't find it, but just the same he looked. He went through each and every page but he did not find the consent form. He did find the pre-op checklist. It did have a check signifying that informed consent had been obtained and was in the O.R. at the time of surgery. The form was initialed J.B.

It was time to make rounds. He returned Frank's chart with a smile of thanks. The last smile was hers. He was still four charts behind: AL KOZAR; FRANCINE BAUMAN; DONALD RUDOLPH; CONSTANCE JOHNSON.

* * *

Dr. William Goodman and Edie Robinson were waiting for Dr. Richardson just outside of Mike Kreevich's room. The senior resident had some sample pages from the patient's brain-wave test. Together the three of them studied the long sheets of paper. Each sheet contained sixteen lines of ink. Each line represented the electrical function of one small area of the brain. Together the sixteen channels gave a second-by-second picture of the electrical activity of the patient's brain. They shuffled through the pages and located three seizure discharges. Those three bursts revealed exactly what they had thought they would find. All three of the abnormal bursts were identical. Bursts of high-voltage spikes coming from the speech area on the left side of the brain, just where the old fracture had been. Each burst of uncontrolled spikes was followed by a slow return to normal waveforms, which took several minutes.

Bill Goodman told him that overnight they had recorded four other seizures and they were all the same. Seven out of seven.

Goodman also had the CAT scan. Paul looked at it briefly. It showed a scar in the area of the speech center. Paul took the CAT scan and one sample of the EEG and led them into the room. Mike Kreevich still had sixteen electrodes attached to his head and was still being monitored by the EEG machine. Normal waking activity, Paul noted.

Paul stood next to the bedside and after exchanging a few pleasantries he got down to business.

He showed Mr. Kreevich the EEG and explained how the seizures were caused by those jagged spikes and how those spikes came out of the part of his brain that was responsible for speech.

He explained how the burst of spikes caused him to lose the ability to speak and how that ability did not come back until many minutes later, when the curved lines of brain function had returned to normal.

Next Paul showed him the CAT scan. "This is like a series of cross sections cut right through your brain," he said. "This part is your brain itself. And you can see both sides look the same. Except"—and now he pointed to one small dark shadow—"for this one area on the left. This is a scar. It's from here that the seizures originate. This is also where your speech center is located." Slowly, painstakingly, he wanted Mr. Kreevich to understand it all, to be informed.

"We have not been able to stop your seizures."

"I know. I wish you could."

"We've tried every combination of medication."

"I know. Dr. Baker has tried everything."

"Do you know why we can't control your seizures?"

"No."

"It's because of that scar."

"The one you showed me."

"The same one. It's causing the brain cells to fire abnormally."

"Can't you do anything about the scar?" Mr. Kreevich asked.

"If it were anywhere else, we could cut it out."

"But why can't you cut it out?"

"If we did, you would probably never be able to speak again."

"Oh, brother."

"There is one thing we can try. It is experimental."

"I'm willing to try anything. I can't go on like this, having all these seizures every day. I can't do nothing."

"What we would do is make a small series of cuts across the scar."

"What good would that do?" the patient asked.

"It would relieve the pressure on the normal brain."

"Would it stop the seizures?"

"Probably. Or at least make them easier to control."

"That's wonderful. When can we do it?"

"We can't guarantee that it will help, Mr. Kreevich. We think it will, but there are not guarantees."

"I know, I know."

"And there are risks."

"Risks?"

"You could lose your speech."

"Just like removing the scar?"

"Yes. Not as likely, but there is a risk."

"How big a risk, Doc?"

"One out of twenty."

Mr. Kreevich did not hesitate. "Let's go for it."

Paul was not satisfied. They went through it all again. The

problem. The proposed experimental solution. Dr. Lenhardt would do the surgery. Dr. Baker would assist him. He reviewed the possible benefits. He spelled out the risks.

Mr. Kreevich was still interested.

Paul took out three informed-consent forms for experimental surgery. The procedure was called dicing of a cortical scar. Paul read it to Mr. Kreevich and asked him if he understood the benefits and risks. He said he did.

Mr. Kreevich signed all three forms.

Bill Goodman witnessed them.

So did Edie Robinson.

Paul gave one copy to Goodman to put on the chart and he took two. When he had done this two years ago with Frank McCormick he had taken only one, the one he couldn't find now. This time he took two. He'd give one to Chris and keep one himself. They'd never misplace both of them.

There was one new patient to go over. She had been worked up by Edie Robinson. The three of them sat in the small conference room and the senior medical student told the story. It was not a very long one.

The patient was named Donna Kolloway.

The name rang a bell with Paul Richardson. He had seen her sometime in the past. Eight, maybe ten years ago. She had bled into her head from an arteriovenous malformation. He did not say anything, not wanting to deprive the student of her chance.

The patient was now thirty-four years old. This was her third admission to Austin Flint Medical Center. The first had been when she had been nineteen and the second when she was twenty-four.

Ten years ago, Paul thought, and smiled to himself. His memory was as good as ever. Especially for pretty women.

Both admissions had been for the same problem: the sudden occurrence of a severe, almost unbearable headache, followed by vomiting and a stiff neck.

"What happened to her?" he asked.

"She had bled."

"Where?"

"Inside her head."

"But where?"

"I'm not sure I understand."

He had gone too fast. She was a student, not a resident. She did look older than most students, almost thirty he guessed, but stilll she was only a student.

"Why do you think she bled into her head?"

"The severe headache she had that was unlike any other headache she had ever had. And it was followed by vomiting and a stiff neck."

"Good. Now, do you think she bled into her brain or into the space outside the brain?"

"Not into her brain, I guess."

"A good guess, but why?"

"I'm not sure."

"Sure you are. You've seen patients with strokes from bleeding into the brain. Did they give histories like this?"

The answer came slowly. "No."

"What was the difference?" It was almost as if he were practicing dentistry, not teaching. One tooth at a time. But the teeth were there. He knew they were.

"They all had some sort of paralysis. One side or the other."

"Give that lady five silver dollars. Bleeding into the brain causes sudden loss of brain function. Bleeding outside the brain does not. What is bleeding outside the brain called?"

"A subarachnoid hemorrhage?" she answered without much confidence.

"And it causes . . . ?"

"Headache."

"And . . . ?"

"Vomiting."

"From . . . ?"

"The blood in the subarachnoid space reaches the vomiting center."

"What else happens?"

"A stiff neck."

"From . . . ?"

"Irritation of the linings of the brain."

Sixty-four silver dollars, he said to himself. It was much more fun than pulling teeth, for both of them.

The rest of the story Paul already knew. The spinal tap had demonstrated the blood in the subarachnoid space. The angiogram had shown a tangle of abnormal blood vessels on the right side of her brain, involving much of her brain on that side. Bill Goodman put one of the old films onto the small view box. Her arteriovenous malformation looked like a bowl of mostacelli with a few thinner strands of spaghetti.

The angiogram had been done during her first admission. Paul was amazed that the hospital had neither lost nor destroyed it. He had seen it during her second admission for her second episode of bleeding. They had nursed her through it. It was late. He had to get to a meeting.

"Has she bled again?"

"No."

"Then what?"

"She has been getting weak on her left side."

"Both arm and leg?"

"Yes."

"Meaning . . . ?"

"A problem on the right side of her brain where her AVM is."

Another sixty-four dollars.

What were the possibilities? Edie could think of two. Bleeding into the brain and expansion of the AVM itself. She knew what they should do to try to tell the difference. A CAT scan. She didn't know exactly why it was so important to tell which was going on.

A medical student was not expected to know that. A resident was. So he asked Bill Goodman the same question.

Goodman was younger than Robinson. Younger and smaller. But he was supposed to know a lot more. He did. If it were a hemorrhage, they might be able to drain it with a simple operation. If it were the AVM expanding, they might not be able to do anything about it.

The CAT scan had been ordered.

Paul's meeting had started five minutes ago.

Everyone was seated around a long table. The dean sat at the head. Paul slipped into a chair next to Gerri Scala near the foot of the table and nodded to everyone.

"Now that Dr. Richardson has arrived," the dean began, "we can get started." He spoke softly but his voice filled the room. "We are all defendants together in a malpractice case. You as individuals and I as head of the medical center. Each

of you played some role in the care and treatment rendered to
Mr. Frank McCormick while he was in the hospital. The
hospital and its various employees, including nurses and non-
professional employees, also participated in his care while he
was a patient here.'' He paused, reached into his pocket, and
took out a pipe. He reached into another pocket and took out
a lighter. He lit his pipe as if it were a historic act worth both
arresting all other activity and recording for posterity. Paul
wished he had brought his camera and a cigar. Not a small
Schimmelpennick, a large stogy. A Winston Churchill special. He was sure Churchill had started to smoke his cigars
because of meetings like this one. The dean went on and on.
He talked about the need to work together, to support each
other, to present a united front, to win the case. To cooperate
fully with the defense attorney. So that was who the one
stranger was, the hospital defense attorney. It was important
that each of them study the chart from beginning to end. ''My
office,'' the dean announced, ''has made a copy of the entire
record for each of you.'' Paul was startled. When, he wondered, had Dean Willis taken the chart out of Medical Records? Why had that not been recorded? Could someone else
have pulled the chart for such administrative tasks without
signing it out?

The dean was done. He introduced the lawyer. His name
was Charles Connors. He was from the old established Chicago firm of Miksis, Smalley, and Cavaretta. He was a senior
partner. Connors looked to be about fifty and very conservative. A three-piece pin-striped suit, a little gray over the
temples. Not a wrinkle on either his face or his pants. Nor a
hair out of place, not an ounce overweight. Paul hated him on
sight, but he listened to every word. Connors was good. He
outlined the issues as cleanly as possible. It was old hat to
Paul. He had been an expert so many times, but it was
obvious that it was new information to many of the others.

Paul looked at Gerri. She was staring at Connors and
virtually hanging on each word. So were John Corrigan and
Floyd Baker. And Don Lenhardt. And even Dean Willis. His
pipe had gone out and was resting on the table.

Malpractice, Connors explained to them, consisted of two
separate issues. Negligence and injury. Without either, there
could be no case. Negligence consists of one or more devia-

tions from the accepted standard of practice. That was the key. As long as whatever was done fell within the accepted standard, there was no negligence. In an experimental setting, the issue was no different. The standard was the accepted standard for such experimental programs.

The second step was injury. If you did something that was negligent and it caused no harm, you were not liable for any damages. You could give the patient the wrong medicine and if it didn't hurt him, there was no case.

The defense in a malpractice case could be based on defending either one or both issues. As far as Connors could tell, both issues could easily be defended here.

Were there any questions?

As several hands went up, it was Dean Willis who acted as mediator.

"Dr. Corrigan."

"Are we all individually covered by the hospital policy?"

"Yes."

"So we don't need individual lawyers?" Don Lenhardt asked

"I would say not," Connors answered cautiously. "Especially since we are, I assume, going to present a united front and not start pointing fingers at each other. It should be easy to defend."

"Easy!" Don Lenhardt shouted.

"Of course. Did you deviate from the accepted level of care?"

"Absolutely not!"

"Did you, Dr. Richardson?"

"No, sir."

"Did anyone in this room?"

There were several heads that shook sideways and a couple of nos.

"I thought not. The plaintiff will have to prove that you did. And—and this is important—he will have to find experts who will testify that you did. Experts with reasonable credentials."

"But what about the informed consent?" the neurosurgeon asked.

"What about it?"

"There isn't one."

"There isn't one on the chart at the moment," Connors corrected him. "There was one. Dr. Richardson obtained it, as he will testify, and Nurse Baumer witnessed it. Remember that. That is our defense. Don't ever contradict that. And besides, it is the truth and Dr. Richardson has another copy which he will be furnishing for us very, very soon. Am I correct?"

Paul nodded.

"Now, one more thing. The patient has not been injured or suffered in any way." It was not clear whether that was a question or a statement. Gerri Scala was tempted to say something, but she could not. Frank was still her patient. Whatever he said to her was privileged. She could not talk about it without his permission.

It was the dean who ended the meeting by reminding them all that the hospital was self-insured for the first two million dollars and for all legal expenses.

The meeting was over. Paul wanted to say something to Gerri Scala as she rushed out, but the dean stopped him.

"Paul."

"Yes."

"You must find that form and find it quickly."

"I'm trying to."

"We have to abort this mess. Operating without consent. Experimenting without consent. We can't afford such publicity. It'll kill us. The papers will make it sound terrible. You and your research projects. Find it."

"I will. Don't worry."

Gerri was gone. He wanted to talk to her. He had to get home. He had promised the kids he wouldn't be late.

The ride home went by quickly. Rush hour was nearly over. Traffic was thinning out. WFMT was playing Schoenberg's *Verklärte Nacht*. Its pivotal ambiguity fit his mood perfectly. Beyond romantic but not yet atonal. You could almost hum along, but not quite.

Only Schubert's "Death and the Maiden" would have been more appropriate. The quartet, not the song.

3

It was at breakfast that Carolyn reminded him that he had to be home by six o'clock. They were going to have a very special supper. "Gerri will be here by three. She and I are going to Northbrook Court to pick out a dress for me."

"You are?"

"Yes. You said I could buy some spring clothes."

"When did I ever say a thing like that?" he asked, having taken note that "a dress" had somehow grown into "some clothes."

"Last week," she reminded him.

He remembered but he liked to give her just a little bit of a hard time every once in a while. "Are you sure Gerri will be able to go shopping with you?"

"Yes. We talked last night. She knows just where she wants to take me."

"Dare I ask?"

"Lord and Taylor, and Neiman-Marcus, and . . . Laura Ashley," she answered quickly.

He whined, but Carolyn paid no attention and Joshua had his nose buried in a book. Clothes bored him even more than Upton Sinclair.

"We had a long talk about clothes and things," she went on.

"You could have told me you were going to call her. I might have wanted to say hello."

"I couldn't, Dad. She called me."

Paul returned to his newspaper. He found nothing about

Jackie Baumer anywhere in the paper. The murder had only been the day before yesterday but it seemed as remote as the last White Sox pennant and of less interest to just about everyone in town. What was one violent crime more or less in Chicago? One nurse more or less? Of course the absense of any further publicity might not be a mere coincidence. The tentacles of Austin Flint reached into a lot of places, most of which were important. Willis had been very successful in keeping more sensational things very quiet in the past. What had Sherlock Holmes said? He remembered. The curious matter of what the dog had done at midnight. Watson had protested that the dog had done nothing. That, Holmes had insisted, was what was curious. This was exactly the same. It was the absence of any mention at all that was curious. Or maybe it wasn't.

He went back to his usual morning behavior and began to carefully dissect the sports section. He should have saved his time. The Sox had blown another one. Their starting pitchers couldn't complete a game and their relievers couldn't get started.

As soon as Paul arrived at his office, Chris greeted him with the news that the dean was waiting for him to call and that Tom Ward would be stopping by in about fifteen minutes. There were also calls from half a dozen patients and the mail to go through and . . . Yes, the coffee was ready. He poured himself a cup and went into his office.

The phone rang.

It was the dean. His day was starting both too early and two quickly. "Paul."

There was a strange unfamiliarity in the all-too-familiar voice. "Good morning, To—" Paul stopped himself. It was never Tom. Tom was not authoritative enough. He caved in. "T.B."

"I was wondering if you were going to attend the funeral today."

Paul did not have to ask whose funeral. He answered the question slowly and carefully. "No . . . I don't think so."

"I thought you probably would."

"Why?" Paul asked, wondering how much the dean knew, and more interestingly, how much he would be willing to say.

"She was assigned to your department." He was going to keep it official. "And was also a member of your research team."

"Not really," Paul said.

"No?"

"No. She did help us on some protocols, but she wasn't an active member of our research group."

"Oh."

Paul was not sure what that meant.

"I am certain that you have made arrangements so that the Department of Neurology will be officially represented at the funeral."

Was that part of his job description? "Yes."

"Yes, what?" the dean asked.

"Yes, we will be represented." Paul was not sure how he would manage that. Maybe Chris or Floyd. A diplomatic mission. Where was Haile Selassie when you really needed him? He had loved going to funerals. And he had always looked so official.

"I will leave the choice up to you, Paul. I am sending one of the associate deans, probably Lynn Morris. A woman is more appropriate."

"Why?" Paul asked. He could hardly hide his aggravation.

"Why? That's obvious. She was a woman and the women here who are activists will all be there, so it's better that we send a woman. And besides, no matter which man we send, it would probably result in rumors. She was—how shall I say it?—a bit promiscuous."

"How the—"

"And we are fortunate that she was," the dean went on.

"Fortunate?" Paul's voice betrayed both his bewilderment and his anger. He had never been a good poker player.

"Of course. In all probability, she picked up some misfit who came back here and, after doing God knows what, killed her. That being the case, we are not involved."

"Not involved?" Paul echoed softly.

"No. She brought in a guest. She breeched our security system."

That, Paul realized, left the hospital without as much as a single smudge. The perfect solution. An outsider. And even better, an outsider brought in by the victim. Not someone who slipped in past the medical center's so-called security system to randomly attack some unsuspecting victim. The ideal answer. But was it true? He hoped he'd learn some more from Tom Ward.

"I am sure," Paul said precisely, "that gives you a great deal of solace. I will make certain Neurology is well-represented. I'm confident that whoever goes to the funeral will also gain satisfaction from knowing that attendance there will not serve to focus official suspicion on them." With that, he hung up.

Chris buzzed him again. Tom Ward was there waiting, and he had a phone call from a patient. "Is anyone from our department going to the funeral?" he asked.

"Yes."

"Who?"

"Floyd Baker."

She then answered his question before he asked. "If you only listened to one-tenth of the rumors in this place, you'd know that they were lovers. And Bill Goodman."

"Were they involved too?"

"No, but they had worked closely together since he became senior resident and he's going as the representative of our residents. And Dr. Corrigan will be there as well as Edie Robinson. And Dr. Chiari is going to officially represent you and the department."

"Why?"

"He thinks that the department should be represented, and all things considered, it would be more politic if he went instead of you," she said.

"And," she continued, "I have sent flowers from the department. I tried to charge them to the grant, but no luck, so I—"

"Used my American Express number," he finished her sentence.

"Of course."

"Of course. Thank you, Chris. Put through the call and send Ward in," he said, and hung up.

The call didn't take very long. It was an old patient of Paul's. Mrs. George Kell. She just wanted to talk for a couple of minutes. To get some reassurance and a small change in her medicine. He easily complied with both her requests.

By the time he hung up, Tom Ward was seated opposite him, sipping some coffee.

"Your office is neater."

"Yes, and now I can't find a damned thing."

"Just tell Chris. I'm sure she never loses anything."

Paul wished that were true. "Tell me, Tom, what happened to Jackie?"

"She did pick up some guy."

"Where?"

"One of the near North Side singles' bars."

"Do you know who?"

"No, he was not a regular customer. An out-of-towner, we think. Here for business. That's all we know. We don't know where he was from, or what business he was in. There were only three major conventions in town this week. And the description we have is great."

"Yes?"

"Around thirty. Medium height, medium build, medium weight. Dark hair."

"That leaves me out."

"You are over thirty, but we could be wrong about that."

"I am also not of medium build and weight and I am mostly bald."

"I guess we won't be able to pin it on you. What's your blood type?"

"A-postive."

"Definitely not you. The murderer is either AB or O."

"How do you know that?"

"From the semen."

"That's not my field," Paul said, "but I always thought you could tell exactly which blood type the guy was by examining the semen."

"You can."

"Then why either AB or O?"

Tom shook his head. "I didn't think I'd have to draw you a picture. Two men had made love to her that night. Both within six hours of her death. One was type AB, the other type O. By the way, are you going to the funeral?"

"No."

"It's better that way."

"Are you?"

"Of course. I have to see who will be there."

"What is this, a grade-B mystery? The killer was discovered by showing up at the funeral or returning to the scene of the crime?"

"No," Tom laughed. "But sometimes people show up unexpectedly and we do get leads." He got up to leave. "One more thing, Doc."

"Yes."

"We are pretty damn sure it was an outsider, so let me solve this one."

"That, believe me, will be my pleasure, Tom."

He had gotten the same advice twice now. They were both probably right. He was better off not going to the funeral. He had his own work to do. What difference would it make to Jackie now? She was dead. Not forgotten. Just dead.

Another dream. This was the second one in three days. Gerri Scala hoped she showed no unusual response. She was supposed to be a neutral observer. Yet she could feel herself beginning to squirm as soon as he started. She hadn't felt this uncomfortable with a patient since her residency.

"I am in a city. It's not the same city as my other dream. There's a lot of water. Canals. Not like Venice. More like Amsterdam. I was there once, with my father. You know that. I told you all about that trip."

A pause. A block in the flow. Filled, Dr. Scala was certain, with associations, loose pathologic associations, tied to his memory of that trip and his father. Associations being filtered out of their communication and perhaps even out of his consciousness. It was frustrating. It would be exciting to tap that flow, to hear his next thoughts, to interpret them. But not with Frank, and certainly not now. He was much too sick. Too unstable. Too fragile.

"I am outside a room.

"The room is on the fourth floor." Same floor, she noted. Perhaps it means something. Four. But what? She had to concentrate and not free-associate herself.

"But somehow I can see inside. A man comes into the room. Everything is very tidy. So very tidy." Just the opposite, she thought, of his other dream. Perhaps this one would not get as messy.

"The man has lots of gray hair. Like my father." Again the hair seems to be important, she thought. Thankfully it was not long and blond this time.

"He looks like my father." Like my father. Not *is* my father. The difference again was not missed.

"He is very neat. Very precise. Like Dad. He takes off his jacket and places it over the chair by the door. Then he does the same thing with his tie.

"He sits on another chair.

"He unlaces his shoes."

One detail at a time. All so neatly told.

"He puts on a pair of black leather slippers and slides his shoes under the chair. The same chair where he hung his jacket.

"He goes over to the bed.

"He lies down on his back.

"He smokes a cigarette.

"Then another."

No blood, no gore, she thought.

"Then he reaches into the bedside table and takes out a gun."

Here we go.

"It's a revolver."

A gun is almost always a male sex symbol.

"It has a very long barrel.

"It seems beautiful. It glistens."

And had to be this time.

"He puts the gun in his mouth."

She cringed.

"He pulls the trigger.

"It explodes in his mouth." What overt symbolism. Right there on the surface. Yet not to be explored.

"He is dead.

"There is a smile on his face.

"My father is dead." No longer *like* my father, but my father.

He paused. She wondered if the dream had ended. She waited. She had to.

Frank went on. "I am now in the room. I look around. Except for the blood and the brains splattered over the wall behind the bed, the room is very tidy." Tidy again.

"I go up to the wall.

"I reach out."

Not again. Please.

"I touch the splattered mess.

"I taste it.

"The blood tastes good."

Again.

"Like blood always does.

"The brain tastes terrible. Rotten. Spoiled. The brain was sick.

"I gag.

"I look around the room for a message.

"I find one.

"It is written next to the phone.

"Two words." He stopped.

A long pause. Very dramatic.

"Two words." Repeated. Why? For emphasis, or did it occur that way in the dream?

"A name."

Whose?

"Paul Richardson." Then quickly, as if he had to get it over, "I looked back at the body. It was no longer my father. It was me.

"I could still taste the rotten brain in my mouth."

He stopped.

She knew the dream was over. Where to start? What was the least dangerous? Was Frank dangerous? Was he violent? He had never been violent before. Now he was waiting for her.

"Paul Richardson," she said. Not knowing exactly why. It was probably safer than either the homosexual or oedipal content of the dream. "What does Paul Richardson mean to you?"

"He rotted out my brains."

"In what way?"

"That operation," he said after a pause. "It was all his idea. He invented it." Not a rush, but individual declarative statements. Stated flatly, without emotion. A defused version of a charged issue. But logical in its own way. Very logical. Tidy.

"It was his idea, not Dr. Lenhardt's."

Dr. Scala listened.

"Not yours. Not my father's. His. And you all agreed."

So did you, she thought to herself. You signed the permit. The missing permit. She said nothing. This was a treatment session, not a courtroom.

"I never agreed to it. I never signed anything."

But you must have, she thought. Paul wouldn't have lied about that. Others, maybe, but not Paul.

"It's your fault. All of you. You plotted against me."

Paranoia again.

"I hate you all. But I hate him the most."

"Who?"

"Dr. Richardson." There was no hatred in his voice now. No emotion at all.

"My brain is smeared up against my skull. I can smell it. It's rotting inside me. He did it to me. You all did." It was the lack of emotion that frightened her the most. His affect was almost as cold as if he had been reading words at random from a dictionary. Such detachment was unusual even in schizophrenics.

Their time was up. It had been up ten minutes ago. Frank got up. Quietly. And left.

She carefully wrote it all down. She recorded as much as she could recall word for word. The gun. The suicide. The body of his father becoming his own body. The homosexual nature of the method. Freud had always taught that paranoia was related to homosexuality. That smart SOB.

And now the object of that paranoia seemed to be Paul. Should she tell him? Should she tell the police? After all, Frank had known Jackie Baumer. His dreams were full of such violence.

She thumbed through her records. The reports from the halfway house noted no change in behavior. Of course, Frank did not blame them. Still, there was no evidence of any actual violent behavior on his part.

She wrote one last note: "It may be safer to put him back on Haldol. Will discuss with P.R."

Most of the mail had been routine. An article to review for *Neurology*. It was a study of the treatment of dystonia by Stanley Fahn. He read it and filled out the form. He recom-

mended that they accept it for publication. An invitation from
Bob Feldman to give a paper in Boston the next spring. It was
impossible for him to accept all of the invitations he received.
He decided to pass it on to Floyd Baker. One piece of mail
was different. It was a mailgram from the FDA suspending all
testing on 0511-807. That saved him some time. He had just
started to write up a protocol for submission to Human Investigation. It seemed that the drug caused liver injury, so all
investigators were being instructed to suspend all use of the
drug. So much for 0511-807. There were also a couple of
letters from patients. He dictated answers. Then he saw the
letter from Jackie Baumer.

He looked at the envelope carefully. It was postmarked
Wednesday at nine A.M. She must have mailed it in the
evening before she had gone out to . . . The envelope was
still sealed. It had been typed and marked "PERSONAL AND
CONFIDENTIAL." Chris had not opened it.

Had she paid attention to the return address? Had she
recognized the embossed JSB?

He opened it very carefully. It was a formal typed letter, a
business letter.

> Paul Richardson, M.D.
> Chairman, Department of Neurology
> Austin Flint Medical Center
> Chicago

> Dear Dr. Richardson,
> I am writing to inform you that Dr. William Goodman
> has been systematically removing patient charts from their
> proper channels and thus creating possible problems in
> retrieving the missing charts when needed.
> This came to my attention over six weeks ago. At that
> time a patient named Phyllis Masi, who had been dis-
> charged one week earlier, was readmitted to the neurol-
> ogy service. Dr. Goodman had been her resident during
> the first hospitalization and was responsible for dictating
> the discharge summary.
> When she was readmitted as an emergency, the sum-
> mary had not been dictated. The chart could not be
> located. When Medical Records had come to the floor to

pick up the chart after her previous discharge they had been unable to find it. Dr. Goodman was on vacation and unavailable.

Late on the night of her readmission, I finally located the chart along with six others. All of the charts belonged to patients of Dr. Goodman. I discovered them above the false ceiling in the conference room.

Since I am well aware of your policy in this matter, and since information available in the missing record was crucial to the care of this critically ill patient, I felt I had to bring this to your attention.

I informed Dr. Chiari of this at the time, but he took no action.

> Jackie Baumer
> P.M. Charge Nurse
> Neurology

Paul recognized the signature. He was not an expert in handwriting analysis, but he had seen it often enough to be sure it was Jackie's. A little messier than usual, but her handwriting had always been a bit messy. She was probably in a hurry. She had other things she wanted to do. It must have been one of the last things she had done before she was killed. She must have mailed it Tuesday evening. It must have been picked up Wednesday, gotten to the hospital Thursday, and slowly found its way from the hospital mail room to Neurology.

What a pathetic last act. Jackie wasn't—correction, hadn't been—a troublemaker. The problem with the charts must have been significant for her to have blown the whistle like this.

Why hadn't she just called him? He knew the answer to that question. He might not have talked to her. He had stopped returning her calls three months ago, since all she ever wanted was to pursue their relationship, a relationship which was, as far as he was concerned, dead as . . . A bad choice of metaphors.

So she wrote to him. But not an official memo sent through official channels. She had used her own stationery. He'd bet she had not sent any official copies to associate deans or other administrators. She had done it the right way. Quietly, personally. It was a delicate matter to be dealt with within the department.

She had gone to Bud first. He had done nothing. Why? He knew how Paul felt. And why had Bill done it? In the ceiling, of all places.

Paul would never have thought of hiding charts there, or of looking there for missing charts.

How had Jackie known where to look?

Chris buzzed. Herb Adams was waiting for him to go over the design of some experiment. And he had a meeting with Dean Willis and Dr. Corrigan in twenty minutes, and then rounds at two o'clock.

It didn't take very long for Herb and Paul to go over the experiments. They wanted to find out if the sclerosing agent JNF-2 was safe even in the presence of fresh blood. They could not use abnormal blood vessels in their study since they could not get experimental animals with arteriovenous malformations, but using normal blood vessels was an acceptable alternative.

First they would anesthetize the animals with a fast-acting barbiturate. Next they would open each skull and expose the brain. Using a special needle they would then puncture one of the large veins in the brain and run a small catheter through the needle and into the vein. In one-half of the animals they would inject a fixed dose of JNF-2. One-tenth of a milligram in two-tenths of a cc of normal saline over ten seconds. In the other half they would withdraw the needle, allowing some bleeding to occur, and then inject the same amount of JNF-2 in the same volume of saline over the same time period. The only remaining question was how long to wait to remove the catheter or the needle.

"A minute and a half," Herb replied.

"Based on what?"

"According to our own data, at least ninety percent of all sclerosis occurs within forty-five seconds and ninety-eight percent in sixty seconds. So it is unlikely that any leakage of blood after a minute and a half could have very much of an effect."

"Okay," Paul agreed. "Then what?"

"We will replace the bone flap and wake up the animals."

"How many will we lose?"

"About ten percent."

"That's acceptable," Paul said. "When do you want to compare the responses?"

"Corrigan says that the acute reaction will be over in forty-eight hours, so I was planning to sacrifice them at the time. I'll take the brains from both groups to see if those with bleeding had any more brain injury than the others."

"How many animals in each group?"

"I'd like to start with ten, so even if I lose a couple we'll have enough."

"Do me a favor."

"What's that?" Herb asked, knowing it was more an order than a favor.

"Start with twenty animals in each group. And only kill half at forty-eight hours. Kill the other half after one week."

"But in Corrigan's studies—"

"I know, but sometimes things take longer in the brain."

"Shall we use guinea pigs or rats?" Herb asked.

"Rats, they're—"

"Cheaper."

"That's right."

"But it's drug-company money."

"I don't care whose money it is. There is no reason to waste it."

"We could do fewer animals."

"No."

It was settled and Paul was off to his meeting.

For once, Paul was not the last one to arrive. He and John Corrigan both had to wait for the dean, who had just finished sharing lunch with the board of trustees.

"Sorry I'm late, fellows," the dean began, "but you know how these luncheons with the board go."

Paul didn't, but he smiled just the same, and watched as John Corrigan nodded knowingly.

"Our meeting today should not take very long. The board is very pleased with the proposal that John has put forward on behalf of a large consortium of private corporations. The president of the board, Frank Lane, asked me to express his personal satisfaction to you. I am sure you will be hearing directly from him in the near future, John.''

"I am looking forward to that," John said.

"There seem to be only a few minor details to be worked out," the dean continued.

"I'm not sure those details are so minor," Paul said.

"You're not?" the dean asked.

"No. I'm not."

"Paul, I'm sure no one here understands our need for an active research program as the very foundation of the academic endeavor of this institution any better than you do. I don't have to explain it to you.''

If you don't, then why are you? Paul said to himself. He knew he would have to listen to the dean's speech and grin and bear it. After the dean was through, he would get his turn.

"Our role in this city as one of the two great teaching hospitals is dependent not only on our excellent clinical facilities and patient-care programs but also upon the scientific-academic-research activities of the medical center. These aspects are all interrelated and interdependent.''

Paul had heard all this before. It had to be part of the speech Willis had just given to the board.

The dean went on. And on.

"All of this obviously costs a great deal of money. Traditionally at outstanding medical centers such as ours, about two-thirds of all research dollars comes from the federal government, mostly as research grants from the National Institutes of Health. I need not detail for all of you the economic . . .''

It *was* his board-of-trustees speech. Paul was certain of it.

". . . as a result, there is much less research money available and . . .''

The bottom line at last.

". . . we are forced to look elsewhere for research funds.

"We are most fortunate that Dr. John Corrigan in his position as senior vice-president for development with Dillinger Chemicals has been able to put together a consortium of Chicago-based companies, including his own firm, as well as Pierce Manufacturing, Zarilla Chemicals, and several others who together have pledged a total of eleven million dollars a year.''

That's one hell of a lot of money, Paul thought.

"For each of the next four years. You must agree, Paul, that we can certainly use this money."

"Absolutely."

"It will help to guarantee our continued growth and success."

"I have no argument with that."

"Then what is your problem? The patents?"

"I don't even have any problem with that. If that's what's required to get the guaranteed research support, that's okay with me. We get the money and they can have the patent rights on any patentable products we might develop or help develop. I and the rest of the members of the Committee on Academic Activities have discussed that thoroughly and we can live with that."

It was John Corrigan who finally said something. "I'm most pleased with that, Paul. So what's the problem?"

"Academic freedom," Paul said softly.

"Don't give me platitudes, Paul," John Corrigan complained.

"That's not a platitude," Paul responded.

"Bull."

"What John means, Paul, is that he needs specifics. He believes in academic freedom as much as you and I do."

"Two simple issues. The first is: who makes the decision as to what research is supported by the . . . ah . . . eleven million dollars a year?"

"The board was very happy with the arrangement and approved it unanimously," the dean announced. "It will be a joint committee of the medical center and the consortium."

"How many members from each?" Paul asked.

"I am not sure," the dean said.

"I am," Paul said. "I've studied their document very carefully. We have six and they have nine."

"What's wrong with that?" John asked.

"Everything. We have to be able to determine our own research priorities."

"That's just not practical," John said.

"Why not?"

"We—the companies, that is—get only one possible return in this investment, namely patents. If you decide to support research which cannot lead to such patents, we get nothing. That would not be a very good investment, would it?"

"Of course not, John," Dean Willis said. "Paul understands that."

"Yes, I understand it. And in fact, from your viewpoint, I even agree with what you said. For you it's right. It protects your investment. But it isn't right for us. In the long run, an arrangement like this would destroy us."

"How?" John asked.

"Since you will support only certain types of research, such as the development of new drugs, the only new faculty we'll develop will be in those areas. The academic needs of our school will become confused with and absorbed by the technical needs of your pursuit of new products. We will become the research wing of a set of second-rate drug companies which cannot afford their own research departments, instead of trying to be a first-rate medical school."

"You're exaggerating, Paul. You have worked with John for three years now. Has he undermined the integrity of your research program?"

"No."

"Then why do you think this will be any worse?"

"Now he neither controls my purse strings nor my research goals."

"The board has already approved the program," the dean reminded him.

"That doesn't mean much."

"It doesn't?"

"No. According to the bylaws, the board does not have the authority to set up panels to oversee research. Only the faculty has that right, and the faculty has delegated that right to the Committee on Academic Activities, of which, I need not remind you, I am chairman. The committee will not, I can assure you, accept the proposed program."

All three of them knew that there was nothing more to say. There would be other meetings. But for now, it was better to stop where they were and say no more.

Paul stayed for a moment after John Corrigan left.

"I didn't mean to challenge your authority, T.B."

"I know that."

"Or John's role. Hell, I know we can use that money, but we must have more say in controlling our future. I'm sure John can understand that."

"Perhaps. He is a bit perturbed now."

"Why?"

"The malpractice suit."

"Why is that bothering him?"

"His company is entirely self-insured."

"So are we," Paul said.

"True," the dean agreed. "But our budget is almost two hundred million dollars per year. A million-dollar decision won't kill us. His budget is less than three million dollars a year. A big award could ruin him."

"What about the consortium and the eleven mil per year?"

"He just put it together. It's not his money."

They started rounds in neuroradiology. Mrs. Kolloway was having her CAT scan. She was on a low table with her head bent forward by a support and held off the table at an angle of precisely fifteen degrees. Slowly the table was pushed into place until her head rested inside a giant horseshoe. The technician then checked a few dials and left the room.

Paul, Edie, and Bill were in the adjacent room watching through a thick leaded-glass window. The neuroradiologist, Sidney Gordon, joined them and pushed a button on the large console next to the window.

There was a ten-second whir, and the first picture appeared on the computer screen. The first cut went through the top of the skull and the upper tip of the brain. It looked normal.

The table moved one and one half centimeters, moving Mrs. Kolloway's head farther inside the horseshoe.

Another whir.

A new section, one and one half centimeters deeper into her brain, appeared on the screen. It was still normal. There was no sign of her anteriovenous malformation.

Another movement of the table.

Another brief whir.

Another computerized image.

This one was not normal. Large dense bright abnormal blood vessels could be seen on the right side of the brain, toward the back.

The next showed more abnormal vessels. As did the following three cuts. Most of the hemisphere was filled with abnormal vessels. There was no evidence of a fresh blood clot.

The CAT scan was over. The technician came back into the room and took Mrs. Kolloway out of the machine and helped her get into a wheelchair to go back to her room. Meanwhile, the neuroradiologist and Paul compared the new CAT scan with the one that had been done two years earlier. There was no longer any question as to what had happened. The vascular malformation was larger than it had been in 1981.

While the three of them walked back upstairs to the neurology floor, Paul made sure that Edie understood what they had seen. The malformation had grown. Its vessels were now larger than they had been before. Larger and thicker. It was these engorged vessels that were causing Mrs. Kolloway to get weaker.

"How does an AV malformation cause weakness?" Paul asked.

"By bleeding," the medical student responded.

"True, but we didn't see that."

"Or spasm."

"Was there any spasm?"

"No."

"Then how?"

"I guess the vessels could injure the brain by squeezing it as they enlarge."

"That is possible, but not likely. There is one mechanism that's more likely."

"I don't know."

"I'll bet you do. Have the vessels gotten bigger?"

"Yes."

"Do they now contain more or less blood?"

"More."

"What happens to the blood in malformation? Does it go to the brain?" Paul asked.

"No, it goes directly from the abnormal artery to an abnormal vein . . . and then it must go out of the skull."

"So if the abnormal vessels get more blood, what happens to the brain?" he asked.

"It must get less blood."

"Right, and that causes loss of function, such as weakness. So to stop her progressive weakness, we will have to do something to stop the vessels from getting bigger. Exactly what, I'm not sure."

Mrs. Kolloway was already back in her room. She was happy to see Paul Richardson. She wanted to show him pictures of her two children.

"My son is seven. We named him Paul after you."

"Why me?"

"Don't you remember?"

"What?"

"The other doctors wanted to tie my tubes. They said pregnancy would definitely kill me. You took the time to tell me about all the possibilities. You sat with me and my husband and explained it all so very carefully. And you let us make our own decision. I have two wonderful kids. Thanks to you."

Paul changed the subject.

"You may have another decision to make. You and your husband. Your malformation is getting bigger and stealing blood from your brain. We may have to do something to make it smaller."

"Whatever you think is best, Dr. Richardson."

"No, Donna. This decision will also be yours. I think we will have to do another angiogram to get some more details on the individual abnormal vessels, and then we will try to figure out what the options are, and when we know, we will all sit down and discuss it with you."

"And my husband?"

"Of course."

Mr. Kreevich was scheduled for surgery on Monday. Don Lenhardt had gone over the entire procedure with him and had him sign three informed-consent sheets. Floyd Baker had done the same thing.

Nothing like overkill, Paul thought. They had not only closed the barn door after the horse had escaped, they had locked it and even nailed it shut.

"Dr. Richardson."

"Yes, Edie."

"I'm not sure I understand about her pregnancies."

"Oh. There's an increased risk of bleeding from a vascular malformation during pregnancy and also a risk of it expanding like Mrs. Kolloway's is now. But the risk is not overwhelming. Some doctors are too authoritarian. They tell patients what they have to do and tell them that they must never get pregnant because of that risk. I guess I'm just not that sure of myself. I have enough trouble running my own life. . . .

"Bill."

"Yes, sir."

"Make sure you do two things. Explain all the possible risks of an angiogram to Mrs. Kolloway, and then go over the other neurologic problems of an AVM with Edie. Things like seizures, migraine headaches, and noises in the head."

"Will do."

Paul wondered if Bill Goodman had recognized how much he had ignored him. He hoped not. He had to talk to Bud. Charts in the ceiling. What craziness.

Paul stopped in the library to look up some reference material for the CPC and after finding two journal articles and giving the librarian requests for three others that were not there, he headed back to his office to meet Bud Chiari.

As soon as he got there he knew he was in for trouble. Chris had left early. She had left him a list of phone calls he had to return before he went home and a pile of patients' records to go with most of the phone calls. Since Bud was already in his office, Paul did not get a chance to get started on his phone messages. "How was the funeral?"

"It was a funeral. The hospital was well-represented. So was this department. You probably were not missed."

"Good."

"Conspicuous by your absence, but not missed."

"Okay, Bud. Don't rub it in."

"Why should I do that?"

"For the best of motives. You don't like to see me make mistakes, so you make a point of reminding me of my past errors."

"It's called teaching. I learned it from a grand master—you."

"But in different areas," Paul reminded him.

"So I just generalized your technique a bit," Bud said.

"Who else was there?" Paul asked, changing the direction of their conversation.

"Floyd."

"Of course."

"And Bill Goodman."

"That I knew."

"And John Corrigan."

"Why was he there?"

Bud shook his head. "Didn't you know?"

Paul obviously didn't.

"She worked part-time for him, for Dillinger that is, re-viewing charts and reports for some of their research products. She's done it for three or four years."

"Oh," Paul responded.

"Red Wilson was there too."

"The operating-room nurse?"

"Yes. She was Jackie's ex-roommate and"—Bud paused—"Corrigan's mistress."

"His mistress? That sounds so old-fashioned."

"It was. He paid for her apartment."

A kept woman, Paul thought.

"Floyd should have stayed at the hospital. Jackie played him for a fool."

Paul knew if he just sat and listened, Bud would tell him the entire story.

"She was such a groupie. I'm sure she just went to bed with him because you let him be first author on that article on Huntington's disease in the *New England Journal of Medicine*. You get famous in neurology and Jackie would go to bed with you."

"You're famous."

"Not famous enough for her. After all, I never was first author in the *New England Journal*."

"Gee, if I'd known that was the prize, maybe I would have made you first author."

"You should have been, Paul."

"No, I'd already slept with her."

"I'm being serious. Why was Floyd first author? It was your project. We had initiated it before he even came here."

"He asked."

"That's no reason."

"And he did a lot of the work."

"So what? It was just a simple biochemical analysis. Any technician could have done it. He supposedly did it to learn the technique. And for that he gets fame and . . ."

"Jackie Baumer."

"He's welcome to her," Bud said.

"But not to the fame?" Paul asked.

"Not when he didn't deserve it. You have always been too damn soft about some things."

"He asked."

"Did he also ask to leave my name off the paper?"

"No."

"But he did."

"He did?"

"Darn it, Paul. Don't you check anything anymore?"

"Bud, I'm sorry. When I told him to write it up, I went over the final draft, but . . ." Paul hesitated.

"You never saw the front page?"

"No," Paul admitted.

"I was left off, and I did help set that entire project up in the first place."

"What can I say?"

Bud did not answer. "Paul, do you remember the first time we met?"

"As clearly as if it were yesterday."

"Well, it wasn't. It was twelve years ago. I was a first-year student taking a seminar course with you and I came up here to this office to talk to you and you were having the same problem."

"I was?"

"Yes, with a student. Carol . . ."

"Carol Voss."

"You let her be first author—"

"Because it would help her get a better residency."

"That was the story."

"I'd forgotten. At least she didn't get Jackie Baumer thrown in as a bonus," Paul added as a feeble attempt at humor.

"No, not Jackie."

Paul had not expected that. When had Bud learned about that old affair of his? It was ancient history.

"I also remember one other thing."

"Yes?" Paul said.

"You threatened to fire a resident over a missing chart. You went so far as to dictate a memo, and then found the chart yourself."

"You remember that day better than I do."

"For good reasons."

"What reasons?"

"It meant more to me then and now."

"Now?"

"Yes. Don't go off half-cocked about the charts."

"But—"

"Trust me, Paul."

"Do you know what I remember so clearly about that day?" Paul asked.

"No."

"You had read the *Three Other Plays*."

Bud was puzzled.

"Sartre. *No Exit*. The only English edition was *No Exit and Three Other Plays*. And you had read all three of the others. I never even got through *The Flies*, much less *Dirty Hands*."

Bud smiled. He didn't remember that part of their first conversation. He was sure he had never told Paul that he had read Sartre in French, not in English. He probably never would. Paul was sensitive about his own limited facility with languages.

It was getting late. Bud had to get home. So did Paul. But first Paul had to return all those phone calls. He tried. One after another. He started with Mr. York first, Mrs. Mayo second, and worked his way down to Frank Overmire. Fortunately, at least the call to Laverne Webb was short. He completed the last of them and then he went home.

The shopping spree had been a success. Carolyn was wearing a new outfit: sweater, blouse, and pants. There were two more in her closet. Joshua had two new sweaters. They had even picked up a pair of new shirts and ties for Paul. Shirts with matching ties at that. He wondered if he would be able to keep them straight.

Dinner was also a hit. The entire evening went well. Gerri fit in perfectly.

At 10:30 she called it an evening. She had patients to see in the morning. Paul walked her to her car. "We didn't get a chance to talk," he said.

"I know."

"When can we get together?"

"I'm not sure."

"How about dinner tomorrow night. Just the two of us."

"I don't know. Let me think about it."

— 4 —

The sun rose bright and clear over the lake and flooded the city. It was a bright yellow morning sun yet its rays were still cool. A perfect late-spring morning. Gerri was sorry she had scheduled six outpatients. She wouldn't be free until almost two. It would have been a perfect morning to play in the small flower garden in the backyard of her apartment.

The morning was equally radiant in Highland Park. To Paul it was a perfect day for a double-header, but the Sox were out of town. In Oakland of all places. What were the Philadelphia Athletics doing in Oakland? Gerri was right. If you were going to keep moving teams every decade or two, you could not expect the fans to develop any meaningful loyalty.

Paul had no professional obligations until Monday. Floyd and Bud were on call for the weekend. He and the kids went to services and then had leftovers for lunch. Paul remembered to again compliment Carolyn on her chicken. He was learning.

After lunch, Carolyn and Joshua had things they just had to do. She had to go to the library to study and he had to go to a friend's house for some sort of tournament. Space Invaders or something. Paul knew just what he had to do—look through his basement office to see if he had put a copy of Frank McCormick's signed consent form there.

First he had to pick the right music. Music to search by. Something noisy. A Mahler symphony. But which one? The Fifth? Too funereal. So was the Second. He decided on the Third, played by the Chicago Symphony Orchestra with Solti conducting. He felt a bit guilty that he still preferred the now ancient Bernstein–New York Philharmonic version, although there was no doubt that Sam Magid's violin solos were better.

He put on the two records, turned up the volume, and started hunting. It was amazing what he found. He had not searched through the basement in a couple of years. Certainly not since Bobbie had been killed in that accident. Bobbie must have saved everything and put it away carefully in these file cabinets. There were things there he hadn't seen in years. Some short stories he had written as an undergraduate at the University of Michigan. They were not exactly Hopwood material but they were not bad. Mostly he found old letters. Letters to Bobbie. Letters from Bobbie. Most of them were twenty years old and even older. Letters full of youth, enthusiasm, and love. Kids today did not write letters. They made phone calls. It was their loss.

Paul was startled out of his reverie by the telephone. It was Gerri. "Do you still want to take me out to dinner?"

"I guess so."

"Don't sound so enthusiastic."

"It's not that. I was just doing something."

"What?"

"Reading over love letters."

"Whose?"

"Mine. Bobbie's."

"If you'd rather not, we can skip it."

"No. I can't think of anything I'd rather do."

"That may not be as much of a compliment as it seems."

"No," he laughed. "I guess not. Where would you like to go?"

"La Grillade in Highwood. I feel like some good fish. I'll pick you up."

"That's a lot of driving."

"No it isn't. I'm already in Highland Park. I came up to buy some yarn at the Yarn Yard. They have the best selection of good yarn in the area."

"Are you done?"

"Yes."

"Come over now. The kids will be home soon and they—"

"Okay," she conceded, "but I didn't call to see them, not this time."

Paul was only partly right. The evening did involve a lot of driving. But not for Gerri. At eight they dropped the two teenagers off at their party and then drove up to Highwood.

The fish was good. So were the conversation and the wine. Paul had ordered a Vouvray. He told her about the one affair he had had during his marriage. It had happened so many years ago, yet he still had a scar from it. And now he had another. Then he told every detail of his brief affair with Jackie. Some she had heard before, some she had not. She listened to every word.

It had started almost nine months earlier. Bobbie had been dead for almost one year. He had made love to one other woman in that time, in Israel that summer, and it had just not worked out. It was too complicated for him and for the kids, especially Joshua. A serious relationship was too painful. It just ended.

And then he was home, back in the routine, and the kids were completely involved with school and the synagogue and the youth group. It was a great relief that they had both worked things out remarkably well and had become less dependent upon him, less tied to him, more independent. He had not been as successful as they had. It was all so damn healthy, but it left him so alone at times, and so empty. And there was Jackie. Young, sexy, and willing.

"Not just for you."

"I didn't know that then."

"You must have been the only one in the hospital who didn't."

"Perhaps. In any case, we became lovers. It was safe. That was her end point. She didn't want any more then. Neither did I. At least that's what I thought. But I was wrong. Sex with her was all right. Not great. But even if it had been great it wouldn't have been enough. Not or me. So I broke it off."

"And there was little old me."

"Yes. I thought you represented just the opposite. And then you said no. You weren't interested in our reaching any kind of an understanding, in anything with any kind of commitment. I was so disappointed."

"I didn't mean to hurt you," she said.

"You didn't. It was screwing Jackie again that hurt."

He ordered some more wine. A split. And went on. "It was degrading. It's one thing to make love not knowing what will ever happen, whether there is any future or not, but it's something else to know there will never be any feeling or any meaning and still go out and do it."

"Paul, I'm sorry."

The wine came.

"Why should you be sorry? I'm the one who did it. It's funny. Physically that was the best time we ever had. It was hell for me when it was over."

Paul poured the wine. They both sipped it slowly.

"Say something."

"There is nothing to say, Paul. It's over. Let's try to forget it."

"Say something else."

"Paul, what kind of wine is this? We've never had it before."

"A Vouvray. Do you like it?" he asked.

"Yes. It is a little on the fruity side, but I do like it."

"It was Bobbie's favorite."

"Is that why we've never had it before?"

He nodded, adding, "And why we are having it tonight."

"Meaning . . . ?"

"I thought you were more Freudian than that," he replied.

"That was a leading question, wasn't it? I didn't mean to pry."

He smiled. "I meant you to." He poured the rest of the wine into their glasses and took a sip.

"So are you going to answer my lead?"

"The answer's simple. It's just not quite so simple to say. I might as well start with the bottom line." He took a deep breath. He might as well get right to the point. "You are no longer competing with Bobbie. It's almost as if you can both exist inside of me without either diminishing the other."

"Paul. That makes me very happy."

"Good. Finish your wine, it's time to pick up the kids."

After he dropped them off at home he drove Gerri back to her apartment and went in with her to make love.

It was perfect.

Slow, sensual. They undressed each other. They held each other. When he entered her he felt at peace with himself and with her. They were as one. He felt no need to hurry. The end would come and it would be exciting, but there was no need to rush it at all. They both knew it and relaxed into a slow crescendo. Almost Brucknerian. With a long climax and a satisfying coda.

That did not end it. Fortunately for them, it rarely did. As they lay back on her bed side by side sharing the afterglow, they both knew that for each of them this was the best part. No matter how good the sex had been.

They barely touched, but felt closer than when he had been inside of her. They talked again of Bobbie and he told her stories he had not dared to think about in the last year and a half. Funny stories. Sad stories. Pointless stories.

"Hell!"

"What's wrong?"

"It's four A.M. I gotta get home." With that he jumped out of bed.

"Will you ever be able to stay the whole night?"

"Sure," he said as he pulled on his shorts.

"When?"

"When Joshua goes to college."

"You son of a—"

"That's only four years from now."

"Only."

"We will go away together."

"When?"

"To a meeting or something."

"When?" she persisted.

"Soon." He was dressed. They walked to the door and embraced.

"Jackie could not make love slowly." It was a fact, not a comparison, and she realized it and was not offended. "She had to rush through to the climax. Then she was ready again. It was just an act. For both of us."

"Paul, try to forget about it. Please."

"There is one other thing," he said.

"What's that?"

"Your car is at my house."

"I know. I planned it that way. You can pick me up for brunch at about eleven."

Sunday is invariably a busier day than Saturday at any private hospital. The reason is not hard to understand. Emergency admissions are equally spread out throughout the week except for the Saturday-night brawlers, who usually go to Cook County or Michael Reese or the University of Chicago. But not Austin Flint. However, on Sunday, the private patients who didn't want to be admitted on Friday or Saturday and waste the weekend come rolling in.

This Sunday was no exception. It was especially busy on the neurology service. There were four new patients admitted, and several of the patients already in the hospital suddenly went sour.

Mr. Kreevich had a succession of seizures, one right after the other for several hours. Floyd Baker, Bud Chiari, and Don Lenhardt all came in to see him. There was no simple answer as to what to do. If they treated his seizures aggressively, they could stop them, but then he might have too much medicine in his system and it might interfere with the surgery the next morning. If they didn't treat him and seizures continued, the brain might become two exhausted to allow them to study it accurately during surgery.

Fortunately, the seizures stopped during their debate. They had decided to treat him fairly vigorously, but before they gave him the intravenous Valium, his seizures stopped. The mere threat had been sufficient.

John Corrigan and Herb Adams were also at Austin Flint that night, getting ready for the week's experiment. They spent four hours opening the skulls of rats, perfecting their technique, so that when it really counted the animals would have every chance of surviving.

Gerri Scala also went in at about 10:30 to see Frank McCormick in the ER. He was very nervous and upset. His brain was rotting. He could smell it. She had meant to tell Paul about it. She would tell him Monday. They had had more important things to talk about. She started him on Haldol.

Edie Robinson also came into the hospital on Sunday. She worked up two of the new patients. One of them was a twenty-six-year-old wife of a Hell's Angel with a two-year history of seizures and two black eyes, both complicated by four months of pregnancy.

By 11:30 all was quiet again and everyone headed home.

Edie never got there. She was attacked just outside the nurses' residence, struck from behind several times with what Detective Ward later called a blunt object, and knocked out. And then much of her hair was cut off. There was no rape. Not even an attempt. And no robbery either. Just some locks of black hair crudely and rapidly sheared off and left beside her on the hard-packed mud.

The security guard found her when he made his 11:45 check. She was just regaining consciousness.

She spent the next two hours recovering in the ER. Their final diagnosis was a slight concussion. Also some bruises, some superficial hematomas, and in addition, some lost hair—but no permanent damage had been done to her, physically at least. To be on the safe side, they even did a CAT scan on her. It was normal.

5

At the same time that Paul Richardson pulled his car out of his driveway, Marv Rickert began to cut the skin on the left side of the newly shaved and cleansed scalp of Michael Kreevich. First he made a long incision beginning one centimeter above the patient's left ear and cutting upward toward the top of the scalp and stopping just before he reached the midline. Then, using the same scalpel, he made a second cut starting from the uppermost end of the initial one and moving anteriorly to just above the patient's left eyebrow. Once the skin flap was retracted and the underlying connective tissue cleared away, Marv looked across the head of the patient to his chief, Don Lenhardt. The latter nodded once, permitting the resident to saw through the bone of the skull and then to open the dura, the thick membrane covering the brain. The routine procedure of exposing the brain was now completed. What came next would not be routine.

Floyd Baker had stood near the operating table and watched each step. Next to Floyd was a fourth-year medical student who was just starting his rotation on neurosurgery. Floyd remembered him. He had taken neurology the previous fall. "Ray," Floyd began, "it won't be like the textbooks."

"Huh?" Ray responded.

"The textbooks all show the same picture of the brain as if the convolutions of all brains are absolutely identical. Unfortunately, things are not that simple."

"They're not?"

Ray Coleman had never been a fast learner.

Floyd started again. "All brains are organized in the same manner, Ray." The student nodded. "Each area of every brain carries out a specific function, and the textbooks show you just where each of those functions is located. But once you open up a skull, that all goes out the window. The convolutions never look like the drawings in the books. No two patients have the same hills and valleys."

"They don't?"

Floyd could feel Ray's disappointment. "I'm afraid not. A person's brain surface is as individual as his fingerprints, but much more difficult to trace out."

It was not going to be easy, but Floyd was going to explain it to him. He started at the beginning. The brain feels no pain. Housed within its protective linings, cushioned by fluid on all sides, and surrounded by thick bones, it has lost its need to feel pain. This one missing attribute was what made it possible for them to carry out their experimental procedure on Mr. Kreevich. To operate on a patient's speech area, you first have to find it. In order to find a patient's speech area, the patient has to be awake and alert. The surgeon has to be able to map out the fingerprint of his alert, awake, pulsating brain.

There was a vague flicker of understanding in Ray Coleman's eyes.

Mr. Kreevich was awake. That Ray saw.

Mr. Kreevich was alert. That Ray understood.

Only the pain fibers of his scalp and his skull had been anesthetized while Dr. Rickert had carefully worked his way down to the brain.

"Wouldn't it be better if he was asleep?" the student asked.

That was it. He'd had it. "From now on, just watch me carefully," Floyd answered.

The senior neurosurgeon now took charge. He inspected the surface of the brain. The scar was easy to locate. It was right there in front of him. A dense pink contracted depression on the surface of the brain, it began on one convolution and bridged the valley to extend to the next one. Finding it was easy. The next part was what took time, skill, and patience.

Floyd Baker turned away from the operating table and in two steps reached the twelve-channel portable EEG machine.

He picked up the thin wires of the sterilized electrodes, checked their connections, and watched as the nurse carefully handed them to the neurosurgeon, who in turn placed them on the brain surrounding the scar. There was a total of ten electrodes, which Don and Marv Rickert put into position one at a time. If they were lucky and a spontaneous seizure occurred, they could record which electrode it came from. But they could not rely on luck, on the fortuitous occurrence of a seizure. Especially not today, with the brain exhausted by yesterday's series of seizures. The green-gowned surgeon made sure the electrodes were placed correctly. When Floyd signaled him that the machine was recording the brain's electrical activity, Lenhardt picked up the single stimulating electrode.

The room was silent. There was no idle conversation. They talked as little as possible. The patient was awake. They communicated by prearranged signals and mere nods and gestures whenever possible.

"Mr. Kreevich . . ." The loud crisp tone of Don Lenhardt's voice filled the room with authority. There was no question as to who was in charge. "We are about to begin. Sometimes I will need you to talk continuously. It's best if you recite something you know by heart. It can be anything. A nursery rhyme, the alphabet, counting, whatever you want, but you must talk continuously, whenever I instruct you to talk. At times, you will feel something. A part of your body may move or feel hot or tingle. Each time you feel something, tell us. We are going to begin."

Don placed the stimulating electrode well behind the scar and fired the first burst of electricity. There was no movement. Mr. Kreevich reported no sensation. The surgeon then looked up at the large mirror in which he could see Floyd Baker seated at the EEG machine. Floyd's signal told them that no seizure discharge had been triggered. That was as expected. They had started in one of the brain's quiet, silent locations, one of the dark, uncharted places on the map of the brain. He slowly moved forward toward the part of the brain that was not silent, toward the part that controlled sensation, then the area for movement, then the one for speech.

Millimeter by millimeter. It was slow work.

First he located the sensory field.

"A burning sensation. I felt it. It was hot." Mike Kreevich said.

"Where?"

"It was so fast I wasn't sure."

"We will do it again for a little longer period of time," Dr. Lenhardt said. Floyd nodded and Lenhardt triggered another low-voltage burst.

"My face, the right side of my face and my right thumb."

"Very good." They were in the right spot. They were at the level of the scar but about a centimeter behind it. They had located the beginning of the sensory brain. They continued anteriorly. The sensation became stronger. Never painful. Never unpleasant. In fact, strangely pleasant. As they got to the scar itself, the response changed.

No more pleasant burning. The right thumb twitched, then the wrist jerked, and the lips pulled to the right. Just in front of the sensory cortex, they had located the motor part of the brain. Right where the textbooks all said it should be. They had done this sort of procedure many times now, but it was still exciting.

The movements became weaker, more fragmentary, and stopped altogether. They had reached the front edge of the motor section of the cortex; next should come the speech area itself. Broca's area. Named after the French surgeon who first demonstrated that speech originated there.

"Now, Mr. Kreevich, start talking. Something you can say over and over again. Anything you memorized early in your life."

" 'The outlook wasn't brilliant for the Mudville Nine that day.' "

As Mr. Kreevich recited, Don Lenhardt fired the probe, waited, looked in the mirror, moved it forward, and once again pressed the trigger. As he got to the midway point in the scar, he fired again.

" 'But Flynn preceded Casey and so did Jimmy . . .' " The speech stopped for a few seconds and restarted. " '. . . Blake.' "

They had found the speech cortex. The neurosurgeon moved the probe forward very carefully. Twice more he pressed the button and twice more the poetry stopped briefly, only to restart where it had left off.

He reached the front of the scar. " 'Somewhere in this

favored land the sun is shining bright . . .' " He pressed the trigger once more. " 'But there is no joy in Mud . . .' " The speech stopped and did not restart. The neurosurgeon looked in the mirror. Floyd Baker was nodding and raising his fingers one at a time. They had found the focus. They had triggered a seizure lasting seven, eight, nine, ten . . . He kept counting. Twenty-seven seconds. They had found the focus just where they knew it would be, in the middle of the speech area. Just where they did not want it to be. It was too easy to strike out in this region.

The process continued. They had to make sure that they had located the only active site. By the time Floyd signaled that they had all the information that they needed, it had taken them almost two and a half hours. The mapping was done, the fingerprint was complete. Don Lenhardt stood back from the operating table, the nurse draped him with extra sterile towels so he could not get contaminated, and he walked over to the EEG machine. Marv Rickert waited at the operating table.

There, on an eight-by-ten sheet of white paper, Floyd Baker had plotted out each stimulus and each response. The sensory map for the face and tongue, the motor map, the speech area. Each point was now fixed in space. No longer unknown. Through the anterior part of the tracing, he had drawn the scar and at the upper edge of the scar, right in the middle of the speech area, the seizure focus.

It was right smack in the most sensitive part of the speech area, one part of the brain that they could not cut out unless they wanted to deprive Mr. Kreevich of the gift of speech once and for all, as if he were permanently having seizures. Even his seizures had never been that out of control.

Ray Coleman was still there, looking blankly at the map that Floyd had so painstakingly constructed.

Seizures, Floyd explained, giving it one last try, travel across the surface of the brain, moving from region to region. There was one fortunate physical limitation. A collection of brain cells which is less than two millimeters across cannot build up enough activity to produce a seizure. Speech works differently. It does not move along the surface. Messages come in from deep within the brain to reach the cortex, and then, once the response is generated, it travels back down into the fibrous depths of the brain.

"So what can we do?" Floyd asked.

"I don't know," came the answer.

"It's obvious. If we make a series of shallow cuts very close together, the remaining areas of the brain between the cuts won't be able to cause seizures." If the theory was correct and if you were very good, very precise, very careful, and very lucky, he added to himself.

"We did this once before," Floyd continued.

"Did it work?" the student asked.

"Shush," Floyd answered.

"Why not?"

"Shut up," Don Lenhardt whispered firmly. "He's awake."

Floyd agreed with the answer. Ray didn't need that answer. If there was one. No one was sure why it hadn't worked. Don had been careful, precise, sure of himself and his technique. The patient had not been lucky. He had permanently lost his ability to speak.

It had been Paul Richardson's idea to try it the first time, but this time it was Don who wanted to attempt it again. Well, Mr. Kreevich didn't seem to have much other hope. The theory was logical. The basis for the surgery was reasonable. Whether it would really work was the only thing that remained as yet unproven.

After a short whispered conference with Floyd, the neurosurgeon shrugged off the extra towels and went back to the operating table. "Mr. Kreevich."

"Yes."

"We are going to start." Marv removed the electrodes and Don picked up a small sharp scalpel. He started at the front edge of the scar and made a single incision, starting one-half centimeter above the scar and ending one-half centimeter below the scar.

The incision was planned to be just deep enough to block the fibers which went across the outer mantle of the brain from cell to cell, but not deep enough to get those fibers which headed deep into the brain substance before turning to deliver their vital messages.

Then he made a second incision, parallel to the first, about a millimeter behind the first one. There was a small amount of bleeding. He carefully put the slightest pressure on the spot, and the bleeding stopped. Then he made a third cut, parallel to the first two and about a millimeter behind the second one.

Over and over again he repeated the same process. He made a total of thirty-four cuts before he was done. It was an exhausted Don Lenhardt who left the operating room while his senior resident closed up.

Soon they would know whether the mighty Casey had struck out again.

As they were leaving the OR, Floyd decided to try one last question. "What are you going to specialize in?"

"Orthopedics."

"Good choice."

It was a typical Monday morning. Traffic on the Edens was terrible. Paul's car moved toward the medical center at a snail's pace. Stop-and-go from Lake Avenue all the way to the junction. It gave Paul a lot of time to think and listen to WFMT. He whistled along with Barber's Overture to *The School for Scandal*. It turned out to be a morning for Americans. Copland followed Barber. Part of the *Red Pony Suite*. And Ives followed Copland. One-third of *Three Places in New England*. Rehearing this minor masterpiece served to strengthen his conviction that Ives was almost as overrated as Barber was underrated.

The news began and he changed stations. He had not learned his lesson. Old habits die hard. He had already read the sports section and knew the Sox had lost, so why hear it again? In switching so quickly, he missed his opportunity to hear about the attack on Edie Robinson. Not that WFMT gave many details. Not even the name. But an attack on a medical student at Austin Flint, just outside the same building where a nurse had been killed a mere five days earlier, was local news that even WFMT could not ignore.

He was still whistling Barber when he walked into his office and found Tom Ward waiting there for him. This was becoming a habit.

"We've got our man, Doc."

"That's great."

"Yeah. We were a bit too late, but it looks like we've got him."

"Too late?" Paul asked.

"Sure, he struck again last night. Right here. Didn't you hear about it?"

"No . . . no, I didn't."

"It was somebody you know."

"Not—"

"No, Doc. It was a medical student. A girl named Robinson." Paul was relieved and at the same time agitated. Ward took out his notebook. "Robinson, Edith. Age twenty-nine. A big girl."

"Is she . . .?" Paul asked, half-afraid to finish his own question.

"She's okay. Got knocked out." He looked down at his notebook again. "She was attacked at about eleven-thirty last night outside the residence hall. Struck with a blunt object, half a dozen times. She was out for about fifteen minutes. She was taken to the ER. A resident of yours examined her. A Dr. William Goodman. She was also seen by a neurosurgeon. The chief, in fact. Dr. Donald Lenhardt. They did some X rays and a scan of some sort."

"A CAT scan."

"That's right. Everything was okay. So they discharged her at two-oh-five."

"What happened?"

"It looks like somebody was waiting specifically for her."

"How do you know that?"

"Well, that's not as quiet a time as you might think. Nurses coming off the three-to-eleven-thirty shift are coming in around then. So somebody is entering that building every couple of minutes. Your neurology P.M. nurse, June Stephens, had just come in a couple of minutes earlier.

"Somebody was waiting in the bushes, as far as we can tell."

"Was he . . . ?"

"We can't even prove that it absolutely was a he. Most likely it was, but we can't be sure. Real life ain't like Sherlock Holmes. We can't look at the partial footprints in the grass and hard-packed mud and say it was a hundred-and-ninety-pound male who was between five-foot-ten and six-foot-one."

"And had red hair and was right-handed," said Paul, completing the nondescription. "And of course there were no tobacco ashes to analyze."

"What? Oh. Tobacco ashes. No. None. Not that they would have been any help anyway."

"So somebody was waiting for her."

"That's the way we've got it figured."

"Who?" Paul asked.

"The same guy who killed Jackie Baumer. At least that's what we're going on."

Paul repeated his question. "Who?"

"Not so fast, Doc. I'll get there." Tom Ward put his notebook away. The rest he knew cold. There was no further need for notes. "As you know, there were basically three possible scenarios. The first, a random act of rape and murder. We doubted that from the very beginning. The other two were something related to Ms. Baumer's sex life or something related to her professional life. The first seemed more likely."

"Why?"

"The kind of crime we had. Tied up in her own bed. Recent intercourse. Multiple stab wounds. It's too messy for anything else."

"That could just be a cover."

"Sure, but that's not likely, Doc. Believe me, I know murder, and this one is a sex crime. Very few people can kill somebody like this, and most of them either have screwed-up sex lives of their own or are tied up sexually with the victim. If you excuse the pun."

Paul had not noticed it and preferred not to say anything.

"So I figured we had to find somebody who knew her."

Paul just listened and said nothing.

"The list was not small, Doc. And we found the right one. Fred Sanford."

"Sanford," Paul repeated softly. He didn't know anyone by that name.

"He picked her up in bars a couple of times. He's a bigshot executive with an oil company. She was into power. He was into some weirder things. We had a complaint about him a year or two ago and suddenly the dame dropped it and went off on a first-class trip to Hawaii, bruises and all.

"We caught up with him this morning about three.

"He was with Jackie Baumer last Tuesday night. He admitted that much to us. Of course we had his semen type.

AB-positive. He also admitted to being into bondage. But he said she was alive when he left her at eleven or so. We didn't really expect him to admit to killing her. We're still questioning him. He has no alibi for last night. Says he was just driving around from ten until twelve and then visited a couple of bars. We're checking out on that too."

"How did you find him?"

"His initials were in her diary. They first appeared just about the last time yours did. I hate to tell you this, Doc, but I think she dug him more."

Paul shuddered.

"Anyway, we had his initials and a four-digit number. For a while that stumped us. Then we figured out that they could be the last four digits of a phone number, and bingo! We figured out the name of the oil company on Friday, but it wasn't until late last night that we got a hold of somebody who knew whose private office number that was. Fred Sanford. F.S."

"I hope you're right."

"I think we are."

"I still have my doubts. It contradicts Antonelli's law or at least the Richardson corollary to it."

"Richardson I know, but not Antonelli," Ward replied. "Wait a minute—wasn't there a Johnny Antonelli who used to pitch for the Milwaukee Braves?"

"Yes there was, and this was also a John Antonelli, I think, but not that one. He was a minor character in a paperback mystery I read by Lawrence Block. His law was that whenever a doctor's wife gets killed, the doctor did it. Don't worry about the evidence, it's always the doc."

"Like Sam Shepard?"

"Yes."

"But Jackie Baumer wasn't married to any doctor."

"That's the Richardson corollary. If there is a murder in the medical center, somebody from here did it."

"You read too many mysteries."

"Maybe."

"You still planning to write one someday based on your cases here? You've got some great stories to tell."

"No. I don't think so."

"Maybe it's better that way. You could let Dr. Chiari be

your emanuwhatsis and write them, making you the hero. I gotta go.''

"So long, Tom.''

Another murder. Solved so easily. Writing a mystery was a tantalizing idea, but Paul knew that he would never even make a stab at it. He had tried to write fiction so many times, but he had realized that that was something he just could not do. He had learned that slowly over time. Not with the suddenness with which he had discovered that he could not hit a curve ball, but with the same finality.

Perhaps his corollary was wrong.

But why had Sanford attacked Edie Robinson? He had forgotten to ask Tom that question. He hoped Tom knew the answer to that one.

What phrase did Paul always use? Some composer. Bruckner. As reliable as Bruckner. If you missed it the first time, he always repeated it for you. That was just what Frank was doing. It was the same story he had told her in the ER last night. The same theme. It was not a time for analysis or insightful interpretations. She had to be more directive than that. "How do you know your brain is rotting, Frank?''

He stopped his rambling. Nothing like a direct question to get an answer. "I told you before, Dr. Scala.''

"Tell me again.''

"I can smell it.''

"What does it smell like?''

"Like a rotting brain.''

She waited. She knew he would say more.

"No. It's more like burning rubber. The smell starts way back in the back of my nose. That's how I can tell it's my brain. I know some anatomy—the back of the nose goes right into the brain, doesn't it?''

"Yes,'' she agreed.

"That's where the smell starts. Right back there. Right where my nose and my brain become one.''

"Is it there all the time?''

"No. No. It's not burning all the time. If it was I'd go crazy. I couldn't take that. I wouldn't have much brain left. My skull would be like a burned-out frame of some old factory torched by some arsonist. No, not a factory. An abandoned warehouse full of tires, old rubber tires. Tires of all types. Tires of all sizes. Radials, whitewalls . . .''

He was rambling again.

Freely associating.

She let him run on, paying at least as much attention to the rapid pressure of his speech as she was to the specific content. And yet when she listened carefully she recognized that it all seemed to have an internal logic once you accepted the premise. More manic than schizophrenic.

"How often do you get this smell?"

"Every day. Two, maybe three times a day."

"Does anything seem to bring it on?" She was acting less and less like a psychiatrist.

"No, they just come. They come and go. All by themselves. I can be doing anything. I can be watching TV or eating or working around the house or anything, even sleeping."

"How long do they last?"

"I'm not sure. They can't be too long. I've tried to time them but it never works. As soon as the smell starts, it takes over my entire brain. I can't think of anything else. I can't do anything else. Time has no meaning. Whatever I see, I don't see. If people talk to me, I hear them but I don't really hear what they've said. The smell is everything. It is me. I am that smell."

She said nothing and once more the pace slackened and came to a halt.

"When did these start?"

"Two months ago."

"Why didn't you tell me until now?"

"At first I only had a few. I wasn't sure what they meant. And then they got worse and I was frightened. I still am. You have to help me, Dr. Scala. You have to."

Time for some positive support. "I gave you some medicine last night."

"Yes," he said anxiously.

"Did you take it?"

"I did just what you told me to."

"Which was . . . ?" It seemed childish but she knew she had to double-check to make sure that Frank had understood the directions and was following them.

"I took two last night and two again this morning." Ten

milligrams plus ten more milligrams, she thought. "And I will take one at noon and one after dinner and then one three times a day."

He had repeated her instructions almost verbatim. She was pleased.

"Will it help me?"

"I think it will," she said.

"Will it stop the burning?"

"Your brain is not burning."

"But the smell?"

"Sometimes when the brain isn't working just right it seems as if you are smelling something, but there is no real odor and nothing is burning," she told him.

"But my brain isn't working right. It's rotting away!"

"It isn't rotting, Frank." She hated that phrase. The imagery disturbed her.

"But you said it isn't working right."

"Yes," she admitted.

"Why isn't it working right?"

She hesitated. "I'm not sure. I am going to discuss this with Dr. Richardson."

"No," he shouted. "No. You can't do that. I won't let you. Never."

"But why?"

"It's all his fault. It's because of him that my brain is rotting."

"We don't know that."

"I do."

It was better not to argue with him. Not to provoke him.

He was calming down. "I trust you, Dr. Scala. I don't trust him. Not anymore. Don't tell him anything and don't ask his advice. You can take care of me. You can help me. You must help me, by yourself."

His session was over. She reminded him to take his pills. After he left, she wrote out her process notes and wondered what to do next. Frank didn't want her to tell Paul anything. Normally she would follow a patient's wishes in a matter like this, and not just for the legal reason that the patient was the only one who had a right to authorize such a flow of information. No, it was not just the legal rights of patients that had to be respected. It was more the entire bond of a psychiatric relationship, of that faith between doctor and patient. That was a two-way street. She had as much of an obligation to it as he did. Maybe more. So often patients didn't follow advice, didn't take medicine, and then lied about it. Still, that didn't make any difference.

She hoped that he was taking his medicine.

There was one major difference here. Frank was on a re-search protocol. They were not just treating him. They were studying him. She had to report on his progress to the group, and especially to Paul. It was his project. She wasn't sure what she could do. Frank had known she would be reporting to Paul. She had explained it all to him. He had even signed a release-of-information form.

She leafed through the chart.

It was there. Signed and witnessed. Still, he had told her not to.

She knew what she would do. She would tell Paul she had had to start Frank on Haldol. Paul had to know that. But she would not give him any details. And if Frank had any more problems, she would refer him to Bud or Floyd Baker. Proba-bly Floyd. He was part of the team for this project. She finished her note.

It was time for her next patient.

Paul had not been sure what to expect. He was relieved that Edie Robinson was feeling well enough to come to the hospi-tal and make rounds. Her face was bruised and she had a black eye. She had not tried to mask her injuries with makeup. Her dark hair did hide the scalp bruises fairly well, but not the facial ones. And her hair was different. Shorter. Less feminine. In fact, almost masculine. Why had she . . . ? Then he remembered. She hadn't cut her hair. He had. Fred Sanford.

It was a morning to take it easy. There were two new patients. Edie told him about the first one. She talked more slowly than usual. Her swollen lower lip was obviously both-ering her.

The patient was a twenty-seven-year-old white female who had had seizures since age sixteen. She had been on anticon-vulsants for nine years and was now on Dilantin and phenobarb. She had been admitted because of three seizures.

"Describe the seizures," Paul said.

"They begin with a strange feeling in her stomach, which then seems to spread up toward her throat."

"What's that called?"

"An aura."

"Right. An aura. The manifestation of abnormal activity in one part of the brain which precedes a generalized seizure and therefore serves as a warning or aura. What follows her aura?"

"A grand-mal seizure."

"How good has her control been?"

"In general pretty good. Only one seizure every year or so," she answered.

"And then three in one day?" he asked.

"Yes."

"Why?" He was going too quickly. "Why do pateints who have seizures and are fairly well controlled suddenly begin to have seizures again? In general?" Paul got up and went to the blackboard and wrote out the list and explained each of the possibilities.

1. NONCOMPLIANCE. "The most common reason. Not taking the medicine. Either accidentally or intentionally."

2. OTHER MEDICATIONS.

3. EXCESSIVE ALCOHOL.

4. INFECTION.

5. HEAD TRAUMA.

6. PREGNANCY.

7. SEVERE EMOTIONAL STRESS.

8. GOK. " 'GOD ONLY KNOWS.'

"Which of these apply to our patient?"

"Most of them," she said.

"Most of them?" Paul echoed her answer.

"She is pregnant. She does drink a lot. Her husband beats her. She's thinking of leaving him and isn't sure what to do. She's worried about the baby. She does use recreational drugs and she admits that she doesn't always take all her medication."

"Let's take it a bit more slowly, Edie."

Edie did just that. She took her time and relayed the entire story. She had gotten much more information than Bill Goodman had, and the two physicians listened carefully as the senior student gave all the details. She had spent most of Sunday evening with her patient.

The patient was married to a Hell's Angel. They bounced around the country on his motorcycle.

They drank a lot.

How much?

They got drunk once or twice a week.

They took drugs.

What?

Whatever they could get their hands on.

He beat her.

When?

Whenever he felt like it. Usually he hit her in the stomach and whipped her backside. But now out of consideration for her baby, he was hitting her on the face.

Paul winced. Maybe that was the sort of thing that Jackie . . . He didn't want to complete that thought.

He had knocked her out a couple of times in the last two weeks.

She was four months pregnant and she was scared that he might hurt the baby.

"So why doesn't she just leave him?" Paul asked.

"She likes it," Bill said, usurping the answer. "She's into that sort of thing."

"She is not."

"Come off it, Edie. She's been with him for years. She must dig it. She didn't even want to be admitted. She's only here because you talked her into it. Those tattoos are a giveaway."

"Tattoos?" Paul asked.

"On each breast," Bill answered.

"Dare I ask what they are?"

"The one on the right breast—" Bill began but was interrupted.

"You men are all the same. Sure she has obscene pictures on her body. So what. She's frightened. She feels trapped. You should be helping her, not staring at the pictures on her . . . tits."

Paul knew she was right.

Bill was not as sure. "Those pictures on her tits, as you so quaintly put it, are important. We are not voyeurs. She did that to herself. I asked her. She's proud of them. It's her life-style. Her husband wasn't the first man to beat her. The guy before her was into leather and God only knows what else. She's crazy. She has been for some time. We'll patch her up and she'll go back to him. It happens every time."

"She will not."

She probably would, Paul thought. Bill was right. That was the usual course. It was not very helpful to sit here and argue.

"What are we doing to evaluate what happened to her?"

As Edie told him what they were doing, he wrote the appropriate test on the board.

1. NONCOMPLIANCE
   Blood levels of Dilantin and phenobarbitol
2. OTHER MEDICATIONS
   Toxic screen
3. EXCESSIVE ALCOHOL
   Tests of liver function
   Blood-alcohol level on admission
4. INFECTION
   Spinal tap to look for signs of infection.
5. HEAD TRAUMA
   Brain-wave test
   Spinal tap to look for fresh blood
6. PREGNANCY
   No workup necessary
7. SEVERE EMOTIONAL STRESS
   Ditto

They went to see her but she was down in the EEG lab getting her brain-wave test.

Bill Goodman started to say something about the tattoos, especially the one on her left breast. That was the one that really got to him, but Edie was still angry so he decided to let it pass.

"Who worked up the other patient?" Paul asked, filling the void.

"I did," Bill replied. His presentation concisely summarized a long, complex story. The patient was a thirty-four-year-old man named Maurie Rath who had had seizures since age sixteen or seventeen. The seizures were always the same. "The first thing he notices is a strange feeling as if something is happening that has already happened before."

"What's that called, Edie?" Paul asked, interrupting.

"*Déjà vu.*"

"That's right. And what's that a sign of?"

"Abnormal function in the temporal lobe."

"Very good, Edie," Paul said. "It's another type of aura. Often such discharges produce a distorted variation of the usual function of that area of the brain. If it's in the visual area, the discharges might cause flashing lights or some other visual phenomenon. The temporal lobe carries out a variety of functions related to memory, so that discharges there may start with an episode of *déjà vu.*"

Bill Goodman went on to tell the rest of the story. The *déjà vu* episodes were often followed by generalized seizures. Over the years, the patient had been on every anticonvulsant in the book. He was now on Dilantin, Tegretol, and Valproate and was still having two or three seizures a week. He was here for two reasons. The first was an entirely new problem. During the last few months he had been having sudden episodes of jerking of both arms. They were also planning to evaluate him for possible surgery for his uncontrolled epilepsy.

The three of them went to see the patient and sat by his bedside.

Paul introduced himself and asked Mr. Rath to tell them all about his seizures and Mr. Rath proceeded to do so. They did not learn anything new. Paul had not expected that they would. He was sure that Bill Goodman had extracted the history carefully and thoroughly. That was not his purpose.

He sat back and listened.

Five minutes.

Ten minutes.

The story went on.

Mr. Rath was talking more slowly. He, too, was now more relaxed.

Twelve minutes.

Then it happened.

It took less than two seconds. Paul hoped that Bill and Edie had not missed it. There was nothing more to see. He thanked Mr. Rath.

"But I haven't finished."

"I know," Paul told him. This was always the hard part. Patients did not know what was really important and what was not. "Dr. Goodman knows most of the rest, I think, and I'll be back soon to talk to you some more." That and a hasty retreat.

"Did you see it?"

Both Edie and Bill nodded.

"Describe it."

Edie went first. "He was talking. Then all of a sudden both arms jerked."

"How many times?"

"Once."

"Was that all that jerked?"

"No, his head twitched a bit."

Very good, Edie, he thought. "What's that called?"

Edie wasn't sure.

Bill was. "Myoclonus." He was right.

"No one has seen it before," Bill added.

"That was probably because no one really got him to relax. Going into relaxation, from tension to relaxation, often brings out myoclonus," Paul explained. "But now that we've seen it, what have we learned?"

Neither Edie nor Bill was sure.

"We learned that we don't have much more to learn."

Paul could see that neither of them had learned very much from what he had said. "That kind of myoclonus can be seen in epileptic patients but means nothing."

Somehow, his explanation did not seem to enlighten them any more. He started again. "There are two real possibilities here. The first is that these jerks could be due to an area of irritation of the cortex like the *déjà vu* episodes. If that were true, it would mean that Mr. Rath has at least two separate areas of epileptic activity and . . ." Paul hesitated. He waited.

"He probably wouldn't be a good candidate for surgery," Edie said.

"That's right. Now, the other possibility is that it's the kind of myoclonus that can occur in patients with seizures, without there being any new abnormal focus. The jerks we saw look exactly like that kind of myoclonus. How can we prove it?"

"He is having an EEG later today," Bill said.

"Right. If he has an episode during the EEG, that will probably answer our question.

"Myoclonus," Paul went on, "always reminds me of my first patient with myoclonus." It was a form of *déjà vu* for both Paul, who had retold this story many times before, and Bill, who had heard it more than once during his residency.

Paul knew Bill had heard it more than once, but he told it anyway. It had happened when he had been in the Army, during the early part of the Vietnam war, at about the same time that LBJ had increased our troop commitment to sixty thousand and promised to have the boys home by Christmas or something. Paul was seeing a consult in the hospital and was idly watching a young female patient walk down the hall when suddenly both her arms jerked just like Mr. Rath's. Unlike the myoclonic jerk they had just witnessed, this young woman's legs also jerked out so that she landed on the exact part of her anatomy that Paul had been observing so carefully.

Edie was not amused.

Bill was.

Paul hurried to make a long story not quite as long as usual.

The Army doctors thought she was hysterical. Paul was sure she had a seizure disorder. The other doctors attributed her hysteria to the ongoing Army investigation of her alleged lesbian activity. Paul became convinced it was due to hereditary epilepsy. Her mother had seizures. So did one aunt.

She was an operating-room nurse and had been for eight or nine years. The Army was going to give her a dishonorable discharge. She was a lesbian, and as such was an obvious security risk. She might give the Vietcong the secret of a new surgical approach to hemorrhoids.

She was a career officer. She wanted to stay in the Army.

Paul turned out to be right. She had myoclonic seizures. The EEGs showed it. She responded well to medicine.

She still had to go.

Paul managed to get her a medical discharge instead of a dishonorable one.

A victory. A minor one, but a victory.

Edie was not impressed.

It was time for another hasty retreat.

Once he was back in his office, Paul sat with a cup of coffee and a package of peanut-butter cheese crackers he had

gotten out of a machine for thirty-five cents. When he had
been in the Army they were only a dime. Of course a dime
then still had silver in it. That dime now would be worth over
seventy cents. That would be two whole packages of crackers.

He went through the mail rapidly, as if he expected another
postmortem missive from Jackie Baumer.

There was none, so he worked his way back through the
mail one letter at a time, but only after turning on the radio.
A concert from the BBC, English chamber music. A string
quartet by Frank Bridge. It was boring. But he had work to
do. He should have gone to the funeral. Perhaps he'd go
when they dedicated the headstone. No one else would be
there from the hospital for that ceremony. He could be like
Walt Whitman. Whitman had been the only one to show up
when a headstone was finally put on Poe's grave. Edgar Allan
Poe. Such was fame. Poe had started it all. He had written the
first real detective story. "The Murders in the Rue Morgue."
The first locked-room mystery. Set in Paris. He should get
some work done.

Once he finished the mail, he started to pull together his
material for his presentation to the Committee on Human
Investigation. He was interrupted by only one phone call.
Gerri Scala.

"Paul."

"Yes, lover."

"Paul, please."

"Right now?"

"Be serious."

"I am."

"Paul, this is a professional call."

"Are you becoming a professional?"

"Sometimes you are absolutely impossible."

"I know."

"I'm calling about a patient."

"Who?"

"Frank McCormick."

"What's with him?"

"He's not doing as well."

"In what way?"

"Paul, he doesn't think I should tell you the details . . ."

"Why?"

"And neither do I."

"What the hell . . ."

"Look, Paul. He is not feeling well. He's worried. He doesn't . . . trust you."

"Me?"

"The surgery was your idea."

"True."

"And he thinks it might have hurt him, so he asked that I not give you the details."

"And you agreed?"

"Yes."

"So why did you call?" he asked.

"I wanted you to know."

"Why?"

"You are the project director."

"I'm glad you remembered."

"You are hurt."

"Don't be my shrink."

"You are a bastard sometimes."

"What did you do for him?"

"I put him on Haldol."

"Good." Not *very* good. Just good.

She waited.

He waited.

She was better at waiting. There were some advantages to psychiatric training.

He apologized.

She accepted his apology.

It was time for his meeting.

Neither John Corrigan nor Herb Adams was terribly enthusiastic about the experiments they were starting, but they both knew they had to be done.

First they anesthetized the rats.

Then they shaved part of the scalp and removed some of the skull, exposing the brain and its blood vessels. Now it got tougher.

In each animal they searched carefully for a large vein. Then just as carefully, using the dissecting microscope, they isolated that vein, and making sure not to cause any blood loss, placed a number-twenty-five needle into the blood vessel. Next they threaded a fine catheter through the needle into the vein. They did this to all forty rats.

In one-half of the animals, the needle was slowly removed until the bevelled end was half outside the vein and blood began to escape from the vein and collect around it and over the brain.

Last came the final experimental step, the injection of the experimental agent JNF-2 directly into the blood vessels.

It was slow and tedious.

One rat at a time.

One blood vessel at a time.

In the first group of animals who had already bled when the needle had been removed, the catheter was immediately pulled out after the injection, allowing for some further leakage from the puncture site.

In the second group, the catheter was kept in place for five minutes until all the blood inside the punctured veins had clotted. Only then was the catheter withdrawn. The protocol worked. None of the puncture wounds bled.

After that the last steps were simple. Covering over the scalp defect to make sure the area would stay sterile and waking up the rats.

For the first time all day they could relax.

"That went well, Herb."

"I don't think we'll lose any of them."

"That should make Richardson happy."

"The injections went so easily," Herb said, ignoring John's sarcasm. "Much easier than the last time."

"How can you remember? That was almost two years ago."

"I remember. The first time, I killed almost half the animals. Paul was pissed. We were using guinea pigs then at seventeen bucks a throw. But the injections were so difficult. The stuff was so thick. The needles got plugged. Then I had to increase the force, and bang, I ruptured so many blood vessels. Now the stuff flows so much more easily. It's hard to believe that it's the same agent."

"It is. But we changed the adjuvant."

"The adjuvant?"

"Sure, the JNF-2 itself won't go into a solution, so in the manufacturing process we have to add an adjuvant to make it soluble. We changed the adjuvant in all of our products about a year ago.''

''It sure makes it easier to work with.''

''It's an old adjuvant. In fact, it's the one we've been using off and on for the last eight to ten years. The one you worked with two years ago was a modification which just didn't work out as well.''

They were done.

Paul would be very pleased. They had lost no animals at all.

In twenty-four hours they would study the acute effects and then they'd know if they could use JNF-2 safely in the presence of recent bleeding.

The successful completion of the first stage of the lab experiment was not the only thing that pleased Paul that afternoon. The Committee on Human Investigation unanimously approved the project on surgical implants in Parkinson's disease. It had gone rather easily. Paul presented the hypothesis in a very straightforward manner.

Parkinson's disease was due to a loss of dopamine in specific regions of the brain.

The adrenal gland made chemicals much like dopamine.

In animals, implants of tissue from an adrenal gland to the brain could replace dopamine lost as a result of brain injuries.

So it was worthwhile to see if an adrenal implant would do the same in a person with parkinsonism.

They all agreed.

They asked only one question. Was it safe?

Paul thought it would be.

They had done the implant over a year ago and the patient was doing fairly well. There had been no problems with the surgery. Of course his schizophrenia had not been helped and might even be worse, but the procedure itself seemed safe enough.

They all agreed.

6

"Is it always this hard?" she asked. "This darn difficult?" She paused, but he, of course, said nothing. He merely sighed. Not that she had really expected him to say anything. He was such a master at saying nothing and she had become equally adept at interpreting his sparse grunts and sighs. Who else had such a broad range of inarticulate utterances? Who else had at his command at least fourteen different classes of guttural throat clearings, each with a distinct set of meanings? No one else. Only M. J. Rotblatt. Had he learned them from Franz Alexander? She hoped so. Perhaps they were a direct link. A nonverbal inheritance, handed down across the generations. From Freud to Alexander to Rotblatt . . . to Scala. Another sigh. That made it three. She knew what that meant. She had to go on.

"I've read so many articles about the process of termination."

He cleared his throat.

Disapproval. She was wasting his time. Beating around the bush.

She stared up at the ceiling. Dammit, she thought, next time I'm not going to lie down. I'm going to sit up and look at him. "Why is it so hard?"

An interested cough.

"I've been lying here on this couch four times a week for five and a half years. Week in and week out, and now we're through. My analysis is supposed to be over and yet I can't seem to cut the cord. I wish we had more time. I like coming here week in, week out. Except when you . . . ah . . . go on vacation. I don't even go on a vacation except when you do.''

A very interested sniff.

"You and your damn vacations. They always seem to come when I need you. Oh, I know you think I'm just like any other patient, I set up crises so that they happen just exactly when you are about to leave town, to try to get you to stay instead of deserting me. But this time it's different. I had no control over it at all. I sure as hell didn't want to find out. That detective just told me. He just came out and told me that Paul had been making love to Jackie Baumer. How could he have done that? And how in the world could I still have gone to bed with him?''

"You already knew that they had been lovers."

A whole sentence. It must be part of the termination process.

"No. No. I didn't. I did but I didn't. Sure, he had told me about their little affair. But this was different. This was something he'd never told me about. This was recent. Not last year. But since we've been together. He never told me about it until I confronted him.''

A deep breath, a question.

"Three months ago.''

."Ah.'' A shared insight.

"You're as bad as he is. All men are alike. You probably think he had every right to go off and screw her because I turned him down.''

Not so much as a sniff.

"Well, you at least know why I turned him down. I couldn't say yes. I couldn't offer him a complete life. I couldn't then and I can't now and I never will be able to and that's the truth.

"All these five and a half years of analysis haven't changed that one damn bit. It's funny. I guess we all have to learn the limits of analysis. Well, I've learned them. It can't make reality go away. I'm never going to be able to have children of my own. That's it. Well, at least I can say it now. I guess I can thank you for that.''

"Does Paul want to have more children?''

"I don't know.''

"Why don't you know?''

"I've never asked him.''

"Why not?" he asked.

It was her turn to be silent.

"How old is he?"

"Forty-five."

"Most forty-five-year-old men are not interested in starting families. Especially not if they already have one."

"That still didn't give him the right to go to bed with that whore."

"Why are you so damn pejorative?"

"About what?"

"About them being lovers."

"They didn't make love. They fucked. It was a pure animal act. They fucked."

She was crying now.

They both knew why.

She was no longer angry. "He lowered himself to her level. He's better than that. He did the same damn thing my stepfather did. Paul's no better than he was."

"I doubt that."

A judgment. A real judgment. Termination was remarkably different.

"I suspect that Paul was hurt when you turned him down." And a full sentence.

"I had to do that. And we both know why."

"Did Paul?"

"No," she admitted. "But why did he pick her to make love to?"

He waited for her to answer her own question. She did. "Because she was available."

"Is that the only reason?" he asked.

"No, I guess not. Other women were available too. I'm sure."

"So there must have been another reason."

"To punish himself," she said slowly.

A grunt. The grunt of assent.

"At the same time he acted out . . . and . . . and he got back at me and . . . he also punished himself. He knew he was degrading himself by making love like that. He said it himself. He made love to her when there was no future to it. It was a meaningless act. No, not just meaningless. It was self-destructive."

"When you and Paul make love, is it like that?"

"Of course not."

"Why not?"

"Because we mean something to each other now and . . . and into the future."

"You have a past, a present, and a future."

"You're damn right."

"A complete relationship."

"Yes."

"Even without children."

"Yes. No. Yes. I don't know."

"You are not incomplete, Gerri."

"You are not a woman, Dr. Rotblatt."

"I will see you next on Friday."

"Friday?"

"Yes, it's time we were down to just twice a week. We haven't got very much longer."

"But I'm not ready."

"You are, Gerri, and we really don't have much choice in the matter."

Paul was not entirely sure what purpose was being served by Tom Ward's daily visitations. It seemed to be part of a game he was expected to play without ever having been given a copy of the rules. The police were still trying to pin it all on Fred Sanford. There were several aspects that were not entirely clear to Paul. There would never be a better time to see what the rules allowed. "There are several things I just don't understand," he began. When Tom said nothing, Paul continued. "You said that some out-of-towner had picked Jackie up in a bar the night she was killed, or vice versa?"

"That's right, Doc."

"But Sanford wasn't an out-of-towner. He was somebody she knew beforehand."

"Right again."

"If I'm right again, why am I so confused?"

"What's the problem?"

"She picks up a stranger and gets herself killed and you are fairly sure it's this Sanford guy who certainly wasn't a stranger and obviously didn't just pick her up that night."

"You really are basically straight, aren't you?"

"I'm not sure what that has to do with all this."

"It explains your confusion."

"How so?"

"She made love to two men that night."

"I forgot that."

"Man one was probably the out-of-towner. Blood type O. Man two was our friend Fred Sanford with blood type AB."

"That makes the unknown visitor to our fair city innocent," Paul realized.

"I wouldn't really call him innocent. But he certainly didn't kill her."

"You still looking for him?" Paul asked.

"Yes."

"Why?"

"If nothing else, he was probably the last person to see her alive except for the killer. Knowing precisely when he left her would help us narrow down our time frame."

"One other thing."

"What's that, Doc?"

"Edie Robinson. How does she fit in?"

"She was a friend of Jackie's."

"So?"

"There you go again."

"Are you saying that you used the term 'friend' as a polite euphemism?"

"I'm not exactly sure what you mean, Doc. But I was being polite. They were more than just casual friends."

Paul understood. You didn't have to draw him pictures.

"It's possible she knew who Sanford was. That she could have fingered him for us. Or identified him even."

"But you had Jackie's diary."

"He didn't know that. You're the only who knows about the diary, and you only know about it because I told you."

"You're wrong there. Two of us know. Me and Dr. Scala. Thanks to you."

"True. But Sanford didn't and still doesn't," Tom said, ignoring Paul's last remark as well as he could.

"I don't know," Paul said. "Something's wrong. Why didn't he just kill Edie?"

"Doc, that's not as strange as you might think. Remember how he killed Jackie. First he beat her up, then he killed her.

There was no reason to beat her up first. But he did it. That's how he operates. Sure, a logical killer would have just killed her if that was what he had to do to protect himself. But this is no exercise in logic. Ask yourself this question. How did he know about her?''

"I don't know."

"Speculate."

"Jackie told him."

"Or?" Tom persisted.

"He met her. Through Jackie. With Jackie."

"Bingo. Now it makes sense. He equated her with Jackie. So he had to kill her the same way."

"But he didn't," Paul objected.

"No. He didn't. He was probably interrupted."

"By whom?"

"We don't know."

"But isn't that important?"

"Sure. And we're trying to find out, but there are so many people around here it's almost impossible to track them all down. We're still trying to discover the whereabouts of everybody on the night Jackie Baumer was killed."

"I was at home that night. With my two kids."

"We know that. We even know that the hospital called you twice and that you were home both times."

"I'm glad to see how much faith you have in my word."

"It's part of my job. I have to check out everybody."

"Everybody?"

"Everyone who knew Jackie. Your team was easy. They were all here. Some patient of yours went sour."

"Rogovin."

"That was the one. Everyone was here." He took out his notebook and found the right page. "Lenhardt, Baker, Goodman, Chiari, Rickert, Robinson. They all were here with the patient. Corrigan and Adams were in the lab finishing up some experiments. Scala was in the ER with some psychiatric patient of hers. You are the only one with an alibi," he concluded. "It is a good thing none of them are suspects."

"Tom, I've got work to do."

"So do I, Doc. So do I."

Paul spent the rest of the morning working in his office. He divided his time between administrative work on the next year's budget, getting ready for his clinical-pathologic conference, and returning patient phone calls.

It was the life of Mortiz Kohn that intrigued him. Kohn had gotten his M.D. from the University of Vienna in 1861. He then served as an assistant to Hebra, one of the greats of Viennese medicine, one of the first great dermatologists.

In 1869 Kohn married Hebra's daughter.

In 1881, following Hebra's death, he was given the chair in dermatology.

When had he become Kaposi? And why? Had he done more than just change his name? Had he converted to Catholicism? Yes. He had. Why? To marry Hebra's daughter? To get a job in anti-Semitic Vienna? Or both? The textbooks didn't have an answer. Certainly the latter, at least. Even Gustav Mahler had had to convert to get a job.

Kaposi né Kohn completed Hebra's path-setting textbook on dermatology and later wrote his own.

He described a dozen new diseases, including Kaposi's sarcoma. That had always been a rare disease. Dark hemorrhagic nodules which occur late in life when the immune system is no longer working normally. Now Kaposi's sarcoma was no longer rare. It was being seen in a new setting. AIDS. Acquired immune deficiency syndrome. The most recent of the world's venereal epidemics. A strange new disease spreading mostly among homosexuals. It somehow knocks out the immune system so the patient gets diseases that people with normal defenses never get. Rare infections and tumors like Kaposi's sarcoma.

It was the phone. Mrs. Kell. She just wanted to check her medicine schedule. Was she taking the right medicine? Yes. At the right times? He listened to her recite the schedule. Yes. She was following the right schedule.

Another phone call.

Another patient. John Mostil. Paul had all he could do to remember him. He had seen him only a couple of times and that had been at least three years earlier.

"It's getting worse. I'm beginning to shake as badly as my dad did."

Paul remembered. Mostil had a familial tremor. His father had had the same problem. "Usually it's stress that brings out your kind of shakiness," Paul said.

"That's it. I was just promoted and I have to give talks to groups of people. That's when I shake like a leaf. Is there anything I can take?"

"Yes."

"What?"

"It's called Inderal. It should help. Have your pharmacy give me a call."

Back to the budget.

While Paul was whiling away his morning in the office, Herb Adams was in the laboratory checking the rats. It was now twenty-four hours since they had been treated. They were all still alive. That was a great improvement over the previous experiment with JNF-2.

Don Lenhardt, along with Marv Rickert and Ray Coleman, joined Paul for the start of rounds at 12:30. They were there to see Mr. Kreevich. Don and Marv didn't particularly like what they saw.

Mr. Kreevich was resting quietly in his bed. His scalp was covered by a clean white bandage. His eyes watched them as they walked to his bedside.

"Good afternoon," Paul said.

Mike Kreevich looked at Paul but said nothing.

"How are you feeling?"

No answer.

"Do you hurt anywhere?"

Again no response.

Paul shook his head. He had to start somewhere else.

"Mike!"

The patient looked at him. It was hard to resist the tendency to shout when the patient didn't respond, even though it was obvious that he had not suddenly become deaf.

"Lift up your right hand."

Mike Kreevich lifted his right hand.

"Now lift your left hand."

He lifted his left hand.

"Put your right hand on your left ear and close your eyes."

This time the patient hesitated.

Paul repeated the order, carefully enunciating each word.

Mike did it step by step. He lifted up his right hand, reached over his head and touched his left ear, and then closed his eyes.

"You can put your hand down now."

He did and he opened his eyes.

"Stick out your tongue."

Mike shifted in bed but he did not stick out his tongue.

"Open your mouth and stick out your tonguge."

The same lack of response.

Paul tried one more thing. He reached into his pocket and took out his keys. He held them in front of Mr. Kreevich and shook them. Mike Kreevich watched him; his eyes focused directly on the keys.

"What are these called?"

The patient continued to watch Paul intently.

"What am I holding?"

He only licked his lips.

Paul called it quits and walked out of the room.

They all gathered in the hallway just outside Mike Kreevich's room.

"What's his problem?" Paul asked, looking directly at Ray Coleman. The student just shrugged his shoulders.

"Marv?"

"He's aphasic."

"What kind of aphasia?"

"Expressive."

"Meaning . . . ?"

"That he can understand and follow orders but he can't initiate any speech."

"Perfect. He can follow complex orders. But he says nothing. The only order he couldn't follow was to stick out his tongue. And that is part of aphasia, if the aphasia is severe enough."

Don Lenhardt frowned.

"Where's the injury that causes that kind of aphasia?"

"Right where we operated," Don said.

"Yes. But that is what we would expect," Paul added, and turned to Edie. "What could the problem be?"

"Maybe the area is just swollen," she suggested through her own swollen lip, which looked better than it had on Monday.

"Possibly."

"Or injured."

"Another possibility. Can you think of a third?"

She thought. "Maybe the surgery didn't work."

"Meaning . . . ?"

"He may be having more seizures."

"So . . . ?"

"We should do an EEG."

He looked at Bill Goodman.

"I'll get one done this afternoon."

Marv and Don left to see their other neurosurgical patients. Ray trailed after them. As they departed, Paul heard Don say, "I never should have let Richardson talk me into that operation."

Paul had not remembered it that way. He was tempted to say something but didn't. They were gone. Instead he discussed Maurice Rath's seizures with Edie and Bill and the three of them looked through his EEG. He had had two myoclonic jerks during the EEG and there was no evidence of a new area of brain injury. That meant that he was still a good candidate for surgery. The question was what they should do next. They decided to do a Metrazol test. Metrazol, Paul explained, was a brain stimulant, a convulsant, a drug that could cause seizure even in normal brains.

"How will that help us?" Edie asked. "It causes seizures in normal people."

"We will give him a much lower dose. A dose that can cause a seizure from an abnormal brain but not in a normal one. We will be monitoring his brain waves and hopefully we will reproduce his usual type of seizure and see just where in his brain it comes from."

They next stopped by to see Donna Kolloway. Her arm and leg were no weaker. She was stable. She asked if they knew what they wanted to do. No, they didn't. The doctors were all going to put their heads together and decide what they felt was safest.

Edie also brought Paul up-to-date on her other seizure patient. She had therapeutic blood levels of both Dilantin and phenobarbital, so she must have been taking her medicines.

"What about her spinal tap?" Paul asked.

"It was normal," she told him.

"No sign of infection?"

"No."

"Or bleeding?"

"No."

"Is that all you're going to tell him?" Bill demanded.

"Yes." She was adamant.

"Chief, you should have been there for the spinal tap."

"I don't believe this," Edie said.

"When we prepped her," Bill went on, ignoring the senior student, "and got her into position, I saw her buttocks for the first time."

Edie walked away. Bill continued, "She has tattoos on her butt."

"So what? She's got them elsewhere."

"It's what she has tattooed on her ass that's significant."

"More dirty pictures?"

"No. Words."

"What?"

"Guess."

"Abandon all hope, ye who enter here. No, that's too literate."

"Names."

"Names!"

"A long list of lovers past and present. And get this. When anyone is out of favor, the word 'Void' is tattooed across the name."

"What happens if an old lover ever makes a comeback?"

"What do you mean?"

"Well, if a lover of mine wrote 'Void' across my name on her derriere, I might take it personally."

Paul stopped by his lab before going back to his office.

Both Herb and John were there. They were both in good spirits, especially John Corrigan. "The rats all look good, Paul. Come and take a look." His enthusiasm incited a pang of jealousy in Paul. John's joy was a special kind of happiness that came when an experiment worked just right. Nothing else that Paul had ever experienced was the same. Some people didn't understand why John still worked in lab himself. After all, he could afford to hire technicians to do the work. Paul understood. If he could only find the time, he'd go back to the lab. But for the chairman there was never time for anything.

The three of them went over to the first observation cage. The cage contained two rats. Both of the rats had bandages on their heads. Otherwise they looked normal and moved around their cage without any sign of weakness or of paralysis.

Herb removed the top of the cage and reached in, picking up one of the rats. Paul did his best to suppress his squeamish distaste. Orwell was right. Rats were one of man's basic fears. Paul watched as Herb placed the rat so that it was hanging from a shelf by its front paws. It held on for ten seconds without any difficulty. Next he placed the rat on a thin horizontal rod. The rat grabbed the rod with all four paws. But Orwell hadn't been one hundred percent right. He had suggested that an uncontrollable fear of rats was irrational. That just was not true. There was nothing at all irrational about it. John Corrigan flicked a switch and a slight electric shock was sent through the rod. Immediately the rat scurried across the rod to the nonelectrified pad at the end. Perched on that small island of safety, it began to survey the room. For a long moment its small piercing eyes rested their gaze on Paul. He tried not to look back. He remembered the hero of *1984*. They had used rats to torture him. What was his name? He couldn't think of it. Not with that damn rat staring at him like a rodent version of Big Brother.

Herb picked the rat up and put him in a maze.

John timed him.

Someday he was going to design a maze with electric shocks at both ends and no rewards at all. That would show the rats who was in charge.

"Fourteen seconds," John told them.

"Normal," Herb added.

For a rat.

They were done. There were no signs of weakness or loss of balance.

"He looks pretty good," Paul agreed.

"Pretty good?" John said. "He's normal."

"His motor system does seem to be intact," Paul agreed.

"He tests out fine on the other maze too," Herb informed them both.

Paul nodded. "He may well be normal, then. Of course our testing is fairly crude. Still, he does look awfully damn healthy. Do they all look that good?"

"Yes," Herb said. "I've tested them all for motor responses, balance, maze reactions, the whole routine. They all test out okay."

"That is very encouraging," Paul said.

"Encouraging. Is that all you can say?" John asked.

"All right. It looks downright exciting. It looks as if there is no evidence of significant brain damage. But it's still too early to be sure."

"Don't be so damn skeptical."

"I'm not skeptical. I just don't like to be enthusiastic until I'm sure."

"Well, I'm sure. We've done these studies ourselves at Dillinger and I can assure you there will be no brain damage."

"I know, but I want us to make doubly sure before we inject any more patients with fresh bleeding. Mr. Rogovin—"

"Paul, we don't know exactly what happened to him. Not for sure anyway."

"True."

"Patients died from AV malformations long before we ever invented JNF-2."

"That is also true," Paul admitted. "We will be cutting his brain this week. Maybe then we will know something more definitive."

Paul watched as Herb put another rat through its paces. Meanwhile, John poured them each a cup of coffee, remembering to put powdered cream substitute and sweetener into Paul's before he handed it to him.

"Has Carolyn decided where she's going to school?" John asked.

The question caught him by surprise. "No. Not yet."

"Is she still limiting herself to the Midwest?"

"Most likely."

"Well, if she changes her mind and wants to go East, let me know. We have a lot of connections out there and could probably be very helpful to her."

Paul was pretty sure Carolyn did not want any help and he was absolutely certain that he didn't. Still, John was just offering to do them a favor. They didn't have to accept his offer. He was probably exaggerating his influence.

"The corporations we have been working with have given a number of very prestigious schools one hell of a lot of money. When they ask that a particular applicant be given very serious consideration, the schools listen. So if she changes her mind, just give me the word.''

"I don't think she will, but thanks for the offer," Paul answered. It was time for him to leave. He had a clinic to get to.

He was halfway through his clinic when he got a call from Tony Muser, the endocrinologist. "Paul."

"Yes."

"I hate to bother you in the middle of a clinic."

"It's okay."

"We've got a big problem."

"A patient?" Paul asked.

"Worse."

"Worse?"

"Dean Willis."

"What's T.B. up to now?"

"He's trying an end run around the Committee on Academic Activities."

"You're kidding?"

"No."

"He's trying to make sure that our committee won't have control over the research set up by the consortium grant."

"He can't do that," Paul complained.

"I'm not so sure. He met with the Committee on Committees today."

"Those stooges."

"That's right. They went along with him. I haven't seen the exact wording of their resolution but apparently they pulled the carpet out from under us," Muser explained.

"That SOB."

"You really didn't think that he would allow a little issue like academic freedom to stand between Austin Flint and all those millions of dollars."

"It's more like academic survival than academic freedom."

"You don't have to convince me, Paul. It's the dean who's sabotaging us. What should we do?"

"We should call a meeting of the committee as soon as possible."

"How about tomorrow at noon?" Muser aked.

"That's fine with me. Why don't you notify everyone else?

We'll meet in my office. I'll try to call Willis and get some more details."

Paul saw three more patients and then got through to the dean.

"What is this business about taking authority over research away from the Committee on Academic Activities?"

"No authority has been taken away from anyone."

"No?"

"No. The Committee on Committees reviewed the bylaws in detail. They make no mention of a direct grant program for goal-directed research."

"Of course not. They were written before we—"

"So the Committee on Committees decided that the present administrative structure did not apply to this new program. As a result they approved of a new committee."

Just what this place doesn't need, Paul thought.

"The new committee," the dean continued, "will be chaired by John Corrigan."

"I can't believe that. John isn't even paid by us. He's paid by Dillinger Chemicals!"

"Paul, he owns Dillinger Chemicals," the dean said, correcting Paul's mistake.

"He does?"

"He and his wife. She's a Dillinger. She inherited the company. She's president of Dillinger."

"That's even more reason why we can't put him in charge."

"He's a brilliant man who knows both us and the corporations involved. He was the obvious choice."

"Can I see the exact resolution and the bylaws?"

"They will be circulated in the usual way."

"A month from now."

"Yes."

Paul knew how to beat this bottleneck. He called Chris. Chris could call the dean's secretary and tell her what she needed. They were old friends. Paul would have the papers he needed the next morning.

It was after five by the time Paul got through seeing all his patients and returning phone calls from six others. Mrs. Kell had called again but she didn't answer when he tried to call her back.

He was sure that Chris had gone home, but he heard

someone typing in the outer office and walked out to see who it was. It was Floyd Baker.

"What are you working on?" Paul asked.

"A rough draft of the paper for the Handbook. It's due in four weeks."

"I'd forgotten that I had committed us to that."

"I've finished the literature review and I'll have this draft on your desk tomorrow," Floyd informed him.

"Good. I'll be able to get to it by the weekend."

"Paul?"

"Yes."

"The dean called me."

"Why?"

"I'm not sure."

"You're not?"

"No. I know what he said, but I'm still not sure why he wanted me. He appointed me to a committee."

"Which one?"

"Yours."

"The Committee on Academic Activities."

"Yes."

"Why?"

"I don't know," Floyd admitted again.

"What did he say exactly?"

"First he talked to me about our research program with Dillinger Chemicals and how their grant to the department pays most of my salary. Is that true?"

"Yes."

"I didn't know that."

"What difference does it make?"

"I don't know. The dean seemed to think it was very significant."

"It isn't. We have a contract with them. They guaranteed us so much money each year and we guaranteed to do certain work. How we spend that money and who does that work and who exactly gets that money is up to us, up to me as a matter of fact. Whether your salary comes from that fund or some other fund is a matter of bookkeeping. Nothing more."

"Okay, I believe you. But the dean seemed to put more emphasis on it."

"He would."

"He did. Then he talked about the committee and asked me if I'd like to be on it. I said I would but I thought that the members were elected by the faculty."

"Only half," Paul said.

"That's what he told me. One-half are elected. One-half and the chairman. One-half he appoints."

"With the advice of the Committee on Committees," Paul added.

"That's right, Paul."

"I didn't know there were any openings."

"Lollar resigned," Floyd reminded him.

"But he was an elected representative," Paul argued.

"The dean said that he appoints all replacements."

"That may well be."

"It is. He read me the bylaws."

"That's strange. It's almost as if that conversation were meant for both you and me."

"It was. He told me to tell you about my appointment."

"So you accepted."

"Of course. It's a great honor and it should be interesting."

"It may be much more than that."

"How come?"

"We are about to go to war with the dean."

"He didn't mention any war."

"Of course not." Over the next ten minutes Paul explained the problem of the drug companies' influence from his viewpoint.

"But why me, Paul?"

"I'm not sure, but I can make a good guess. He thinks he can control you."

"He does?"

"Sure. If this becomes a real shooting war, there is going to be a lot of pressure put of all us. You're not tenured."

"No."

"And, as he reminded you, we don't really pay you."

"But my contract is with Austin Flint, not Dillinger."

"And you should remember that at all times. Even if Willis doesn't." There was one more thing they had to talk about. "Floyd."

"Yes."

"Why were those missing charts so important to Jackie?"

The transition did not surprise the younger neurologist. It was as if he had been expecting to talk about them all the time.

"I'm not sure I know. There were a lot of things we never talked about. But I don't think it was just the issue of the charts generally but one chart in particular."

"Whose?"

"Phyllis Masi's. Jackie never cared if she had trouble finding a record on somebody who wasn't acutely ill. That sort of thing always happens one way or another. But this was different. Masi has very severe myasthenia and is allergic to a host of drugs. Her old chart was an absolute necessity for anyone who wanted to treat her."

"What happened to her?" Paul asked.

"She did okay. Thanks to the nurses. They remembered what not to give her better than the doctors. Then Jackie located the chart."

"So no permanent harm was done," Paul suggested.

"No."

"Of course, that doesn't change the issue."

"No, I guess not," Floyd said.

Paul was not sure he should say anything more, but he did. "I'm sorry about Jackie."

Once again Floyd was not surprised. "Thanks for saying something, Paul. Most people haven't said anything. As if she didn't mean anything to me. I know she had her problems, but still she meant a lot to me and I . . ." He stopped. "What has that detective told you?"

"Not much."

"What?"

"That it was probably somebody she knew and let into her apartment."

"Is that all?"

"Yes."

"I don't know. The poor kid. I warned her. She was getting better. She hadn't done it in a couple of months. Why did she have to . . . ? It's my fault, in a way."

"Your fault?"

"I had told her that I was going to go out with someone else. She was the one who wasn't willing to make any . . . ah

. . . changes. How the hell was I supposed to know what she was going to do? I should have guessed. I should have——"

"Floyd. Don't blame yourself. You did what you had to do. You were honest with her. She did what she did. You had no way to know she would do it. And no way to predict the results."

"I don't know, Paul."

"I do. I've been through it."

"You have?"

"Yes. And it's not your fault. It's no one's fault. It just happened."

"I wish I could be so sure."

"Dad, you should have been there today."

"Where?"

"In my English class. You know old Ms. Holloman," Joshua said with a distinct emphasis on the "Ms."

Paul was happy the emphasis was there and not on "old." After all, he was sure that Joshua's English teacher was not more than a couple of years older than he was himself. "Yes, I remember Ms. Holloman."

"Well, thanks to you, I stumped her today. I really knocked her dead. I asked her about that stuff you told me. I asked her who was the Nobel Prize winner for literature who worked in Chicago as a bus driver."

"She didn't know." He said it triumphantly. "She just guessed. Ernest Hemingway. Sinclair Lewis. Then I told her. Knut Hamsun. Was she ever surprised."

"I didn't even know you were paying any attention to me."

"I was listening."

"Apparently."

"She went on to talk about the Chicago school of authors. Guys like Saul Bellow and——"

"Saul Bellow!" Paul said with obvious disbelief. "He may live and write here but I wouldn't call him a real member of any Chicago school. Bellow could live anywhere, put his characters anywhere, and his novels would be the same. He's no longer from the Chicago school. Not in that sense. He's University of Chicago, not Chicago."

"Then who is?"

"Nelson Algren," Paul began, "and James T. Farrell, Harry Mark Petrakis, William Brashler, and the great Ring Lardner."

Joshua had not heard of any of them, so Paul told him about them and about their stories of Chicago. He ended by quoting Nelsen Algren, who once had contrasted his own works with the popular novels of Harold Robbins and complained that Harold Robbins was worth forty million dollars while Algren was trying to find his bookie to collect the seventeen dollars and sixty cents the bookie owed him.

Joshua decided to read *Knock on Any Door* and something by Petrakis. *A Dream of Kings* probably.

"If you're interested, I have another question for your teacher."

"Yeah?"

"Ask her who was the only Nobel Prize winner in literature to be tried as a Nazi sympathizer and collaborator."

"Who?"

"The same guy."

"Knut Hamsun?"

"The one and only."

"Wow. She'll never guess. The old bat."

This time the emphasis was unfortunately on the "old."

While the kids were getting ready for bed, Paul called Gerri. He told her about his whole day, from Tom Ward through Floyd Baker, including Dean Willis and Tony Muser. She did the same thing, with the exception of Dr. Rotblatt, but that was expected. Her analysis was a private matter. Paul did ask her one question.

"Why did you keep Frank McCormick's chart for three weeks?"

"When?"

"When you signed it out from Medical Records last year."

"I remember now. I just forgot I had it. I signed it out on a Friday to go over at home over the weekend, and that was the first weekend we ever made love."

"I remember that."

"I should hope so."

"I do. Very clearly."

"So do I, Paul."

"Good."

"Are you sure you don't want to come over tonight?" she asked.

"I can't."

"I know, but I can wish, can't I?"

"Tell me about the chart."

"I never got to it that weekend and I forgot I had it. It just sat around my office until Medical Records called me and reminded me, and I finally reviewed it and signed my notes. Why are you asking?"

"I just wondered. You didn't notice if the consent form was in it?"

"No."

"I thought not," Paul said.

"Maybe."

"Maybe you noticed it."

"No, maybe I'll come over to your place," she suggested.

"Gerri, we agreed. I have a seventeen-year-old daughter."

"And fourteen-year-old son, you chauvinist," she replied. "And they both know we are lovers."

"I know that."

"And you are right and I love you for it but I'd still rather be with you."

"You know how to arrange that."

"Don't, Paul."

"I'm sorry."

"Good night, love."

7

"I am on a beach. I don't know how I got there. Or why I'm there. But I'm on a beach.

"It's not a beach that I know. It's not the Oak Street Beach. That's for sure. It's not any beach on Lake Michigan. It's not any beach I've ever been to before. Just the same, there is something very familiar about it. Maybe I've been there before in a different dream and I just don't remember it. At least I can't bring up the memory."

He certainly is beating around the bush, she thought to herself. Is it because he doesn't want to get down to the substance of his dream? Or is his mind wandering, perseverating as part of his disordered thinking?

"Like an old acquaintance. That's it. Not a real friend, but someone or something I knew once. Like an old top-forty song. Or maybe—"

She decided that it would be better to move him along. This was not the time for free associations. "I think I understand, Frank."

"You do?"

"Certainly. It's like picking up a book you read once many years before. It's familiar even though you cannot recall the specific details."

"No. That's not what I mean."

The midst of a dream was not the best place for an argument, even if this wasn't a true analytic session. "You may be right. A melody is more like a visual image. They are both primarily emotional. A book is more intellectual."

139

"Yes. That's it. It's more a feeling than just a memory."
He paused.

She waited. Had he lost his place, his train of thought?

"Did I tell you that it's a saltwater beach? Not freshwater. An ocean somewhere.

"I can tell by the smell. I recognize the smell. The smell of salt water. It's such a pleasant smell. It drives away the bad smells of the world."

He stopped. His mind was obviously pursuing this thought one way or another, but he was censoring it.

She did not ask him anything. Perhaps the medicine was working, driving away the bad smells of his private world.

"There are lots of shells on the beach. No other people, just shells. And it's hot. Very hot.

"I walk along the beach. Right at the edge. I have all my clothes on. I walk along the edge of the water. The waves come in and wash up my legs. I can feel the cool water. My clothes never get wet."

At least this dream started pleasantly enough. Then she remembered that the previous one had been so neat and tidy in the beginning.

"There are lots of sand castles being washed away by the surf. I walk along the shore and I pick up some seashells."

Frank had been to the Riviera once with his father, she remembered. When he was ten or eleven. A good age for seashells and sand castles. Too young for bikinis and topless sunbathers.

"In the distance I see some people sunbathing. Women."

I may be wrong, she thought.

"I cannot see them very clearly and even though I'm walking right toward them, they never get any closer.

"They're like a mirage.

"Then I see someone else." His tone changed.

"A man. He's fully dressed.

"He's walking toward me.

"The whole beach is like an oven."

It was no longer a continuous narrative. Each sentence was pronounced in isolation. Like a series of pistol shots. Her own metaphor disturbed her.

"He's far away.

"I stop.

"He keeps getting closer.

"His face is hidden in a shadow.

"The shadow moves with him.

"Despite the shadow, I know he is grinning at me.

"The heat is worse.

"It scorches my cheeks.

"My pants are wet from the waves.

"Beads of sweat pop out on my forehead.

"My armpits are very wet.

"So hot. So damned hot."

Heat stroke is one of the complications of Haldol, she thought. But this is just a dream.

"He stops.

"I start to walk toward him.

"He's an Arab."

An Arab. Why an Arab? He's never mentioned Arabs before.

"I can tell that much.

"A grinning Arab.

"He's not sweating.

"I am.

"He has a knife.

"The sun is so bright.

"Its rays are everywhere.

"They hit the knife blade.

"They are the blade.

"The sun races from the knife blade right to my forehead.

"It's like a bolt of white-hot lightning.

"The sweat pours off my forehead into my eyes, blinding me.

"I can't see anything.

"It's as if my eyes have been pulled out of their sockets."

Like Oedipus, she recalled. Oedipus at Colonus. Oedipus on the beach at Colonus. Oedipus, no longer the king. Oedipus, eyeless and sightless.

"The rays of the sun are much brighter now. Like cymbals crashing into my skull, crushing my brain."

Here we go again.

"I can feel it being crushed, squeezed, mangled."

At least you can't smell it, she said to herself. No odors. It was more intellectual this time. At least so far.

"The white heat of the knife blade is now piercing my

eyes. It feels like a pair of stilettos. One in each socket, burning into my brain.''

She waited for the smell.

"The sea seems to open up before me.

"A great sheet of flames comes out of the sea.

"It leaps out at me.

"I take the gun out of my pocket.''

What gun?

"It's a revolver.

"I aim it carefully.

"He's grinning at me.

"He does not move.

"I shoot the Arab.

"He falls.''

His speech had become a rapid staccato. More like an automatic weapon than a pistol.

"I shoot again.'' His phrases were closer together.

"And again.'' More forceful.

"And again.

"The gun is empty.'' Quietly. The climax had passed.

Slowly, "Six shots.

"Blood is spilling out from everyplace on the body. From the nose, the ears, the grinning mouth.''

"She is still smiling at me.''

She?

"She has long blond hair. It looks just like your hair. It is your hair. The hair is bleeding.

"She's naked. I can see her breasts. They remind me of . . . breasts. Her nipples are bleeding.

"She is dead.

"My mother is dead.

"The sun is red. It is bleeding. It's raining blood.

"That's it. That's all I remember,'' he concluded ever so calmly.

"How are you feeling, Frank?''

"Good.''

"Why?''

"I don't know. Maybe that medicine is helping me. I don't know. My time is up, isn't it?''

"Yes.''

"See you Friday.''

"Yes."

With that he got up and left, departing as abruptly as if they had just completed an intellectual discussion of *Being and Nothingness*. He made no attempt to prolong the session, no complaint that she had not helped him understand his dream, none of the usual tricks employed by patients. On the contrary, he just told his tale and departed like some ancient itinerant poet, leaving Dr. Scala to interpret it on her own. She had only a few minutes before her next appointment to put her thoughts together and then record them in the process notes. She wrote down as many details as she could remember, including the inconsistencies of seeing through blind eyes and of course the sexual ambiguity of the object of his violence. First an Arab. Then a naked woman with long blond hair. Then the hair became not just hair but her hair. And the breasts too, but that he had censored. And then it became his mother. Like Oedipus, he was blinded for seeing his mother, but Frank was punished beforehand, out of sequence. And he shot her. With a pistol. As good a phallic symbol as there was.

Taken in reverse order: he saw his mother; she was naked; she was a blond; he took his gun and emptied it into her; he was blinded by the sun. By himself, the son. Very much like Oedipus.

But he felt better.

His brain was no longer rotting. He no longer complained of smelling it. Thank God for Haldol.

It was time for the next patient. From a sick schizophrenic to a depressed housewife who sometimes wanted to kill herself because her husband only wanted to screw other women. She ought to kill him. Gerri's own destructive thought process surprised her. Perhaps violence was contagious.

Paul was a little surprised that Tom Ward was not already in his office waiting to see him as soon as he arrived at the hospital. He had been getting used to their daily conferences. On the other hand, he was not at all surprised that Chris had already gotten the papers from the dean's secretary.

He turned on WFMT. Obviously a Haydn symphony. He had no idea which one. A mature one. One of the London compositions? More likely Paris. What a glorious phenomenon. In Papa Haydn's day, you needed fifty musicians to hear this allegro movement. All Paul had to do was turn a switch and then half-listen. It had been reduced to good music to work by.

The memo said pretty much what he had expected. The Committee on Committees had met in executive session with the dean to discuss contractual arrangements with commercial concerns made for the purpose of furthering the research activities of the medical center. They made it all sound so formal and innocent. And of course they made absolutely no reference to any specific contract. It was just a general policy statement. All very well-engineered and absolutely properly construed.

The committee concluded, unanimously of course, that such arrangements were not covered by any single existing administrative body. It therefore created a new committee. The Committee on Commercial Research Development, CCRD for short. The committee charged CCRD with complete control of all aspects of such contractual relationships, which they then listed.

Paul read through the list.

1. Determining institutional needs. That was probably acceptable.

2. Assessing institutional resources to be allocated to such ventures. Very reasonable. No standing committee had that overview.

3. Negotiating all contractual arrangements, including overhead. Paul could live with that.

4. Defining research objectives. But not with that.

5. Directing allocation of funds within the institution. And certainly not that. That was not their prerogative. It was his. That right belonged to the Committee on Academic Activities. Not to Willis and his circle of cronies.

It was the last part of the memo that was most devastating. The members of the committee were to be appointed by the dean with the advice of the Committee on Committees and with each serving no less than two years or more than six years. The rules for chairman were the same.

It would be a packed committee. Picked by the dean to do whatever he wanted it to do. The charges were all beautifully general and vague: determine, assess, negotiate, define, allocate. No specific mechanisms were spelled out. No checks and no balances. Just vague, general responsibility.

There was only one possible loophole. The resolution had passed because this situation was "not covered by any single existing administrative body." Was that really true?

He read the bylaws and the charge of his committee. They said nothing about contracts for research development. The dean could probably get away with it.

He took the papers in to Chris and told her to make copies for the members of the Committee on Academic Activities. He'd give them out at the meeting.

Tom Ward walked in just as he was pouring himself some coffee.

"Sorry I'm late."

"Late?"

"For our daily meeting."

"Do we have a daily meeting?"

"It's on your calendar."

He looked at Chris and she nodded. "What am I," Paul asked, "your therapist?" He hoped that Tom had not picked up any of the displaced anger in his voice.

"No," said Tom as they walked into Paul's office and he closed the door. "You're not my analyst. And if I wanted one, I'd go to Dr. Scala. She's got the training and she's one hell of a lot better-looking." He had picked it up. "You're my sounding board, my inside source on the way this place works. I trust that role doesn't compromise you?"

"I'm sure you cleared this with Dean Willis first."

"No."

"No?"

"No," Tom repeated.

Paul was pleased. He was tempted to apologize, but didn't. Instead he got down to the business at hand. "What's new?"

"It may not have been Freddie Sanford."

"Why not?"

"He may have had an alibi. At least for Sunday night."

"When Edie was attacked?"

"Yes."

"That doesn't have to be tied in to Jackie's murder."

"No, it doesn't have to be," Tom agreed ever so slowly.

Paul understood the way Tom emphasized "have." "But you believe that it is."

"Yes. I don't have any real proof, but I think they are tied together in some way."

"Can't you prove he was with Jackie by typing the semen you found in her?"

"No."

"Are you sure?"

"That's what the lab people tell me. Once you mix up two samples, you can tell the general type of each of them but when you run the rest of the tests, the HAL—"

"HLA," Paul corrected him.

"That's it, HLA. Well, you can't tell which one of the blood types it goes with. In fact they even tell me they can't do some of the tests accurately."

"I'm sure they're right," Paul said. "All you could tell would be who it wasn't."

"And maybe not even that. The results get very confusing with mixed samples," Tom said.

"That makes it a bit harder."

"Around here it's never easy, Doc. I wanted to check out a few things with you."

"Shoot."

"It's Jackie Baumer's diary." With that he took out his notebook.

"I'm not sure I should hear all this."

"You're not going to hear it all. Much of what's in there is not really any of your business, but there are some things I'd like to go over with you."

"Go ahead."

"She used initials throughout the whole diary."

"Like F.S. for Sanford?" Paul asked.

"Yes," the detective replied. "So far we have identified a number of sets of initials that appeared in the diary as being those of specific individuals from the medical center."

"How can you tell they're from here?"

"The initials had no number after them."

"No phone number. She could just page us," Paul said, remembering the number of unanswered pages, "or call us through the hospital operator."

"That's right."

"So?"

"I'd like to make sure we have the people straight. P.R. is . . ."

"Me."

"That we figured out."

"Brilliant deduction."

"And F.B.?"

"Floyd Baker."

"You sure, Doc? There are other F.B.'s here. There's a Fern Bell, a Frank Bolling, and a Fred Bruchell."

"Where . . . ?"

"The computerized list of employees and students."

"Oh. Well, it is Floyd."

"We were pretty sure of that. E.R.?"

"Edie Robinson."

"How sure are you, Doc?"

"I don't know it as an absolute fact. But it's Edie."

"D.L.?"

"Don Lenhardt?" Paul answered.

"There are other D.L.'s in the medical center. But they are both older women. G.S.?" he asked.

"Gerri!"

"Dr. Scala," Tom said.

"B.C. This one has us beat. The only B.C. we found on the list is a Bill Cunningham and he's . . . how shall I say it?"

"Of a different sexual persuasion."

"That's right."

"B.C. is Bud Chiari. You have him as A.C. His first name is Arnold but everyone calls him Bud."

"J.C. We had a little trouble with that one. There are six J.C.'s here."

"John Corrigan. She used to work for him."

"Thanks, Doc."

"That's it? You're going to leave it at that?"

"Sure."

"But . . ."

"But what?"

"Were all those people involved with her?"

"In some way."

"You know what I mean."

"Is that something I should tell you?"

"Yes!" Paul insisted.

"Okay, Doc. I'll tell you what you need to know. G.S. was only mentioned in reference to you. And B.C. in reference to nonsexual matters."

"One more thing," Paul said. "F.B. was serious about her."

"And she about him."

"He thinks she sort of reformed over the past few months."

"She did. Sort of."

Rounds on the neurology-neurosurgery-protocol patients took Paul only a few minutes.

Donna Kolloway was unchanged and was waiting to hear what procedure Dr. Richardson thought would be the best for her.

Mr. Kreevich was still unable to speak. His EEG had been done. Bill Goodman showed it to Paul. There was no evidence of any seizure activity. The surgery had been a success. The patient could not speak. More anticonvulsants would not help. The EEG showed changes right in the speech area. Large slow waves instead of normal rhythms. Were they due to swelling or did they reflect permanent injury? Only time would tell.

The tattooed lady was doing well. Her bruises were clearing up. She had been seizure-free since admission. They had no reason to keep her any longer. She was planning on going home the next day. Back to her husband complete with motorcycle, black leather jacket, chains, and God knows what else.

De gustibus, Paul thought to himself.

The Metrazol on Maurie Rath was scheduled for later in the afternoon.

The research meeting for once started on time. Bill Goodman presented Mrs. Kolloway's story again. Most of them were already quite familiar with it, but it was best to refresh everyone's memory before any decisions were made. Paul only half-listened to Bill's concise reduction of a life into a five-minute synopsis.

Then they looked at all the pictures, including the angiogram and the CAT scans.

Now came the hard part.

"What can you do surgically, Don?"

"Nothing," the neurosurgeon said. "I hate to admit it, but even with the operating microscope, I don't think I can do much. There are just too damn many abnormal vessels. I could try to take out the whole hemisphere, but even then she'd still have some abnormal vessels and . . ." He stopped, shrugging his shoulders.

"She would be paralyzed on the left," Paul said, completing the prediciton.

"Yes, paralyzed," Don concurred.

"John?" Paul continued the survey.

"JNF-2."

"How much would she need?"

"I reviewed all scans with Don and the neuroradiologists." With that he got up and put a film on the view box. Don and Floyd went up to the view box. Paul did not. He could see it in his mind. "There are six distinct veins which have enlarged in the last few years."

"Are they the ones with red arrows?" Edie asked.

"Yes," Don answered. "And there are two others which are just about as big but not enlarging, as far as we can tell."

"Marked in blue," Floyd added, looking at the film.

"That makes a total of eight major trouble spots," Paul said.

"Yes. Several are quite long and tortuous. I figure a total of eleven injections," Don said.

"How much JNF-2 will be injected?"

"Half a cc each time. Five and a half cc's. We've used up to eight cc's on patients before with no signs of toxicity," John added.

It was a fact Paul already knew.

"Don, can you reach all of them?"

"Yes, I think so."

"How long will it take?"

"Four hours. From skin to skin."

"What will the mortality be?"

"From the surgery itself?" Don asked.

"Yes," Paul answered.

"Virtually nil."

"The morbidity?"

"From the surgical technique itself, less than one percent."

"From what you inject?"

"I don't know."

"Less than one percent," John Corrigan said.

"Then what happened to Sam Rogovin?" Paul asked.

"He had just bled," John said. "She hasn't bled in years."

"I thought you said bleeding doesn't make any difference," Paul reminded him.

"It doesn't as far as JNF-2 is concerned."

"So what happened to Rogovin?"

"Who knows, Paul?" Don Lenhardt said, interrupting their dialogue. "We were all there when he went bad. Everyone but you. I didn't know what happened to him. Neither did Bud or Floyd. Maybe we will see something at brain cutting. We'll just have to wait and see."

"So what do we tell Mrs. Kolloway?"

"JNF-2," said Don Lenhardt.

"Floyd?"

"JNF-2."

"Gerri?"

"This is not exactly a psychiatric decision."

"I know that, but how does she feel about having to do something that may involve some risk?"

"I'm not sure."

It was unlike Gerri to be evasive. Paul persisted. "Come on, you've talked to her, haven't you?"

"I've talked to her three times now, and it's hard to say." She spoke very quietly; then suddenly her voice became harsh, almost angry. "She knows she's living with a time bomb in her head, to use her phrase, and she has two small children and she wants you to do something about her time bomb, but . . ." She stopped for a moment.

"But what?" John asked. "That sounds like she wants us to do something."

"Oh, she does."

"So what's your hesitation?"

"She thinks Paul walks on water. She'll do anything he suggests."

"Anything?" Paul asked.

"Paul."

"Sorry."

"What's the problem?" John persisted.

"She'll agree to anything Paul suggests. That's not really informed consent."

"Come on, Gerri," Paul protested. "That's not really true. I will explain both the pros and cons."

"I know you will. But she'll know what you want her to do and she trusts you. So she'll do it. Just because she has faith in you."

"Is it wrong for patients to trust me?"

"No. Of course not. You know that's not what I mean."

"Look," Don said, "if you are worried that Paul has too much influence over her, I'll explain it to her."

"That won't help," Gerri said. "She won't agree to anything without talking to Paul."

"So what do you suggest, Gerri?" Paul asked.

"JNF-2, and both of you tell her about it. It won't change how she feels or what she does, but it'll make me feel better."

"John?"

"JNF-2."

"It's unanimous," Paul said, counting his own unarticulated vote. "I'll talk to her later today."

For the rest of the hour they discussed the Parkinson's-disease protocol. Don Lenhardt talked about the surgical aspects, Herb Adams about the tissue culture, and Paul about the approval they had received from Human Investigation.

Paul's second meeting took longer, but accomplished very little. Paul gave out copies of the memo from the Committee on Committees, along with copies of the bylaws. Muser was incensed. So were a couple of the other elected members. The members who had not been elected by the faculty seemed mostly disinterested in what they perceived as a direct power struggle between Paul and the dean. Paul couldn't expect to win them all. Any White Sox fan knew that. But that wasn't the issue.

Floyd said absolutely nothing. His silence bothered Paul. According to the bylaws, Paul could only vote to break a tie, not to make one. The way he counted noses, Floyd was the key vote. An appointed member in the seat of an elected mem-

ber. If they had an issue on which to vote and Floyd went
with the dean, it would be six to four. If Floyd went against
the dean it would be five-up and Paul could make it six to
five and the good guys could win one. If only they had an
issue on which they could vote.

As far as Paul could tell, however, they had no such clear
issue. The end run had been successful. No one stood between the dean and the end zone, and he had five guys
running interference for him. The faculty senate would accept the memo in one week. The game would be over.

After the meeting, Paul went down to EEG along with
Floyd to watch the Metrazol test on Maurie Rath. By the time
they got there, the baseline brain-wave test had already been
run. Bud Chiari showed it to them as well as to Bill Goodman
and Edie Robinson.

It was definitely abnormal. There were frequent spikes
coming out of the right temporal lobe. They could be seen on
virtually every page. That frequency, Paul explained to Edie,
meant an average of one abnormal discharge every ten seconds. And once every fifteen pages or so, there was an
abnormal discharge from the left hemisphere.

"That," Paul said, pointing to one of them, "is the hooker."

"Most of them are on the right," Edie said.

"Yes."

"Doesn't that mean the seizures come from the right side?"

"Statistically, yes, but it's possible that the seizures might
come from the left, and if that's true and we cut out his right
temporal lobe . . ." He stopped to let her finish the thought.

"He would still have seizures," she said.

"That's right."

With that, Bud Chiari went into the room where Mr. Rath
was while the rest of them went into the adjacent room where
they could both watch the EEG and also observe Mr. Rath
through the observation window.

Mr. Rath was lying on a bed. A series of fine wires was
attached to his head and then to a disk. From the disk a thick
wire carried the signals through the wall and into the EEG
machine.

The technician turned on the machine. A broad stream of
paper began to roll out of it. The paper had twenty-four

freshly drawn lines on it, each one drawn by a separate pen. Each pen transcribed the electrical activity of one small part of Mr. Rath's brain so that they were able to observe a total of twenty-four separate samples of his brain's function simultaneously. The top twelve came from the left side. The bottom twelve from the right. Every few seconds, three or sometimes four of the pens recording activity from the right half of his brain suddenly jerked, recording a sudden burst of seizurelike spikes. Once every two or three minutes, a similar event occurred in two or three of the upper set of channels.

The rest of the time, the pens waved back and forth slowly, recording the normal background activity.

It was time.

Bud Chiari began injecting something into Mr. Rath's IV.

The technician recorded the exact time when the injection started.

Dr. Chiari signaled as he pulled the needle out of the IV tubing.

Again the technician recorded the event.

They waited.

Their eyes moved back and forth from the EEG machine to the patient. Back and forth. As if they were in the front row at Wimbledon. And it were match point. Featuring a long volley of ground strokes from the baseline.

Connors against McEnroe.

Back and forth.

Ten seconds.

Twenty.

Back and forth.

Thirty.

Paul and Floyd noticed it at the same time and pointed it out to Edie and Bill. A few small spikes on two of the channels. Both on the right. They were about half a second apart. As they watched, the spikes continued. They got closer together. They came in pairs, then triplets, then short runs. More pens became involved. A true crescendo.

Back and forth.

Forty seconds.

Maurie Rath smacked his lips. He opened his eyes and looked around the room and smacked his lips again and then passed out.

Six channels were now jerking with continuous spikes.

Suddenly they stopped jerking and began a slow, wavelike motion.

Mr. Rath moaned.

One minute and twenty seconds.

They watched.

At two minutes and forty seconds, he woke up. He had had a brief seizure from his right temporal lobe. Just what they had hoped for.

Four more times they repeated the procedure.

Four more seizures occurred.

All four came from the right side.

That made it five out of five.

It was no longer just a statistical guess. It was a medical fact. His seizures came out of the right side of his brain.

Mr. Rath was a candidate for surgery. They might well be able to do something to help him.

While Paul and the others were observing Mr. Rath having Metrazol-induced seizures, John Corrigan and Herb Adams were at work in the laboratory.

Herb tested each animal as he had the day before.

Then John took each rat, stuck a needle into its heart, and injected one cc of a clear fluid. Within seconds, each rat collapsed and was dead. Next John carefully opened each one of the small skulls, removed the brain, and handed it to Herb.

Herb examined each brain, made some notes in his notebook, and then put each brain in a small vial filled with formaldehyde.

All afternoon they repeated the same steps.

Test.

Sacrifice.

Remove.

Observe.

Record.

Fix.

Test.

Sacrifice.

Remove.

Observe.

Record.

Fix.

This was what the world knew as research.

It had the same regularity as an assembly line.

By the time Paul got to Mrs. Kolloway's room, she and her husband had already spent an hour with Dr. Lenhardt discussing the proposed surgery. But Gerri had been right: they wouldn't agree to anything until they talked to Dr. Richardson.

What did he recommend? He was as nondirective as possible. Yet, no matter how objective he was, the mere fact that he was telling them about the new procedure meant to them, to her, that he wanted her to agree.

She did. So did her husband.

The last thing Paul did that night before he left was stop by Bud Chiari's office. "That Metrazol test was very convincing."

"Yes, he should be helped by surgery," Bud replied.

"Don't sound so overwhelmingly convinced."

"Look, we all thought surgery might have helped Mr. Kreevich, and now he can't say a blessed word."

"I know," Paul said. "And we pretty much talked him into it. But it's still too early to be absolutely certain."

"I guess so," Bud agreed.

"Bud, there was something else I wanted to talk about."

"What?"

"Those charts in the ceiling."

"Yes?"

"Did you ever do that when you were a resident here?"

"No, but a lot of the residents did."

"Why?"

"Why? Because sometimes they were overworked and got behind in dictating them and it was more convenient to keep the charts where they could get at them without having to leave the floor and run down to Medical Records."

"I don't believe it."

"Why not?"

"It's so dangerous."

"Dangerous? It's probably safer than keeping them in Medical Records."

"Safer?"

"Sure."

"How can that be?"

"The residents only did it on our own patients, and the nurses all knew where the records were. They could get them out of the ceiling faster than they could get them up from Medical Records. And they always got the right chart. They would not pull the wrong chart."

Paul was still skeptical. "They didn't know where Miss Masi's chart was."

"I know."

"Why not?"

"It's not part of the routine anymore."

"That's right. There's a policy now and Bill violated that policy—"

"Paul, take it easy. Let me find out exactly what happened."

Paul shrugged his shoulders. What else was there to do? He'd let Bud look into it. Why not? Bud had already been doing just that. According to Jackie's letter, Bud had known about it for weeks. But how had he known about Jackie's letter? He wanted to ask. He did.

Bud hesitated.

"Bud!"

"From Chris."

"Chris?"

"Sure. She saw the letter on your desk and told me. I think she wanted to warn me. She and I go back a long way."

"So do you and I."

8

Whenever he could, Don Lenhardt, like every other senior attending surgeon in the medical center, let someone else carry out the menial duties associated with a surgical procedure. The preoperative checklist was one of those routine tasks that he readily delegated to someone much lower on the pecking order. Either the circulating nurse or the research protocol coordinator was ordinarily given that responsibility. Not anymore. At least not for a while. As of now he changed his routine and started doing it himself. He knew that Mrs. Kolloway had signed an operative-consent form and an experimental-procedure-consent form. He had watched her sign them the night before. Marv Rickert had been there too. He had seen her sign both of the forms. They had both also seen her husband sign both of the same forms. And they had both countersigned each of the documents as witnesses.

Both forms were on the chart.

He marked off the appropriate box on the checklist.

There was another, similar set on the chart. They had been obtained by Paul Richardson and signed by both Donna Kolloway and her hubsand. And witnessed by Bill Goodman. There was no place on the checklist to mark off a second set of permits. Still, he was pleased to see them. In any court in the world, two sets were better than none.

Mrs. Kolloway had already been put under by the anesthesiologist. She was seated in an operating chair with her head held in place by a heavy metal frame. Her head had been shaved earlier in the morning so that the smooth, shiny tight skin of her bald scalp reflected the glare of the bright lights of the OR.

By the time Don Lenhardt finished scrubbing, Marv had already cleansed her scalp. Don watched while his senior resident cut through the scalp and the underlying connective tissue, exposing the bone of the calvarium. Once Don saw that there was no more bleeding, he signaled the resident to begin the opening of the skull itself.

First Rickert looked over his shoulder at the view box on the wall of the OR. There was a single X ray on it. It was from Donna Kolloway's angiogram and had been carefully selected with the help of Sid Gordon, the neuroradiologist. This one film gave the best overall picture of the abnormal collection of blood vessels sitting inside her brain. Different films may well have shown some of the vessels in better detail, but this one showed them all. Superimposed on the white wormlike figures which made up so much of the X ray was a trapezoid drawn in with a red crayon. It was the smallest simple figure that could be constructed and still give them access to all of the important abnormal blood vessels which they planned to inject with JNF-2. Marv took a black felt-tip pen and placed four dots on the right side of her head. He looked back at the X ray. One of the dots was in the wrong location. He washed it off and painted on another one about a centimeter higher.

He stepped back so that his chief could have an unobstructed view of what he had just done. The senior surgeon nodded his approval.

Marv took the pen and started to draw the four lines of the geometric figure that was staring down at him from the view box. If he did it correctly they should be able to get at all of the veins and arteries through this one opening.

As soon as Rickert had connected the four dots, Lenhardt took another look. It was easier to be sure once the lines were all drawn in. "It looks good."

That was the signal for Marv to really get to work. First he drilled holes at the corners of the figure he had just so painstakingly drawn. Then he passed a small saw blade through each pair of holes and carefully cut along the lines connecting the holes. In a few minutes he had converted his hand-drawn figure into a slab of bone detached from the rest of the skull.

He removed the slab of bone and prepared it with bone wax and gave it to the nurse to save. They would use it later when it was time to close up. The only layer remaining was the thick dura which covers the brain. If his measurements had been right, when the dura was opened and the brain exposed, the major part of the malformation should be in the upper third of the field, with three large abnormal vessels extending down and toward Mrs. Kolloway's face and one down and back behind her ear.

It was time to find out. Marv Rickert took a dural pick and lifted the dura away from the brain. A few clean cuts with a dural scissor and he was done. He lifted the dura.

There it was, precisely where it had been on the angiogram, but ever so much more impressive. It stood out grotesquely, a mass of tangled reddish-blue vessels in the upper third of the exposed area. There were one, two, three veins extending anteriorly and . . . there it was—one extending posteriorly. That one was just barely covered by a thin layer of brain. They couldn't see that sort of detail on the angiogram. He had done his job well. He smiled. So did Don. Marv could recognize his boss's smile above his mask.

It was now time for Don Lenhardt to get to work. He scanned the brain carefully. All the abnormal vessels were right where they had seen them. They looked swollen and distended. Their walls looked as if they might rupture sometime soon. They hadn't done that recently. There was no evidence of any fresh bleeding. The brain was clean. In fact the surfaces of the brain looked normal. Smooth and pink and glistening, they reflected the bright lights of the OR much as her scalp had done less than an hour earlier.

Lenhardt nodded to John Corrigan, who had been relaxing in the back of the OR. There were now five of them gathered around the one draped skull. Two neurosurgeons, one anesthesiologist, one scrub nurse, and one biochemist.

John Corrigan took the syringe from the scrub nurse. He carefully drew up one-half cc of clear fluid into the syringe and gave it back to the nurse.

"Number-twenty-five short needle," Don said.

The nurse put a twenty-five short needle on the syringe and handed it to the neurosurgeon.

Now it started.

They had agreed on the order of injections. They would move clockwise after beginning, with the one large vessel traveling down and behind the ear. Don suddenly and deftly plunged the needle into that partially buried vessel and injected.

In the observation booth above the OR, Floyd Baker sat with another copy of the same angiogram that was on the view box in the OR. It had the same red design drawn on it, and each of the vessels had been numbered sequentially.

In his notebook he wrote, "Vessel one. One-half cc. Injected at 9:07."

Don held the needle in place for two minutes while John Corrigan loaded another syringe. This time Marv Rickert asked for the needle. Another twenty-five short.

Marv found the next vessel and injected it.

"Vessel two. One-half cc. Injected at 9:17."

The two surgeons continued to alternate injections. First Don Lenhardt, then Marv Rickert.

In the end they had treated eight individual vessels. Four of them had required only one injection apiece. The other four each took two. That made a total of twelve injections, one more than they had originally planned on. That had been Don's decision. One of the vessels was larger than it had looked on the X ray. Lenhardt and Rickert had used a total of six cc's of JNF-2—one half of a cc per injection. That was well within the allowable dose range.

It took them just over two hours.

By the time they were finishing the injections, the once reddish-blue vessels were now a grayish blue. No pulsations could be seen in them. The brain itself looked no different. It was still a healthy pink.

Don Lenhardt took one final look at the entire field. He inspected each vessel as well as each of the twelve injection sites. They were done. There was nothing more to do but close up and wait and see.

John's part was through, so he left. So did Floyd.

Don watched as Marv closed up. First he closed the dura. Then the nurse gave him the piece of bone he had so carefully removed almost three hours earlier, and he just as carefully put it back into place. Next the connective tissue was sutured together, and finally the skin flap was put in place.

It was done.

Four hours. Skin to skin.

Estimated blood loss: seventy-five cc.

Mortality: none.

Morbidity; so far, none.

They'd have to see how she looked when she woke up. They all knew that Rogovin had looked normal when he woke up. That memory had become part of their collective unconscious.

Paul was not disappointed when he got to his office. Tom Ward was already waiting for him as soon as he arrived, even though he was ten minutes early.

They had coffee and talked about the White Sox and their highly touted pitching staff, which was not throwing as well as expected. The million-dollar contract given to Bannister was not paying off and Lamarr Hoyt couldn't buy a win. It wasn't like the '59 staff with Early Wynn and Billy Pierce and Donovan and Shaw. With Lown and Staley in relief. And Barry Latman. Paul reminisced about the two games he had seen Latman pitch that year. No one seemed to remember Latman anymore. That was too bad. He had been a good pitcher who helped them in the pennant drive.

"I'm afraid you may be right, Doc."

"About Barry Latman? Of course I'm right. He won eight and lost five, with a good ERA. Three-point-seventy-five."

"I never doubted that. You know every baseball statistic there ever was."

"Not quite," Paul said.

"But I was referring to something else."

"To what?"

"Jackie Baumer."

"Meaning . . . ?"

"Her murder may well be tied in with the medical center."

"How come?" Paul prompted, very anxious to learn the details.

"Well, it's hard to explain. Call it an old cop's instinct."

Paul sipped his coffee and listened. That was exactly what Tom wanted him to do.

"At first it smelled like a sex crime pure and simple. Of course that didn't mean it didn't involve people from this medical center. As we both know she . . . she was involved with several . . . ahm . . . people from here."

Paul said, "Yes." Just to say something. Why did it always have to get back to Jackie's sexual proclivities?

"But there were some problems. First there was the attack on Edie Robinson. Was that really done by the same person?"

It was not a question Paul was supposed to answer.

"I don't think so anymore," Tom went on. "Why? It doesn't feel right. Edie's not bisexual. We assumed that it was a guy who knew both Jackie and Edie and made it with Jackie and then went berserk. But would he have gone after Edie?"

"Only if she could have fingered him," Paul said, adjusting his language to the situation.

"But we talked to her before, and she hadn't fingered anybody in particular."

"Maybe she could still have identified him."

"Right. So what would he do?"

"Get her."

"How?"

"How should I know?" Paul answered.

"He wouldn't have stalked her in the bushes and then either attacked her there or tried to drag her to her apartment to finish his routine. That doesn't fit. He would have tried to visit her in her apartment. He got into Jackie's place, so he probably could have gotten into Edie's. She might have let him in. She didn't suspect anyone in particular. No one talked to her about coming over on any pretext at all. Except for one of her female classmates. A Ms.—"

"No names, please."

"Okay, Doc. Anyway, no one made any attempt to get into her apartment. And I don't believe her attacker was stopped in the midst of a sexual attack. He most likely was interrupted, but probably before he could kill her, not rape her or whatever."

It made sense to Paul. He had never accepted the easy solution of a deranged outsider.

"Of course it is rather too much of a coincidence to have Jackie's lesbian lover attacked four days after her murder and consider her just a random victim who happened to be at the right place at the wrong time," Tom continued.

Richardson's corollary was holding up.

"So what are we left with?" Tom asked.

Another question Paul was convinced he was not supposed to answer.

"A sex crime," Tom replied to his own question.

"A sex crime?" Paul said. "But I thought you said that it wasn't a sex crime."

"I said it couldn't have been a pure-and-simple sex crime."

Paul was not sure what Tom was getting at, and his expression reflected his lack of comprehension. He felt a lot like one of his own students on teaching rounds when he made one or two too many assumptions as to what they already understood.

"Oh, it was a sex crime all right, but not a random one with any victim who just happened to make herself available at the convenient time. It just wasn't an outsider only Edie could recognize. No, it was a sex crime with a specific motive, a motive which in some way directly involved our little Jackie. So it was someone whom she knew." He paused, then added, "Someone from the medical center. Someone Edie may have known about without realizing what she knew. Or more likely a love triangle in which the third party knew her but she didn't know him or her, at least not consciously."

When Paul made no comment, Tom continued, "That's why I went over her diary again."

"Am I a suspect?"

"No."

"Is Gerri Scala?"

"No."

"Is—"

"Yes. Whoever you were going to ask about, the answer is yes."

"Why not Gerri?"

"That, my good friend, is not as easy to answer as your first two questions. The best reason I can give you is that I trust you and I trust your judgment."

"Are you really convinced that it was some local love triangle with Jackie as the hypotenuse?"

"It's our best bet."

Paul was not so easily convinced. He once again reminded Tom of the malpractice suit and emphasized the significance of the missing form that Jackie had witnessed.

"In a way I wish I could buy that, Doc. But it just doesn't work that way. Somebody trying to pull off that kind of scam might kill. After all, there could be one hell of an amount of money involved in that sort of an action. But they wouldn't have killed her like this. That just doesn't figure."

"You're probably right," Paul admitted grudgingly.

Tom nodded. "So are you, by the way."

"What do you mean?"

"One page is missing from Frank McCormick's chart. And it's a good bet that it was stolen."

"How did you find that out?"

"When they get a record in Medical Records, the very first thing they do is count the number of pages and then they write that number down on the bottom of the last page. That's so that when they have to make a copy they know how many pages they have to copy."

"I didn't know that."

"Not very many people do. Except for the clerks who work there."

"And one page that was originally counted is now missing," Paul guessed.

"You got it. We ran a new count and came up one short."

"That's great," Paul said enthusiastically.

"I thought you'd like that."

"Wait a minute. They don't bother to number each page, do they?"

"No."

"Damn."

"What's the problem?"

"Then there's no way to prove which exact page was removed."

"It has to have been the one that is not there. The one you are looking for."

"I wish it were that simple. It could just as easily be some other page. Some page that no one would ever miss. A page that you couldn't even be sure existed. Some page with just one order on it. Or just one nursing note. Or God only knows what. I'm sure it was that form, but that'd never stand up as a defense in court. Any lawyer worth his salt would punch that defense so full of holes it would look worse than the left side of the Sox infield."

"I guess you're right."

"By the way, Tom, why were you so interested in that particular chart?"

"Just checking all the angles, Doc. I can't afford to overlook anything. Not in a case like this one."

It occurred to Paul that Tom was beginning to believe in the Richardson corollary.

Paul walked over to the neurology floor to see his patients as well as one new patient whom the dean had asked him to see. That was the kind of request that invariably bugged him in the long run. It was probably some bigwig donor who wasn't sick enough to be in the hospital in the first place. Or worse yet, his neurotic wife, who was afraid she had M.S. Tom was probably right about Jackie's murderer. After all, if some guy found out that she had indelibly etched a "Void" across him, it might be enough to trigger some violence. Especially in some of her playmates. How had he ever let himself . . . ? The question was one he could not answer.

Still, it was one heck of a coincidence. Maybe he just wanted the whole thing to have absolutely nothing to do with her sex life. That way he wouldn't have to think about it. Coincidences do happen. No one goes around killing people just to win a malpractice suit. Mr. Kreevich was better. He was no Demosthenes or William Jennings Bryan. Or Winston Churchill, for that matter. But he was talking.

"Good morning," Paul said as he stood at the side of the bed.

"Hel-lo," Mr. Kreevich said very precisely.

"Not bad," Paul responded, talking more to Bill and Edie than to the patient.

"How are you feeling today?"

"I . . . am . . . fine."

"Where are you?"

"In . . . the . . . hos-pital."

"What hospital?"

"The . . . hos-pital."

"What is the name of the hospital?"

"Flint."

"And why are you in the hospital?"

"Sick."

"In what way are you sick?"

"Seizures."

"Tell me about your seizures."

"Bad seizures."

"We know that, Mr. Kreevich." And then, as gently as he could, "Please try to describe your seizures to me as fully as you can."

Mr. Kreevich stared at Paul.

"Describe your seizures to me."

"Talk-ing . . . speaking . . . then . . . then . . . all stops. . . . It starts . . . it . . . sleep . . . tired . . . so tired."

"That was very good, Mr. Kreevich." Paul reached into his pocket. "Now tell me, what am I holding?"

"Key."

He tried something else. "And this?"

"Pen." It was pencil.

"Are you sure?"

"Pen . . . Pee . . . No . . . Pen . . . cil . . . pencil." There seemed to be a touch of actual pride in his voice.

Next Paul held his wristwatch in front of the patient.

"What is this?"

"A time."

"A time. Are you sure?"

Mr. Kreevich looked intently at the watch as if he were sure that the correct answer was there right in front of him. "Hour. . . . An hour. . . . What hour? . . . Such an hour. . . . No. . . . Watch. A watch."

"What is this part of the watch called?" Paul asked as he pointed to the band.

"The watch."

"Which part of the watch?"

"The watch-watch."

"Is this the watchband?"

"Yes."

"One last thing." Paul then pointed to the stem of his watch. "What is this part called?"

"The part."

"The part?" Paul sighed. "Is it the band?"

"Watch."

"What do you do with it?"

"Watch . . . it. . . . No . . . No. . . . Turn it. . . . Turn it."

"Why do you turn it?"

"To . . . to . . . to . . . wind it."

"To wind what?"

"The watch."

"And what is it called?"

"The turner."

"Thank you."

"Thank you."

As soon as they were outside Mr. Kreevich's room, Paul went over what they had heard. There was no doubt in anyone's mind whether Mr. Kreevich was significantly improved. He could now talk. He could produce words, words that made sense at least most of the time. However, he was far from normal. He still had several real problems. Was his fluency back to normal? No. Was he able to construct complete sentences? No. He spoke in a telegraphic manner, using either single words or short phrases. All nouns and verbs. No adjectives. No adverbs.

That was not his only problem. He had trouble finding the correct name for even rather simple objects. He sometimes substituted a wrong word. "Pen" instead of "pencil." "Time" instead of "watch." But he always used related words, not just random substitutions. His mind was obviously on the right track. He understood what they wanted from him. It was finding the exact word that was the problem.

At times he repeated what had previously been a correct answer, but since the question had changed, what had been correct was no longer acceptable. What was that called? Did Edie know?

She didn't.

Bill did. "Perseveration," he said.

Mr. Kreevich could understand the function of something and even describe it in his own telegraphic style and yet still not be able to come up with the right word for that particular object. He knew what a watch stem was. Somewhere in his brain he understood the concept of a stem and what it did. What had he called it? "A turner," Edie recalled.

What was his problem called? Aphasia.

What kind of aphasia? Broca's Aphasia. Paul told them that Broca, who was not a neurologist but a surgeon, had been the first one to demonstrate that aphasia resulted from a lesion of a specific region of the brain. A region which now carried his name. Broca's area. That was the exact spot where they had operated.

The brain of Broca's patient, Paul told them, still existed. It may be the most important brain in the history of neurology and it still could be seen and examined. It had never been cut. It was kept intact in a jug. In Paris. They should read about that brain. He told them about the article in *Revue Neurologique* that had a CAT scan of the brain of Broca's patient. And about Broca. There was an excellent book about him, by an American neurologist named Schiller.

It was time to get on with the next patient, Maurie Rath. He too required surgery for his epilepsy. Of course his operation would be much less risky than the one they had carried out on Michael Kreevich. It was simply a matter of where they would be operating. There was rarely any problem in taking out the anterior part of either one of the temporal lobes. Unlike Broca's area, neither temporal tip carried out any unique, exclusive function. They both seemed to do pretty much the same thing. As long as a patient had one left, no one could tell if the other one was there or not.

They went over the results of the Metrazol test with the patient. They discussed the operation. It would probably help him.

"Will it stop my seizures?"

"It might. There is about a sixty-percent chance that it will."

"But if it doesn't?"

"It will still probably help you."

"How?"

"By making it easier to control your seizures with medicines."

"Where do I sign?"

"Not so fast." First Paul went over all the possible complications and even the real possibility that the surgery might do no good at all. He made certain that he warned him that it might even do more harm than good.

"Where do I sign?"

"Right here."

He signed.

Bill Goodman acted as the witness.

There was only one more follow-up to see: the tattooed lady.

"She went home," Bill told him.

"She did not go home," Edie objected vociferously.

"She didn't?"

"No, she didn't."

"I don't know. She sure as heck isn't still here. She was discharged. I wrote the discharge order myself. And a new patient has been admitted into her bed," Bill said.

"She was discharged on schedule," Edie said. "But she didn't go home to that bastard of a husband of hers."

"Where did she go?" Paul asked.

"To a sheltered home for battered women."

"How did that happen?"

"Well, a number of us talked to her. I guess I started it on the day she came into the ER. I think the only reason I got her to agree to come into the hospital was that I told her she didn't have to go back to him. There were other places she could go. It got him ticked off. But it made her feel safer. For the first time in her life she realized that there might be an alternative.

"A couple of the nurses also did a lot of talking to her. Finally we convinced her that she didn't have to put up with him. There was somewhere else to go where she and her baby would be safe. A place where he couldn't get at them."

"Will she stay there?"

"I think so. She's all right. She's had a tough life. Both of her parents abused her something awful. They both took out their frustrations and anger on her. And they both had plenty, especially her father. But she knows that they were wrong, that she didn't deserve that kind of treatment. Not from them and not from her husband.

"It won't be easy for her, but I think she is going to make it. I even arranged some supportive therapy sessions for her."

"With whom?"

"Me."

Paul was surprised but immediately realized that he shouldn't have been.

"She can't afford to pay a real psychiatrist. They never

can. So a lot of us medical students have set up an alternative. We do get supervision from Dr. Landis, the psychiatrist.''

"I don't know whose idea it was," Paul said.

"The program?"

"No. Getting our patient into it."

"I guess that was really my idea," Edie informed him.

"Well, it was a brilliant idea. I can't think of anything that anyone has done for one of our patients that could be more important. I congratulate you, Edie. Let me have the names of everyone else who helped you. I want to send each of them a little note thanking them. I'll even send a copy to the nursing office. So often we neglect the real problems that our patients have to deal with because we get so wound up in the purely medical issues."

"Dr. Richardson."

"Yes, Edie."

"I didn't think you cared."

"Why not?"

"You seemed more interesed in her . . . her . . ."

"Artwork?" he suggested.

"Yes."

"Just a little gallows humor. Something to relieve the tensions of this place. But that didn't mean that we didn't care. Not at all."

Bill broke in to tell him about the new patient the dean had asked him to see. She was a forty-two-year-old woman named Wright. She had multiple sclerosis. She had had it for a decade or so. Was the diagnosis certain? Yes. She had the classic clinical course of recurring attacks and remissions involving first one part of the brain or spinal cord and then another part, with each episode leaving its mark. All the tests for M.S. were positive. She had been getting progressively worse for the last year. She was no longer able to walk on her own.

She had become desperate. So had her doctors. Four months ago they had put her on high doses of steroids.

"How high?" Paul asked.

"Forty milligrams of Medrol a day."

"For how long?"

"Continuously."

"You're kidding."

"I wish I was."

" 'Were,' not 'was.' "

"That too," Bill said. "They did one other thing when she didn't get any better on the steroids."

"Don't tell me. Let me guess."

"Okay."

"They put her on some other immunosuppressant agent to make sure that they poisoned her immune system."

"Bingo. Would you like to guess which one?"

"Cytoxan."

"Double bingo."

"Don't tell me what happened next. They saw her once a month or so and now she's running a fever. They screwed up her ability to fight off infections and now she has some blasted fungus infection like cryptococcus and they sent her here to us so I can try to save their asses and her life. Especially the former."

"You're correct, except for two small details. She has aspergillosis, not cryptococcus, and Dr. Chiari is supposed to save her life. You're only supposed to help."

As if he were responding to a cue in a some second-rate musical comedy, Bud arrived with Mrs. Wright's CAT scan.

"Does it show an abscess?" Paul asked.

"Not really. Here, take a look."

They all did.

"It looks like Swiss cheese," Paul said. "She's riddled with abscesses. She must have a couple of dozen."

"Only nineteen that we could see."

"She's going to die," Paul said.

"I know," Bud said. "But we'll try to treat her with amphotericin B in big doses."

"Well, if the aspergillosis doesn't get her," Paul concluded, "the amphotericin probably will."

"I know, but what other choice do we have?" Bud asked.

They all stared at the CAT scan. It was a good time for gallows humor, but no one could think of anything very funny to say.

"Did they explain the risks to her?"

"I don't know," Bill said.

"Did they tell her they were experimenting with her life?"

"I don't know."

"Were they really experimenting?" Edie asked.

"Yes."

"But I've read articles on high doses of steroids in M.S. And even one or two on drugs like Cytoxan."

"Yes. But it's still experimental as far as I'm concerned. The value has not been proven. Nor has the safety. But since the drugs are available, every Tom, Dick, and Harry who reads an article and probably only remembers the title and not the ambiguous results feels he has the right to use the damn drugs any way he wants to. Well, he doesn't. Not as far as I'm concerned. That's human experimentation without safeguards. No protocol. No approval from a human-investigation committee. Probably no informed consent. The Nazi school of experimentation," he concluded.

"Paul, you are exaggerating just a bit," Bud said.

"I am?"

"And also jumping to conclusions."

"That may be true. Although I doubt it."

As he started back to the office, Edie stopped him and handed him a list with four names on it: two nurses and two LPN's. "There's still one thing that bothers me a lot," she said.

"What's that?"

"You never bothered to ask her name."

"Whose?"

"Emily Verban."

"Who?"

"Your tattooed lady. Her name is Emily Verban. She has a name and you never bothered to learn it. Why not?"

He knew he had no appropriate answer. "We all make mistakes. Saying that this kind of error is better than killing patients is no excuse. I've learned a lesson. You may have made me a better doctor. That is, if I'm still educable at my age."

Gerri was waiting in the parking lot. Paul hadn't really been with her since Sunday. They hugged and kissed, not passionately but certainly more than merely politely, and then drove off for lunch. They had a whole hour and forty minutes to spend together. What a luxury.

"If my apartment were closer, we could go there and make love," she said.

"You only want me for my body."

"That's not true," she protested.

"It's not?"

"I love your kids too."

"Don't try to fool me. You women are all the same."

"Who else wants your body?"

"Let's go to Chinatown."

"Don't change the subject."

"I'm not. We're in my car driving somewhere for lunch and I want to know where we're going. 'Where' is the subject. 'Lunch' is the object. And unlike you, I am merely hungry."

"Who?"

"No one. I was just kidding."

"Chinatown," she said.

They decided on the Chinese Deli, an inexpensive and rather drab storefront restaurant where they ordered beef chow fun and pan-fried noodles with chicken. These dishes almost made Paul believe that it was actually possible that noodles were not invented in Italy but had been smuggled back to Italy from China by Marco Polo. Before his first meal at the Chinese Deli he had always believed that story to be apocryphal. Now he wasn't sure.

"How did Donna Kolloway do?" she asked.

"I don't know. They should be finishing up about now."

"Why does she worship you?"

"She recognizes my talents."

"Paul."

He told her the story. How the other doctors had wanted to sterilize her because of her malformation and how he had told her the odds and let her make her own decision.

"You ass."

Paul was startled by her outburst. "What did I do now?"

"You think you're so damn smart all the time."

"I—"

"But you're not. Not this time. Damn you." She removed her glasses. "Look at my face," she demanded.

"There are other parts of you I'd rather look at."

"Stop it. Look at my face."

"Okay. I'm looking."

"What's wrong with my face?" she asked.

"Well, as I have pointed out before, your nose is a trifle too large for—"

"Schmuck."

"No. No. 'Schmuck' means 'penis,' not 'nose.' Your understanding of Yiddish—" This time he interrupted himself. It was not one of their games. The tears on her cheeks were real. He had never seen her cry before. He was lost. Why?

"Paul, please look at my face," she pleaded.

He looked at it. No longer a wisecracking lover but the observant clinician. It was a pretty face. Her nose was a bit too large. Her right naso-labial fold was slightly decreased. He'd never seen that before and the lower eyelid of her right eye was a bit lower than the one on the left. That was something he'd never seen. No, he'd seen it before, he just hadn't observed it.

"You have a very mild and undoubtedly old injury to your right facial nerve," he told her.

"Very good," she congratulated him. He felt the sarcasm through her tears.

"Is it due to an injury of the nerve or the brain?" she asked with a sob.

He looked again. Without asking, she went through the necessary steps.

She closed her eyes forcefully. They closed nearly normally, but not quite. No good neurologist would miss the asymmetry.

She wrinkled her forehead. It wrinkled normally.

She smiled broadly. The right side of her face lagged behind.

"Your brain," he said.

"What else do you know about me?"

"That I love you."

"Not that, Paul. What else do you know medically?"

Medically. He had not been her doctor. He knew so little. Then he remembered his convenient lie. "You have migraine headaches."

"Located where?"

"The left side of your head."

"What else?"

"I don't think I know anything else."

"You do."

Paul was puzzled.

"My darling, what did we do last Saturday night?"

"Made love."

"Good observation!"

"Cut it out, Gerri."

"I'm sorry. We made love. You certainly don't want me to get pregnant, all things considered."

"True."

"So what precautions did you take?"

"None."

"A typical male. You left it up to me."

"Yes."

"What precautions did I take?"

"I don't know."

"I know you don't. You never once bothered to ask me."

"No."

"So."

"Probably birth-control pills."

"Is that what you believe?"

"Yes. After all, you don't have an IUD. You've never had to put in a diaphragm. So I assume you're on the pill."

"But I have migraines."

"True."

"And?"

"The combination of the pill and migraines can result in a stroke, so you, being smart, wouldn't take birth-control pills."

"Give that man a cigar."

"Gerri!"

"Paul, put it together," she begged. The tears were now sobs.

The contest was over. Paul knew. "You have an AV malformation on the left side of your brain, causing migraine headaches. You've seen a doctor for it, so it must have caused more than just occasional headaches. Seizures. No. If it had caused seizures, you'd still be on medications and I'd probably know. So you must have bled once."

She nodded.

"Long ago. Years ago," he added.

"When I was nineteen. I was an undergraduate then at Brandeis."

"And you went to a neurosurgeon."

It was a statement, not a question, but she answered it. "Lenhardt. He was in Boston then."

Paul understood the tears, the anger, the sarcasm, the pain. "That bastard."

"I'll never even have a bastard," she said quietly. "He told me if I ever got pregnant it would kill me. So I had my tubes tied. You never even noticed the small scar. It's pretty well hidden in my hair down there."

"Still, I should have seen it. I have examined that area pretty—"

"Paul!"

"I'm sorry. Just one of my feeble attempts at humor."

"This is not the time."

She choked back the tears and told him the whole story.

The noodles got cold.

She went through all the details. How she had dropped out of school for two years and then finally worked things out with a therapist and decided to go to medical school and become a psychiatrist. And now, to find out she'd made a mistake, that she'd been lied to.

If it had been different, maybe they could have gotten married and had a family.

"So that's why you won't make any commitment to me."

"It's part of it."

"You don't even know if I would want to start another family."

"No."

"You never even bothered to ask me. You're no better than I am. No. You're worse. You just made up your mind, and that was it for both of us."

"Yes."

"I have to get to a brain cutting," Paul said.

"Is our discussion over?"

"What discussion? I'm not even sure you want to talk about this with me. You've already made up your mind."

She said nothing.

"Maybe I *am* just a body to you."

"Paul."

They rode back in the car listening to a tape of the last movement of Beethoven's Ninth. Paul put the tape on and sang along with it. Schiller had never sounded that bad before.

They were both glad not to be talking.

By the time Paul got to the brain cutting, they had already started. The brain was lying on a wooden cutting board resting on top of the metal table in front of the neuropathologist Charles Risberg. Students, residents, and attending physicians from Neurology, Neurosurgery, and Pathology were gathered around the table. Everyone was there but Floyd Baker. The odor of formaldehyde was just beginning to fill the room.

Paul had missed the recitation of the clinical history, but he already knew Rogovin's history by rote. He had arrived right on time, however, for the real action. He took his place at the table and . . . Something was wrong. There was no evidence of any recent bleeding on the surface of the brain. But Rogovin had bled just two days before his surgery. And Paul couldn't see any abnormal blood vessels. That JNF-2 might be good, but it wasn't that good.

"As expected from the history," Dr. Risberg began as he picked up the large knife, "the external surface of the brain is entirely normal."

Normal? Whose brain was it? He turned to Bill Goodman and asked him.

"Jackie Baumer."

No wonder the room was so quiet. He'd forgotten that they were scheduled to cut Jackie's brain today.

He could almost feel the first long cut across the frontal lobes. And the second, which reached the ventricles and spilled the formaldehyde they contained onto the cutting board.

The stench was overwhelming.

It burned his eyes. It was more than he could stand.

Charles Risberg was working faster than usual. Twelve cuts. Thirteen slices. All laid out on the cutting surface. All ready for a final close examination and then for Risberg to take his small scalpel and carve out small samples for even further study. They didn't need Paul for that. They could look at this one without him. He walked outside the room to take a few deep breaths of untainted air.

Jackie's brain. It bothered him much more than he thought it would. He had been to brain cuttings hundreds of times. What difference did it make whose brain it was? Jackie's brain or the brain of Broca's patient. It was a brain. No more. No less. There was no trace of the person it had once been.

No remnant of Jackie, her hopes, desires, or memories. This was infantile. Paul waited until he was certain they had taken all the necessary samples and disposed of the rest. He reclaimed his seat only when Risberg had started on the next brain.

Despite the obvious interest in the second case, the discussion was subdued. Even Don Lenhardt was restrained. Rogovin's brain was not normal. There was evidence of rather recent bleeding over the surface of the brain, but not enough to have killed him. Most of the abnormal vessels were a dull grayish blue in color and firm and rubbery. JNF-2 had done its job. The abnormal vessels were sclerosed.

Before Dr. Risberg went into action Paul summarized the three possible things that could have happened to Mr. Rogovin. Spread of the sclerosis to normal vessels, causing a massive infarction. Some adverse reaction to the chemical, causing necrosis of the brain. A hemorrhage directly into the brain itself.

Risberg started cutting one slice at a time. There was no spread of the intravascular coagulation. The normal vessels were wide open.

There was no infarction.

Nor any massive necrosis.

The cause of death was obvious. There was an enormous hemorrhage from one of the abnormal vessels deep in the brain. The hemorrhage had blown its way through the brain, ruptured into the lateral ventricle, rushed like a tidal wave into the third ventricle and then the fourth ventricle. Sudden pressure there in the fourth ventricle was always fatal. No wonder they could do nothing to save him.

"Well, you can't blame JNF-2 for that," John said.

"Of course not," Don Lenhardt agreed. "And that hemorrhage could not have been due to anything I did. Our needles were no place near the site of hemorrhage."

"Not so fast, guys. It's not that clear."

"Come on, Paul," John said. "How could JNF-2 have caused that?"

"Two ways. It could have caused some sort of injury to the walls of some of the blood vessels, and one of those injured walls might have ruptured. Or maybe everything worked just right but the sclerosis acted as a block to blood flow, and pressure built up in some other vessel and it ruptured.''

"You must admit there was no evidence of tissue damage,'' John said.

"That's true.''

"Those other possibilities are just conjectures.''

"We shall see.''

"How?''

"The microscopic slides,'' Paul said. "When will they be ready, Charles?''

"One week,'' Risberg replied. "Give or take a day.''

Paul spent the rest of the afternoon in his office reading and answering some correspondence. He didn't even argue with Dean Willis when he called. He told the dean about the M.S. patient with aspergillosis. He did not believe they could help her. He didn't mention the issue of whether or not she had been informed of the risk of chronic high doses of steroids and Cytoxan.

They wanted to hold a meeting of all the defendants in the lawsuit Friday night after dinner away from the medical center. Paul offered his house. It would be easier for him that way. The dean agreed.

They didn't talk about Jackie Baumer. They also didn't talk about the control of research.

When Don Lenhardt saw Mrs. Kolloway at five o'clock she could do everything she could do before surgery.

The surgery had been a success so far. He told her that everything was going to be fine. He knew that it was not that simple. If one of Paul's conjectures was right, she could be in for one hell of a lot of trouble. She could develop some necrosis of the walls of one of those damn vessels and that could result in a hemorrhage or maybe the sclerosis might cause increased pressure. It could be her brain being cut next week.

Paul was probably wrong. Hopefully.

As he drove home, Paul pondered the same problem. He was not so sure he was wrong. At least they had helped Emily Verban and he had remembered to write letters to all the nurses who had been involved. And Gerri had a mess like that in her brain. He tried not to connect what she had told him with what he had just seen at brain cutting. He should have missed the entire session.

9

"I finally told him," she said, but even as she said it she was angry with herself. It was the one thing she had wanted to talk about most and she had waited until her session was almost half over before she brought it up. She was acting just like any other patient, expressing her own ambivalence in such a childish manner.

"Ech . . . ech." He cleared his throat twice. That meant he was dissatisfied with her, more impatient than angry.

"I told him that I could never have children. I told him yesterday at lunch. I hadn't meant to, but he told me about this patient of his with a malformation in her head like the one I have inside mine and why it hadn't really been necessary for her to have her tubes tied. Dammit. That meant that I didn't have to have mine tied. It was such a shock. I blurted it out at him."

"And . . . ?" A direct question. She was beating around the bush.

"He got angry."

"Why?"

"I don't know."

"Come on, Gerri. This is not your analysis. Don't pull that on me."

"Because I'd been holding out on him. Because I hadn't told him before. Because I never let him know why I haven't been willing to think about anything permanent."

"That's a good start, Gerri. Did Paul say very much?"

"No. He just yelled at me."

"That's understandable."

"I guess so."

"Did he say whether or not he wanted another family?"
This clearly was not analysis. "No."

"So you still don't know the answer to that question, do
you?"

"No."

"What did Paul say?"

"He was pissed. He attacked me for making a decision
about us by myself. He made it sound as if I didn't care about
him."

"Do you?"

It was even getting hot for directive therapy. "Of course."

"Are you sure?"

"Yes."

"Absolutely?" It was beginning to resemble a third degree
more than any kind of psychotherapy. "I'm not so sure,
Gerri."

"You're not! Well, you're not me. I've never cared more
for anyone."

"Than whom?"

"Ca . . . I mean . . ."

"You do mean Carolyn, don't you?"

The game was over. "Yes."

"You knew that all along."

"That I loved those two kids, yes. But there's nothing
wrong with that. They are both very special. And I think they
love me in a way. Especially Carolyn. We talk more often
than Paul and I do."

"That's what I mean. It isn't just that you can't have kids
of your own, of your husband's, of Paul's."

She was crying again. It was the second time she had cried
in two days. She hadn't cried during therapy for almost two
years.

"It was that at first. It really was. You know that. I've
been that way for twelve years now."

"You don't have to convince me."

"We have worked on it for years. But it never has gone
away. It's a fact. I can't have kids. I always wanted to. Sure,
I'd be able to adopt children, but that's different. Thanks to

you, I feel better about myself, and maybe someday I will get married.

"But you are right. I've known it for months. I really do love his two kids. And I would be marrying him for the wrong reason. Paul deserves better than that. I care for him too much to do that to him. I can't marry him to live with them. Carolyn will be in college next year and Joshua in three more years, and then what would we have?"

"So now he believes that you won't consider marrying him because you can't mother a new child for him."

"Yes."

"Is that any fairer?"

Gerri checked her watch. Their hour would be over in less than five minutes and there was something else she wanted to talk about.

"I want to tell you about a dream."

"Gerri, your analysis is over. We stopped dealing with your dreams months ago."

"It's not my dream."

"It isn't?"

"It's the dream of a patient of mine. I wanted your opinion."

"Gerri, I'm not your supervisor. I'm your therapist. We have so few hours left to us and we still have work to do for you. Here we finally get down to the one issue which means something to you and you try to avoid it by talking about one of your paients' dreams."

"You're right. I'm sorry."

The mood was broken. As far as Gerri was concerned, they might as well have discussed one of Frank's dreams. Instead they just rehashed what they had already discussed. She knew that Dr. Rotblatt was right. This was an issue she had to face.

They started rounds in the surgical intensive-care unit. Mrs. Kolloway was there. She probably didn't need to be in the ICU. The ICU was designed for patients who needed special monitoring. Mrs. Kolloway didn't. Her vital signs were all stable. ICU's were also designed for swift action if anything disastrous happened to a patient. If something disastrous happened to her, there was probably nothing they could do.

Despite these truths, which both the neurologists and the

neurosurgeons recognized, Mrs. Kolloway remained in the ICU. It made everyone feel more confident and safer. Paul was not certain that it was anything more than a form of supportive therapy for the staff.

She was happy to see Paul Richardson and show off for him. She was at least as strong as she had been prior to surgery. In fact, she thought that she might even be stronger.

Paul examined her thoroughly. Her left arm and leg were not any stronger, but she was right—they were no weaker. If only they would stay that way. The image of yesterday's brain cutting was still fresh in his mind.

It was Bill Goodman who brought it up as they walked down to Neurology. "Do you think she'll hemorrhage?"

"I don't know."

"That hemorrhage we saw at brain cutting yesterday was scary."

"It was also unusual. That's the frightening part. I don't remember having seen one exactly like it before."

"That means it must be a complication of your experiment," Edie said.

"Don't jump to conclusions. We aren't sure yet. I have not been around long enough to have seen everything. What happened was unusual, but was it unique? Was it something that could never have happened if we hadn't injected something foreign into Rogovin's brain? I can't say that."

Mr. Kreevich had continued to improve. Paul showed him his watch.

"Watch."

Paul pointed to his watchband.

"Watchband."

Then to the stem.

"Watch winder . . . winder . . . no, stem."

Paul took out his pencil and pointed directly to the hands. "What are these called?"

"Fingers . . . pointers . . . no, hands. Big hand and little hand. Hour hand and . . . minute hand."

He could even describe his seizures in complete sentences. True, the sentences were still rather short, but they were complete.

Paul was pleased. At this rate, Mike Kreevich might recover completely.

A repeat EEG had shown much less evidence of injury and there were no spikes at all. That was pretty good evidence that the surgery might have done the trick.

They talked to Mrs. Wright. She was still running a fever and had a headache. It was not a terrible headache, but it was always there. Day and night. It never went away.

Other than that, they didn't find out anything new. Paul sat by her bedside and talked to her. She didn't know why she had been transferred here. She knew her M.S. was bad but it had been getting worse for a couple of years. As far as she knew, nothing else had happened to her. No one had ever told her any different. Fortunately her doctors had at least tried to help her with the Medrol and the other medicine, even though it hadn't worked.

She blessed them for trying. No one else had tried as hard.

Had they told her about the Medrol? Of course.

About the risks? "What risks?"

What risks? The phrase echoed inside Paul's head. He did not answer. It was too late to give a fragmentary answer.

Did they tell her it probably would help? They had said that they couldn't make any guarantees. It was possible it might not help. They had told her that. She knew it might not work. Nothing worked all the time. Didn't he know that? He made it sound as if they had experimented on her. The very idea!

Paul left it at that. He would talk to Bud. Bud would have to let her know what had actually transpired.

"Is that such a good idea?" Bill asked him.

"She has to know what happened to her, what is going on now. She has a right to know. We have an obligation to tell her."

"But . . ."

"But what?"

"She could sue her other doctors."

"Yes, she could."

"But shouldn't we try to prevent that?"

"Why?"

"There are too many malpractice suits already."

"Yes, because there is too much malpractice. What she does with the information is her business. If she sues, so be it. I can't help it. In fact, I think that might be the right thing for her to do."

They had one new patient, an old friend of Paul's. Oscar Felsch. He was sixty-four years old and had had Parkinson's disease for nineteen years. He had been Dr. Richardson's patient ever since Paul had finished his residency in 1968. He had been one of the first patients Paul had ever treated with L-dopa when it was still experimental.

They went to the bedside and Paul reviewed Mr. Felsch's history with him.

The first medicine Paul had put him on was L-dopa. That had been in early 1969.

Then Symmetrel was added in 1971.

He was switched from L-dopa to Sinemet in 1975.

Bromocriptine was added as an experimental drug in 1980.

Pergolide, another experimental drug, was started in 1981.

He was still on Sinemet and pergolide, but the medicines just weren't working anymore, his parkinsonism was getting worse. He needed help to get out of a chair. He couldn't roll over in bed at night. His voice was getting softer and softer.

Paul discussed the options. They had one more new drug to try. It was called mesulergine and it was related to bromocriptine and pergolide, but there was still a chance it might help. The other was the operation.

He told Mr. Felsch about the risks of both. Mr. Felsch wanted to have the operation. He didn't think another drug would help. Paul was not as pessimistic. They would try the new drug first, for at least a few days, and then they'd see.

"That's it," Bill told him as they left Mr. Felsch's room.

"What about Mr. Rath?"

"He went to surgery at ten-thirty."

"Anything to report?"

"No," Bill said.

"There is one thing, Dr. Richardson."

"What's that, Edie?"

"Emily called."

"Mrs. Verban. How is she?"

"She's fine. She likes it at the shelter. Her husband came to see her and she told him she wasn't going home with him. He got angry, but nothing happened. She doesn't ever want to go back to him."

Paul didn't have to say anything. Edie could see the approval in his eyes.

* * *

Frank no more than sat down when he launched into a rush of words. "That medicine you put me on, the Haldol, it's just not working. I keep on taking it, just like you told me to, but it's not doing me any damn good."

Gerri was hesitant to ask him the necessary questions, but she did. "How can you tell?"

"Those smells. They're back."

She didn't have to ask the next question.

"My brain is rotting again. It's burning up inside of me. I can smell it. You can smell it too. I'm sure that you can. Everyone can. But you won't tell me. You don't want to scare me."

"Frank, I don't smell anything like that."

"Don't lie to me, Dr. Scala. I trust you. I trusted him, too. And look at what he did to me."

She didn't have to ask him who the "he" was. She hoped that if she just waited it out, without arguing, he would start to calm down.

"Everyone can smell it. The smell is so strong. But no one says anything. They all lie to me."

He was beginning to slow down. The rush was over.

"Why do they all lie to me?"

He had never been this paranoid before. Perhaps the Haldol was not doing him any good.

"Whenever I smell it, they all smell it too. Do you know how I can tell?"

Gerri shook her head. She wasn't sure she wanted to learn exactly how paranoid he had become.

"I'll tell you. It'll become our secret. They look different. They no longer look the same to me. They don't talk the same. They become farther away from me. Then when the smell is gone, they come back. They look normal and they talk to me normally. But they all lie about it."

"How often do you smell it?" she asked. There were some facts she needed to know, and relying on Frank's train of thought would not get her these facts.

"Every day. Three or four times a day . . . at least. Maybe more."

"Wasn't it worse than that before?"

"No. No. It's worse now. The smell is worse than ever. It's closer to my nose. More of my brain is gone."

She waited.

He took a deep breath and started, "My nose was gone." This was a new twist.

"It was as if I had been born without a nose. I was in a strange town. A different town. Not one of the other towns."

It was another one of his dreams. He had just slipped into it as if the barrier between dreaming and the rest of his life didn't mean very much to him anymore. No nose. She wondered if he understood the symbolism of that image. Classically that was tantamount to being without a penis, castrated, impotent. Perhaps in this dream he had lost his gun. She hoped so.

"The town is full of rubble. Like there may have been an earthquake. It's like before, but different. I've never been there, but it seems familiar to me. There is one other difference. The other dreams were full of colors. Reds and blues and yellows and greens. Especially reds. Bright reds. Dull reds. But there is no red in this one. There was no color at all. It was like watching an old TV set without color. Not a new small one, but an old one. A black-and-white. That is what it reminded me of the most."

"Just like old TV," he repeated.

"Or a movie," she suggested, hoping to interrupt his reverie.

"No, not a movie. An old set without any color."

As soon as he answered, she knew she had made a mistake. He was angry that she had broken into his train of thought.

"The city was old, and full of broken-down buildings. Like a slum. Only worse. The streets were full of rubble. Or did I already tell you that once?"

She nodded, not wanting to sidetrack him any further.

"Suddenly I'm not in the city anymore. I'm at a fairground or a carnival or something like that. An amusement park, maybe. Not one of those little corner traveling carnivals, but a real amusement park. With a real Ferris wheel. A giant one. Like the one they had here in Chicago in the 1890's at the Columbian World's Fair. The one built by Ferris himself. I've seen pictures of it. This one was like it.

"There were only a few people there. I'm waiting for someone. To meet someone. I don't know who. I'm waiting. Someone tries to sell me some balloons. I don't buy one. Everyone keeps away from me. It's as if I give off a bad smell. But I can't smell it. I have no nose. I'm all alone. Alone in a crowd.

"Then I'm not there anymore. I'm in a long tunnel. I'm running. There is water in the tunnel. Lots of water. I'm running. Other people are running. I'm trying to catch up with them. They are chasing me. There are lights in the tunnel.

"They stop.

"I stop.

"She is running again.

"I chase after her. But she isn't the one I want.

"It's her tunnel I'm in."

She let that one pass. How could he not understand what he had said?

"I shoot at her.

"My shot explodes in the tunnel. Its noise fills the whole tunnel."

Dream on.

"He shoots at me.

"When I shoot it's always at her. She has long blond hair. My bullets go into her every time. I never waste a shot. But it never hurts her.

"When she shoots back, it's not her. It's him. He doesn't have any hair.

"My gun never runs out of bullets.

"It just keeps shooting.

"Over and over again.

"He only shoots at me a few times. He shoots me through the nose. Now I can smell it. At first I think I must be in a sewer, it smells so bad. There's a real stench. I'm bleeding from my nose. But I can smell.

"There is blood, but it's not red. It's black.

"Then I know what I'm smelling. It's my own brain I'm smelling as it drips out of the hole in the back of my nose.

"I keep firing. I want to shoot him. But all of the bullets go into her.

"The more I fire, the worse the smell gets.

"The more I shoot, the more of my brain oozes out.

"Then I know it's my last shot.

"I aim right at your mouth.

"I shoot.

"This one doesn't miss.

"He is dead.

"The fat man is dead."

Frank stopped.

Gerri knew that it would not be worthwhile to wait. "What fat man?"

"The fat man.

"Paul Richardson.

"He is dead.

"Paul Richardson is no more." He stopped.

"I think we ought to increase your Haldol," she said.

"He murdered my brain so I killed him. That's justice."

"What good would that do, Frank?"

"Plenty. It makes me feel good."

"What does?"

"Shooting at you and killing him. All at once. It's wonderful. But I couldn't shoot you. Not really. I don't even own a gun.

"You know I wouldn't hurt you, Dr. Scala."

"Yes."

"Or anyone else."

She considered him thoughtfully.

"I can't hurt anyone. I never could. People hurt me. They always have. My father. My mother. No, not my mother. Not you. But everyone else. My father. Dr. Richardson." He sobbed. "I should hurt them back but I can't. They're . . . too big. And I can't. I can't." His voice trailed off.

"Frank, it's best not to hurt people."

"I know that."

"I do think you need more medicine." She gave him his new instructions and made arrangements to see him first thing on Monday morning.

It didn't take Paul very long to learn why Tom Ward didn't stop by his office until almost noon, three hours later than his usual early-morning visit. Tom let him know as soon as he sat down. "You may well be right, Doc. We have to look at the entire case in a different way now. The two attacks were not related. The mugging of that medical student had nothing to do with the murder.''

"You're kidding," Paul responded.

"No. I'm not. We caught that guy."

"I thought you already had him."

"Oh, you mean Sanford."

"Yes."

"He didn't attack that Robinson girl. We found that out yesterday afternoon by plain old-fashioned policework. Nothing fancy. We know he goes to a variety of pickup joints every once in a while and we were checking them all out. One by one. And we found out that he had an alibi for Sunday night. He was with somebody else he picked up."

"Why didn't he just tell you her name?"

"His."

"His?"

"Doc, you shouldn't let the world amaze you."

"It doesn't. It just takes me by surprise from time to time," Paul said. "I'm still not sure why he didn't just tell you."

"Some guys are still that way. He didn't want to come out of the proverbial closet."

"Even if you charged him with murder?"

"We haven't officially charged him with murder yet. And this had nothing to do with Jackie Baumer's death. He still could be guilty of that. He probably is. This was just Sunday's mugging. And that one he's out of. He's got an alibi that would hold up in any court."

Tom paused.

Paul guessed. "Would you like some coffee?"

"Yes."

He debated and then got up himself and walked to the outer office to get two cups of coffee. The coffeemaker was empty. He looked at Chris and she recognized his look. The coffee would be ready in five minutes.

Paul went back into his office. "I thought you said you caught the guy."

"We did."

"Who?"

"I'll get to that. Once we knew it wasn't Sanford, we were

back to 'go.' There were always two possibilities. The first was that it was tied into the Baumer business. The other, that it wasn't. Number one was a natural assumption, but still an assumption. So I decided to follow up on number two and see who else in Ms. Robinson's life could have a motive unrelated to Jackie Baumer. It didn't take very long. I tried to get in touch with her all evening and she wasn't around.

"I finally got through to one of your residents, who told me she was visiting some tattooed lady."

"Emily Verban."

"That's the one. At first I thought he was talking about something really weird. Don't get me wrong. Nothing surprises me, Doc. Not even tattooed ladies. Then he told me the entire story and it made sense."

"Emily Verban?"

"Not Emily. Peter. Her husband. He was a definite possibility. After all, he had a history of uncontrolled violence toward women and Edie was trying to talk his wife into leaving him. Besides, whoever mugged her, as far as we know, hadn't actually tried to kill her. Just beat her up a bit.

"So I paid a little call on him. I found him at a bar up near his place, up around Bryn Mawr and Broadway. We got to talking about things. Usual bar talk. The Cubs. The Sox. Women. Dikes. That did it. He told me the whole damn story about Edie and his wife. How the dike nurse—I don't think he likes to think about women as doctors—was poisoning his wife against him. Then he told me he'd taken care of her."

"Tom. Wasn't that entrapment or something?"

"Entrapment? Hell no. He never even talked to a cop. I finished my beer. We talked about how the Cubs were letting us all down again and I paid my bill and left. No cop would have paid for his own beer."

"That's all?" Paul was surprised.

"Not quite all. I did do one more thing. I stopped at a pay phone and gave the cops an anonymous tip. Something I'd overheard in a bar. I wanted them to know. This guy might be dangerous. But I didn't want to get involved.

"They picked him up around one A.M. He almost confessed before they read him his rights. He's proud of what he did. Protecting his home from dike-bitches."

"Does Edie know?" Paul asked.

"I just told her. She thinks that she will press charges unless Emily tells her not to, and that probably won't happen. When we told Mrs. Verban about it this morning, she really got ticked off. She said she'd kill the SOB. Edie was the first person who had ever sincerely tried to help her. If I was him I'd stay away from her."

"So where does that leave us?"

"A good question," Tom replied.

"Are we back to square one?" Paul asked. "Or is Sanford still a suspect?"

"Both," Tom said, then added, "There is one thing you can do for me, Doc. One thing that we can't do ourselves. At least not very well."

"What's that?" Paul asked, his interest tempered by Tom's hesitancy.

"Well . . . it may not be that easy."

"Tell me."

"I'd like you to find out exactly who around here might have had a motive to kill Jackie Baumer."

"I am not going to investigate her past sex life."

"No, Doc. I didn't mean that. Not that kind of motive. That I'll investigate. I want you to evaluate other kinds of motives, just in case."

"I don't know." Paul's voice reflected his lack of enthusiasm.

"You'll do a better job than we would."

Paul knew that was true.

"And you can do it easier, more efficiently, and without ruffling people's feathers."

That too was true, but not sufficient.

"And maybe you owe it to her."

"How do you figure that?"

"Well, you said so yourself."

"What do you mean?"

"It could all be related to that lawsuit of yours."

Paul knew that Tom was right. There were certain things that he could do better than the police could do, and this was probably one of them. And maybe he did owe Jackie something. But he had to know where to start.

"Who do you figure has a sex-related motive? Aside from me and Fred Sanford?"

"Around this place, Dr. Baker and Edie Robinson."

"That all?" Paul asked.

"Yep. Now you can get to work so you can tell me who has any other kind of motive."

It was only after Tom Ward left that Paul realized they had never gotten their coffee. He went out and got himself a cup.

Paul did not get started on his new assignment immediately. He had other work to do. First, he still hadn't completed his presentation for the CPC. And he wanted to read those bylaws again, just in case there might be some loophole.

He was able to work for about twenty minutes while listening to a Mozart piano concerto on WFMT.

The phone rang. It was his direct line.

It was Gerri.

"I have to talk to you, Paul."

"So talk."

"Not on the phone. In person. How is your schedule? Are you free from two to three?"

"No, but I'm reasonable."

"Can I come by?"

"Yes."

Ten more minutes of work, accompanied by an overture by Rossini, from one of his comic operas. Paul never remembered which overture was which. He figured that it didn't make much difference. Rossini himself hadn't kept them straight. He was forever switching tunes from one opera to another. Sometimes even entire overtures. No wonder Paul couldn't be sure which one he was hearing.

Just as Ray Norstrand was about to tell him which opera it was from, the phone rang again. It was Chris. Herb was there to talk to him about the implants.

He hung up. He'd missed the announcement. They were playing something else. Vivaldi, maybe. He turned it off.

Paul and Herb got right down to business.

"I've spent two days checking all the adrenal lines and I've picked out the four cell cultures that look best," Herb told his boss. "I've brought all the biochemical data, the immunological data, and both regular photographs and micrographs with me."

"Let's go over it, then," Paul said.

The review took them over an hour. The choice that they had to make was obvious. They had to choose one of the four cell lines to be used for the implant on Mr. Felsch. The trouble was that the choice was not easy. There were so many parameters. They compared the cell lines biochemically to see which one was most likely to make enough dopamine if it actually grew in Mr. Felsch's brain. Paul went over all the data and then did some calculations and wrote down the samples in the order in which he ranked them:

1.	Leibold	302
2.	Weaver	296
3.	Gandil	290
4.	Schalk	282

The order was identical to the list that Herb had already prepared.

Next came the immunological comparison. This would hopefully predict which cells were least likely to be rejected and would therefore be most likely to survive inside Mr. Felsch's brain. Once again Paul and Herb came up with identical lists. Unfortunately, the list did not parallel the one based on biochemistry.

1.	Schalk	9
2.	Leibold	18
3.	Gandil	18
4.	Weaver	33

Then they compared the pictures to see how healthy the cells looked. This, they hoped, was a predictor of how well the cells would reproduce and grow, if not rejected. Again they agreed with each other.

1.	Weaver	9
2.	Gandil	4
3.	Schalk	3
4.	Leibold	2

Finally they looked at the last factor, the ability of the cells to survive under adverse circumstances, such as a decreased

supply of oxygen. This, perhaps, would predict their ability
to survive the transfer into Oscar Felsch's head.

1.	Gandil	277
2.	Weaver	272
3.	Leibold	266
4.	Schalk	253

There was no right answer. They needed cells that would
survive sugery intact like the Gandil cells, and not be rejected
like the Schalk cells, and then grow like the Weaver cells.
And of course, even if the cells did all that, if they didn't
produce enough dopamine like the Leibold cells, they wouldn't
do any good. What Mr. Felsch needed was dopamine, not
new cells that didn't make any dopamine. He already had
brain cells that didn't make dopamine.

No one knew which one or two of these predictors meant the
most. This was the kind of decision Paul had to make. And
he did.

"Leibold," he announced. "I've never been convinced
that it matters too much how the cells look in culture, so we
can leave that one out and . . . Nuts, there is no right answer.
Last time we went with survivability and growth, so this time
we'll go with dopamine production. Herb, what were those
figures last time?"

"We used a different Schalk line that time. The dopamine
production was two-nineteen, immuno six—"

Paul interrupted, "Two-nineteen. That's lower than I remember. That's quite low. Lower than any of these. What
would be the lowest end of the scale?"

"Two hundred."

"So that was really just plus nineteen, as opposed to
Leibold, which is at plus one-o-two, over five times as high."

"Yes."

"Why such a great difference? The other Schalk is two-
eighty-two now, or four times as high. That is strange." Paul
hadn't really expected an answer to his question, but he got
one.

"I think it's my fault."

"Your fault?"

"After the surgery didn't seem to help McCormick, I went

over my techniques again and I discovered that I had used six-percent glucose in the media and most of the other investigators in the literature used seven-and-a-half-percent solutions, so I increased to seven and a half percent."

"That shouldn't make such a difference."

"Maybe not, but they all make more dopamine now."

"True. But is that the only difference in your technique?"

"Yes."

"Are you sure?"

"Hell, yes!"

"Don't get so defensive, Herb. I was just trying to help figure things out. By the way, where do we stand on the JNF-2 animals?"

"I've sacrificed the first group and fixed the brains. The slides will be ready Monday or Tuesday."

"Good. How about the chronic animals?"

"They look fine so far. I'll check them again this afternoon with John and Floyd. And then again Monday or Tuesday."

Herb picked up his notebook and the photos and went back to the laboratory, leaving Paul alone in his office. Paul did not turn on the radio or try to get any work done. Gerri would be there any minute. If only he had a cigar to smoke. Maybe he should try pipes again. He could be like Holmes and sit back with a calabash and puff his way through a three-pipe problem. Of course, he didn't own a Persian slipper to store his tobacco in.

Why had Herb been so defensive? Had he screwed up somehow in the cell cultures? Made some technical mistake? Was he afraid that he had done something wrong in the lab and that that had made Frank McCormick worse? It was possible. If the cells were making something else instead of dopamine, something like methyl dopamine, that might make schizophrenia worse.

The change in glucose by itself couldn't account for it. He was going to have to go over the notebooks.

Was it safe to operate on Felsch?

Would the Leibold adrenal tissue take inside Felsch and work?

Who knew?

The figures all looked pretty good.

It was the previous ones that looked bad.

That might have been a factor in the results on McCormick. Maybe the McCormicks were right to sue.

Is that how Herb felt?

Had he killed Jackie?

What a crazy connection. His logic was as loose as Frank McCormick's. That didn't make any sense at all. Or did it? Without the consent and without Jackie, they had no defense. If there was no defense, there would be no reason to check Herb's lab data. The case would never get that far. If it was actually Herb's fault, he could hide it by eliminating the investigation.

Would he do a thing like that? No.

How did Paul know that? He didn't.

If Herb had screwed up and his mistake had been the only error and it came out in a trial, Herb could end up driving a cab for a living.

This was getting him nowhere.

It was 2:20. Gerri was late. Was she ever late for her analysis? He doubted it. He was sure she was always on time for M. J. Rotblatt. That unluck— He never finished his thought.

"Hi, Paul."

"Gerri. You're late. I was going to pretend I was your analyst and start without you."

"Paul, your jokes are getting worse."

"Let's just say they fit my mood."

"I'm sorry."

"Why? You did what you felt you had to. You don't owe me any apologies."

"I didn't want to hurt you."

"No. You just decided the ground rules of our relationship and never told my why. It's your life. You have the right to run it any way you want to."

"You're being impossible."

"Yes, I guess I am. After all, I like to be treated like a mature adult."

"Paul!"

"Look. All I knew was that you turned me down. Why? As far as I could tell, it was because I was too old for you to want to spend the rest of your life with me."

"That's not true."

"Or you just didn't care enough."

"I never—"

"I know you never said that. One way or the other. So now we come up with another reason. You can't have kids. So what?"

"So what? I've spent half my life dealing with that. I used to feel like I'd never really be a woman."

"That's bull and you know it."

"I do like your sympathetic approach," she said bitterly.

"And I like the way we share our problems."

"Oh, go to hell."

"I . . ." Paul stopped himself. He had gone too far. They both had. There was no reason to go on this way. Gerri began to twist the end of her hair with her right hand to refrain from adding any more fuel to the fire.

"Are you coming to the meeting tonight?" he asked.

"Yes," she said. "I'll be there at eight o'clock sharp."

"I'll see you then, I guess."

"I guess you will," she said.

Paul wanted to apologize, but he also wanted her to and he didn't feel like initiating the process, and she didn't. After a brief pause that seemed to drag on longer than a Wagnerian interlude, she left. He neither turned on WFMT nor read.

He definitely was going to get either some cigars or a pipe. One or the other. He tried to get his thoughts back to the problems of the day but couldn't. The lab seemed remote. So did Oscar Felsch and even Jackie Baumer. Gerri didn't. Yet he didn't understand what was going on. At least Mike Kreevich was better. He could say "watch" and name the parts: hands . . . stem . . . band. Time. Paul was behind schedule once again.

Traffic was better than he had a right to expect it to be on a Friday night. So was the music. He listened to part of the new Haitink recording of Shostakovich's Fifth. It was so good he was tempted to buy it.

He got home only a few minutes later, well ahead of when the kids had expected him. Once again, Carolyn had fixed a fairly extensive Friday-night menu. Joshua had set the table for four. Carolyn had invited Gerri when they had talked during the week. When? Monday or Tuesday. He told them another small lie.

"She got tied up at the last minute and told me to apologize. But she'll be here after dinner with a bunch of other people from the hospital."

"When?" Carolyn asked.

"About eight."

"How many?"

"About eight."

"Dad, the house is a mess."

"So what?"

"You're impossible. What am I going to serve?"

"This isn't a party."

"Coffee," she decided. "And I'll make a cake or something. No. I have a better idea. You'll go pick something up. Entenmann's. I really don't have time to bake. I would have this afternoon if you had told me."

"I don't believe this."

"After we finish dinner, Joshua and I will clean up and you'll go to the store."

"Yes, sir, boss lady."

"Dad," Joshua said, "get some of those chocolate crumb doughnuts."

"Any other orders?"

"No."

"Let's have dinner then."

"Wash your hands and get your yamulke."

He had remembered the time correctly. Eight o'clock. He had even guessed the number correctly—eight.

Carolyn made a perfect hostess. Gerri offered to help but was told she was a guest. The dean, John, Herb, Floyd, Don Lenhardt, and Charles Connors took coffee. Gerri and a young associate of Connors' named Terwilliger had tea. Joshua even waited until everyone had had one pass at the Entenmann's before he took his doughnut.

Then the kids disappeared and everyone else got down to work. They went over Frank McCormick's records with a fine-tooth comb. Page by page. Note by note. Word by word. Order by order.

"Even though we do not have a copy of the signed consent

form . . ." Mr. Connors began. "Or have you located your copy, Dr. Richardson?"

"Not yet," Paul said.

"Well, despite that fact, we do have a very strong defense. The pre-op checklist is there, and consent form is clearly checked off."

"Yes, but," Don Lenhardt protested, "Jackie did that."

"True. And the plaintiff might try to construe the fact that she was the original witness to casting some doubt that she could properly check informed consent on the checklist, but it is a double bind. If she did witness it, perhaps it was improper for her to carry out the checklist. But, and that is a big but, if they want to admit that she witnessed it, then it must have existed."

"Unless," Mr. Terwilliger said, "they claim that the McCormicks refused to sign it and she knew that they had refused. Perhaps she had witnessed that refusal."

"That's possible," Connors agreed.

It was 11:30. Carolyn and Joshua had long since gone to bed. Floyd helped Paul serve cold drinks while Gerri and Herb cleaned up the coffee cups. John and Don wanted more coffee. Paul showed them where the coffee was and John made some more.

It took them another forty-five minutes to wind it all up. The last item was the choice of expert witnesses.

"Why do we need experts?" Gerri asked.

"To say we didn't make any errors," Connors explained. "We'll need a psychiatrist, a neurosurgeon, a neurologist, and someone knowledgeable about this sort of procedure, and last an expert on hospital policy to testify about the pre-op checklist."

"I will get that one," the dean said.

"Good. The rest of you think about names for the rest and let me know."

They were done.

Gerri left last.

"Carolyn was disappointed that you missed dinner. So was Joshua."

"I'm sorry. Will you apologize for me?"

"I already did."

"Were you?"

"Was I what?"

"Disappointed," she explained.

"No. Not really."

"I guess that says a lot."

"No, it doesn't. I didn't know you had been invited so I wasn't disappointed. I couldn't be."

"Would you have been?"

"I don't really know."

"It's not you," Gerri said.

"It isn't?"

"No, it's me."

"For someone who has been analyzed—"

"I haven't been analyzed."

"But you are terminating your analysis."

"Not because I want to."

"Rotblatt said your analysis was complete."

"He and I have different opinions on that issue."

"Is that the sort of issue on which mature adults can differ?"

"Yes and . . . no."

"Why no?"

"The analyst has the last word."

"So you are done."

"I don't agree, but we have to be done and I won't start again with someone else. I don't have the time or the energy. Okay?"

"It's okay with me."

The dishes were all put away.

"Paul, don't be so hurt. I do care about you."

"I know that."

"Good night."

She kissed him lightly on his cheek and left.

He looked in on Carolyn and Joshua before he went to bed. They were both asleep. He watched each of them for a minute or two and realized how much Gerri had lost. He cursed the SOB who had told her what to do. That SOB had been Don Lenhardt. He wondered if Lenhardt even remembered the incident. He had to be more gentle with her.

10

"Your dad's girlfriend sure doesn't look Jewish." Paul heard the comment by one of Carolyn's friends from the synagogue youth group and waited to hear her answer. He didn't want to butt in—just listen. That was one of the best features of the kiddush after services at Beth El. You could stand around in the crowd and listen in on a conversation without appearing to be eavesdropping.

"So what? She's still very pretty," Carolyn said. Luckily they were standing near one of the serving tables. Paul surveyed the selection.

"And her name doesn't sound Jewish."

"I guess it doesn't." And then Carolyn caught on. "She is Jewish, though. She showed me the pictures of her bat mitzvah."

I've never seen those, Paul thought as he picked out a small florentine. That wouldn't have too many calories.

"I don't know," the voice went on. "My dad says he never heard of a Jew named Scala."

It was Joshua who continued the defense. "Who cares what your dad has heard of? There are lots of Jews named Scala."

Not so many, Paul realized. Gerri's grandfather had converted.

"Jews have all kinds of names," Joshua added.

"We even know some Jews named Cortes," Carolyn added. "They're from Kansas City. They're descended from *the* Cortes." No one could have missed her emphasis.

"The one who conquered Mexico?"

"Yes."

"Wow. I read a book about him. He only had a few hundred Spanish . . ."

Paul walked away from both the conversation and the food-laden table. They had defended him better than he could have. The very idea that he would go with someone who wasn't Jewish was an affront to them both. Bobbie would have been proud of them. They had saved his name. Or hers? Wasn't it really Gerri whom they had defended?

When he finally sat down on Sunday night to catch his breath, that overheard conversation, despite its ambiguity, stood out as the highlight of the weekend. Not that the weekend had been bad. It was just different. It had been the first weekend in three months during which he had not been alone with Gerri. At least it hadn't been the same disaster that the previous weekend without her had been. That was when they had had their one discussion about their future and she had gone off by herself to Wisconsin. That had also been the last time he had made love to Jackie.

After services and the kiddush, Paul and his defenders had driven to Comiskey Park and watched the White Sox win, thanks to a home run by rookie left-fielder Ron Kittle. Then they had dinner out—at Connie's on Twenty-sixth Street. Real Chicago-style thick pizza, in a class with Uno's and Geno's. No—better than Geno's.

After dinner they continued northward, making one more stop: at one of the small theaters on Halsted to see *Inherit the Wind*. He and Bobbie had taught their kids right. Carolyn and Joshua had been raised on live theater and they both loved it. All the way home they talked excitedly about the play, the Scopes trial, the pizza, and the White Sox.

"Do you think they have a chance this year, Dad?" Carolyn asked.

"I'm afraid not," Paul answered.

"Don't be so sure. They could still do it," Joshua proclaimed.

The optimism of youth. "I hope you're right, Josh."

Sunday was no less hectic. They had brunch with some friends and after half-watching the Sox lose a tough one, thanks to four errors, they drove back to the South Side to the Candlelight Dinner Theater to see *Camelot*. They didn't get home until after eleven.

As they were getting ready to go to bed, the phone rang. Carolyn answered. It was for her. Paul straightened up the kitchen and made himself a cup of instant coffee. She was still on the phone laughing and gossiping when he was done.

He picked up a book to read, or rather, to reread. *The Maltese Falcon*. Who came first, Humphrey Bogart or Sam Spade? The chicken or the egg?

Peter Lorre had also been perfectly cast, and Sydney Greenstreet, to say nothing of Ward Bond and—

Carolyn handed him the phone. Gerri also wanted to talk to him.

"Hi," she said.

"Hi," he replied without much enthusiasm.

"You certainly had a busy weekend."

"Yes."

"Carolyn enjoyed it."

"Yes."

"And the Sox won."

"A squeaker. Four to three. It was a good game," he said.

"Carolyn liked the peanuts."

"And the scoreboard," Paul added.

"Yes, and the scoreboard," Gerri agreed. "You had a good time?"

"Yes," he answered.

They both paused, and then started talking at once. She stopped.

"What did you do?" he asked.

"Not much. I stayed around my apartment. I cleaned it. I caught up on some paperwork. That's what I wanted to talk to you about."

"Cleaning your apartment? I only do light dusting. No stoves. No windows."

She laughed. More than she should have. It hadn't been that funny.

"No, not about cleaning my apartment. I did that last night. It was about Frank McCormick. I was going over my process notes."

Only shrinks called them "process notes." Part of the

therapeutic process. Why couldn't they write "progress notes" like the rest of us? Paul thought.

"I wanted to tell you about his dreams. They've become so violent, Paul. Awful." She outlined the dreams for Paul, reconstructing them from her memory and her process notes. She was most careful in her retelling of the first two. She told him about the screams in the middle of the night on the quiet street in some unknown town and the discovery of the dead woman whose body had been shoved up a chimney and whose head came off and whose blood Frank tasted. She told him about the gore, about the victim-lover being her and then his mother, and pointed out the sexual connotations: the woman being stuffed up a chimney was obviously a symbol for intercourse. Obviously. Paul tried to remember exactly what Freud had said while he listened to her interpretations. Then he remembered: at times a cigar was merely a good smoke. Maybe a body up a chimney was just a body in a chimney? He decided not to introduce that possibility. At least not then.

Gerri was still describing the scene. "So the blood dripping out of the chimney must be a sign of lost virginity."

"Not his mother's?"

"No. Nor mine."

"To that I can attest. But whose?"

"His."

Then she went on to the second dream. There was an obvious progression. The first time, the violence was over by the time Frank got to the scene. In the second dream he was an observer. She told him about the gun in the mouth, explained the homosexual connotations, and concluded that the victim was Paul, Frank's father, and Frank himself, all at once.

Paul listened. "Process" was the right word after all. Frank might be changing but he sure as heck wasn't making anything that Paul would have called progress. Paul would have used the term "regression." Why was she telling him all this? Hadn't her patient told her not to? Had she called just for this? This could wait. Had she called to tell him she had spent the weekend alone? If she missed him, why didn't she say it?

The third dream.

Paul wondered how many there were. Even his own dreams bored him. What were Gerri's dreams like? Did he really care? Personally he paid more attention to his conscious thought patterns.

He had thought more about Bobbie than about Gerri these past two days. Was that evidence of further progression? Would Gerri classify that as regression? He had missed some of what she had said.

"He did the violence this time. On a beach. He shot someone, an Arab."

"Why an Arab?" he asked.

"The victim didn't stay an Arab very long."

"What?"

"The Arab turned into me and then into his mother."

"Oh, brother."

"In his latest one he starts at a Ferris wheel and ends up in a tunnel."

"The tunnel I understand," Paul said. "It's a chimney substitute. But what does a Ferris wheel stand for?"

"I don't know, Paul. But once he was inside the tunnel he started shooting his gun and kept firing and never ran out of bullets. He had a gun that never stopped firing."

"Even I understand what that means. It's enough to make a grown man jealous."

"Paul, you've never had any problems. At least not with me."

"No."

"In fact, just the opposite."

"Oh, really?"

"I've told you before."

"What?"

"That it's better with you than with anyone else."

"No, you haven't."

"I haven't?"

"No."

"Well, it's true."

He wasn't sure how to respond. Was this like an opening of two no trump, a demand bid? Did he have to answer? Three clubs?

"I'm glad." A weak response.

She understood. "I think he may be dangerous."

"To whom?"

"To you."

"Me?"

"Yes, you. He blames you." She explained Frank's fear that his brain was rotting inside his head and the fact that he believed it was all Paul's fault.

"How dangerous?"

"I'm not sure."

"Could he have killed Jackie? Made it with her and then killed her?" Paul asked.

"I suppose he could have killed her. If I wasn't worried about that possibility, I probably wouldn't be talking to you about this now. But I'm sure that he never made love to her. He's never done that. Ever. I don't think he could."

"She did have long blond hair, like you."

"Is that why—?"

"No, and you know it."

"I'm sorry, Paul. It still hurts."

"We both have our little pains."

"He wouldn't have gone to bed with her!"

She was proud of that fact. Even her schizophrenic patient had better sense than he had had.

"But," she added, "I'm not at all sure that he might not be capable of violence of some sort."

"I'll tell Tom Ward tomorrow when I see him. He can look into it."

He didn't read any more Dashiell Hammett, but he still didn't get any sleep for several hours. He spent most of the night tossing in his bed and thinking.

When he finally did get to sleep, he dreamed. His dreams for once were filled with violence and screams and blood. The blood of Jackie Baumer. The blood of a violated virginal Jackie. Even she must have been virginal once. The dreams shifted from place to place. From Paris to a giant Ferris wheel. Like the one he had seen so often in pictures of the Columbian Exposition.

All in all, it was a night that could have been spent better in some other activity. He would have been better off had he been up all night at the bedside of a sick patient. He missed those nights. And those solitary decisions. That was when he had learned about medicine. And about himself.

— 11 —

The alarm radio went off at 6:30, forcing some late-Romantic sonata for piano and violin into his consciousness. Paul thought that it was most likely Brahms. It was not his idea of how to start the day, but he didn't have any alternative. Nor did he have much choice about getting out of bed and starting the family on their work week. The luxury of choice was not his. That was the one thing that made him most envious of the great fictional detectives. They had true freedom of choice. If a client presented himself, they could either take on the case or reject it and just sit around in an apartment in Baker Street or on a houseboat in Florida and wait for a case that appealed to them. And if that wasn't enough, each of them only worked on one case at a time. If you could even call that work. They were all such lucky SOBs—except for Maigret. He had to take the cases as they came along and he had other responsibilities to boot. Of course, he got to live and work in Paris for all his troubles. And walk those magnificent broad streets on rainy spring evenings with the smells of . . .

Time to get up. His dreams, which had been vivid enough to be all but palpable, were rapidly fading. It was now easier for him to remember Gerri's retelling of Frank McCormick's nightmares.

First he made certain that both Carolyn and Joshua were up and about. Yes, he agreed they could each take a shower and he would wait his turn. He put his head back down for just a moment.

When he woke up again, it was well after seven and Brahms was no longer coming out of the speakers.

He recognized the music. He knew it. And for once, he also knew the performer. Not that it was very difficult. It was Berio's *Folk Songs*, sung as they were written to be sung, by Cathy Berberian. He was tempted to sing along but they were too beautiful to ruin. If he could fall in love with a woman by merely hearing her sing, this was the woman. And this was the music.

Maybe they will play another of the songs, he hoped, knowing that that was unlikely. Much to his surprise, they did. They seemed to be playing the entire song cycle. When the third song started, he knew he had to get up. He turned up the sound and let in just barely enough water to shave. He'd brush his teeth during something else.

He shaved very slowly. It took him three songs.

Removing the traces of lather with a washcloth took most of the two songs of the Auvergne.

They were playing the entire suite.

Why?

Was it Berio's birthday?

Or had he died? That was much more likely. WFMT might celebrate Beethoven's birthday. But not Luciano Berio's. They did something like this when a composer died.

Paul had to make a decision. He'd take his shower that night. He changed into clean underwear and fresh socks while Cathy began the Azerbaijan love song that was the last song of the set. He hated making the bed. But he hated coming home to an unmade bed even more. He made the bed.

The love song was over. Paul was finishing getting dressed. WFMT told him the news. It was not Berio who had died. It was his former wife, Cathy Berberian. She was dead.

Dead at the age of fifty-seven. One of his heroes was gone. He turned off the world and brushed his teeth.

Joshua and Carolyn were already having breakfast. He could hear their incessant chatter as he got downstairs and went into the library to pick up his briefcase.

Paul did not hear the chattering stop.

He did hear a low moan, but he didn't pay very much attention.

The moan got louder. He wondered.

He heard a crash and turned.

It had been more of a thud. He started toward the kitchen.

A scream. Joshua was screaming. Paul dropped his briefcase and tore toward the kitchen.

He saw Joshua first. Pale. Shaking. A silent scream still on his lips.

Carolyn? Where was she?

He saw her. She was stretched out on the floor. A kitchen chair, obviously the one on which she had been sitting, was on the floor beside her. Orange juice was dripping from the table.

Carolyn was on her back.

Her arms were bent at the elbows.

Her fists were both clenched.

Her legs were extended.

Her jaws were clenched.

Her eyes were wide open and unseeing, the irises jerking up into her head so that Paul could barely see them.

Both of her arms twitched rhythmically in time with her eyes. Her head bounced up and down in a series of forceful spasms as if her neck were also keeping time with the same unheard drummer.

He counted the spasms. One. Two. Three a second.

Paul knew all too well exactly what was happening. He had seen such things hundreds of times during his professional life. But this was not part of his professional life—this was his own daughter having a seizure right there on the kitchen floor, during breakfast. For a moment he remained frozen in place.

Joshua had never seen anything like this before. He looked at his father, his eyes asking him to somehow stop it, to make his sister okay. His eyes begged it, demanded it.

The convulsion went on and on.

Seemingly forever.

Paul recognized the plea and terror in his son's look. He hoped his eyes had not betrayed his own fright.

The jerking continued.

Carolyn's eyes were all but lost to view.

"Dad, what—?"

"It's okay, Josh. She is having a convulsion. But she'll be fine." I hope to God.

Just when it seemed as though it would never end, suddenly it did. Carolyn's arms relaxed. Her jaws opened. Her eyes rolled back into view, stared straight ahead, seeing nothing, and then closed. She let out a low moan and began breathing. Deep sighing breaths. They sounded wonderful.

The convulsion that had gone on for an eternity—an eternity of perhaps thirty or forty seconds—was finally over.

Paul quickly pulled off Carolyn's shoes. And as he did so he glanced at Joshua. God—was he as white as Joshua? As scared? Probably more. He knew what it could be. A brain tumor, a catastrophe inside Carolyn's head. Please, God, don't take her away too.

Paul peeled off his daughter's socks. Then he took his keys out of his pocket and stroked them against the sole of her left foot. The toes all curled down. He repeated it on the right. Down again. "No toe signs," he said, as if he were demonstrating an important physical finding to a group of residents and students. "No evidence of any injury there."

"Joshua, get my reflex hammer from the library and my ophthalmoscope."

Joshua ran off and Paul stayed kneeling next to Carolyn. Her breathing was softer now, less deep. The transition back to a normal respiratory pattern was almost complete. Her eyelids were flickering. Soon she would be awake.

Joshua was back with the hammer and scope.

Paul took the hammer and tested her reflexes.

The ankle reflexes were normal.

So were those at the knees. And the biceps and triceps reflexes.

"All normal," he announced.

Carolyn's eyes were open. They were glazed. She was looking around the room as if in a daze.

"Carolyn."

She said nothing. She looked at her father without showing any sign of recognition.

"Carolyn."

"Yes."

"Where are you?"

"Where am I?"

"Yes, where are you?"

"I'm . . . I'm lost."

"No. You're not lost," he told her, and then he repeated, "Where are you?"

"I don't know."

"Who are you?""

"I'm . . . I'm . . . Carolyn. Carolyn Richardson, and I live in . . . Highland Park."

"How old are you?"

"Sixteen."

Not too bad. "Where are you?"

Her eyes were less glossy now. She was beginning to focus on Paul's face.

"Dad, what happened?"

"It's okay, Carolyn."

"What's okay?"

"You are."

"What happened? Where am I?"

"You had a seizure, a convulsion, but you're fine now."

"I'm not."

"You're not?"

"No. My head hurts. It hurts so. Like it's exploding." She began to cry.

"Dad, what's wrong?" This time the question came from Joshua.

"She'll be fine, Joshua. Believe me." This was said slowly and firmly, admitting to none of his own panic. "It's common to have a headache after a seizure. It's nothing to worry about." Unless something actually was exploding in her head. Oh God.

"Where are you?"

"I'm at home. In the kitchen."

"What do you remember?"

"Nothing. I was reading the paper and eating something. A bagel I think. I'd had something to drink."

"Orange juice," Joshua said.

"Yes and then . . . I don't remember anything else."

"Then she started making a noise," Joshua said. "It started soft. I thought she was humming. It got louder."

Carolyn stared at him bewildered.

"Then she grabbed her neck."

"What do you mean? No, don't explain. Show me."

Joshua bent both elbows and lifted his arms in front of him

so that his clenched fists were just next to the upper part of his neck. "Like this," he said.

"Then?"

"She fell over."

"And?"

"I screamed. I don't remember exactly what happened next. I'm sorry."

"It's okay, Josh. You did just right. You did great. Your description is perfect."

"I thought she might have swallowed something wrong and she was choking. I was going to do a Heimlich."

Paul smiled.

Carolyn was crying. "My head hurts so. It's pounding. Is it going to burst?"

"No. It's all over. You're going to be perfectly fine," he reassured her, and then he turned to his son. "Joshua, call my office. Chris is probably there already."

Joshua dialed the number, said hello to Chris, and gave the phone to his father.

"Chris."

"Yes."

"What time will Bud be in?"

"Nine."

"What does he have scheduled?"

"A meeting with—"

"Cancel it. Or at least delay it."

"Why?"

"There's a patient he has to see."

"Who?"

"Carolyn. She had a seizure."

"Oh no."

He looked at his daughter. She wasn't crying anymore. She was holding her head. "She's all right. I'll be there around nine."

"He'll be waiting for you."

Paul hung up. "How's your headache?"

"A little better. I'm so tired."

"Rest. Joshua, get her a pillow while I clean up this mess. Then I'm going to take her to the hospital. I'll drop you off at school. We'll let her rest ten minutes, then we'll go." Paul stood up. He felt shaky. He had been kneeling in the exact same position for over fifteen minutes. His legs were stiff. He felt dizzy.

He needed to sit down and catch his breath.

He knew what it had to be. That damn botched delivery. That was the most common cause of seizures that started during adolescence. Most seizures were not due to brain tumors, hemorrhages, malformations, or severe infections. The cause was usually something much less dramatic. A few minutes of decreased oxygen supply to the brain during birth, and then years later the seizures started. That's what had happened to Carolyn. Some stupid resident had loused up what should have been a normal delivery. It had to be that. It just couldn't be anything else.

Carolyn was resting, her head on a pillow.

Joshua and Paul cleaned up the kitchen.

"Dad, aren't you going to look in her eyes?" Joshua asked.

"No, I'll let Dr. Chiari do that. He's going to be her doctor. Not me."

The kitchen was pretty much back in order.

Paul helped Carolyn put on her shoes and socks and the three of them got into the car together.

"I am in some other city. It's not Chicago but it's in America.

"I'm happy. I had gotten up with a bad taste in my mouth but I was happy.

"And I know what I have to do but I am still happy."

This was the first dream in which he started out happy. Gerri doubted if it would make any difference. Had Paul called that detective yet? Probably not. It was still early. She hoped he wouldn't forget.

"I go inside the building. It's not a big building, not a high-rise. It's just an average apartment building.

"The lobby is empty.

"There is an elevator but I use the stairs.

"I am outside the apartment. No one is home. The door is locked. I unlock it. It's dark but I know where all the furniture is so I don't turn on the light. I walk across the room and sit in a deep-cushioned chair in the corner.

"I take out my gun and wait."

Like the image of himself in his dream, Frank waited.
And while he paused, his air of happiness dissolved.

"The door opens and she comes into the apartment.

"I see her before she sees me.

"She smiles at me.

"The smile is beautiful.

"I recognize her.

"I recognize you."

If it were not so disturbing, it might become monotonous.
No matter how Frank's dreams started, they always involved
the same cast of characters. Didn't she have the right to pick
whose dreams she appeared in? If she did, she'd pick Paul's.
She caught herself. Her own nervousness was making her
mind wander. Gerri recognized that something was wrong.

"She . . . I mean *you* see the gun and tell me to put it
away.

"You are standing only a few feet away from me.

"Your hands come up along the sides of your body, pressing your clothes against your skin."

Gerri's clothes suddenly felt very tight. She should have
worn a looser sweater or a baggy sweatshirt.

Her skin felt prickly.

"You run your fingers along your breasts, then you take
your hands and cup your breasts."

I would never do that, she thought. They're hardly large
enough to cup. Her throat felt very dry.

"You put your hands up to your throat. You're wearing a
blouse. Like the one you're wearing today, with buttons up
the front. It's buttoned up all the way to your neck.

"Your fingers fumble with those buttons and then you
unbutton the top one.

"And the second one.

"And the rest.

"One by one."

The medicine was not working. Had Paul made that call?
Maybe she should do it herself. Where was that detective?

"There are no more buttons."

Frank was telling this one more slowly than he had to. He
needed more Haldol. The dream had started with a bad taste.
Neurologically a bad taste isn't much different from a bad

odor. Maybe it was the same as his odor. He hadn't dwelled on it. He'd just mentioned it in passing.

"Slowly. Very slowly you pull the blouse out of your skirt."

As slowly as you are telling it? she wondered to herself. Why are men so interested in slow strip-tease acts?

"Then you shrug your shoulders and the blouse falls to the floor.

"You are naked under the blouse.

"You wear no bra."

I always wear a bra.

"Your shoulders are lovely.

"So are your breasts.

"They are beautiful.

"So firm.

"So much larger than I had imagined."

Dream on.

"They are so inviting."

"Frank."

He started talking a little faster. "You shake your head and swirl your long blond hair. It shimmers down your back.

"We are talking.

"You are smiling at me.

"I'm still happy. Very happy.

"Your fingers are at the zipper of your skirt. There's a button and a zipper. First you undo the button. Then the zipper."

Her throat was getting drier again. His increased speed didn't help. Maybe she should switch him from Haldol to Thorazine or Mellaril.

"Your skirt falls to the floor.

"You step out of it.

"You are wearing a half-slip.

"You push the half-slip down and step out of it.

"You are wearing only panties.

"Bikini panties.

"Your legs are . . . beautiful.

"Lovely curves."

Prolixin. That's what he needs. Injectible Prolixin. Each shot would last two weeks.

"You are wearing bikini panties."

And you are repeating yourself.

"They are transparent."

Depot Prolixin. Large doses.

"I can tell now. You are a real blond."

Weekly injections, you bastard. She caught herself. Her reaction was all wrong. He was sick. He needed her help. His dream was telling her how much he needed her to be open to him, to offer him her help.

She swallowed. It was not easy.

"You put your thumbs inside the top of your thin panties." Again he was speaking slowly and very softly.

"Your thumbs pull your panties away.

"And all the way down.

"You bend down and step out of your panties.

"You are now completely naked."

When did I take off my shoes?

"You stretch out your arms to me."

He really does need my help, but he cannot ask for it.

"You lick your tongue over your lips."

Her lips were so dry she felt like licking them, but she couldn't let herself do it.

"You walk toward me.

"Your outstretched arms reach behind me.

"I can smell your perfume.

"Its smell is all around me.

"You lean forward to kiss me.

"You, the smell, your breasts, your blond hair. They are all around me. Swallowing me.

"I pull the trigger.

"The bullet enters your stomach.

"Your stomach begins to swell.

"It gets so big and swollen.

"You are bleeding.

"You are dead.

"I can still smell you.

"It was easy."

She waited.

He was done.

They were both spent.

She started. "Why is it so hard for you to accept my help?"

"You know Dr. Richardson."

"Of course I do. You knew that all along."

"No, I didn't."

"Of course you did."

"I didn't."

"Frank. You were referred to me by Dr. Richardson."

"Yes."

"And he told you that he wanted to have a psychiatrist to work with you and that I would be that psychiatrist."

"Yes. But I didn't know."

"What?"

"That you two are . . ." He stopped.

"Are what?" He had to say it.

She asked it again. "Are what?"

"Lovers."

"What difference does that make?" she asked, suppressing the more natural question as to what was the source of his knowledge. Did he know or had he made a good guess?

"You're on his side."

"No, I'm not. This is not a baseball game. You against Paul Richardson. Dr. Richardson wants to help you."

"He wants to help himself."

"That's not true."

"He doesn't care about me. And now, you don't."

"So you killed me." In a blatantly sexual way. That was better left unsaid.

"Yes."

"To drive me away."

"No."

"To take me away from Dr. Richardson?"

"Yes."

"I have to be either yours or his?"

"You can't belong to both of us. You have to belong to me. I need you."

"I'm sure you feel that way. But it's not true. You are my patient. In that relationship I do belong to you. My private life has nothing to do with that, Frank. Nothing at all."

"That's not true. He'll poison you against me. He'll ruin everything. He'll rot your brain." He sobbed and then went on. "And you won't smell like perfume anymore."

Enough was enough. "Frank, tell me about the smells."

"It's my brain. It's so bad I can taste it sometimes."

That's what she had been afraid of. The smell had been that taste. It had become a taste.

She asked him all the necessary questions. One at a time.

He did need more medicine. She gave him his new instructions and another appointment.

This dream was the most disturbing of the five. It bothered her more than any one of the others. It was not just that she was the target of his sexual fantasies and his violence. That had been true before. It was something else. The directness? Maybe. The lack of object confusion. That was it. She was the sole object from beginning to end. It wasn't his mother becoming her or vice versa. It was her from beginning to end. And what an end. Shot with his gun so her belly began to swell. Instant pregnancy. With bleeding again.

He had killed her. Because he hated Paul and she loved him. That wasn't what he had said. He had said "lovers," not "in love." He had killed her because she was Paul's lover. Could he kill her just because of that? Could he have killed Jackie because she and Paul had made love?

How would he have known about Jackie and Paul?

How did he know about her and Paul?

Paul had better talk to that detective.

She dialed Paul's number.

Paul knew very well what he shouldn't do. No doctor, no matter how good a clinician, should take care of his own family.

He told Bud what he had seen, what he had found during his own examination, what Joshua had described, and then left Carolyn in Bud's hands. She was the patient and Bud the doctor. She had a right to have her own doctor, one who was not her father.

He went back to his own office, told Chris that he didn't want to talk to anyone, and sat at his desk. For once, Tom Ward wasn't there, though. There was a note from him, a scrawled message forewarning Paul that he would come by later in the day.

It took forever.

Five minutes.

Paul paced his office like a caged animal, not knowing

what to do with himself. The hands of his watch were frozen in place.

Watch.

Watchband.

Crystal.

Stem.

Minute hand.

Second hand.

He knew all the parts.

Only ten minutes.

How could it be only ten minutes?

A neuro exam always took him half an hour and he was fast. He paced some more. Stopped. Turned on the radio. Heard a few bars. Changed stations. Turned it off.

Fifteen minutes. This was crazy.

He had to do something. He called Gerri. There was no answer.

He told Chris to try to get Tom on the phone.

He waited.

The phone rang.

"Hi, Doc."

"Hello, Tom."

"I hope everything'll be okay."

"Thanks, Tom."

"How is she?"

"She's fine."

"Good."

This was not what Paul wanted to discuss. "Tom, I think we may have another suspect."

"Who?"

"Frank McCormick."

"The patient you guys did that operation on?"

"Yes."

"Why him?"

Paul wondered how much he could say without violating McCormick's rights as a patient. How specific could he be? "It's hard to explain it, Tom."

"A hunch? There's nothing wrong with that, but—"

"No, it's not a hunch. It's more than that. He's still a patient and there are some hints he may be tending toward violence."

"Has he done anything violent?"

"Not as far as I know, but he has had some dreams." In his mind Paul could see the look on Tom Ward's face as he heard a half-suppressed groan. "His dreams are not just violent and gory; he sees himself actually killing people."

"Anyone in particular?"

"Yes."

"Who?"

"His father, his mother, me."

"You?"

"Yes, me."

"Why you?"

"He blames me for his getting worse."

"Is he worse?"

"He must be or I wouldn't be calling you."

"But why would he have killed Jackie Baumer? She doesn't exactly look like you."

"No, but in his dreams he did kill some women who looked like Dr. Scala. And Dr. Scala . . ."

"Is a blond like Jackie," Tom said.

"Yes."

"That's a pretty flimsy connection."

"Not really. They both saw him in the hospital."

"Okay, Doc. It's not much to go on, but I'll check him out."

"Thanks."

Twenty-two minutes. What the hell was taking Bud so long?

He tried Gerri again, but again there was no answer. This time he left a message with the departmental secretary. No, she didn't know where Dr. Scala was or when she'd be back.

More pacing.

He looked at the radio.

Nothing would fit his mood. Not even Beethoven's Ninth with the original cast.

Twenty-six minutes.

Bud came in with Carolyn.

"Her exam is normal," he announced. "I can't find evidence of anything. She doesn't take any drugs. She doesn't drink at all. Nothing."

Paul told him about her birth. Carolyn listened as intently as Bud. She had never heard all the details before.

Bud agreed that a mild birth injury could well be the cause of her seizure. "I've already talked to Neuroradiology."

"And . . . ?" Paul asked.

"She's scheduled for the CAT scan at ten-forty-five, then at two-thirty she'll have her EEG, and after that I'll see her again and decide what to do next. She'll have to go on something. Do you prefer Dilantin or—"

"Bud. That's between you and Carolyn. You're her doctor."

"Thanks, Dad," Carolyn said.

"Yes, thanks, Dad," Bud said.

It was time for another wait.

Carolyn was exhausted. It was 9:45. Paul would take her down to the CAT scan in forty-five minutes.

Forty-five minutes until he would see images of her brain to see if . . .

It was like being back in the Army. Hurry up and wait. If it moves, salute it. If it stands still, paint it. Don't volunteer for anything. And wait some more.

"How is your headache?" Paul asked.

"Much better. It's almost gone. Is there someplace I can lie down, though? I'm so sleepy."

"Yes, on my couch."

"Don't you need your office?"

"You just lie down. I'll work around you." Not that he really thought he would get very much work done.

Paul watched as the two radiology technicians put Carolyn on the table of the CAT scanner. She was wearing a hospital gown over her blue jeans. She could not see him through the one-way observation window, but he smiled at her despite this limitation. Carefully the techs elevated her head and checked the angle.

Then they started the IV. The neuroradiologist, Sid Gordon, came in and talked to her. He explained just what they were going to do to her and then joined Paul in the observation room.

"Paul."

"Sid."

"She's a good patient."

"She's a darn good kid."

The table was in place. The technicians left the room. Sid flicked several of the numerous switches.

They both heard the first whir and went over to the monitor to watch the pictures of Carolyn's brain.

The first one showed the top of her skull and just a small section through the very top of her brain. Not enough to mean anything at all.

There was another whir. One-point-five centimeters deeper; less than one inch farther inside her brain.

Paul waited.

It took about ninety seconds for each new picture to appear. Each minute and a half seemed as long as the seizure itself had. Maybe even longer.

Paul felt a hand slip into his and grasp it. He didn't have to wonder whose it was. It was Gerri.

"Bud told me you were here," she whispered.

The second cut began to appear on the monitor, like the computer printout which it was, line by line, beginning at the top.

Normal.

No mass.

No edema.

No tumor.

No blood.

No abnormal vessels.

Sid Gordon didn't say anything to Paul. He knew he didn't have to.

There were tears in Paul's eyes.

So far, so good. Donna Kolloway's first two cuts had been normal, he reminded himself needlessly.

Another whir.

Another wait.

Another ninety-second epoch.

"Paul, is it normal?"

He'd forgotten Gerri wasn't a neurologist. She was no expert in reading these things. "So far, so good."

She squeezed his hand harder.

An eon later, the next picture began to appear. Line by line on the monitor. Top to bottom.

Normal. No tumor. No abnormal vessels. No nothing.

Three more to go.

Two more.

One more.

And then suddenly they were done. It took them all a long moment to realize it. All the cuts were done and they were all normal.

"It looks clean, Paul," Sid Gordon said. Paul and Gerri were hugging each other with tears streaming down their cheeks.

"I think we should still do an infusion study just to be on the safe side."

"Yes, yes," Paul agreed. "Tell her it looks good so far."

"Of course." Dr. Gordon went back into the room with Carolyn. Paul and Gerri watched while he said something to her and then injected some dye through her IV tubing.

There was one more set of cuts to be made, but they were the icing on the cake. Carolyn would be okay. She'd need to take medicine to make it less likely she would have any more seizures, but she'd be okay. No tumor. Nothing disastrous, and they both knew it.

They stood hand in hand and watched as the new sequence of images paraded across the monitor. One right after the other, separated by a mere minute and a half.

"Joshua. I have to tell Josh. He must be beside himself. I'll have to call school—"

"No, he's in your office. With Chris."

"How?"

"I called your office this morning a little after nine and Chris told me everything. I know Josh. I was sure he was worried half to death so I drove up to his school and picked him up."

"How did you get him out of school?"

"I told them I was his mother."

"You could be."

"I could, couldn't I?"

"Yes. We'd all love it. It's not much of a proposal, I know."

"It's a beautiful one, Paul. I just don't know."

"Because you can't . . ."

"No. But I still don't know." Her ambivalence was obvious.

"I'm sorry I ever hurt you."

"I know. It's not that. It's—"

"It's normal," Sid said. "Perfectly normal."

"Thank God," Paul said. He and Gerri went to join Carolyn and share the news with her.

Bud had already gotten the official reading of the CAT scan from Neuroradiology by the time the three of them got back to the office. Joshua hugged his sister, then his dad, and after Paul told him that everything was really okay now, he announced, "I'm hungry."

"Hungry?"

"Sure. Carolyn had her . . ."

"Seizure."

"Yeah, that, just as I was starting my breakfast."

"Are you hungry?" Paul asked Carolyn.

"No," Carolyn said, "I'm tired."

Gerri came up with the solution. She would take Joshua to lunch and Carolyn could stay with Paul and relax. In three minutes she was asleep. The two doctors watched her breathe for a few moments and then walked across to Bud's office.

"The EEG will probably show something," Bud said.

"I doubt it. It'll be normal."

"Come on, Paul. The chances of it being normal are very small. Five, maybe ten percent of all epileptics . . ." He said the word before he realized he said it. He had meant to say it less bluntly.

"You know what's been wrong with your training?" Paul asked.

"Other than learning from you, nothing."

"That is the problem."

"Come off it, Paul. You're the best darn—"

"That's not what I meant. But it is the problem. This is a real medical center. All we see are complicated problems. You haven't seen very many of the day-to-day common problems of neurology."

"Like the teenager with one seizure."

"Right. The single fit. I saw a lot of them during my two years in the Army. Over half had normal EEG's. So will Carolyn."

"Maybe."

"I bet you a cup of coffee. Or better yet, a month's supply of coffee for the office."

"You're on." Then, in a more serious tone, "I suppose, then, I will start her on Dilantin."

Paul would not have chosen Dilantin. He would have preferred Tegretol. It had much less of a tendency to cause acne and increased facial hair and problems with her gums. Much better for a pretty teenage girl. But Dilantin was a legitimate choice. Probably the one most neurologists would make. All he said was, "Good."

"I think she'll do very well," Bud added.

"So do I."

"With the medication, the chances are she'll never have another one."

"I know. That will make her happy, but that was not my main worry. I was worried about . . ." He stopped.

"There is one thing that won't make her happy. She won't be able to drive for a year," Bud said.

"You tell her that. You're her doctor." There were advantages to relinquishing authority, and this was one of them. No driving at all for a year. Carolyn would be disappointed. Driving had given her both freedom and responsibility and she had thrived on both. She had also done the car-pooling for Joshua. They had no mother for that. Paul would have to make all kinds of arrangements.

They went back to Paul's office and watched her sleep for a while, and then Chris brought in some coffee and doughnuts. Paul was hungry. He, too, had missed breakfast. They once again returned to Bud's office.

Paul was on his second doughnut when Bud started talking again. "Paul, I wasn't completely honest with you last week."

"What?"

"I lied to you last week."

"You did what?"

"Lied."

"About what?"

"About the charts in the ceiling."

It was not the time for any cross-examination or a Socratic dialogue. Paul wasn't even sure he cared. He merely listened.

"It was so long ago. I remember it as if it were yesterday. It was during the second year of my residency. I was acting as chief resident. I wasn't supposed to be chief resident yet, but you had asked me to do it as a favor."

Paul remembered. One senior resident was sick, the other a bust. The service was falling apart. Bud had done a great job putting the pieces together.

"You were on service. I was so pleased that you had asked me, that you trusted me that much. You said you'd always be available to help me. All I had to do was call. Anytime day or night. But you were even busier than I was and things were so hectic here. I got behind. So damn far behind. There was all that dictating to do and Jill was sick, she was afraid she might lose the . . . Shit."

Paul had never heard Bud swear before.

"Why beat around the bush? I put some of those damned charts aside to dictate and forgot about them and then one of the patients got readmitted weeks later when I was at the American Academy of Neurology meeting presenting my first paper."

Paul remembered that presentation. Bud had done brilliantly. Better than Paul had done with his own debut.

"Of course they couldn't find the records and the patient was delirious. They gave him antibiotics for his sepsis and he died. He was a borderline addisonian. Whenever he got into any kind of trouble he needed steroids. It was on his old record, but they didn't have the records. I had carefully hidden them, so he never got steroids. As a result he died. In shock. And now you know."

So that explained why Bud's elation had disappeared so completely as soon as they got home from the meeting.

That was seven—no, eight years ago. There must be some sort of a statute of limitations.

"Paul, say something for God's sake."

"I'm sorry, Bud. I was just thinking about . . . about that time. I remember that meeting, your presentation, and all. I never understood why you seemed so depressed when you got back here."

"Depressed. Hell, I was more than depressed. I was ashamed and scared."

"Scared?"

"Scared to death. That you'd fire me."

"I didn't."

"Because you didn't know."

"Who did?"

"Alice Simmons. She was the nurse in charge, and two other nurses. I'm not sure you remember both of them. They were only here a short time. One was named Dente and the other was Red Wilson."

That was the second time he had heard her name in the last week. She had been Corrigan's mistress. Or still was. She had also shared an apartment with Jackie Baumer at one time. Did Bud know that? He must. That meant that Jackie in all probability had known all of this. Did that give Bud a motive? That was insane. It also meant that Jackie had to have known about Red and John Corrigan. That gave him a motive. That, all things considered, was not quite so crazy.

"Well?" Bud said.

"Well, what?"

"Well, are you going to do anything?"

Paul looked at his watch. "In half an hour I'm going to wake up Carolyn and take her for her EEG."

"That's not what I mean."

"Perhaps not. But that is what I'm going to do."

"And that's all?" Bud hesitated. "I suppose there is still a chance that you might fire Bill."

"Yes, I might," Paul agreed.

"What is the difference between what he did and what I did?"

"There are several differences, Bud, and you know it. The first is the one that even the world outside of medicine would understand. Those people who never stayed up nights trying to save lives. At that time it was not official departmental policy that anyone who did such things would be fired. I don't believe in retroactive policies. They are unconstitutional or something.

"Besides," Paul continued, "I'm not sure steroids would have made any difference. Of course, that's really irrelevant to the issue of stashing away charts. But it wasn't irrelevant to me at the time, or to you, I suspect. But to Mr.—"

"Holcombe," Bud said, finishing Paul's sentence for him.

"You remember his name."

"I'll never forget it. But why do you recall him so well, Paul?"

"He died on Neurology. We had a thorough mortality conference on him. I met with a pathologist and an internist. Lehner, I think. Anyway, we decided he died from gram-negative shock. The major problem was that he had been given the wrong antibiotics, but it was an honest error.

"We wondered why he hadn't been given steroids. The missing charts explain that. Lehner was sure that made no difference. I wasn't, but who was I to argue. He's the endocrinologist. That's his ballpark, not mine."

"I was never entirely convinced that it wasn't my fault. I wasn't at that conference," Bud said.

"No, I guess not. Your name wasn't on the record for his final admission. There was no reason to tell you."

"Did you know about the records then?"

"Yes."

"How?"

"Alice Simmons told me. She was an old friend."

"But you never said anything to me?"

"No."

"Why not?" Bud asked.

"There was no reason to. The patient hadn't been hurt by it. There had been no definitive policy. So I just made a policy and let everyone know what it was."

"I still have that memo," Bud said softly.

"When did you find out you didn't kill him?" Paul asked.

"Never."

"But—"

"Look, I know what Lehner said. I pored over that report. But in my heart . . ."

"That's why you're a good physician. That and the fact that I trained you."

"Dad." Carolyn was in the doorway. Her voice prevented Bud from answering him.

"Yes."

"I'm thirsty."

"Let's get you something at the coffee shop on the way to your EEG. Some orange juice?"

"Ugh!"

"A milk shake?"

"That sounds better."

"Did you say something about a milk shake?" It was Joshua. He and Gerri were back.

"Yes. You want one?"

"Sure."

"You just had a tuna-fish sandwich and french fries and some ice cream," Gerri said.

"It was only a small scoop."

Gerri laughed.

So did Carolyn.

The four of them went to the coffee shop.

They left Carolyn at EEG and Paul went onto the floor to see his patients while Gerri took Joshua back to Paul's office.

Rounds took only a couple of minutes.

Mrs. Kolloway was out of the ICU. She was back on Neurology. She felt that her arm was stronger.

Paul examined her. She was right. It was stronger. With the AV malformation no longer shunting the blood away, her brain was getting more oxygen and functioning better.

So far, so good.

Mr. Felsch felt that he was worse. His walking, he told them, was slower. His arms and legs were stiffer, his voice softer, his balance worse.

Paul examined him. He, too, was right. The implant was probably the only hope they had to offer him.

Mrs. Wright, the patient with M.S., was also worse. But it wasn't her M.S. that was the problem—it was the aspergillosis. She, however, didn't tell them about it. She couldn't. She was in a coma.

Mr. Kreevich was better. His speech was normal. They talked about the '44 Brownies and the '44 series and Whitey Kurowski and Stan Musial and the rest of the Cardinals.

Mr. Rath was still in the ICU. Paul would see him tomorrow.

Carolyn and Paul got back to the office at the same time. She had brought her entire EEG with her. "Do you want to see how my brain is?"

"Sure."

"It's normal," she told him.

"Only modern medicine could come up with an answer like that."

"Oh, Dad."

"You take that into Dr. Chiari's office. He's waiting to see you."

Joshua was waiting in his office. He had found the chess program on the computer. He had set it at level three. As far as Paul could tell, Joshua was winning. He should let Joshua answer those letters from Amsterdam. George wouldn't have a chance.

Paul watched.

It took Bud only fifteen minutes, then he and Carolyn came into Paul's office. She was carrying her prescription. "I can't drive for a year, Dad."

"I know."

"But Bud—I mean Dr. Chiari—says I most likely won't have any more seizures if I take my medicine."

"How often?" Bud asked.

"Three a day."

"Every day," he said.

"Every day," she echoed him.

It was time to go home. It was only four, but they were all exhausted.

No sooner had they left than Herb Adams called to talk to Paul. Chris told him that Paul had already gone home. There was something wrong in the lab. That, Chris told him, could wait.

Herb agreed. Half of the rats had died and some of the others didn't look too good. He had wanted to ask Paul if he should just end the experiment right then. That was what he decided to do. He sacrificed the remaining rats and took out their brains and put them in formaldehyde.

Paul had been right. The reaction took longer than twenty-four or forty-eight hours.

Gerri was waiting for them when they got home. Her car was in their driveway. Dinner was on the kitchen table. She had stopped and picked up some cheese and fresh breads at Gourmet International, the one in Crossroads Shopping Center, just south of Clavey Road. She had remembered everyone's favorites: Morbier for Carolyn, Boursin for Joshua, aged Gouda and Double Gloucester with onions for Paul, and some Brie for herself. The Brie was just right, a touch overripe. There was wine for the two of them, a Vouvray. And lemonade for the kids. A perfect light supper. Just what the doctor had ordered. No one ate very much.

After supper the four of them played games. First, the London Game. Carolyn won. During the entire game they talked about London and what they'd each do next time they went there. Then they played Clue. Paul won. It had been Miss Scarlett. He had never trusted her. She had done it in the library with a lead pipe. A little perverted perhaps, but none-theless true.

Carolyn almost fell asleep as Paul began to deal the cards for a second round.

It was time for bed. Carolyn kissed everyone good night and headed upstairs. So did Joshua.

"I'm tired too," Paul said. "I think I'll go to bed."

"I'll stay," Gerri said.

"Thanks for the offer, but I'm afraid I'm not quite up to it," Paul said, and then added, "That was not a pun."

"I know, and besides, it was not an offer either. I'll stay downstairs for a while, and if anyone wakes up and needs anything, I'll be here."

"Thanks. We couldn't have gotten through it without you."

"Yes, you could. You are amazingly strong, Paul."

"Perhaps we could have, but it was better with you."

"Thank you. I know it was better for Joshua. He was so frightened. He was afraid he'd never see Carolyn again."

"You are great with them."

"Get to bed."

"Yes, sir."

He kissed her lightly on the lips and went upstairs.

It was after two in the morning when she went home, and before she did, she did something she had never done. She went upstairs and looked into Carolyn's room and then Josh-ua's. She could see each of them breathing regularly and also see her own shadow cast across their rooms as she stood in each doorway with the hall light behind her.

She watched longer than she had meant to and left much more quickly then she had to.

— 12 —

"Carolyn, did you take your medicine?"

"Dad, I'm not a baby. I'm seventeen years old."

"I'm sorry."

"I did just exactly what Dr. Chiari told me to do. I took two of those pills last night and two this morning. I take two more tonight and then three a day after that."

Paul took the leftover bread out of the oven where he had been warming it and put it on the kitchen table with the rest of the cheeses.

"How are we going to get to the synagogue this afternoon?" Joshua asked. "Carolyn can't drive," he said, adding an unnecessary explanation.

"I'll try to get home early, or . . . ." Paul tried to think of another solution.

"I've already called my friend Susan. She'll pick us up at ten to four," Carolyn said.

"Oh," Paul said.

"I was hoping Gerri would still be here this morning," Joshua said. "I wanted to thank her for . . . everything."

"You can call her," Paul told him.

"I'll wait until Friday. She's coming to dinner."

"She is?" Paul asked.

"Yes, I invited her at lunch yesterday."

As soon as breakfast was over the three of them cleaned up and Paul dropped them off at school. Hopefully, WFMT would play something uplifting. The finale of the Shostakovich

Fifth or some Copland. Nothing somber. Nothing too intellectual. Something joyous.

He smiled. They had chosen brilliantly. *Pictures at an
Exhibition*. That was an art exhibit he would really like to
have seen. The pictures of Victor Hartmann. They were
playing the episode based on a picture of two Jews from the
ghetto.

Something was wrong.

It wasn't the notes. They were all correct. It was the
orchestration. It wasn't Ravel's. It was someone else's. Close
enough to sound almost like the Ravel one, but not quite. A
true rip-off. For once, he paid close attention to the announcement. ''Orchestrated by the conductor, Leopold Sto-
kowski.'' Who else?

He had a tape of *Pictures*. He was sure of that. He found it
among the others stuffed in the glove compartment. The
Ravel orchestration, conducted by Bernstein. He played it
twice as he drove in to the hospital.

''I'm sure that it must have been the hottest night of the
year, or any year. Our air conditioning was broken. It had
been for months.

''I was in my own room. Upstairs, in the back of the
house. I picked that room because it was out of the way,
away from everyone else. Away from all the arguing and
bickering. I could be alone there and pretend I was somewhere else, whenever I wanted to. But it was always the
hottest room in the whole house. Always.'' She paused.

He made no response. There was no need to. This was an
old story she had told several times before in various different
shades of the truth. They had dissected it more than once.
Why now? Why again? Why use what little valuable time they
still had left to them to rehash this? When he knew that, he
might say something.

''It's like a dream. I wish it had been a dream. Maybe it
was a dream.''

That possibility had occurred to him. But whether it was a
dream, a half-truth, or some mixture of the two probably no
longer mattered. Either way, she believed it had happened
and had been working her way out of that tangled belief for
two decades.

"I didn't sweat much as a kid, but I was covered with sweat. I even had to take off my pajamas. I sometimes did that in the summer, when it was very hot.

"Then I did something I'd never done before. It was just unbearable in that room. I needed some air. I could not catch my breath.

"So I opened the door.

"I remember how the cross breeze cooled me off. How it evaporated some of my sweat.

"I even felt a slight chill.

"It made my nipples hard. I remember that. I never told you that before." She had, but she had forgotten that fact or suppressed it. He had not.

"I went to sleep. It was a deep sleep. I hadn't slept in two nights.

"Then I woke up with a jolt.

"I was still cool but my nipples were no longer erect. I remember that.

"I was naked in my narrow bed.

"And he was in the doorway looking at me.

"I was stretched out on the bed, looking up at him. I was stark naked. My legs were apart. He was staring at me.

"I don't know how long he had been there.

"He didn't move.

"I didn't move.

"Maybe if he thought I was still asleep, he'd go away.

"I was only twelve. No—thirteen.

"Then he took a step forward.

"He was inside my room.

"I still pretended to be asleep.

"There was more light in the room now. The closer he got to me, the more light there was. The light came from one bare bulb hanging in the hall.

"I could feel my nipples getting hard again.

"He was halfway between the door and my bed.

"I watched him through half-open eyes.

"He was staring at me."

She sobbed very quietly.

This was the part where what passed for actual events became confused, or perhaps she had lied sometimes to make it easier.

"I opened my legs a little further.

"He stood there.

"The shadow of his head was right on my . . . body.

"On my . . ." She couldn't say it.

"He moved his head.

"The shadow was gone.

"The light was shining on me.

"I was covered with sweat again.

"He knew I was awake. And I knew that he knew."

Dr. Rotblatt also knew this. Gerri had told it this way once before. So far this was the version he had believed was the closest she could ever come to any historical truth.

"He was standing next to my bed.

"My bed was so narrow.

"I spread my legs further. It was as if I were getting ready for a pelvic. God, I hate being examined by gynecologists.

"So far apart that my heels were both off the bed.

"The light was very bright.

"And we looked each other straight in the eyes.

"We never said a word.

"I swear to God we never said a word.

"He licked his lips.

"I did the same thing.

"I licked my lips."

She sobbed again.

"I did it again.

"So did he. The bastard. I was only twelve. I was just a little kid. What the hell did I know? He should have known better. He . . . The SOB.

"He sat on the bed.

"He sat on the bed, right between my legs.

"His shadow took up the whole room now.

"I closed my eyes and prayed for my nipples to go down.

"But they didn't.

"I wanted my legs to go back together but they wouldn't budge.

"I couldn't move.

"I felt frozen—like a cold piece of marble.

"Then he ran his hands up my legs.

"He touched me . . . there.

"My nipples got harder.

"I hated it. I hated him.

"I wanted him to go away, to leave me alone.

"But I got wet.

"I could feel what he did to me with his fingers. With his . . .

"I was crying. I know I was crying.

"He kept on doing it.

"I . . . I . . . It felt good.

"He stayed there looking at me until I stopped crying. Then he got up and left.

"That morning, when he came downstairs to breakfast, I was already downstairs. When he kissed Mom, I felt sick. I tried to get up, but I couldn't. I vomited right there."

Why today? he wondered. He cleared his throat. It was his first intrusion. She understood that she had to explain. "I guess it is because Carolyn had her seizure during breakfast."

"You don't think Paul—"

"Of course not. But anytime something bad happens during breakfast, it reminds me of that breakfast, that morning. I never have anything more than coffee for breakfast."

An insightful "Ah."

When she said nothing, he knew he needed to do more than just grunt.

"So you blame yourself again," he said.

"I do not."

"You are not that important."

"I am too. I . . . Oh, hell."

"Gerri, everything that happened was not your fault."

"It was too. I could have screamed. I didn't have to spread my legs for him. God. I didn't even know men did things like that to little girls."

"That's not what I meant and you know it."

"My mother blamed me. He cheated on her."

"But not because of you."

"He said it was my fault."

"He was a schmuck. Probably still is."

"He'd be sixty-four years old now. No one has heard from him since he left us."

"And that wasn't your fault either."

"I'm afraid."

"Ah." It was a question.

"Paul will leave me. I know it's crazy. But I'm afraid he'll think I'm dirty and he'll leave me. And I'll be alone again and everyone will blame me like they did before. This is crazy.''

"Gerri. It *is* crazy. What happened happened. It happened because he was sick and unhappy and knew that the marriage was all but over. It was a parting shot. Hell, you were the only one in the family he hadn't destroyed already.''

She was crying, but she knew what he said was true. Too bad knowing it and feeling it deep inside where it mattered were not the same thing. Not even for a psychiatrist.

"Your mother never recovered from it. You think that she knew and blamed you. Your two brothers did blame you. Or at least that is what you think. You raised them and they still resented you. Well, there's nothing you can do to change that.''

"Sometimes I feel like a piece of crap.''

"When you're with Paul?''

"No.''

"When?''

"When I'm alone and it's quiet and I can hear the swishing in my brain and then I remember. I heard it that night.''

"God did not put it there to punish you and it didn't start that night.''

"Well, that's when I first heard it.'' She was adamant. That's how psychopathology was. Even a shrink's.

"You were born with it.''

"Yes.''

"So it didn't start that night.''

"Why did Paul have to f . . . screw her again?''

"I don't know.''

"Why her?''

"You knew they had been lovers before.''

"Yes. She even told me he wasn't good in bed. She was wrong.''

"No, she wasn't. For Paul it has to mean something. We're not all like your stepfather, you know.'' That was called reinforcement.

"She was the last woman I was ever tempted to make it with.''

"I know.''

"That was years ago. I never really liked it, but I didn't

hate it. Not like I hated making love to men. Thanks to you,
that's all over now. She never told Paul. I'm sure of that.''

Things must be back to normal, Paul thought: Tom Ward
was there waiting for him in his office.
"Tom."
"Hi, Doc. He's got an alibi."
"Who?"
"McCormick."
Paul had almost forgotten. Crazy Frank. Killing Gerri in
his dreams. Gerri and Paul both. The former at least was
fairly good evidence that he was worse. For a brief instant
Paul was almost willing to consider the notion that Frank
McCormick might have a point in suing them.
"I'm glad," Paul said.
"I thought you said he might have done it."
"I did. But I'm glad he didn't. It could have been our fault
if he had actually killed her."
"I don't follow you."
Paul realized the truth in Tom's statement and started at the
beginning in order to draw the entire picture for him.
"So if he'd actually killed her, it would have proven that
he was made worse by the surgery," Tom said once Paul
finished his explanation.
"Yep."
"But he didn't. He was with his dad all night."
"That's his alibi?"
"Yes."
"His father!"
"Yes."
"Is that much of an alibi? His father?"
"In this case, yes. His father is very worried that he might
get violent. And blames you personally. I didn't really under-
stand why when I talked to him. Now I do. He wouldn't
protect his son if he was killing people."
"No, I guess not."
"You know, Doc, if he had killed her because he was
crazier, that might make it easier for them to win the lawsuit.
And if his son were that crazy, they'd put him away and the
father would get the money."
"You're even more suspicious than I am," Paul concluded.

"It's part of my job description."

"Are you back to Fred Sanford?"

"No."

"Why not?"

"He, too, has an alibi. He left Jackie's about ten. She called in, you remember, about half an hour later. By that time he was with a male friend of his."

"He certainly had a busy night."

"True."

Paul nodded, not knowing what else to say.

"Say, Doc," Tom began, signaling a change in direction, "what did you find out for me?"

Paul decided to play it straight. He told Tom that there had been a problem in his lab that could possibly have made McCormick worse. He did not mention Herb by name, but Tom understood the implication and knew who could have been involved. Paul also told him about the missing charts, again mentioning no one's name. He stopped. He had nothing more he wanted to say.

"Tell me, is everybody here crazy?"

"No. Of course not." The question bothered Paul. "Why do you ask that?"

"We've been following up Jackie's sex life. It's like one of those soaps on TV, only more so. *General Hospital* brought to you live from Chicago. Is everybody here like that?"

"Doctors are no worse than anyone else, Tom."

"Are you sure?"

"I'm not saying we're exactly like everybody else. There are some differences. On the average, doctors are brighter than most other people. We also work harder. We live more intensely and many of us play more intensely, and . . ." Paul stopped.

"And . . . ?"

"We are more vindictive."

"That I learned before."

Things were back to normal. Paul met Edie and Bill to make rounds. They started with Mr. Kreevich. His speech was completely normal. He could even spell words. Spelling, Paul explained, was the best test for aphasia. Kreevich could spell both forward and backward without making errors.

"World" was the usual test word. "D-l-r-o-w," Kreevich answered, and then added on his own, "L-l-a-b-e-s-a-b."

"What do we do next?" Mr. Kreevich asked.

"A couple of things. We'll get another brain-wave test to see whether there is any seizure activity, and if there isn't, we'll start to decrease your medicine a little. We can't send you home on this much."

"I know. It really knocks me out. And my gums are sore and bleeding."

"That's the Dilantin," Paul said, thinking about Carolyn for longer than he wanted to admit.

"But it's great not having seizures."

"Ain't it the truth," Paul said, consciously quoting Burt Lahr. A reference that surprisingly went unnoticed.

Mr. Rath was not doing as well. He was now four days post-op. He was out of the ICU and back on the floor, but unlike Mr. Kreevich, he was still having seizures. He had had three yesterday and he was running a fever.

"How high?" Paul asked.

"One-oh-one," Edie said.

"What's the source?"

"We did a spinal tap to make sure he didn't have meningitis."

"And . . . ?"

"He didn't," she said.

"What else could he have?"

"An abscess in his brain where they operated."

"A possibility. How do we rule that out?"

"A CAT scan, I guess," she answered.

"And an EEG," Paul added.

"They've both been ordered," Bill informed them.

"What are the commonest causes of a post-op infection, Edie?"

"Wound abscess."

"How does his wound look?"

"Perfect."

"What else?"

"From brain surgery?"

"From any surgery."

"A urinary-tract infection from being catheterized."

"Correct."

"He did have some cells in his urine," she remembered.

"That's the source," Paul said.

"Why would that cause him to have seizures?" she asked. "He started having seizures again right after the fever started. If the infection was in his brain, I could understand it. But a bladder infection? How could that make his seizures worse?"

"It couldn't," Paul agreed. "Let's look at his chart."

The three of them studied it in detail. It was Bill who said it first: "The surgeons did it again."

Paul immediately knew what he had discovered. Edie did not. "What?" Edie asked.

"They gave the Dilantin intramuscularly," Bill told them both.

"What's wrong with that?"

"It just stays in the muscle. If it never gets into the blood, it can't get to the brain and the patient has seizures," Paul explained.

"Have we changed the order?"

"No," Bill admitted. "But the nurses on our service have a standing order not to give it IM." He looked at the nursing notes. "And they are giving it IV."

"And no more seizures today?" Paul suggested tentatively.

"No. He's had no more seizures today."

"I should have seen him yesterday," Paul said, as much to himself as to them.

Mrs. Kolloway was continuing to improve.

Mr. Felsch wasn't. His voice was softer. His movements were slower, his limbs stiffer. He was beginning to have difficulty swallowing. The surgical experiment was all they had to offer him. They would discuss him at the research meeting on Wednesday and then perhaps operate on him by the end of the week.

Mrs. Wright was also doing poorly. The amphotericin was not helping. She was in coma. Paul examined her. Her respiration came in an alternating rhythm. First slow, then faster, then slower, then faster. It was a cycle with an ominous meaning of its own. He opened her eyes. She looked straight ahead. The pupils were equal. He took hold of her head and suddenly twisted it to the right. Her eyes, like those of a well-made Raggedy Ann doll, went to the left. With his thumb Paul pushed hard just above her eye where the nerve that goes to the forehead comes out of the skull. He pushed so hard his knuckle turned white. It even hurt him. She never moved. She never moaned. She made no response.

"Well, Edie, what do you see?"

Edie seemed hesitant to say anything.

"Don't worry," he assured her, "she can't hear us."

"She didn't respond to pain."

"That's right. What else?"

"She has doll's-head eye movements."

"One more."

"And . . . And . . . I don't know."

"Six-sixty-seven ain't bad. Bill?"

"Cheyne-Stokes respiration," the resident said, using the time-honored eponym that described her breathing pattern.

"I knew that," Edie complained.

"I'm sure you did," Paul reassured her, and then, to make certain that she understood: "Now put it together."

She did. She was able to tell him that Mrs. Wright's coma was due to the fact that she had abscesses on both sides of her brain but that the brain stem, that deep part of the brain which carried out vital functions, was still working well.

"Is that good or bad?"

"Good. There is no immediate threat to her life."

"I wish I was as sure about it being good," he said. "We can't help her and she could go on like this for some time."

There were no new patients.

Rounds were over.

As he walked past the nursing station, one of the nurses gave him a message. He read it. "Meet me for lunch at 11:30 in the coffee shop. Jerry." Jerry?

"Who left this message?"

"Someone called and one of the aides took it," the nurse answered. "She didn't catch the last name. It was a lady who called. Must have been someone's secretary."

A secretary indeed. Gerri'd really love that. Any secretary would have said "Dr. Scala."

It was almost 11:30. He'd have to hustle.

She was already seated at a table when he got there.

"How's Carolyn?" she asked before he had a chance to say anything.

"She's okay."

"She is more than okay. She is exceptional. She held up so well yesterday. And so did you."

"What choice did I have?"

"None," she said.

"That's right," he agreed.

They ordered chicken-salad sandwiches on kaiser rolls. The one thing the coffee shop did well was make chicken salad. Most people agreed that it was the only thing.

"Frank is worse," she said. She wanted to bring him up-to-date on yesterday's session.

"He's innocent," Paul replied, much to her surprise.

"What?"

"I talked to Tom Ward, and he checked it out, and Frank has an iron-clad alibi. He was with his father the whole time. He could not have killed Jackie."

"Oh." She seemed almost disappointed. "I'm still worried about him."

The waitress was back. They had no kaiser rolls. Just bread. Whole wheat? No. Just white bread. Toast? She wasn't sure. Some days they couldn't do anything right.

"He's worse."

Paul didn't want to hear any more about Frank. He wanted to talk about the two of them. "Gerri, I'm sick of hearing about patients who aren't doing well. The world seems suddenly full of them. I . . ."

"You just feel guilty."

"Guilty?"

"Yes. It was your theory."

"Oh, don't give me that analytic b.s. I was hoping you wanted to have lunch with me. Paul Richardson. Forty-five-year-old lover. Not with the other Paul Richardson. Physician, teacher, scientist, troubleshooter, and general busybody."

"I'm sorry I'm disappointing you, but I want to talk to you about a patient of yours. Something is very wrong with him and I need your advice. I am going to tell you about him."

"So, tell me."

The waitress was back. They had found two kaiser rolls. And, she added, the tuna salad was quite good today.

He'd forgotten. It was Tuesday. The coffee shop didn't serve chicken salad on Tuesdays. It was a tradition. Meatless

Tuesdays had ended everywhere in the whole country in 1946 except the Austin Flint coffee shop. He hated tuna salad. Gerri actually liked the tuna salad. There was certainly no accounting for taste.

"Listen to what he told me today."

What choice did he have? He couldn't even enjoy his sandwich.

"It was another dream."

Paul hated listening to dreams. Of course, there was that one dream of his own about the blond with the big—

"Paul."

"Yes."

"Please listen to me."

"Okay. Lay on, MacDuff."

"You may even like this dream. It's sexy and it involves me."

"That's not a bad start."

"That's what scares me, Paul. At least in part. There's no confusion here. The object of his violence doesn't switch from you to his father to his mother to me to one of the other three again. It's me from beginning to end. That's different."

Her words had had an effect. He was interested.

"He's in an apartment building and walks upstairs and goes inside an apartment. My apartment."

"Are you sure?"

"Yes."

"How?"

"I come in later."

"No, that's not what I mean. Is it really your apartment? Did he mention anything that definitely identifies it as your apartment? The furniture. The pictures on the wall. That oversize bed in the undersize bedroom."

"No."

"That's good."

"Why?"

"That means he's probably never seen your apartment and it's all just a fantasy, a dream. He hasn't actually been to your apartment. He doesn't know what it really looks like."

"Let's hope he never does."

"You are scared."

"Yes, I am."

"Why?"

"Listen to me and you'll understand. He's sitting in my apartment waiting for me. He has his gun out."

"Shall I comment on the symbolism?"

"Not when it is that self-evident."

"Go on."

She resumed talking. She told it in much the same way Frank had, as a series of individual sentences, as if each of them represented a different still shot in a sequence of pictures. Not a smooth motion picture, but a series of frozen images. "I come in.

"He is waiting there.

"I start undressing."

Paul said nothing.

"I undo my blouse. Very slowly. One button at a time until I am naked from the waist up."

The tuna was too dry. He needed something else to drink. He saw their waitress and ordered two more iced teas.

"I keep stripping until all I have on are bikini panties, and he can see my blond hair through them."

"This is getting better."

She ignored him. "I take them off and walk over to him and put my arms around him."

"And . . . ?" Paul asked rather coldly.

"He shoots me. In the stomach."

"What?"

"He shot me. My stomach swelled up. He made me pregnant. And I bled as if I had still been a virgin. He made love to me and got me pregnant—real virility there—and killed me."

"That's not what happened."

"Paul, I heard him describe it."

"That wasn't his dream."

"It certainly was. Virtually word for word. He told it to me just like that."

"I know, but . . . Look, I'll bet you I know exactly what he said when you were standing there in front of him naked except for your panties with your big breasts and long blond hair."

"Smart guy."

"Would you like to bet?"

"Yes."

"What?"

"You name it."

"You're on," Paul said with a voice that reflected either excitement or something less polite. He paused for effect, then said, "And she was a real blond."

"How did you know?"

He laughed. "It's not Frank's dream. It's Mickey Spillane's. No, Mike Hammer's. It was the single most famous line in all of literature when I was in high school. More famous than 'To be or not to be,' or my favorite ' "Shut up!" he explained.' You'll find it in the last scene of *I, the Jury*. Mike Hammer goes to her apartment. She's the killer. She strips and reaches around him to get her gun. Believe me, there was no hidden sexual symbolism there. And then he killed her. Plugged her in the gut. No virgin impregnation. He just shot her. And like you, she was a real blond. Frank just borrowed it, that's all.

"Paul, why would—?"

"Tell me about that other dream."

"Which one?"

"The Vienna one."

"Vienna?"

"The one with the giant Ferris wheel. The Ferris wheel from the Prater. How in the name of heaven could I have missed that one? I love that book. I must have read it a dozen times. And seen the movie almost as often. Describe it to me again."

"The city is full of rubble," she began.

"Postwar Vienna."

"First he goes to the Ferris wheel, then into a sewer, and he starts shooting at me and—"

"I remember his gun never runs out of bullets."

"Yes."

"And they explode in your tunnel," Paul added.

"More or less. Then he hits me with his last shot. But it's not me who got killed."

"Of course not."

"It's you."

"No, it's not. It's Harry Lime. What did he say, exactly?"

"He said it was you."

"His exact words?"

She thought. "The fat man is dead."

"Orson Welles."

"Orson Welles?"

"Yes, he was the fat man. He played Harry Lime in *The Third Man*.

"Paul, why—?"

"Why? That's obvious. Tell me about the Arab on the beach. God, that one was so obvious; more literary, too. A Nobel Prize winner."

She told him. About the heat. About the Arab with the knife. About his shooting the Arab, and the dead body turning into his mother."

"Is that what he said?"

"Let me think." It only took her a couple of seconds. "No, I guess I jumped to a conclusion. All he said was—"

"My mother is dead."

"That's right." She was surprised.

"Camus," he said.

"The Stranger," she said, no longer surprised.

"Yes. His mother was dead. Tell me about the first one." She did.

"Dammit." He was aggravated at himself. It was worse than the intramuscular Dilantin. "I should have recognized it immediately. I should have recognized them all. Dammit. That's Poe. *Murders in the Rue Morgue*. The opening sequence."

"Even the tasting of the blood?"

"No, he did add a few details."

"And the rotting brains?"

"A few arresting details. But that doesn't change it. Those weren't his dreams at all. He stole them."

"Why?"

"To convince you that he was worse."

"Why?"

"To win his lawsuit. He has to be worse to get any money."

"So he made it all up." She wasn't completely convinced.

"I'm sure he did."

"Maybe he just incorporated that stuff into his dreams?"

"Gerri."

"No, I guess you're right." Then she added, "I'm glad."

"Why?"

"That means he's not worse. He's not a dangerous maniac. He couldn't have killed poor Jackie.

"It's strange," she continued. "I was so convinced. She was a blond, like me. A real blond. And I was convinced he might have killed her."

"He still might have."

"Paul, why?"

"For the same reason. Look. He made up the dreams or stole them so you would think he was crazier. Why would he do that? No, don't answer." She hadn't intended to. "I'll tell you. So he could win a lawsuit. 'Look what they did to me and how nutty I am. I'm nuttier than a fruitcake.' Except he's only a little nutty, a cunning type of crazy. Not mad as a hatter."

"Then—" she started.

"Don't interrupt. As they say on the sports broadcasts, I'm on a roll."

"I hate that expression."

"So do I."

"Then why do you use it?"

"Language evolves," he said unconvincingly.

"Go on."

"Yes. He kills Jackie. Why? It's a perfect crime. He's got us caught in a dilemma. If we can't prove he did it, the only real witness to the informed consent who is not a party to the suit is out of the way, our innocent murderer is free, and we have no real defense. If we prove he killed her, it's even better: only a real nut would kill her like that. Off he goes. But not to jail, to some funny farm."

"Paul!"

"I forgot I was talking to a shrink. I'm sorry."

"You're forgiven. This time."

"He's been there before. They'd give him some Thorazine or some Haldol. Some group therapy. Maybe some advanced basket weaving. Who knows? Perhaps he always wanted to learn to weave baskets. At the worst, in a year or two he'd be out and rich. That murder would convince any jury he's insane and we must have done it to him. An updated version of Frankenstein reborn without the benefit of Mel Brooks or Madeline Kahn."

"But, Paul, he has an alibi."

"Some alibi. His father. The only other person who would profit from the lawsuit."

"Oh, Paul."

"Pay the bill, will you? I'm going to call Ward."

"You didn't eat your lunch," she reminded him.

"I hate tuna salad," he complained.

"Then why did you order it?"

Once he got Tom Ward on the phone, Paul discovered that it wasn't very easy to convince him that his newest theory had any merit to it. It was obviously the rapid reversal that bothered the detective the most. First he was supposed to believe that McCormick had killed Jackie Baumer because he was insane and could not control his violent behavior. The only objection was that he had an alibi. He was with his father. Now he was supposed to subscribe to a new theory. Frank McCormick was no longer a psychopathic killer acting on uncontrollable urges. Now he was a cold, calculating, premeditated murderer who specifically stalked Jackie Baumer, not because of her sexual behavior or her blond hair, but because of some missing piece of paper. And of course that meant they could no longer believe his alibi, since his father would also profit from the crime.

"You really should write detective novels, Doc."

"It's all possible."

"Is it?"

"Yes."

"How would he know about that paper?"

"He signed it. So did his dad. They both knew that Jackie had been the witness. She was there. It was just the four of us."

"Okay. But how would they know it was gone?"

That stopped Paul for only a moment. "He took it."

"He?"

"Sure. His chart was in Gerri Scala's office for weeks just sitting there. He saw it, went through it, and took it. That explains everything."

"Except why he took it."

"The lawsuit."

"You already told me that, but—and this is a big but,

Doc—how would he have been clever enough to know that the missing consent form could help his case?''

"A smart lawyer. One who may not be too ethical."

"Is his lawyer smart?"

"You can bet on it."

"Is he ethical?"

"He's a lawyer, isn't he?"

Paul no sooner started to work than Herb Adams called.

"You were right, boss."

"In what way."

"That JNF-2 project. The rats looked fine at twenty-four hours and at forty-eight hours but they started dying after about five days. By day seven they were all dead."

"All?"

"Not all, but over half."

"Christ, and we just gave that stuff to another patient." Damn it all. Some days nothing went right. And those were the good days.

"How's the patient doing?" Herb asked.

"Fine. Of course, she hadn't bled," he reminded himself aloud, "and that was what we were testing for, wasn't it?"

"Yes."

"Didn't you say that all the rats died?" Paul asked.

"Yes, but I meant all the experimental ones. The ones with bleeding, not the others."

"What did the brains look like?"

"Not good, but I'm no expert on neuropathology."

"What did you do with them?"

"They're all in formaldehyde. They'll be ready to examine in a week."

"Good," Paul said. "We'll have to present this at the research meeting. As far as I'm concerned, we better stop using JNF-2 in anyone with any evidence at all of recent hemorrhage."

"Shall I present the data tomorrow?"

"No, we won't have time. We have to talk about the Parkinson project. You'll have to present all that. It'll probably take the whole hour." He thought for a moment. "We'll do it next week. We'll have examined the brains microscopically by then. It'll be better that way."

"Okay, boss."

"Did you ever tell John about the changes in technique in the culture project?"

"No."

"Floyd?"

"No. Why do you ask?"

"I just wondered."

"Should I have?" Herb asked.

"No, of course not. I was the one to tell. See you tomorrow."

Chris came into his office and reminded him that he was late for clinic. He had three patients to see. He went to the clinic and saw them quickly. He got only two phone calls while he was there. The first was from Dean Willis reminding him that the new committee of which he was not a member would like all the minutes of his committee that had anything to do with corporate research contracts. He said that he would send them. There was one other thing: Tom Ward had mentioned that he was being very cooperative and helpful. That was appropriate, but he should stay in the background.

For once Paul wished he'd scheduled more patients. They kept him busy without causing this kind of aggravation.

His wish came true. The nurse told him that two extra patients had shown up, without appointments. Paul told her that he would be happy to see them.

The second phone call was from Mrs. Kell. It was her fourth or fifth irrelevant call in a week. What was really bothering her? he wondered. Why was she badgering him? He asked her, but more gently. "Because I'm dying," she told him.

"What?"

"I used to smoke."

"Yes, I remember. Two cigarettes a day, and you never inhaled."

"Sometimes I cheated and did."

"Two cigarettes won't—"

"I coughed up some blood."

"When?"

"Four weeks ago."

"Why did you wait to tell me?"

"I'm frightened."

"I'm going to admit you to the hospital."

"When?"

"As soon as we get a bed for you."

"Will you be my doctor?"

"For a while."

"I'm an old lady. I don't want to die in a crowd of strangers trying to make me suffer."

"You aren't going to die."

"Dr. Richardson, you do understand."

"Yes."

It was Floyd Baker who was waiting for Paul in the office when he got back from the clinic.

"We've got him."

"Who?"

"The dean."

"How come?"

"He can't name that new committee."

"He can't?"

"No. I've been reading the bylaws. He can name the chairman of any newly formed committee, and with the advice of the Committee on Committees he can name the membership and he can even create new committees."

"So?"

"There is one exception."

"What is that?" Paul demanded.

"It's an old bylaw. It goes back to the time of the Second World War."

"Like meatless Tuesdays."

"What's that?"

"Nothing. Just another relic of history. Like Red Points and Lucky Strike Green. Go on."

"Well, it seems that there were a number of industrial contracts with this place during World War Two and a special bylaw was passed. Here, let me read it to you." Floyd picked up a thick old notebook and opened it to a place where he had put a marker. "Here it is. 'All contracts with any profit-making external agency must be governed by a committee of the faculty. Said committee must have at least half of its members elected by the faculty meeting as a whole.' "

"The Committee on Academic Activities is the only committee that fits that description," Paul said.

"I think that's true," Floyd agreed.

"I've never seen that bylaw."

"No one else on the committee has either. I checked with Muser. It last appeared in the 1956 set of bylaws."

"What happened?"

"That's hard to say."

"Was it ever revoked?"

"Not as far as I can tell."

"Just conveniently omitted."

"Apparently."

"Is it still in force?"

"I talked to the hospital lawyers."

"Miksis, Smalley, and Cavaretta?"

"Yes. I talked to a certain Mr. Ramazzotti. He's the expert on our internal affairs. He hadn't heard of it. But I read him all the documents that I had and he was of the opinion that it was still in force."

"Fantastic. You and I will pay a little visit to our dean."

"I don't know. I . . . ah . . . I'm not much when it comes to a confrontation with a dean or someone like that."

"If you prefer not to, I'll do it myself. Just give me the papers."

"Here they are," Floyd said as he gave the papers to Paul. "The key pages have clips on them."

Paul nodded. He began to look through them. Floyd had done a great job. He'd even checked with Miksis *et al.* He'd hoist the dean on his own whatsis.

"What's scheduled for the research meeting tomorrow?" Floyd asked. "Should I prepare anything?"

"No. We're going to talk about the Parkinson project. Herb will present all the data. The cultures are all doing well. Better than last time. Herb thinks its because he made an error in technique before."

"I know."

"You do?"

"Sure, too much glucose."

"And how do you know?"

"I'm not sure."

"Did he tell you?"

"No, Herb never mentioned it."

"John?"

"No." Then he said, "It was Jackie. She knew. I don't know how she found out, but she did and she told me. It was a couple of months ago."

"Did you ever tell anyone?"

"No."

"Don't."

It was almost time to head home. The phone rang. It was Joshua. They were at home. He wanted to know if he should go to the synagogue. Carolyn was taking a nap. Could he leave her alone? He did have a ride. Both ways. But was it safe? After all . . . Yes, it was safe. The medicine just made her tired.

Was he sure? Yes.

On the way home he listened to the real *Pictures* again, and after that to WFMT. They played a Beethoven piano concerto. Number One, with Rubinstein. Paul always preferred that to the "Emperor."

Herb had a motive. Not much of one, but Jackie had had something on him. Something that could have hurt him professionally. Had she used it? How had she found out? Probably from Herb. How? He didn't want to know.

Thank God Frank McCormick had probably done it. He didn't have to worry about other suspects. It didn't make any difference that Herb had a motive. Or Bill Goodman either. Those damn charts. He had to talk to Bill about them.

Did those charts really give Bill a motive? He had gone to the funeral. So had John. And Jackie must have known about him and Red Wilson. That sure as heck gave him a motive. His wife owned the company. A divorce would cost him more than just a not overly happy home. And of course he was also involved with the hidden charts.

So was Bud.

Why did hidden charts always come back to Bud? And now he was Carolyn's doctor. This was getting him nowhere. Let Tom Ward solve it. And if not Tom Ward, someone else. Maigret. Or Philo Vance. Or Lord Peter Whimsey. Not him. He was a conceited prig. Maigret. He could sit in the hospital coffee shop, drink bad coffee since they served nothing stronger, talk to the nurses, and learn everything about them all.

At least Floyd had done a great job. Paul couldn't wait to confront the dean. It was such fun to win. Too bad the White Sox didn't understand that simple fact of life.

13

Tammy Wright was dying.

No one had to inform Paul. They had started rounds early and had begun with Mrs. Wright, since she now occupied the room adjacent to the nursing station. The instant they walked into her room, Paul knew. He had not looked at the chart. Neither Edie nor Bill had brought him up-to-date on what had happened to her, but he knew. The feel of death pervaded the room. He could sense it. He recognized that it was not the mere feeling of death. It was something much more visceral than that. More primitive. What phrase had Hemingway used? The stench of death. That was closer to what he sensed.

The stench of death. Except she was not at the foot of Kilimanjaro. And as far as he knew, she had no heroic past. And no lover at her side. Just tubes running in and out of her body and monitors beeping quietly over her.

Paul watched as Bill went through the paces. Respiration: shallow, irregular. Pupils: small. Doll's-head movement: absent. Pain: no response.

They all watched as a respirator was wheeled into her room.

Paul refused to watch them intubate her and put her on the respirator. He hoped that it was still possible to die heroically in Africa. It wasn't in Chicago. Not in Austin Flint Medical Center. You could not even die quietly, with dignity. Mrs. Kell was right to be worried about how she would die.

Paul waited outside the room, lost in his own thoughts.

Without the respirator, Mrs. Wright had two, maybe three days left. With the respirator, maybe weeks or months more of agonal function, if you even chose to call such activity functioning.

Kilimanjaro was, he recalled, a snow-covered mountain. Close to its summit, there was the frozen carcass of a leopard, and no one knew, at least according to Hemingway, why the leopard had wandered up that high. What was he seeking? Paul at least understood what Mrs. Wright had been seeking. Nothing much, just a small miracle. And some bastard had offered it to her. And now her decaying body was here for them to watch die.

They were done. From where he stood in the hall. Paul could hear the respirator.

Whoosh . . . *whoosh.*

Whoosh . . . *whoosh.*

Edie and Bill joined him. She was flushed with excitement. It was understandable. She had been allowed to place the endotracheal tube inside Mrs. Wright's trachea. It was the first time she had done that. It was another milestone. Another step in her education completed. The intubation of an unconscious patient who could feel no pain.

The rest of the service was stable. For Michael Kreevich and Maurie Rath that was pretty good news. Both of them were seizure-free. Mr. Kreevich would be going home soon. Mr. Rath's fever was gone. It had been a bladder infection. If he stayed afebrile and free of any seizures, Bill told Paul, they would repeat his Metrazol test.

"Why?" Paul asked.

"Bud Chiari wants to do it," Bill answered. "He thinks that a change in the Metrazol test might predict whether the surgery got the entire focus and how much medicine he'll need when we discharge him."

"It's probably worth doing. Make sure Mr. Rath understands why we're doing it, and the risks."

Mrs. Kolloway was continuing to improve.

Mr. Felsch was continuing to deteriorate. When they walked into his room, he moved his eyes to watch them, but the rest of him seemed frozen. As frozen as that poor leopard. There was no smile of recognition for his doctor. He could not smile. He could barely turn his neck from side to side.

"Good morning, Mr. Felsch," Paul said as he leaned over the bed, his face in front of the patient.

He waited.

It took over fifteen seconds.

"Good . . . morn . . . ing . . . Doc . . . tor." One fractured syllable at a time.

"How are you?" What a dumb question. They could all see that he was terrible. It was as if he had grown very old in such a short time, and was now trapped in a body made entirely of asphalt.

"Not . . . so . . . good."

"Do you hurt anywhere?" A better question. Only the patient could tell you if he hurt, and if so, where.

"No. . . ."

Paul sat down next to the bed and described the experimental surgery to Mr. Felsch step by step. When he was through, Mr. Felsch had one question.

"When . . . will . . . I . . . get . . . the . . . oper . . . a . . . tion?"

"Soon."

"When?"

"Friday."

"Thank . . . God. Bless . . . you. Doc . . ." He paused to take a long sighing breath. ". . . tor . . . Richard . . . son."

"Don't bless me until you know whether it helps you."

"It . . . will."

"I wish I were as confident as you are."

"It . . . will."

As soon as they were in the hall, Bill asked Paul a question. Why had he told the patient that they would definitely operate on Friday? The neurosurgeons had not even seen him yet. They might not want to do it.

"They'll want to. They always do."

Edie looked puzzled.

"They're surgeons. They like to cut. Today, at the research meeting, I'll tell them that Mr. Felsch is a good surgical candidate and they'll have him on the operating-room schedule before they even examine him."

Edie was not convinced.

Nor was Bill.

"When was the last time they refused to operate on a patient

I sent them for surgery? Bill, can you remember a single such patient?''

''No.''

''I rest my case.'' Paul started to leave, when Edie stopped him.

''I have a new patient to present.''

''Tell me about him.''

''Her.''

''Tell me about her.''

''Her name is Susie Nicholson,'' she started. She emphasized each syllable of the name and then repeated it. ''Her first name is really Suzanne, but she prefers 'Susie.' Susie Nicholson.''

There would be no more nameless tattooed ladies. Not if Edie Robinson could help it. Paul appreciated the help. Names were one thing he had trouble remembering. His usual trick was to associate a name with the name of an old ball player he had grown up with. Bill Nicholson. Good old ''Swish'' Nicholson. Twice for the Cubs he led the National League in home runs and runs batted in—'43 and '44. ''Swish.'' He'd have to remember not to call her ''Swish.''

''Susie Nicholson,'' he said.

''Yes,'' she said. Then she went on to tell him about the patient. She was thirty-four years old. Born in 1949. The year Nicholson went to the Phillies, Paul remembered. They won the pennant in '50. Not that ''Swish'' helped much. He never even picked up a bat in the World Series.

Susie had been in her usual state of good health until about one year prior to admission. ''The first thing she remembers is that her neck felt different.''

''Did it hurt?''

''It wasn't really painful,'' Edie told him.

''Numb?''

''No, just different, as far as I could tell. Maybe you can get a better description from her. She prefers men.''

''What?''

''As doctors. At first she wasn't so sure I wasn't really a nurse. And then she wasn't very comfortable with the idea that I was one of her doctors. She got married right after high school. She has three kids. The feminist movement passed right by her. She's anti-ERA. She—''

"Enough. I want to hear about her neck, not her political views or lack of them."

"About nine or ten months ago she realized that her neck was pulling to the right."

Paul nodded.

"Over the last nine months it has been pulling more and more, so that now it's over to the right all the time."

"All the time?"

"Yes."

"Even when she lies down?"

"I'm not sure."

"When she sleeps?"

"I don't know. I didn't ask. Is that important?"

"Yes. Is it painful now?"

"Yes."

"Does anything make it worse?"

"Tension. If she and her husband have an argument or if the kids are too noisy."

"Increased by normal activities," Paul said. "What could she have?"

"A lot of things could make her head turn like that," Edie began.

'Such as . . . ?"

"A tumor pushing on the spinal cord."

"That's one."

"A disk pushing on a nerve in her neck."

"That's two."

"A tumor in the neck itself, or an abscess."

"Three and four." She had done her homework. "Anything else?"

She didn't answer.

"What's it called, turning of the neck."

"Torticollis. I guess she could also have just plain torticollis."

"Right, spasmodic torticollis. Now, what is the single most reliable way for us to tell which of these she has?" This was not a question he expected either of them to answer. "All that it takes is a careful history and examination. Let us go now and see her."

Susie Nicholson looked ten years older than her stated age. She was probably seventy pounds overweight and carried it all poorly. She was seated in the lounge chair watching TV. The Phil Donahue show. Maybe she wasn't as backward as Edie thought. Her left hand was touching her chin. Not holding it up. Not pushing against it. Her left arm was bent across her overly ample bosom and her thumb and first finger were resting lightly against the right corner of her chin. Her head was cocked ever so slightly to the right. Ten degrees at the most.

Paul introduced himself and went to work immediately. "Your neck has been turning for almost a year now."

"Yes."

"It's better when you lie down." It was as much a statement of fact as a question.

"Yes," she agreed.

Her left hand had not moved.

"And it doesn't turn at all when you're asleep." Another fact.

"Not at all." Again agreed to.

Her hand was still in place.

"When you are behind in your chores and the kids are getting in your hair and your husband calls and says he'll be late for dinner, it really gets worse."

"Yes. It pulls more then."

"Let me see. Your neck—is it getting fuller?"

"Yes. I'm . . . worried."

"You think you may have a tumor."

"Yes. My mother had cancer."

"It's not cancer."

"It's not? How can you be sure?"

He stepped behind her and asked her to put her hand down. As she did, her head jerked to the right.

He loosened the neck on her hospital gown and ran his fingers ever so lightly over her neck. "Here is the mass you are worried about. It's a muscle. It's called the sternocleido-mastoid muscle. Here, feel it yourself." She did, gingerly. "You have another one on the other side. Feel it." She did.

"The left one is bigger."

"That's because it's pulling your head over to the right. You have what is called spasmodic torticollis. There is no tumor. No cancer. Just recurring spasms of that muscle. I think we'll be able to help you."

She was far from completely convinced. Her left hand went back to her chin and her head tilted back toward the front.

"Aren't you going to do any tests?"

"Yes. We will do some tests. They will all be normal— then you'll know we're right."

She'd wait until she saw the test results.

They went back to the nursing station and Bill got her chart.

"What should we order?" Paul asked.

"I guess we have to work her up for a tumor," Edie started.

"No. What we have to work her up for is to get her to believe us." Once again he had gone too fast. "Edie, describe what you saw in there. How as she sitting?"

"She had her hand on her chin."

"What happened when she put her hand down?"

"Her head turned much farther to the right."

"And when she touched her chin again?"

"Her head turned more toward the front."

"Your observations were correct, but what do they mean?"

Edie slowly turned her own head left to right and back again.

"That sequence of events only happens in one condition," Paul explained. "Spasmodic torticollis. If she had a spinal-cord tumor or a disk or a neck abscess or anything else, then touching her chin like that wouldn't help.

"So the minute I walked in and saw her, I knew what she had. I knew it would get better when she lies down, and she agreed that it does. I knew that the turning had to go away when she sleeps. And that she'd have an enlarged sternoclei-domastoid muscle. Those things are true in every patient with spasmodic torticollis. They had to be true for Swi . . ." He caught himself. "Mrs. Nicholson. It's not anything magical or mystical—it's just recognizing the symptoms. There's no workup for her disease. That's it. We will get neck X rays to show her that her neck is normal."

"What causes it?" Edie asked.

"We don't know."

"Can we help her?"

"I hope so. By the way, how is Ms. Verban?"

"She's doing well. Her husband's in jail. We talked it over and I pressed charges."

"Oh."

"She's staying at the shelter and looking for some sort of parttime work for the next few months."

There were almost no traces of the mugging left on Edie's face. Only the bitterness of her voice and of course her shorter hairstyle. Why the hell had he cut her hair off? He'd better ask Tom that question.

As he walked back to his office, Paul remembered another line from Hemingway. The western summit, where the leopard lay frozen, had been called the House of God. This was certainly not a House of God. Twentieth-century America had separated not only church from state but also religion from healing, as if that were possible.

It was well after ten when Paul got back to his office. He still had a lot of work to do on that CPC and he wanted to talk to Gerri. There was so much left to be said. The kids loved her as much as she loved them. And hell, he loved her, too. Why was it so hard for him to say it?

Chris had come through again. The library had called to inform him that they had received the articles he requested as well as the two books. She had picked them up. They were on his desk waiting for him. It was time for him to get back to lupus erythematosus. Back to Kaposi. Back to Vienna. The Vienna of Mahler. Of Schoenberg. Of Freud. Of Schnitzler. Schnitzler had been a physician. A physician writer. One of the few great ones. Like Chekhov and William Carlos Williams. Imagine writing a great poem about Paterson, New Jersey. Vienna he could see. Chicago. But Paterson. You might as well try to write a hit song about Gary, Indiana, or Manchester, England.

Back to work.

"Hi, Doc." It was Tom Ward. Back to reality.

"Tom." The policeman was standing in the doorway.

"Can I bother you?"

"It's no bother."

"You sure?"

"I'm sure," Paul sighed.

"It's about that McCormick kid."

"Come on in and sit down."

He did. "That kid is guilty of something."

"What?"

"We're not sure yet."

"How can you tell?"

"You have your own set of rules that apply to your patients."

"Yes," Paul agreed.

"So do we. And one of them is that any suspect who won't say anything without his lawyer is guilty."

"It's like my mother says. If a defendant needs F. Lee Bailey, he must be guilty."

"Yeah," Tom said. "And I can feel it in my bones. I've seen guys like McCormick before. He's guilty of something as sure as I'm sitting here in your office."

"But what exactly is that something?"

"You always were a stickler for facts, Doc, and that's one fact I don't know yet. He's guilty. I'd bet my badge on it. Sometimes I think he's a killer, other times I don't know. At first he was fairly open with us. He told us he lied to Dr. Scala. The dreams were all fake. But lying to your shrink isn't a crime. So why did we pick him up? We didn't tell him very much. Then his father showed up. He is one slick character. Smooth. I'd trust him only as far as I can throw him. And that lawyer, a guy named Arft."

"Henry Arft?"

"You know him?"

"I've met him."

"He's as cagey as they come. Once he showed up, the kid only talked to him. He started acting like Charlie McCarthy. He changed his story. Lie? He never lied. What he told Dr. Scala was all privileged. What right did we have to ask him about his dreams? Who had told us about them in the first place? He did make a few mistakes. He told us he'd never even seen *The Third Man* and never read any Camus. We had never even asked him about either of those. We only asked him about Mickey Spillane. It's the only one any of us had read."

"You never read Poe?"

"Only in high school. Who could remember a short story after all those years? Besides, I don't need cross-references to know he's hiding something."

"Do you think he could just be lying to Gerri to make his case against us stronger?"

"I don't know," Tom answered.

"Did he take the consent form?"

"He denied it. And I believe him on that one."

"Why?"

"Well, Arft said that he requested the chart a year ago—that was before it was ever in Dr. Scala's office—and there was no form in it then. One more thing. Frank knows Dr. Scala told you and you're the one who figured it out."

"How come?"

"One of the guys who was questioning him with me goofed. A guy named Serena. You met him once on that poisoning case."

Paul nodded.

"He let it slip."

"Damn."

"McCormick is really pissed. So is his father. They both blame you for all his troubles."

"Like he was normal before they met me."

"Yeah. I have to get back to work, Doc."

"There are a couple of other things," Paul said. "There are people around here with motives."

"To take the consent form?"

"No, to kill Jackie."

"You have been working on it."

"Yes."

"Who?" Ward asked coldly.

"Herb Adams, for one. She knew something about him that no one else around here knew. He may have done something that screwed up the surgery on Frank McCormick. She knew about it. Maybe she threatened to expose him."

"Who else?"

Paul told him without thinking. "Bill Goodman. Bud . . ." He tried to stop but couldn't. ". . . Chiari."

"Why?"

Paul told him about the charts in the ceiling and his policy.

"Was anyone else involved?"

Paul hesitated for a moment. "John Corrigan. But he had a better motive than that."

"What's that?"

Paul told the detective that Mrs. Corrigan owned Dillinger
Chemicals and that if she learned about her husband's not-so-
little affair with a nurse, it could be a disaster for him.

"Did Jackie know about it?"

"Yes," Paul said. "She had to. The woman had been her
roommate at one time."

"Did Corrigan know that she knew?"

"I guess so."

Tom didn't seem very impressed by Paul's revelations.
"Thanks, Doc. Keep me informed of anything else that turns
up."

"I will. One other thing. Why did Verban cut Edie's
hair?"

"So she'd look like a butch."

"It didn't work. I like her better with short hair."

"You can't win them all."

Once again Paul tried to get back to Vienna. Perhaps
WFMT was playing Mahler, or Richard Strauss, or even
Johann Strauss. No such luck. They were playing a song with
some French tenor or other. WNIB was no better. He would
have even put up with Lehar, but not second-rate Bellini.
Was there any first-rate Bellini? He went back to work *a cap-
pella*.

One of the benefits of being the chief was that the Indians
came to him. Around twelve they all started filing in for the
research meeting. John and Herb. Floyd. Bud. Don and
Marv. Bill and Edie. Not Gerri. Late as always, Paul thought.

"Paul." It was Bud who asked him a question. "Something came up. Can you cover for me Saturday morning?"
Bud knew they had an unwritten agreement that Paul didn't
have to work weekends since his wife had died and he had the
two kids all to himself. "It'll take you about two hours, from
ten to twelve. I usually meet the residents on the floor at
ten."

Paul said nothing.

He could feel the tension in the room.

"I can't . . ." He stopped. He could. There was only so
long he could take advantage of his special dispensation. Bud
was right. ". . . think of any reason not to. I'll be there at
ten. Please tell the service."

It was time to get started. They had a lot to do. More, it turned out, than Paul realized.

"Paul?"

"Yes, John."

"Can I make an announcement?"

"Sure."

"We have to amend the JNF-2 protocol."

"In what way?" Paul asked.

"As a result of the experiments that have been completed this week in your own laboratory, it will no longer be possible to use JNF-2 in any patient with fresh bleeding."

"But we haven't completely finished those studies yet."

"The rats died."

"Yes, but we haven't looked at the brains yet."

"We are aware of that. We can no longer use JNF-2 in any patient with fresh bleeding."

Paul was puzzled. Why this change of face? Just last week, John had opposed Paul's study as totally unneeded.

"We have notified the FDA," John went on.

"Already?"

"Yes. As you well know, the manufacturer must notify them immediately of any adverse reactions in test animals or humans."

"Once the data are all in. Our study isn't finished."

"We felt we had no alternative. And," he added with emphasis, "the FDA made this decision."

They might be right. It was better to be safe than sorry. And there was always some chance of being sued if they were wrong. What with Rogovin's death and the fact that they hadn't studied the slides yet, it was probably a good decision. There was still one unanswered question. "What is your definition of 'fresh'?"

"It must be arbitrary, I'm afraid," John said. "Seventy-two hours was the figure the FDA decided upon."

"I'll notify Human Investigation," Paul said.

"I've already done that."

Herb told everyone about the adrenal-cell lines and handed out Xerox copies of the data on the four he had worked up in detail: Leibold; Weaver; Gandil; Schalk. He discussed each of the factors they had evaluated and what each of them was supposed to predict. Bud was obviously puzzled. It was apparent to Paul that Bud must have noticed the difference between the new data and the results from the previous time they had gone through all this. Paul caught Bud's attention and shook his head. Bud understood and kept quiet.

Herb finished. They had decided to use Leibold. He explained why. Were there any questions?

There weren't.

Bud said nothing.

Bill brought everyone up-to-date on Mr. Felsch. He was a perfect candidate for surgery. Were there any questions?

Just one. When? Friday. They would schedule it for Friday.

The meeting was over. Gerri had become absent, not tardy.

Paul and Bud walked together to Pathology for brain cutting. Bud asked Paul about the changes in the adrenal cell cultures. Paul repeated what Herb had admitted to him.

"Do you think that's the only difference?" Bud asked.

"As far as I know."

"That might have made the experiment a failure," Bud said. "And your old friend Jackie knew about it. Hmm. Do you think that gives him a motive to have killed her?"

"Maybe."

"And to take the consent form too?" Bud asked.

"I don't know. Herb's not an M.D. I don't know if he understands all of the intricacies of a malpractice suit. Would he have known that the missing consent meant we had no defense so no one would ever investigate his lab results? He knows that now. But would he have before we had all these meetings? I don't know. I doubt it, but I'm not sure."

"Brain cutting" was a misnomer. There were no brains to cut. It was a delayed replay of the previous week's session. The same two brains but from a different perspective. Not gross dissection of brains with their released formaldehyde filling the closed room. This time they looked at microscopic sections of last week's brains, projected on a screen. There was no stench of formalin. Everything was sterile and clean. They would finish the same two brains they had cut the week before.

Sam Rogovin.

Jackie Baumer.

Dr. Risberg knew which brain everyone came there to see.

So he started with the other one—Jackie Baumer. He projected one slide at a time.

Cortex: Normal.

Cerebellum: Normal.

Paul watched and listened. Why had it been painful last week and now it was just an intellectual exercise, part of a scientific ritual, devoid of emotion? Was it time? Distance? Was it that no one, no real person, could reside in these tiny specks of tissue? Whatever it was that was Jackie, whatever made her tick, whatever made her what she was, none of that was being projected now.

Risberg had shown them the few slides he had prepared of the brain itself. He was down to the brain stem.

It was all normal. So what? Einstein's brain had merely been normal. So in all probability had Hitler's. And Torquemada's. There were, after all, grave limits to our knowledge.

Risberg was done. Jackie's brain had been studied and had revealed nothing. What more could they have wanted? She had no history of neurologic disease so they had just taken a few random areas to study. They expected to find nothing and that was what they had found.

The slides on Sam Rogovin were very different. It was not a matter of randomly studying one area after another, searching for some sign of abnormality. Here they knew just where the abnormality was. The arteriovenous malformation had been easily visible to the naked eye. That was where Dr. Risberg started.

First he showed them the veins that had been injected with JNF-2. The walls were thin but intact. There were no new areas of rupture. No signs of inflammation. No evidence of necrosis. Nothing there to explain his demise.

Then they went over the clots inside the vessels, the clots formed by JNF-2 and the venous blood. They looked just like they were supposed to look, just like they looked in the experiment animals that they had studied. They consisted of loose meshworks of blood cells and JNF-2 which were tight enough to prevent new bleeding and yet just loose enough that pressure inside the vessel would not build up and cause a new rupture.

They looked at the adjacent blood vessels. Had the thrombosis spread? No, it hadn't.

Next Risberg showed them the other abnormal vessels deeper in the AVM, deeper inside the brain.

He finally projected the image of the one vessel that had ruptured, spewing blood into the patient's brain. The walls of the vessel were obviously the problem. A vein that size normally had a fairly thick wall with many layers of cells. This vein had a wall as thin as tissue paper. No, thinner. It was only one or two cells thick at the most. In some places there was only one flattened, stretched cell, and it was in one of those regions that it had ruptured.

"My God," Paul said. "That's so thin a good cough could have blown it apart."

"It might have," Don Lenhardt said. "He had some irritation from the tube he had in his throat during surgery. He was coughing a lot."

Paul turned to John Corrigan. "The JNF-2 worked perfectly."

"Yes, it did."

"Don't you think the decision was premature? This was a patient with recent bleeding, and nothing went wrong with the JNF-2."

"I'm not sure what I can do. I'll notify the FDA and report this to our own scientists."

As soon as Paul got back to the office, he went back to Vienna. It was a short trip. Bill Goodman came by, as he had been told to do. Paul was not sure how to start. He took the bull by the horns and plunged right in. "Tell me about the charts in the ceiling."

"Do you want me to resign my residency?"

"I didn't say that. I asked you for some information."

"What difference will it make?"

"I'm not sure," Paul said.

"Then what is there to say?"

"Bill, have I been fair to you in the past?"

"Always."

"Well, I will this time too, but I want to know exactly what happened."

"I didn't invent that hiding place. It has a tradition behind it."

"That I know, but I want to know why you did it."

"John Corrigan asked me to."

"Why?"

"I'm not sure. He just asked me if it was possible for him to see the charts before they were dictated. He promised to go over them within a week."

"Why?"

"He said he just wanted to make sure that what was said about his experimental chemicals was true, and if it wasn't, he'd flag it and leave a note so I could correct it in my discharge summary."

"He wanted to write your summaries for you?"

"Not really. You know, a heck of a lot of people write on those charts. Some of them don't know exactly what we're doing all the time. Nurses, aides, students. They write things down that aren't true. He would point out such mistakes and then give me proof. Articles and the like that showed what the errors were. Then I would say whatever I thought I should say in the summary," Bill explained.

"Did he tell you why?"

"Yes, to decrease their legal exposure."

"How long has this been going on?"

"Two years."

"Does he pay you for this added work?"

"Can I take the Fifth?" the resident asked.

"No."

"Yes."

"How much?"

"Fifty per patient."

"You can use that, can't you?"

"Yes."

"Is that everything?"

"Yes."

"But it isn't. It can't be. Phyllis Masi wasn't on a protocol."

"I know."

"Her chart was up there. How did it get up there?"

"I'm not sure."

"Make a guess."

"She was sent home on a Saturday. There were two other discharges that day. Both of them were on research protocols. I was off that day. When that happens, I give the clerk five dollars for each chart they save for me."

"So you think the clerk put all three up there?"

"Yes."

"Figuring that fifteen bucks was better than ten?"

"I guess so," Bill admitted.

"I won't ask which clerk."

"Thank you."

"Have you talked to her?"

"She says she doesn't remember."

"Very convenient."

"That's what I thought."

Paul had learned all there was to learn. He had to get back to the CPC. Bill knew it was time for him to leave.

"Dr. Richardson. Do you want me to resign?"

"No."

"Are you going to fire me?"

"Of course not."

The afternoon slipped by like a well-ordered drawing-room comedy. Scene by scene the different players came and went. Their sequence was not the result of a playwright's clever artifice but rather the careful scheduling of a talented secretary. Paul was so used to the regularity with which Chris ordered his life for him that he hardly noticed either its smoothness or its pacing.

When Paul had been working for twenty minutes, she put through a call from a patient. Twenty minutes later another call. Why twenty minutes? Hadn't Paul once told her that if he couldn't grasp the essence of a paper in that time, it wasn't worth grasping?

The second call was from Dean Willis.

"We are in your debt, Paul."

"How is that?"

"Mr. McCormick has most definitely been lying."

Good news traveled quickly.

"It may be very difficult for them to maintain their suit. They will now need experts to prove that he has been injured, since he has admitted that he intentionally lied to Dr. Scala. That admission will seriously jeopardize their case. We may make an effort to have them drop it altogether. One of the senior partners at Miksis, Smalley, and Cavaretta will be contacting Mr. Arft tomorrow."

Paul was pleased. It would certainly save him a lot of time

if they could avoid the entire process of meetings, depositions, affadavits, and God knows what else.

"It was very clever of you, Paul. *The Third Man* and Edgar Allan Poe. Very clever. What gave it away?"

Paul knew that the dean enjoyed a good story, so he made certain that it was a good one. When he had finished, he made a request.

"T.B."

"Yes."

"I'd like an appointment this week."

"I'm pretty busy. How about Friday at four?"

"Okay."

"What's it about?"

"The Committee on Academic Activities and the new commercial research contracts."

"One has nothing to do with the other."

"That's what I would like to discuss."

The dean hesitated. Perhaps he did owe Paul an hour. "I'll see you Friday at four."

"On the dot."

Ten more minutes and there was another buzz from Chris. Edie Robinson was here to see him.

She had some X rays for him to look at. It was after four and the neuroradiologists had all gone home and Bill Goodman wasn't entirely satisfied that they were normal. She put Mrs. Nicholson's cervical spine X rays on the view box and Paul got up to look at them. They were normal. Just as he had expected them to be. With her neck twisted the way it was, the films were hard to read but they were normal. He took his time and demonstrated the normal features to Edie.

She listened intently and tried to memorize the salient points. Paul was patient and went over it again.

"Will you show me your famous screening test for residents?"

Paul walked over to the door of his office and closed it, revealing a group of five-by-seven framed photographs which were usually hidden by the open door.

"It's this picture." Paul pointed to a copy of an old photograph of a young woman who was naked above her rough burlap skirt and rope belt. Her left arm was an inch or two shorter than her right arm, and ever so slightly atrophied.

Just above each of her ample high, pointed breasts a safety pin was stuck through her flesh. This, he told Edie, had originally been published in the 1890's in an early English neurology textbook by Purvis-Stewart as a typical case of hysteria. It had since been reproduced in many places as the perfect example of neurosis with a hysterical contracture of the patient's left arm. "As you can see, she is a young woman, in her early twenties I would guess. That is the typical age for hysteria. Freud's early cases were all young women. Anna O. All of them.

"Now, what do you see?" he asked her.

She studied the picture.

"She has lovely breasts."

"Yes." Edie was the first student to notice them. No, he was sure others had noticed them. She was the first to mention them.

"Her face isn't right."

"What's wrong?"

"Her eyelids are down too far and her face looks flat."

"Meaning . . . ?"

"Bilateral facial-nerve injuries."

"Is that all?"

"No." She paused.

"What else?"

"Her left arm is shorter."

"Do you think hysteria can do that?" he asked.

"Make one arm shorter? Of course not."

"So what does she have?"

"My God, she's got safety pins stuck in her breasts."

"That is why she was so obviously hysterical. When the eminent Dr. Purvis-Stewart put in the safety pins they caused her no pain."

"I'll bet. He was probably a closet sadist like all those other Victorians."

"No, no. Believe me, the pins caused no pain. Yet her breasts felt other sensations normally. Touch, pressure. To the Victorians such dissociated sensory loss had to be hysterical. Neurologic diagnosis, of course, is like beauty. It is entirely within the eye of the beholder."

She hesitated. "A syrinx."

"A what?"

More confidently, "A syrinx, a long cavity of her spinal cord."

"Where?"

"In her neck."

"Are you sure?"

"I'm not . . . No, darn it. I am sure."

"Sensational. You are also absolutely correct. You are the first senior student to have made the right diagnosis. I'd give you a great big hug except . . ." He paused awkwardly.

"Except I'm a lesbian."

"That wasn't what I was going to say."

"Wasn't it?"

"No. I was going to say 'feminist.' I thought better of it. I was sure that my hugging you would have been interpreted by you as a chauvinistic, condescending act."

"It might have been. On the other hand, I might have liked it. I like positive strokes. Everyone does."

Paul was not sure there was anything else to say.

"Tell me about the other pictures," Edie said.

He did. He told her about Romberg, who wrote the first textbook of neurology, about Duchenne and his early studies of the electrical activities of muscles, about Oppenheim, who was the first Jewish neurologist to be refused a professorship because of anti-Semitism. In Berlin of course. And about Charcot, the first professor of neurology, the father of them all.

"Did you like Jackie?"

Her question caught him off guard but did not completely surprise him.

"I guess so."

"She liked you. She didn't like most of the men she slept with, but she did like you."

"Oh." He had not appreciated that fact.

"She loved me and I loved her. I was the only woman she ever loved. I met her when I was just starting medical school. We became lovers the next year. She loved me. But she still needed men. I never understood that."

Why was she telling him all this? Did he need to hear it or did she just need to tell it to someone? Why him?

"She trusted you."

"I trusted her."

"She sent you a letter right before she died."

"Yes."

"Was it about me?"

"No."

"She said she had written you a letter about . . ."

"About what?"

"I'd rather not say."

"Oh."

"She was angry. I had called her a whore and walked out. She said she would write to you and make sure I never got a residency."

"A woman scorned."

"Yes."

"By another woman." To Paul that was a new twist. But as he gave it some thought, he realized that it was probably no newer than any other variety of hate or revenge.

"What was in the letter?" she asked.

"It wasn't about you. That's all I can tell you."

"Do I get the residency?"

"What?"

"According to local legend, you have said that you would automatically offer a residency to anyone who makes the right diagnosis on that picture."

"That's true."

"So do I or don't I, Dr. Richardson?"

"You do."

"Thank you."

"Will you accept it?"

"I don't think so. I want to be a neurosurgeon. I have to get back to chart rounds."

A woman scorned. But which of them had been the scorned woman? Jackie, whose lover called her a whore? Or Edie, whose lover acted like a whore?

Another suspect.

Edie had made the diagnosis. She had also noticed the lovely breasts.

He had forgotten to tell her Richardson's law: the chances of a woman's picture being put in a textbook are directly proportional to the size of her breasts. He now pondered whether the increased number of women in medicine would result in an obvious corollary for the appearance of naked men in textbooks. Not if they were all like Edie. Of course he knew very well that they all weren't.

It was time to go home. He called first and Joshua answered. No, Carolyn was not napping. She was resting and watching TV. Paul told them he was on his way. He would take them out to dinner. Where? Somewhere in Highland Park. A salad at the Mushroom. Joshua wanted to get whitefish. That was fine. Would they be home by eight? Sure. Good. Why was it important? *Evil Under the Sun* was on cable. With Peter Ustinov as Hercule Poirot. They would all watch it together.

It was while Ustinov alias Poirot was taking his unique morning swim in the Mediterranean that Paul got a phone call from the hospital. It was Dr. Berry, a medicine resident, who had recently started his two-month rotation on neurology and had just seen one of Paul's patients.

"Who?"

"Some old gomer."

Paul shuddered. He was sure Berry didn't even know what "gomer" meant. He'd bet on it. He asked.

"Sure. It's an acronym for 'Get out of my emergency room.' "

He was wrong, of course, but Paul didn't feel like going through it. He could still see the TV. Poirot's swim was over. The murder was about to take place. It was happening too late; the movie was already an hour old. How could you have a murder mystery with no corpse for the first sixty minutes?

"What's my gomer's name?" he asked.

"Kell."

"She's no gomer."

"She came here to die. She coughed up some blood and she sure as hell has something on her chest X ray. And she probably has a metastasis in her brain."

"Slow down and tell me the story."

Paul learned one new fact from Berry's presentation. Mrs. Kell had suddenly gone deaf in her left ear a month ago. She had never told Paul that fact. To Berry that meant her lung tumor had spread to her brain. To Paul it meant anything but that. Metastatic tumors could do a lot of things, but sudden deafness in one ear was not one of them.

There was only one possible explanation that would tie it all together.

"When was her last chest X ray?"

"Ten years ago when she first came to you." Paul could tell that young Dr. Berry felt that he had been lax as a primary-care physician. One chest X ray in a decade. Oh well, he wasn't a real doctor. He was just a neurologist. "It wasn't even done here." A second reproach. "So we don't have the old films for comparison. Not that it would make much difference."

Paul could not remember the chest X ray. Chest X rays weren't his business. But he could remember something else.

"We are going to disappoint her, I guess."

"How's that?"

"She's not going to die."

"Oh."

"No. Get me X rays of her auditory canals tonight and join me on my rounds tomorrow."

—— 14 ——

The phone rang just as they were leaving the house. Carolyn answered it. It was for her. Paul took advantage of the delay to pick out some tapes to listen to while driving. Some Stravinsky, he decided. *Pulcinella, Petrouchka*. He got into the car, started it, and honked. Joshua was ready. A minute later Carolyn came out, books in hand but without her lunch. She ducked back in the house, retrieved her lunch, and got in the car.

"Gerri said to say hello."

"That was Gerri?"

"Yes. Some early-morning patient didn't show up. A Mr. McSomebody. So she called me to talk about dinner tomorrow night. She can't come over early enough to cook, so she's going to bring the salad and the dessert."

"What's she making for dessert?" Joshua asked.

"I'm not supposed to tell. It's a surprise."

"Is that all she said?" Paul inquired.

"No."

It was worse than taking a history from a reluctant patient. "What?"

"She asked me how I was feeling."

"Anything else?"

"She said we might go shopping again on Sunday."

"Oh."

"She . . . We both need some things."

A very reluctant patient. "What things?"

"Clothes."

He didn't want more details.

"Anything else?"

"Some makeup."

"That's not what I meant."

"No, I don't think she said anything else."

They were at the high school. He left them off across from the main entrance and watched them cross the street and head into the school.

Carolyn stopped and looked back at him.

Had she forgotten something?

He let down the window.

"She said she'd see you later."

"Call me?"

"No, see you. 'Bye."

" 'Bye."

As he pulled away he put on the first tape. *Petrouchka*. Except it wasn't *Petrouchka*. Somebody had mixed up the tapes and he knew who that somebody was. No one but him ever listened to Stravinsky. Beethoven perhaps. Tchaikovsky yes. But not Stravinsky

Rite of Spring. It was too early in the morning for that, even if it was Monteux conducting. Too strident for 7:55, and besides, it always made him jealous. Not of the genius of Stravinsky but of the audience who booed it off the stage on opening night. To care that passionately about the score of a ballet that you actually rioted. That was what made him jealous, that degree of passion over a piece of music. And Monteux had conducted that first aborted performance.

He tried hard to listen but it was too early. He settled for the other ballet. It was later and calmer. No original cast here.

An unexpected gift. That was what it was. A gift of time. A missed appointment which gave the physician fifty whole minutes of unstructured time for catching up. And in the private practice of psychiatry there were always insurance forms and bills to bring up-to-date. To say nothing of all the process notes she needed to update or review, or both. Out of habit, Gerri put on some music, accepting whatever WFMT was playing, and went back over her notes on the absent Frank McCormick.

He had seemed more at loose ends, more distracted, for the last six weeks. Then the dreams started, or at least he started telling her about them. That was an unavoidable problem: she had to depend on what he reported to her. The first dream involved a body that had been put inside a chimney. Paul said that was from Edgar Allan Poe. *Murders in the Rue Morgue.* A suitable title. She had read it the night before. She had gone to Kroch's and Brentano's and bought a paperback copy of Poe's short stories so that she could read this one brief tale.

It had started on a dark street in Paris. There were terrifying screams from an apartment. When it was broken into, the apartment was a shambles. All in all, very much like Frank's version.

There was some hair scattered about. Hair pulled out by the roots. But the hair was gray, not blond. There was some blood as well, though not the amount that Frank had dreamed about, or said he had dreamed about.

The body had been stuffed up the chimney. Had that image been born as part of a nightmare in one of Poe's alcoholic stupors? The story itself had not given her the same connotation of sexuality that the dream had. Was it the compression of the material, the setting, the way it was told, or the prejudice of the listener? In Poe, perhaps she hadn't looked as hard. Poe wasn't a patient on her couch bringing his symbol-laden thoughts to her for her interpretation. In reading the story, it had struck her as a womblike image.

But what Frank had described was different. In Poe, it was the body of a young woman that was pulled from the chimney. The corpse never switched identities. Its head didn't come off. And no one stuck his fingers into the blood and then tasted it.

Paul was right. The dream certainly had been purloined, but not verbatim. There had been changes. Alterations which came out of the deranged personality of her patient, out of the depths of his disordered brain. It was those changes that gave his version a different flavor. Those differences impressed her more than the stolen outline. It was the additions that were pathological.

More blood. The tasting of the blood.

She herself as the victim. Was it her? Wasn't it his mother?

Or both of them? Or could it have been Jackie? She had also had long blond hair.

And the image of deflowering a virgin. That didn't come from Poe. At least not from that story.

Frank had been lying to them. But lies so often revealed more than the truth. The exact lies a patient tells are chosen subconsciously and often reflect his innermost thoughts. That bothered her. For the first time she was convinced that Frank was capable of violence. Deep down, he wanted something and was willing to act violently to get it. To get her? No, not her. How could she be certain of that? She couldn't. All she had were a feeling and his words, neither of which was completely reliable. She suddenly felt very cold and very much alone.

She reread the other dreams. She really should have recognized Camus. She knew *The Stranger* backward and forward. Frank had not said the body became his mother. All he had said was: "My mother was dead." His mother was dead. So was the stranger's. That's what started the novel. The whole narrative turned on the mother's death. So did Frank's life. So did hers. Enough free association. The Arab on the beach should have been a dead giveaway.

Paul was right, but there was still so much that was unexplained:

The oral sexuality of tasting the first blood.

The blatant imagery of intercourse. That had not come just from her interpretation. No, it had been there.

The identity of the victims.

The overt hatred.

The direct violence.

The smells. They were independent of the dreams. They were not from Poe or Camus or Graham Greene.

It was time for her next patient. She had not even gotten started on the insurance forms.

Events were proceeding normally at the hospital, at least in the Department of Neurology. Frank McCormick may have missed his early-morning appointment with Gerri Scala but Tom Ward was there in Paul Richardson's office, ready and waiting for him.

Paul did not even stop to pick up a cup of coffee or check

his schedule for the day with Chris, but instead went straight into his office. "What's up, Tom?"

"Not much. We've been chasing our tails with this McCormick kid."

"And?" Paul asked.

"It's hard to be sure with a psycho."

"You sure he's a psycho?"

"I'll let you make the exact diagnosis. You and your lady friend. Let's just say we consider him to be crazy enough to have killed her. But did he? That's the sixty-four-thousand-dollar question."

Another sign of inflation. It was only yesterday that it had been the sixty-four-dollar question.

Tom continued without any further prompting. "Either way he's a good suspect. First you tell me that he's so crazy that he could really have done it to her. Of course his blood type doesn't match the semen, but we're not trying to pin a rape on him. He could have come in after the two other guys and then tied her up and taken a knife—"

"I don't need a blow-by-blow description."

"Sorry, Doc. Anyway, we've been checking him out. He's got no history of any kind of violent behavior. Not in high school, or when he was hospitalized here, or in the state hospital, or in the halfway house where he's been for a while. Or even around his neighborhood. He spends a lot of time just walking around. Lots of people know him. They think he may be a little strange, but he's never gotten mad at anyone. No police record either.

"And there's no history of anything even resembling deviant sexual behavior. That's harder to chase down, but we looked everywhere. We checked it out as best we could. No interest in little girls or little boys. He never even goes into the friendly neighborhood porno theater or adult bookstores. In fact he strikes everyone as basically asexual. He never even looks a second time at girls. Or boys."

"That's what the initial police report said on John Wayne Gacy, and he'd already buried a dozen little boys in his basement."

"I know. It's hard to prove someone isn't a sex maniac, especially if he's clever. But usually you get at least a hint of it. There is no trace here at all."

"Just your friendly, quiet neighborhood schizoid."

"That's what it looks like," Tom agreed.

"So where does that leave us?"

"It means that you're probably right. He isn't a mad sex killer. But he still could be a cold, premeditated murderer trying to hide under the cover of a sex murder. So he didn't sleep with her. We know that from his blood type. That may make him virtually unique around here, but it doesn't make him innocent."

"Actually it makes a good story," Paul began. "They have to get her out of the way because she witnessed the signing. Without that it's just my word against theirs. So he kills her. He makes it look like a sex crime. He may be crazy, but he's no sex maniac. His own doctor will say that he's never even gone to bed with a woman. Or a man. And he's never been violent."

"So why all the dreams?" Tom asked.

"It's his safety valve in case he does get caught. It could happen. Maybe somebody saw him. By some act of God, one of our security guards might have tripped over him. If he gets caught, he pleads insanity. And he's got a treating psychiatrist to tell the world how crazy he was, how he had violent dreams in which he killed and mutilated women. So he cops a plea of insanity and then gets miraculously better. The dreams go away and he's back on the street in six months."

"Very clever," Tom said.

"Too clever. A far cry too clever for Frank McCormick. He just never came across as clever enough to plan anything like this."

"So he didn't do it," Tom complained.

"I didn't say that. He may well have done it, but he didn't think of it. He may well be nutty enough to be manipulated into killing Jackie, but he didn't engineer it."

"Who did?"

"His old man."

"That makes more sense," Tom conceded. "He is one very cool, collected customer."

"And his son's alibi."

"Yeah."

"Very convenient," Paul said. "I remember old man Mc-Cormick. We only talked a few times. Twice before surgery.

Once was when I explained everything to them both and they signed up."

"He says that meeting never took place."

"You sound like Henry Arft."

"That shyster."

"At that meeting that never took place, McCormick's old man asked a lot of questions. I answered them all but I remember how he kept pushing me. At first I thought he was just being perceptive and cautious. Then when he kept pushing beyond the limits of what was known or predictable, I just figured he was a bit paranoid—maybe it ran in the family. He's short, thin, with a thin mustache. He looks like he went out of style with the Second World War. His son towers over him but quakes at his every word. Frank wouldn't sign what he supposedly or reputedly signed or didn't sign until after his dad signed it."

"They're both signing their statements this morning," Ward informed him.

"Any bets Daddy signs his first and reads Frank's before the kid signs it?"

"No."

"Then what?"

"We try to find the loophole in their story. They didn't take the consent sheet. Arft signed an affidavit that it was gone before he and they had access to the original chart."

"Do you believe him?"

"Yes. If it weren't true, he wouldn't have signed an affidavit. He could be disbarred for lying to the court."

Paul knew he would have to accept that. Then he told Tom about the latest suspect, Edie Robinson, the woman scorned. Once again Tom was interested but not impressed.

"McCormick's still our best suspect, Doc."

"You may be right."

"By the way, I checked her diary."

"Yes." Slowly.

"About John Corrigan," the detective began his explanation.

"Oh," Paul continued articulately.

"She knew."

"That I had guessed."

"But she never confronted him."

"Too bad."

"Why too bad? That makes him a less likely suspect."

"I was just fantasizing. It would solve one of my problems if he were the killer."

"What problem's that?"

"It's purely a parochial political one. But one other aspect of this still bothers me."

"What's that?"

"Whoever took the consent form must have known that we had proof that it was there at the time of surgery."

"You did?"

Paul told him about the checklist.

"I didn't realize that. But believe it or not, I don't always work in hospitals. No one but a doctor or a nurse would know about that kind of double-check."

"Or a medical student," Paul added. "Or almost anyone who worked in an operating room."

"That's everybody around here."

"Pretty much."

"Then I guess it doesn't make much difference."

"Probably not."

Another day. Another set of rounds. Once more back to the ICU.

Mrs. Wright was there with a full set of tubes and wires coming and going. Her life, which just two days ago was slipping away undocumented by the paraphernalia of modern medicine, was now being continuously measured and evaluated by the best equipment money could buy. It was being recorded electrically only to be charted and then filed away by a succession of overworked nurses and residents, none of whom had ever met her before she went into coma. The entire scene was enacted every day by three separate shifts. The same machines, the same charts, the same observers, doing their job with perfect efficiency.

Only one thing changed. The body whose chest and veins were pierced by the needles and tubes which counted out the vital information of such interest to everyone else came another step or two closer to that last good night with each changing of the guard. Too bad she had turned the corner toward death before any of them had even met her. She had already become less than an individual before they ever measured her urine output or cleared out her trachea. It was not her that they knew, only her basic physiologic functions, and it was those that they were striving to preserve. There was nothing they could do now to alter the final result. She was on her way to death. She would never again pass go.

The rest of the follow-ups stood out in bold contrast to their inability to do anything to help Mrs. Wright. Donna Kolloway was going home. She was stronger. The noise in her head was so soft now she had to strain to hear it. The relative silence was wonderful. And music. She had never realized before how truly wonderful music could be. Now she could hear melodies without her own accompaniment dominating the foreground. The Who. REO Speedwagon. Meatloaf. The Exploding Plastic Inevitable. Such glorious sounds. She loved them all so much. Didn't he? He agreed he too loved music. She smiled. She had so much to thank him for.

Mr. Kreevich was also ready to go home. Another cure. He had been seizure-free ever since surgery. His speech was normal. Paul put him through all the tests. He could even spell Schoendienst backward. Did Dr. Richardson remember him? Remember him? The redhead. Second baseman for the Cards and the Braves. His home run won the All Star Game in Comiskey Park in '50. The game in which Ted Williams broke his arm crashing into the left-field wall. But Paul was not sure he could spell his name forward, much less backward.

"It's easy. T-s-n-e-i-d-n-e-o-h-c-s."

They may have created a monster.

Mr. Rath was not running any fever. He was once again seizure-free. He was scheduled for a Metrazol test later in the day.

Mrs. Nicholson still had her head turned to the right. Paul examined her again. Once more he told her what the diagnosis was. Not what he thought it was, but what it was. She needed the reinforcement.

Could they help her? Yes.

Back in the hallway he asked Edie what they should do. She wasn't sure.

"Bill."

"I'd start with Artane."

"Why Artane?"

"Because it helps."

"True, but how do you know it helps?"

Neither of them knew the answer, so he told them about two articles to look up. One was by David Marsden from London. The other by Tanner, Goetz, and Klawans. They had both been published in *Neurology*. The former had better data, but the latter, he thought, had a more elegantly stated thesis.

The surgery had been scheduled on Mr. Felsch for Friday at 8:30 A.M. The neurosurgeons had not seen him yet but the operation had already been put on the OR schedule.

Paul went through all the details of the entire procedure with him once again, including the possible risks as well as the potential benefits. Mr. Felsch signed three copies of the form. Bill Goodman and Edie both witnessed each signature. Two witnesses were better than none.

Since Dr. Berry had a clinic of his own and couldn't join them, Bill told him about Mrs. Kell. He too called her a gomer. He added nothing new.

They went in to see her. She looked like a gomer. Old. Thin. Wasted. Depressed. Paul greeted her like an old friend.

She returned his greeting without even a flicker of a smile. Paul vowed to change that. There was one thing to check. He asked her to sit up in bed, and when she did, he walked behind her and looked at her back.

He had remembered correctly. He was right. Where was that Berry guy? He made sure that Bill and Edie saw what he had remembered, and they left Mrs. Kell to her depression. He would tell her when he had all the facts. Paul stopped at the door. "I don't think you have cancer. You're not going to die this time around."

Edie described what she had seen, three large brown spots.

"Called . . .?" he prompted.

"Café-au-lait spots."

"Meaning . . . ?"

"She has von Recklinghausen's disease."

She would be one heck of a resident and she did look better with short hair.

"Bill, what is the commonest brain tumor in von Recklinghausen's disease?"

"An acoustic. A benign tumor of the eighth nerve behind the ear, which . . ."—Bill suddenly caught on—"usually causes dizziness and ringing in the ear but which can on rare occasion start with sudden deafness in one ear.''

"Give that man a cigar.''

"But why the blood and the lung tumor?''

"I saw that once before. It could be a benign lung tumor from her von Recklinghausen's or . . .''

"Something worse,'' Bill reminded them.

"Which is it?'' Edie asked.

"I'll bet on the former,'' Paul said.

"Why?''

Why indeed? Because he'd seen it before? He'd seen cancer of the lung before. Lots of times. More often than he'd seen von Recklinghausen's. "It's too much of a coincidence to have both things at once. It could be two different diseases, but more likely it's just one in two different places.''

Berry had not ordered the X rays Paul had wanted. They ordered them and a CAT scan and Paul would try to locate at least the official reading on the old chest film if not the X ray itself.

"Are there any other new patients on the service?'' Paul asked, already preparing for his weekend duties.

"There is one who might interest you.''

"Who's that?''

"A guy with AIDS.'' Paul was interested. Any new disease was inherently intriguing. "What is AIDS, Edie?''

"Acquired immune deficiency syndrome.''

"Meaning . . . ?''

"For some reason, the patient loses his normal immune defense systems and starts getting infections with bacteria and fungi that most of us can normally fight off.''

"Such as . . . ?''

"Peculiar lung infections.''

"Any particular kinds of neurologic infections?''

"I'm not sure,'' she answered.

"Bill?''

"Abscesses.''

"Like Mrs. Wright?'' Edie asked.

"Yes,'' Paul told her. "Anything else, Bill?''

"Chronic meningitis, especially cryptococcosis.''

"How do you get AIDS?'' Paul asked.

"It's a venereal disease spread by sexual contact. Mostly among homosexual males," Edie answered.

"Not exclusively."

"No, but that's where it was first reported, and it still accounts for most cases."

"It can also be spread by transfusions," Bill added, "and across the placenta to the fetus."

"What really happens in AIDS?" Paul asked.

Edie didn't know.

Bill spoke up. "No one knows for sure. It may be a virus that destroys the T cells so you can't fight off infections anymore. It's obviously contagious and spreads by intimate contact."

"What happens to the patients?"

This Edie knew. "Sixty percent die in the first two years. In the long run, it's probably one hundred percent fatal."

"Does everyone who knows someone with AIDS, knows them in the biblical sense, that is, get AIDS?"

"Probably not," Bill said.

"What percentage?"

"Probably fairly low, but no one knows for sure."

"What's going on with this patient?"

"Chronic meningitis. Probably cryptococcosis. You want to meet him?"

"Sure."

"He's a nice guy. An oil-company executive, named Sanford."

"Fred Sanford?"

"Yes. You know him?"

"No. And I think I'll pass on meeting him. I've got to get ready for my CPC."

The CPC was a real bravura performance, from beginning to end. It was not a work of art, but a CPC was not supposed to be a work of art. It was arresting, entertaining, illuminating, and, Paul was sure, educational, but it did lack the one quality that any real work of art had to have: it was not worthy of a second hearing. In the long run only true masterpieces and sex deserved being replayed. Instantly or otherwise. This was just a great CPC.

He started with two simple facts. The patient had systemic

lupus erythematosus and had been on steroids. Those were the keys. As a result of her lupus her immune system was abnormal and in addition she was on a drug which further altered her already abnormal defenses. Then, and only then, did she develop obvious neurologic signs and symptoms, beginning with psychotic behavior. It was a routine introduction, like a Donizetti overture. Pleasant, professional, competent, but not distinguished.

Then he turned to Kaposi. Kaposi and the Medical School of Vienna. Fin-de-siècle Vienna. The Vienna of Freud and Mahler. The Vienna of the last glorious agonal years of the Hapsburg Empire. Unfortunately, no one was able to attach the Hapsburg Empire to a respirator and extend its glory. He told them the history of the Medical School of the University of Vienna, one of the great jewels of the Hapsburg crown. He talked about Rokitansky, who single-handedly invented CPCs. He mentioned Rokitansky's first autopsy on an embittered deaf composer named Beethoven, but he did not tell them the findings. The medical facts behind his dying defiance of nature made too good a story to just toss out in passing. He would save that for another day.

He told them about the other great Viennese physicians.

About Skoda.

About Hebra.

Then about Kaposi. He told the story of Kaposi's life. His conversion to Catholicism in order to get a job. The same thing Mahler did two decades later to become director of the Opera. He talked about Freud. His house had somehow survived and could still be seen. And about Herzl. He had lived on the same street, but of him there is no trace. But he came back to Kaposi and to his original description of lupus. It was a brilliant rondo, worthy of Mozart, an earlier resident of Vienna.

One of Kaposi's original patients had had the same problems as today's patient. The same signs and symptoms. There was no reason to blame the steroids alone.

Then he took a tangent, a new variation, the pathology of psychosis. He started with Freud, Freud the neurologist, and in the end came back to Kaposi and Kaposi's patient.

Variations on a theme of Kaposi.

It all came down to a few basic concepts. Psychosis occurred in lupus before patients were ever put on steroids. Psychosis always meant bilateral disease. It was not some new exotic infection, set up by modern drugs or modern infections.

Now the grand finale. The diagnosis. A viral infection of the brain made possible primarily because the patient already had lupus.

He made the same diagnosis in both patients. Theirs and Kaposi's.

The coda. Short and sweet. A true recapitulation. Risberg showed the slides that gave the final answer, not just the discussant's educated guess. And Paul was right. One hundred percent correct.

Paul accepted the applause and answered the questions. Then it was over and they were all rushing off to their next duty.

The CPC was over. It had been brilliant. He had been right.

Something else was not. Paul immediately knew what it was. Psychosis always required bilateral disease. To get worse, both sides of the brain had to deteriorate. He was sure of it. And they had only operated on one side of Frank McCormick's brain. Frank couldn't be worse as a result of what they had done. That was as obvious as the nose on his face, or on Gerri's face. Had she been there? He hadn't seen her. She said she'd see him later. When?

If both sides of the brain had to be abnormal to cause psychosis, then changing one side back to normal could help. It could have helped Frank. But it couldn't have made him worse. Paul was convinced. Now he just had to convince the rest of the world.

Paul was pleased to discover that his afternoon was relatively free. Floyd had left the rough draft of a paper for him to go over and Bud the second version of a grant application. There was also the mail to go through. The only important piece was the printer's proof of a chapter he had written, which had to be proofread and returned to the publisher by no later than . . . He rechecked. That was yesterday. He'd do it tomorrow.

First he'd do the grant application, then the paper, and after that there was one other matter he had to settle. He buzzed Chris and asked her to have John Corrigan stop by sometime before four. He wanted to get home at a reasonable hour.

While Paul was working on the grant application, Bud and Floyd did the repeat Metrazol challenge on Maurie Rath. Mr. Rath was once again attached to an EEG machine and Bud Chiari measured out the Metrazol, injected it through the intravenous tubing, and watched and waited at the bedside. Floyd stood in the observation room by the EEG and watched.

Five minutes.

Ten minutes.

Fifteen minutes.

Nothing happened.

Bud drew up some more Metrazol, twice the previous dose, and injected it into the IV.

Floyd noted the time of injection on the EEG paper.

They waited and watched some more.

Another fifteen minutes.

Again nothing happened.

One more try. Bud again doubled the dose. They were up to four times the original dose. With this amount of Metrazol, even a small number of patients without epilepsy had seizures and virtually all developed abnormal discharges in their EEG's.

Bud injected it.

Floyd recorded the time.

One last period of watching.

They watched for thirty minutes.

Nothing happened.

No seizures.

No abnormal brain-wave activity.

Nothing.

Floyd was pleased. Mr. Rath remembered the previous test and the seizures that were a part of it. He had not had a seizure this time. He was very happy. It had to mean that he was better. Bud was also pleased. After Floyd took Mr. Rath back to his room, Bud pored over the EEG page by page. The Metrazol had done nothing. Either Mr. Rath was more normal than normal or something had gone wrong. That was one of the biggest problems with research: something always went wrong.

*   *   *

It was amazing. No one had called for almost an hour. He'd heard the first act of *Turandot* and part of the second. It was the old London recording with Birgit Nilsson and Jussi Bjoerling. None of today's singers could compare with them. He'd even got through half of the grant application. Not bad.

Just as Nilsson started to sing for the first time, the phone rang. It was Gerri. Could he come over tonight? To her house? He wasn't sure he could. She wanted to see him, to talk to him. He recognized the unusual quality in her voice, which struck him as partly an urgency, partly an uneasiness, and mostly some sort of distress. To make love, she added. That was a request she had made before on a weeknight. But those had all sounded different. He could come over around ten, couldn't he? He could.

Act Two was over. He had missed Birgit's big scene.

Act Three started. The phone rang again just as Nilsson began singing. It was Bud.

"We repeated the Metrazol test on Maurie Rath."

"They told me about your idea. It sounds like a worthwhile study."

"I don't know."

"Why not? Did he have a seizure?"

"No, just the opposite. He didn't have a seizure even at four times the usual dose."

"That's great."

"I'm not sure."

"Why not?" Paul asked, his curiosity aroused.

"Even his EEG stayed normal."

"At that dose?"

"Yes."

"That's unusual."

"Paul, would his first Metrazol test prevent him from responding to a second one?"

"No. There can be some tolerance, but not that much."

"You sure?"

"Yes."

"What else could it be?" Bud wondered aloud.

"Sometimes the EEG doesn't change."

"Even at that dose?"

"Even at bigger doses. I've seen it once, maybe twice before," Paul told the younger neurologist.

"I guess that's it."

"Don't sound so convinced."

As soon as he hung up, Paul saw John Corrigan standing in his doorway. "You wanted to see me, Paul?"

"Come on in, John."

Paul switched off what was left of Puccini, which was not very much, and came right to the point. He told John about the hidden charts and their medical and legal implications and then asked, "How could you have asked Bill to do that?"

"Hold on, Paul. I didn't ask him to do anything unethical."

"You didn't?"

"Of course I didn't. I just asked him to put the charts of specific patients aside so that I could make sure that no one had put any false information in them. Misinformation based on incomplete understanding. There's nothing wrong with that, is there?"

"No," Paul admitted. "In fact, it's not a bad idea. Sometimes when they're in a rush, residents do make errors on the discharge summaries."

"I didn't ask him to sequester any charts. Look, Paul, I'm not a physician. I'm just a Ph.D. I don't know about things like access to medical records and such. I just wanted to prevent some mistakes."

"Okay. Enough said."

John stood across the desk from Paul, hesitant to leave. "Is that all?"

Paul thought before he answered. "Yes."

"I was sure you wanted to tell me about my wife and Lehner."

"Lehner?"

"Yes. Well, I knew."

"I didn't."

"There is no need to tell me about such things. My wife and I have an understanding."

"Oh."

The conversation was over. John left.

It was four o'clock. For once he was going to get home early. They would have time for dinner. Then he would drive

the kids to synagogue at six and pick them up at eight and
then go over to Gerri's.

Rite of Spring sounded just right.

It had been a long time for both of them, almost two
weeks. There were so many things they needed to discuss,
but making love had a higher priority for both of them. The
long hiatus increased their desire along with their concern for
each other's needs.

Afterward it was Paul who spoke first. "I wonder if cigarettes really do taste better after making love."

"Didn't you ever smoke after sex?"

"Cigarettes? No. I don't think I've smoked more than a
couple of cigarettes in my whole life. And those I smoked
while I was an undergraduate. That was before I got married."

"And you were such a good boy then."

"I still am," he protested.

"Most of the time."

Her head was resting on his left shoulder and his left arm
was draped comfortably around her, lightly touching her left
breast. He let her remark go by without comment. It was
better that way. He had made a minor mistake. It happened.
Like the Greek soldier who was in a hurry to get home from
Troy so he decided to sail back with Ulysses. A simple,
honest mistake. It was no big deal.

He began to rotate his index finger around her nipple, but it
was obvious this was not the subject in which she was now
interested. He tried a different approach. "You missed the
research meeting yesterday."

"We had a departmental meeting. I do have other responsibilities, you know."

"I wasn't criticizing you. I just wanted to bring you up-to-
date. We're doing another implant tomorrow."

"Not on a schizophrenic?"

"Of course not. On a Parkinson patient. One of mine.
Oscar Felsch. He's been my patient for years. We've tried
everything and nothing works anymore. He told me that now
he only feels good when he sits in the sun. He wondered if he
had been reincarnated as a lizard."

"I think I saw him once. He had some hallucinations from
some new drug." She rolled over and swung her left thigh

over him. He could feel her breasts against his chest wall and her hips against his.

"Who's doing the surgery?" she asked.

"Don Lenhardt, of course." With that he began to rub his hand ever so lightly over her smooth buttocks.

"I hope he does better this time."

"What do you mean?"

"Of course this won't be the first time he's done an implant."

"No, the second, but—"

"It's only first times that cause him a problem."

"I've never had any problem with first times," he remarked.

"Paul, I'm trying to tell you something that may be very important. Try to pay some attention to me."

"I am paying attention to you. To all of you."

"Pay attention to what I'm trying to say."

"It's hard with your hips grinding into me."

"Paul. Don Lenhardt has a drug problem."

"Had." He took his hand off her backside.

"No. Has."

"You can't be right. We went through all that when he first came here. We got his medical record. We even got a statement from his psychiatrist. He was over all that."

"He's not."

"Are you sure?"

"Yes."

"But . . ."

"There are no buts about it. He may not be completely addicted or anything like that, but under certain types of stress he still needs drugs."

"Like what kinds of stress?"

"New procedures. Like a brain implant."

Paul sat bolt upright. It fit. "Are you sure he was on something when he operated on McCormick?"

"Yes."

"What?"

"Some amphetamine and some sort of downer, probably Valium," she said.

"That bastard. That explains why he's so pissed at me. He doesn't want anybody investigating that operation. Even if he didn't do anything wrong, he could still lose his license."

"Are you sure he didn't make any mistakes?" she asked.

"I don't think he did." Paul tried to think back. "I was in the OR. I didn't notice anything."

"Jackie did."

Paul frowned at her.

"She knew he was on drugs. She saw him take them just before he scrubbed in. She told me about it. She was sure he screwed up. She even got mad at him once and told him so."

"When was that?"

"A long time ago. I don't remember exactly when."

"How long ago?"

"Right after the surgery, I guess."

"Does he know she told you?"

"I doubt it. She wouldn't have told him. She hated him."

"That sure as hell gives him a good motive to kill Jackie."

"I guess it does," she agreed. He was still sitting up. "Lie back down so I can rest my head."

He did. This time she put her head on the lower part of his stomach and her hand immediately found its way to his thighs and his groin. She was no longer interested in Don Lenhardt's drug problem.

He wanted to ask her another question, but he never got the chance. Why had Jackie told her? They were never close friends. Or had they been?

She was making love to him. First with her hands and then with her mouth. And finally with both her hands and her mouth. This was not just foreplay. She was completely in charge. He was more an observer than a participant. That was not enough for him. He tapped her on the shoulder. She shook her head lightly. He tapped again. She moved so that he could reciprocate. There was an urgency in her that he didn't recognize. A reckless drive, a demanding need. She finished it the way she started it. So did he. It was over much too quickly. They had made love that way only once before and it had not been like this.

"I'm sure that's better than having a cigarette after sex," he said.

She smiled weakly. He tried to hug her, but she rolled away and crossed her arms in front of her breasts, grasping her shoulders and looking up at the ceiling as if there were some strange creature perched there looking down at her.

"I—"

"Don't say anything," she demanded.

"But—"

"Don't talk about . . . us. Talk about something else. Anything else."

He didn't want to talk about anything else, but what choice did he have?

"Everyone seems to have a motive."

"Who else?" she asked.

He told her about Bill Goodman and Herb Adams and John Corrigan and Bud Chiari and then about Edie Robinson.

"We used to be lovers."

"You and Edie?" he said laughingly.

"No, me and Jackie."

"What the hell!"

"It was a couple of years ago."

"Why are you telling me this now?"

"I—"

He didn't let her answer.

"Why not before?"

"Maybe I didn't think it was any of your business."

"So that's why my going back to her pissed you off so."

"Maybe."

"Why are you doing this, Gerri?"

"What do you mean?"

"We make love better than ever. We seem closer than ever. We even make love like we never do, and then, bang. 'By the way, I used to be a lesbian.' "

"Maybe I still am."

"Still?"

"Sure."

"Are you trying to get rid of me? Well, it won't work. I'm not that easy to dump."

"No?"

"No. I don't care who you used to . . . sleep with."

"Not even Jackie?"

"Not even Jackie. Hell, if you hadn't made love to her you might be the only one in the whole damn medical center who hadn't, except maybe the dean and the chaplain."

"I'm not sure about the chaplain," she said.

"It won't work, I know that trick."

"Huh?"

"Making a bad joke to avoid dealing with something. It won't work."

"It's three-thirty."

"Dammit." He had lost the round. She didn't want to say any more and he had to get home.

15

Another morning, another drive. Forty-five minutes of solitary travel confined in his Cressida with his music and his thoughts. Rodin notwithstanding, thinking was not the sole provenance of muscular young men seated rather uncomfortably on knotty tree stumps. When his life was going at its normal hectic pace, he treasured this time alone, this late-twentieth-century form of solitude. Why would anyone put a phone in his car and lose that one chance of a private world?

Today was different. Gerri had a motive. Paul would have welcomed an interruption to his thoughts, even the sudden dissonant clang of a telephone. Everything WFMT played was wrong. Bartók was boring. So was Janáček. And then when they finally did play one of Richard Strauss's *Four Last Songs*, the wrong soprano was singing. Kiri Te Kanawa. They should only be sung by Schwarzkopf. Those songs belonged to her and had for years.

Could Gerri have wanted to get Jackie out of the way to prevent her from telling him about the two of them? He rejected that notion outright. It didn't make any sense at all. How could he suspect Gerri of murder? And of such a grotesque murder at that? This was not one of Agatha Christie's drawing-room murders in some secluded stately manor without a single drop of blood spilled on the carpeting. This was a real murder with plenty of gore. He had seen the photographs himself. He could still see them, as if they had dug a new furrow all their own deep inside his brain. Gerri

couldn't have killed Jackie that way. And certainly not for
that motive. Maybe if he and Gerri were planning on getting
married and Jackie and Gerri were still . . . lovers. How did
he know that they weren't? He didn't. Jackie might have been
the reason Gerri wouldn't make any commitment to him. No
man could compete with that. But it was all over. Or was it?

Gerri's initials were in Jackie's diary. Tom Ward had told
him that. But not as a lover. Was Tom just protecting him?
That was possible. That might explain why Tom had ques-
tioned Gerri so early. That picture wasn't the reason. It
couldn't have been. Hadn't Tom said the picture was torn in
half? Paul had assumed that Jackie had tried to delete Gerri's
image. What wonderful conceit. Maybe he was the discarded
half. It was a good picture of her. Better than it was of him.

Were Gerri and Jackie still lovers at the time of Jackie's
death? It had been so easy for him to accept Edie's relationship with Jackie. Why not Gerri's? If it was enough of a
motive for Edie, why not for Gerri? Because he loved Gerri?
Hell, somebody loved Leopold and Loeb. Somebody even
loved Eichmann.

Was their affair merely history? Or was it more recent than
that? Was that why Gerri had gotten so angry when Tom told
her about him and Jackie? Was that why Tom had told Gerri?
To provoke her? To gauge her response? Tom had said Gerri
wasn't a suspect. But that probably meant nothing.

He had made mistakes choosing women before. He chose
to go to bed with Jackie. But not to fall in love with her.
Would he have if they had been better together?

This was getting him nowhere.

He had to see that diary.

His trip was over. He was in the parking lot. The radio was
still on. He didn't even know what music he had not listened
to.

Gerri's morning did not start off any better than Paul's. She
wasn't worrying about who might have killed Jackie. She
knew. And he was there in her office, alone with her.

"You fucked me over, Dr. Scala. Or shouldn't I use such
language with you? You can do whatever you want to do, but
I have to be careful. I'm just the patient; you're the god-
damned doctor. The holy psychiatrist. Should I bend down

and kiss the hem of your skirt? Is that the kind of reverence you require? Or should I kiss you . . . somewhere else?'' He paused. The anger was there. No flat schizoid affect this time. You didn't have to be a psychiatrist to feel it. Underneath all the anger, his logic was sound. His anger was neither shallow nor fragile. It was deeply felt and strongly expressed. It frightened her. His attack was directed at her. Straight at her. It forced her involuntarily to remember his dream image of shooting into her tunnel again and again. Paul must be right. Paul . . .

"The most high priestess of psychiatry. You're just another shrink. A shrink who happens to be a woman. You're no different from any other woman. You all look the same with your clothes off.''

How . . .

"And you're just like any other shrink. And I'm the one whose brain's been shrunk. Well, I still have rights. And I told you not to tell him anything, but you did. You told him. Probably while you were in bed . . ." He stopped himself. She wished he'd say the word, deal with it normally. "My dreams were just between us. I told you that. But no, you had to tell that bastard Richardson. I ought to kill him. Maybe you too. Him first." He stopped again. His voice changed.

"Both of you.

"But him first.''

Like a record winding down.

"You can watch . . . naked . . . with your tits . . .''

He stared at Gerri Scala. A glassy look came over his eyes. Was it the imagery of her naked body that had taken over his mind? Or something else? Violence. Sex. Blood. All three. He was licking his lips. Not in a gentle or nervous way, but primitively, hungrily, greedily, as if he wanted to gobble down whatever it was he was tasting. As if any drop was too precious to waste. He smacked his lips over and over. Was it the blood he tasted? Her blood? Or Paul's? His eyes were burning into her.

Except for his lips, he didn't move.

He just stared at her.

Unseeing.

Undressing her.

She was naked and alone.

He was tasting her. She hated it. She always had. Except with Paul.

She felt naked.

And alone. She knew that there was no one in either adjoining office. So did he. No one else in the department saw patients this early.

Was that why he had insisted on seeing her this early? He knew they'd be alone.

Quit tasting me.

She was all but certain he could hear her thought.

The licking stopped.

The movement of his lips changed. The loud, forceful smacking stopped. It was replaced by a gentle sucking movement.

So gentle.

His tongue moved back and forth in a peaceful rhythm.

In and out of his mouth.

Ever so slowly.

In.

Out.

Far out of his mouth.

In.

There was a faint smile on his face.

It wasn't a rotten brain he was tasting.

Licking.

Out.

In.

He wasn't capable of that, she reassured herself.

He had never had a woman, in any way.

How did she know?

Out.

He had told her.

In.

But perhaps he was capable of . . .

Out.

Of sex.

In.

Of rape.

Of rape and . . .

In.

Murder.

Gerri's mouth was dry.

Out.

His eyes were half-closed now, yet they seemed to be burning through her.

Through her clothes. Staring at her.

In.

It had been too hot to wear her pajamas.

She had her legs apart.

She was on her own bed on a hot summer night with her legs . . .

Out.

. . . . apart.

In.

She sat up in her chair.

She put her legs together.

Out.

From ankle to knee to thigh.

In.

As tightly as she could.

The tongue stopped.

Frank's eyes closed.

He was breathing more deeply now, a hint of a smile on his face. He seemed relaxed. Happy. Like a sleeping child.

What did she really know about him? He lied about his dreams. Maybe he lied about other things too. Did she really know what he could do to women? To her?

The minutes passed like hours as Gerri sat frozen in her chair. Her legs were locked together. Her throat and mouth were dry and immobile. She just watched.

His eyes were open now. He broke the silence that seemed to seal the room.

"I tasted it that time.

"My brain—in the back of my nose.

"It was the same smell.

"But it smelled different.

"And I tasted it.

"It was salty. Like blood."

What else would he tell her? How much was he filtering out unconsciously? Or consciously? How much was he just refusing to tell her?

"I like the taste of blood."

The sentences still came slowly, as if he were finding his way out of the dream.

"Your blood."

My blood.

"But it wasn't just blood."

"I know the taste of blood."

"It was more than just your blood."

"My brain. My burning brain."

"I hate that smell."

"The smell. It's all your fault. You and Paul Richardson. I hate him. He ruined me!"

He was back, back to his own abnormality. But he was less frightening now. His eyes looked normal. They focused on her. They were not undressing her, not prying through her clothes and forcing her legs apart.

She relaxed her legs.

"How did he figure out my dreams?" he asked.

She ignored his question. "Frank, how many spells like that do you have?"

"Maybe one a day now."

"That is less than you had before."

"Yes."

"The medicine must be helping you."

"No. I stopped taking it."

"Why?"

"Because it wasn't helping. I stopped when you told the police about me. And now I just have one spell a day. You didn't help me. You said you would, but you didn't."

"What do you dream about when the smell comes?"

"Why should I tell you? You won't believe me. You'll think I just make it up."

"No. I will hear what you say. Even if some of the dream may be borrowed. Some of it is from you. That part I will hear and know came from you."

"I don't believe you."

"I was never in the sewers of Vienna. I was not in *The Third Man*. I believe that your putting me in there means something to you."

"I'm not sure I believe you," Frank whined.

"Let's take your first dream."

"No."

"In Poe's story, the hair was gray. In your dream it was blond. That difference must be important to you. I know it must."

"You're a blond." He laughed. "A real blond. I like blonds. Blond women. Blond doctors. I like you. Blond nurses. I had a blond nurse once. When I was here for that operation.

"I remember that blond nurse. She was nice to me."

He knew Jackie. He remembered her.

"She had long hair. Like yours." He stopped.

"Long blond hair.

"I liked her.

"Her breasts.

"Her . . . taste. . . ."

He stared again.

Again. The same sequence, only more quickly.

Licking his lips.

Smacking his lips.

Sucking with his lips.

Her legs began to freeze again.

He was staring right at her. . . .

Out.

In.

Tasting.

What?

Who?

Her? Or Jackie?

She stopped herself.

He was not staring at her.

In.

His eyes were closed.

He was calm.

Breathing deeply. And regularly.

There was a smile on his face. It was all over. It couldn't have lasted more than twenty seconds.

He started back just where he had stopped.

"Blond hair.

"I love it.

"Blond blood."

The first episode had been triggered by talking about Paul. This one by Jackie.

"You need your medicine."

"No I don't."

"Frank, I think you do," Dr. Scala insisted.

"Why should I trust you?"

"I want to help you."

"No, you want to help Richardson."

"I want to help you get well."

"But you told him."

"Yes, I thought he might be able to help you."

"I need help."

"Yes, you do."

She waited. "Will you take your medicine?"

"Yes."

"Two pills, three times a day."

"You shouldn't have told him," he complained. "You let me down. Just like my mother. She was a blond. Just like you. I hate blonds."

Paul was not yet in the operating room. He never liked to get to the OR early just to watch the neurosurgeons preen themselves while merely opening a patient's cranium; as if the simple task of trephining a skull were the equal of squaring a circle. He would get there in time for the implant itself. The other members of the research team that were involved in this project were there. They were all dressed in Austin Flint's traditional surgical greens, complete with masks and gloves. Each had his own role to play, roles which each of them had spent a lifetime training to perform. Don and Marv were of course in charge of the surgery itself; Floyd, the clinical observation of Mr. Felsch while Herb and John took charge of the adrenal tissue that was to be implanted. They had been at the hospital since five in the morning, transferring the Leibold sample to a special sterilized container. This container had then been placed into another, similar but larger one for transfer to the operating room and now rested in an incubator about six feet from the operating table.

There were others in the room, a scrub nurse, an anesthesiologist, a circulating nurse, and a neuroradiologist, Bob Falk. Only the last three were not gowned. They wore surgical suits of the same green color, and masks, but no gown and no rubber gloves. Their duties would be performed outside the operating field, relieving them of the obligation to adhere to the complete ritual of sterile technique.

Oscar Felsch was seated in a special chair. Only the top of his head stuck up above the surgical dropcloths. His face was hidden by the black rubber mask which carried oxygen into his respiratory system.

He was asleep, in stage three of anesthesia from a rapidly acting barbiturate which had been given intravenously. His head was completely shaved and was held tightly in a vise which was attached to the heavy metal chair in which he sat. The device was designed to make any movement of his head impossible.

Marv Rickert washed his scalp once again with Betadine.

The neuroradiologist turned the switch and projected one slice of the CAT scan onto a large screen.

"The bur hole should be two centimeters in front and three-point-five centimeters above the exact center of the external auditory canal," he said.

Marv repeated what he said, and then, taking a sterile ruler from the scrub nurse, made the measurements and put a small black X on the spot. He moved to the other side of the patient's bald head to repeat the same steps.

Meanwhile the missing chief-investigator was making rounds. There was not very much work to be done. Both Donna Kolloway and Mike Kreevich had gone home. Mrs. Wright had died.

"What happened?" Paul asked.

"Everything," Bill said. "First she went into shock and then she stopped putting out urine and started bleeding. Finally we just couldn't support her blood pressure anymore."

Paul could picture the scene. He had been there himself, all too many times. She had not gone gently into her last good night. Why could she not have at least died in peace? He was certain that the leopard had frozen to death with more dignity.

There was no longer any question as to Fred Sanford's diagnosis. The immune studies had come back showing that he had severe T-cell abnormalities. He definitely had AIDS. Whatever that was. They had also discovered the exact cause

of the infection at the base of his brain. It was as they had
suspected, cryptococcus, a fungus which was able to grow
there because of the inability of his injured immune system to
fight it off.

They had started him on amphotericin B.

"That's what Mrs. Wright was on," Edie said. Her unneeded reminder was as much a question as a statement of
fact.

"True, but it is the best antifungus agent we have," Paul
said.

"Will it help him?"

"Probably. Each patient is different, but most patients with
early AIDS still have some immune responses so that they
can help to some degree in fighting off the infection. Unless
he has an abscess, we should be able to help him." He
looked at Bill Goodman.

"I went over his CAT scan again. There's not even a hint
of any abscess."

"Good. Mrs. Wright had so many abscesses we couldn't
even count them. Sanford should do pretty well," Paul said.

"This time." Bill didn't have to remind them of that. "We
should be checking on his sexual contacts."

"I guess so," Paul agreed hesitantly.

"He has been reluctant to tell me about any of his sex
partners," Bill continued. "I'm sure he'd be more cooperative with the chairman of the department."

Bill was absolutely correct. They did need to trace the web
of his sexual contacts. And Paul was in a better position. He
knew where to start. It would be a complex pattern, leading
from Jackie to . . . "I'll take care of that," Paul told him.

Mrs. Nicholson was on Artane. She was a little better. Her
neck hurt less.

The ear-canal X rays were back on Mrs. Kell. So was the
CAT scan. They were both wonderfully abnormal. They confirmed that she had a brain tumor and that it was not a
malignant tumor. It was a small benign one right behind her
ear that could easily be removed. Paul was happy for her.

"We should tell her the good news."

"I already have." Bill said. "But I'm sure she needs to
hear it from you."

"Let's go and see her."

"She's down getting her hearing tested. That'll take all morning."

"I'll see her tomorrow."

"After you check her old chest X ray. She could still have a malignant lung tumor," Bill reminded him.

"Yes, after that."

With work rounds completed, the three of them headed for the operating room. Paul couldn't believe he hadn't realized it before. He knew that AIDS was a venereal disease. Of course no one knew how contagious it was. It wasn't herpes or gonorrhea. That they knew. But no one knew what percentage of people who had sexual contact with a patient with AIDS went on to get the disease or transmit it. Some did. How many was an unanswered question. And Sanford had known Jackie. So had he and Gerri and Floyd and God knew who else. Jackie's diary. It would all be there. He had to see that damn diary.

Both sides of Mr. Felsch's head had been marked off. Incisions had been made bilaterally. Don did the one on the right while Marv did the one on the left. Then each of them drilled a small bur hole—about one centimeter in diameter—in the temporal bone. Once the bur holes had been dressed with bone wax, the neurosurgeons each made a small cruciate pair of incisions in the dura and exposed the brain itself.

It was time to wake up the patient. "Let him up," Don said.

"I'll stop the barbiturate," said the anesthesiologist. "He'll start waking up in about four minutes."

They waited for the four minutes to pass, and then another four. It always took longer than it was supposed to.

By the time Mr. Felsch was awake, Paul, Edie, and Bill had arrived. They had put on scrub suits and masks, but not gloves and gowns.

"Mr. Felsch."

"Hel . . . lo . . . Dr. . . . Richard . . . son."

"How are you?"

"A . . . little . . . bit . . . grog . . . gy."

"Everything is going well."

"I'm . . . ready."

"Dr. Lenhardt and Dr. Rickert are about to put the needles in place."

"I . . . hope . . . it works."

"So do we."

This was the one part of the procedure that took any real technical skill. Paul and the neuroradiologist looked at the CAT scan and conferred, then Paul did a few calculations.

"Height: twenty-seven centimeters," he announced.

"Correct," Don Lenhardt said. "That was the number Marv and I came up with yesterday." With that he took a small vise from the scrub nurse and attached it to the head frame at the twenty-seven-centimeter spot.

Marv Ricket did the same on the other side. Next they each attached a long needlelike instrument into the vise.

"Angle," Paul said, "forty-two degrees." Don again nodded, and each neurosurgeon made the appropriate adjustment, fixing the angle of the needles at forty-two.

"Which side first?" Paul asked.

"I'll start," Don said.

Paul looked at him. His voice seemed normal. His hands steady. His fingers had a slight tremor. Nothing terribly remarkable, but nonetheless, there was some tremor. Paul was sure that he had never seen it before. Had he taken anything before the operation? If so, what?

Don began to pass the needle into the brain.

"Eleven and a half centimeters should be the best target," Paul said.

"Our calculations came out at eleven-point-seven," the surgeon replied.

"Not much different," Paul suggested.

"I'll start testing at ten and a half." With that Don continued pushing the needle in to the ten-point-five mark.

In one way, Paul explained to Edie, the procedure they were following was just the opposite of the epilepsy surgery they had done on Mike Kreevich. In his case the electrical probe had been used to trigger a seizure and prove they were in the correct location. Here they once again used an electric probe, but this time it would be improvement of the parkinsonian signs that showed them when they were in the right spot.

Don passed a long thin electrode through the needle.

He turned the switch on.

It was Floyd who was now in charge. "No change."

Don switched it off and began inching the needle farther into the deep centers of Oscar Felsch's brain. "Ten-point-eight." He turned the switch on once again.

"No change."

Off.

Another adjustment.

"Eleven-point-four."

On.

"No change. No, the tremor is a shade slower. Three-point-five per second. It was between four and four-point-five, but it's still there."

Off.

"Eleven-point-seven."

On.

"It's gone. No tremor at all."

"My . . . right . . . hand . . . feels better," Mr. Felsch said.

"We're in the right place," Paul announced, to the surprise of no one.

Don turned the electrode off.

"Four-point-three per second. Amplitude seven-point-four."

On.

"Gone."

Off.

"Four-point-four. Eight-point-one."

Don waited for several minutes.

On.

"No tremor."

Off.

"Same readings."

Three times it had worked. Three times Don had sent electricity to that one spot eleven-point-seven centimeters inside the left half of Oscar Felsch's brain and three times the tremor had disappeared from his right arm and his right leg, only to reappear each time he stopped the flow. They were in the right location.

Lenhardt tightened two screws that held the needle in the vise so that it was locked into place and then removed the electrode. Don's tremor was still there. In fact, it was ever so slightly more pronounced. The testing was not helping him. It wasn't supposed to.

The circulating nurse opened up the incubator and lifted out the container and carried it over to John Corrigan and Herb Adams. She opened it. John reached in and took out the vial labeled "Dillinger 307." Herb took out another one labeled "Leibold." Each man opened his vial. John poured the contents of his slowly into the bottle Herb was holding. Herb held it steady while John took a syringe and sucked up the now-combined contents. He then attached a long needle to the syringe and handed it to Don Lenhardt. Don passed it through the fixed needle where the electrode had just been. It was the final crucial step: the injection of the adrenal cells into the brain. This was what it was all about. This was the climax. A simple step any medical student could do. You didn't need a neurosurgeon for this. Just stick in the needle and inject. A practical nurse could do it.

Over the next five minutes the neurosurgeon injected the entire contents of the syringe. One cc each minute. He waited exactly sixty seconds between each squeeze on the barrel of the syringe, making what should have been the simplest of tasks into some sort of ritual. He was done. He took out the entire probe.

It was Marv Rickert's turn to perform the same complex procedure on the other side.

Twenty-seven centimeters.

Forty-two degrees.

The probe. The flashes of electric current.

The tremor stopped at eleven-point-five this time.

Again three trials. Again John and Herb prepared the cells. Then Marv injected them, one cc each minute.

When they were done, they closed the dura and sutured the skin.

"I . . . am . . . no . . . better," Mr. Felsch said. It was the first thing he had said in an hour.

"It will take time, Mr. Felsch," Paul said. "The cells have to start growing and making the right chemicals, just like we told you."

"I . . . was . . . hoping . . ."

"No, it will take time."

"How . . . long?"

"Six months. Maybe less. Maybe more."

Paul knew that his patient would look no better when he left the OR. What he had not known was that Don Lenhardt would look worse. Why was his tremor getting worse? Was it some sort of drug withdrawal?

As soon as he got back to his office, Chris told him that Dr. Scala had called him twice.

"I was in the OR."

"That's what I told her."

"Did she leave a message?"

"No."

"Did she say anything about tonight, about dinner tonight?"

"No."

"Did she say she wasn't coming over or—?"

"She didn't say anything except that she'd be in with patients and then Dr. Rotblatt for a couple of hours and that she'd try to call you between patients."

"So I can't call her now," he complained, not expecting an answer.

"Tom Ward also called."

"I need to talk to him too."

"Should I try calling him?"

"Yes. If he's around, have him stop up here. And get me Mrs. Kell's chart, please."

Paul poured himself a cup of coffee. There was a box of doughnuts next to the coffee. Chris had done it again. Entenmann's. Chocolate crumb-cake doughnuts. He shouldn't. He was trying to lose some weight. He took only one.

His work was waiting on his desk. The paper he was supposed to proofread by the day before yesterday was sitting there. He flipped over the front page without reading it and started with the first paragraph of the text itself at the top of page two. Something was wrong. He remembered his opening sentence. It had been a gem. Maybe not "Call me Ishmael" or "It was the best of times," but it had been a good opener. It had taken him three consecutive morning drives in to the hospital to work it out. He still remembered it: "Viewed from the perspective of the striatal neuron . . ." This wasn't his sentence. He never used the word "posits." He wasn't even sure it was a verb. A posit was something a dog left on a carpet.

He turned back to look at the face sheet. It was his article. The title was the one he had written. The authorship was the way he had sent it in. The acknowledgments were complete and correct. He went back to the opening paragraphs. Only the text had been changed. He read on. It got worse. More archaic verbs, some arcane adverbs, and some adjectives he didn't even know.

"Antipodes," he read aloud.

"What the hell is an antipodes?"

He looked it up. Diametrically opposed pair of objects. Why hadn't the author just said that in plain English? But he had. He was the author. He had written "opposite ends of the same continuum." Another phrase he had liked. Gone. Transformed into "antipodes" by some unseen medical ghost writer. Some twit who had never written a scientific article in his or her life but who owned a *Roget's*. Did he or she even know that Roget had been a physician? Paul was willing to bet against it. And give odds.

What right did they have to rewrite his article?

Where was that contract?

Right in his drawer. In a file labeled "Contracts." He looked. The file was there. Such organization. The contract was in the file. The top one. He read it. They did have the right.

Now he finally understood a comment made by Sir Thomas Beecham. Beecham was said to have hated recording engineers. Why? It was recording engineers who made his art, the ephemeral art of a conductor, immortal. What had Beecham said? That it had taken him forty years to get the horns to play quietly enough, and with one mere flick of a wrist the recording engineer destroyed forty years of hard work.

Paul hadn't quite put in forty years of hard work. Still, he had put in his time. Posits indeed.

Chris buzzed him. Tom Ward was there to see him.

"Send him in."

The door opened.

"What's up?" Tom asked.

"Have a cup of coffee and a doughnut."

"Just coffee. I'm trying to watch my weight," Tom replied.

Had that remark been necessary? Tom went out to the outer office, got himself some coffee, came back in, and sat down in the office. He handed Paul a chart.

Paul glanced at it. It was Mrs. Kell's. Chris had given it to Tom to carry in.

It was Paul who wanted to talk and it was Paul who started. He began where it was easiest. He had found another suspect.

"Who?"

"Don Lenhardt."

"The neurosurgeon?"

"Yes."

"What did he do? Act out some transvestite fantasy in Jackie's bra?"

"Be serious, Tom."

"I am. Look, Paul, most of the motives you have come up with so far have been rather flimsy for this kind of murder."

"Not really."

"No?" Tom paused for a moment of thought. "Let's see, that makes how many suspects now? Five? No. Six. We won't count you."

"Thanks."

"You're welcome. What's Lenhardt's motive?"

"Drug addiction." Paul could see that he had gotten the detective's full attention. Drugs were a motive the police understood. Paul took his time as he told him exactly what Gerri had said to him the night before.

"Jackie really had him where she wanted him," Tom said.

"That's what it looks like."

"I'll buy that one. Lenhardt had a damn good motive. So did Corrigan."

"I'm not so sure of that," Paul said thoughtfully.

"I checked, Doc."

"Yes?"

"She owns the company. Hook, line, and sinker. If she dumped him, he'd be out in the cold, cruel world."

"True, but that won't happen."

"Why not?"

"They have an understanding. An open marriage."

"You sure?"

"Yes," Paul said. He could not tell whether Tom was convinced.

"We also can't forget our little Jackie's lovers."

"Who?" Paul asked forcefully. Would Tom include Gerri this time? He had the diary. He waited.

"Floyd Baker and Edie Robinson.'

He didn't mention Gerri. Why not? Paul had to know. He didn't ask.

"Then the lab business. Herb Adams. Although that seems like a pretty weak motive to me."

"No, I disagree. If that suit were pursued, any mistakes in the lab would become public and his professional career would be in serious jeopardy. Men have killed for a lot less." Paul thought for a moment. "That, by the way, would give John Corrigan another motive."

"How come?"

"It's his chemical we inject. He does the lab work on the project with Herb. Maybe he screwed up in the lab. Maybe Jackie knew it was as much his fault as Herb's. Or more. He could have been the one who made the lab error and was afraid of being investigated."

"So I'll keep him on my list," Tom conceded grudgingly. "Right next to Chiari and Goodman and those charts of yours."

"Don't be so skeptical."

"I can't help it. The whole thing still smacks of a sex crime to me. I'd put my money on either Baker or Robinson."

Again he hadn't mentioned Gerri.

"Although Lenhardt could be the dark horse," Tom admitted.

Paul didn't say anything about Gerri and Jackie. Hell. Tom already knew. He had to know. He had the diary. *The diary*.

"Tom, I need the diary."

"The diary?"

"Jackie's diary."

"I can't give that to you."

"It's not to find her killer. It's . . ." It took him ten minutes to teach Tom about Fred Sanford, AIDS, and the diary.

"Paul, you might . . ." Tom finally understood.

"I know. So might a lot of other people. I have to see that diary."

"I can't get it to you before tomorrow."

"I'll be in tomorrow."

"I'll put it in your mailbox."

He tried calling Gerri. She was in with Dr. Rotblatt. He left a message. He read through Mrs. Kell's chart. He found the old X-ray report. The spot had been there ten years ago. It hadn't changed in all those years. No cancer for Mrs. Kell. He'd tell her in the morning.

"You know why we are meeting for two hours today."

She responded slowly. "I guess so."

"There is no reason to deny it, Gerri. I am going into the hospital this evening for another course of chemotherapy. I don't expect to come back to work." He paused. "Ever."

"I . . . I know that."

"There are loose ends we must try to tie up."

"I won't be seeing Paul anymore."

"How can you be sure of that?"

"I told him that Jackie and I were lovers."

He merely snorted contemptuously. They had been through that issue too many times to go over it again. She and Jackie had never been lovers. Not that Jackie hadn't tried, but they had never been lovers.

"He won't want to be with me again."

"You really have set yourself up."

"I have not."

"Yes, you have. You feel deserted by me. Well, in a sense you are being deserted. I won't be here for you from now on. But it's not like your mother dying all over again or your stepfather disappearing forever. I am not dying just to leave you stranded."

"I know that."

"Do you?"

Gerri said nothing.

"I am neither your father nor your mother."

She bit her lip. She had promised herself that she was not going to cry. "I was all alone when my mother died. She had already divorced that bastard. I was all by myself. I was just barely fourteen with two little brothers to try to help. She divorced him because of what I . . . what he . . ."

"What did you say?"

"What he did to me."

"No you didn't."

"What I did," softly.

A curious "Hm?"

"I . . . I . . . induced him . . . I . . . I seduced him away from my mother. That night. I was naked. I didn't hide myself. I didn't scream. It was all my fault. I had loved him so. He was the only father I'd ever really known. He was so kind to me. Kinder than my mother. I couldn't hide from him. So I . . . I . . . Then my mother sent him away."

"Did she?"

"Send him away? Of course."

"No, send him away because of that."

"Yes."

"Who told her about it?"

Gerri didn't answer.

"Did you?"

"No." She swallowed hard.

"I thought not. Did your stepfather?" he asked.

"No. He would never have done that to me."

"Then who?"

There was no answer.

"No one told her," he said. "She never mentioned it, did she?"

Gerri said nothing.

"She never knew. Your mother never knew. Only two people knew. You knew and he knew. You didn't tell her and he didn't, either. There is only one conclusion, Gerri. She didn't know."

"Then why did she throw him out?"

"Did she?"

"Of course. He wouldn't have left me. I gave him what he wanted and . . ."

"And?"

"I wasn't enough for him. I wasn't any good. He loved me. Not her. Me. And I wasn't any good, so he left. I've never been any good. Men always leave me. I can't give them what they want. I can't even give them children. I'm no good for them; that's why I turned to women."

"Bull." That stopped her. "One woman. Big deal. You were looking more for a mother than a lover. One woman and the few times Jackie Baumer tried to seduce you. Tried and failed, unless you lied to me."

"I didn't. I've never lied to you."

"I know that. But you have sometimes lied to yourself and believed those lies to be the truth. All these years you really believed that your mother knew."

"She didn't," Gerri whispered.

"And she didn't die because of what you did, because you tried to steal her husband, your stepfather. She just died. Period. People do that, you know."

She knew.

"Why do men leave you?"

"Because I'm not good for them. I'm no good in bed."

"Is that what they say?"

"No."

"Then why?"

"And I can't have babies. I knew when I was sixteen that . . . that was the only way I could keep a man. Then I lost that."

"Gerri."

"Yes."

The fact that she was a good psychiatrist didn't keep her from living with such contradictions. Part of her believed that her stepfather left because of her failure as a woman. Another part that her mother had thrown him out because of that same event. She vacillated between these two extremes. Sometimes believing one. Sometimes the other. Sometimes both. Neither was true. "That is not why your stepfather left."

"Then why?"

"Did he leave or was he thrown out?"

"I don't remember."

"You do. Stop lying to yourself."

"He left." She was defiant now.

"If he left, it wasn't because you weren't good enough. It was because he felt guilty."

"It was my fault."

"No. It was his fault. The whole world doesn't revolve around you. Think about it. What happened?"

"He came home one morning about six o'clock. He did that once or twice a week."

"What kind of work did he do?"

"What difference does that make? He was working."

"Humpf."

"He was an accountant," she said. The defiance was gone.

"Working until six A.M.? Once a week? Maybe twice?"

"You bastard," she said flatly.

"He came home at six A.M." He waited.

"I heard him rattling the door. My mother had changed the locks. His suitcases were on the porch. They were already packed. The two of them screamed at each other through the locked door. They screamed about me. My mother called me a . . . a whore."

"They weren't arguing about you."

"They had to be."

"They weren't. You know that. Believe it. Accept it."

"I wanted it to be me. I wanted him to be faithful to me. I wanted to go with him. I loved him so damn much. But I wasn't good enough."

"No one woman was enough for him. He liked having lots of women."

"Yes."

"So your mother threw him out."

"Yes."

"It wasn't because of you."

"No."

"But that's what hurt so much—the feeling that you weren't any more important than any of his other . . . whores. That made you like them. A whore. But you were more important. You loved him. He loved you. He probably did, by the way. In his own peculiar fashion. So the story changed. At first you believed your mother threw him out because of you. Then she got sick.

"Part of you wanted her to get sick. Part of you may even have wanted her to die so that he'd come back to you. But he didn't come back. When she got sicker you became terrified at your own power. But she didn't throw him out because of you and she didn't get sick because of you." He paused. "You are not omnipotent. No one is."

"I know that," she said.

"Then why are you reliving that pain now?"

"You are leaving me."

"Sure, I'm leaving you and everyone else. Not just you."

"I will be alone again."

"Only if you want to be alone."

"I don't."

"No? What did you tell Paul?"

"That Jackie and I were lovers."

"Why did you lie to him?"

"So that he wouldn't leave me later and hurt me more."

"Gerri. He might have left you someday. Men leave women. Women leave men. Fathers leave daughters. It doesn't make the one left behind worthless." This last session was no longer analysis by any stretch of the imagination. The rules had all been cast aside. "My first wife left me. Yet I'm not just a worthless shell of a man because of that."

"I didn't know that."

"Of course you didn't. That's not why I'm dying, either. She remarried. I remarried. I never see her. I never see our son. She took him when she left. Yes, I felt rotten for a while. You always do. But don't keep reliving the past. I'm not saying Paul is the one. But he could be."

"He is."

"Then why?"

"Because I love him and I'm afraid. And I love his kids and that makes me more afraid. I could have it all for once and I'm so damn afraid."

"You are worth it. You do deserve it."

"I wish I could believe that."

"You have to."

Paul tried to call Gerri as he was leaving his office, but she was still in with Dr. Rotblatt. He would try calling again later.

He took one of his shortcuts through the bowels of the hospital to get to Medical Records. He remembered how surprised Gerri had been when he had first showed her some of them. So few people used them now. When he'd first come here in '58 they were the main thoroughfares.

Medical Records had pulled his charts. They were there in a neat pile waiting just for him. It was said with a smile. Would they get one more? Whose? Frank McCormick's. Of course. No problem at all. Did he have the hospital number? He didn't. She just smiled.

He signed the records as quickly as he could. He didn't read the summaries. He didn't check the diagnoses. He didn't go over each of the orders. He just wrote his signature as often as the checklist told him to.

The checklist. Whoever stole the informed consent must not have known about the pre-op checklist.

The clerk brought him McCormick's chart. The consent form was still missing. The pre-op checklist was still there. He reread it. All the checks were there. Including the one for informed consent. It was initialed J.S.B. Jackie had initialed it. Whoever took the informed consent should have taken this too. Having the checklist gave them a defense. Not the best one, but still a defense.

Killing Jackie made sense only if both the consent form and the checklist were missing. If you can take one, it's just as simple to take them both. No physician would have made that error. It had to be an outsider. It all came back to Frank McCormick. It all fit.

It was time to get to the dean's office.

There were two charts left. He finished them, and as soon as he was done, he tried to call Gerri again. She was still not available.

He took another shortcut. This one was his favorite. It saved him at least four minutes. He got to Dean Willis' office on time. Better he should have been late. John was already there. Paul hadn't expected that.

"We settled the case," the dean began.

"What?"

"The McCormick case. We settled it. Very amicably, too. The father agreed to drop this suit and not to enter into any further suits and to have his son remain a patient here."

"For how much?"

"Not much."

"How much is not much?"

"One hundred and fifty thousand."

"Gee, can I have a raise in my departmental budget? Not much of one. Just one hundred and fifty thousand bucks. It's not much. We give that away on nuisance suits."

"Paul. Defending the suit would have cost at least that, most likely considerably more."

"So what!"

"And it is possible that we might have lost the suit," John reminded him.

"We would have won."

"Maybe," Dean Willis said. "We decided not to take the chance."

"We."

"John and I and our lawyers," he answered. "It's better for us all not to receive any adverse publicity on any experimental procedure. Such things always makes us look bad. We were fortunate not to have been too badly damaged by that nurse's murder. We were able to limit the sensationalism of both TV and the newspaper. Don't think for one minute that that was easy. We don't need anything that could stir that up further. John and I have been worrying about this case for over a year. You just got into it. It's not worth fighting it anymore."

Paul knew he had lost. One thing about Sox fans, they knew how to recognize defeat.

"You wanted to meet with me," the dean continued.

Paul nodded.

"About the consortium grant," John added.

Paul nodded again.

Game two was about to begin.

Paul led off. He told them about the bylaws they had just violated. There was one problem of which he was not aware. The loophole had been rescinded five years ago. John showed him a copy of revised bylaws that he just happened to have with him. Paul felt as if he had just smacked into a double play in the last of the ninth with the bases loaded, against the Yankees, with the tying run at third, on a sucker pitch.

It was those damned Yankees all over again. The beloved White Sox of his youth had not been able to beat them. The Yanks had Mantle and Maris and Berra and Ford. All the Sox had on their side were Truth and Justice—neither of whom could hit a curve ball.

The White Sox had won once. That happened in 1959, the same year that he had gotten married. The Sox had lost the World Series. And now he was a widower.

Paul walked slowly back through the regular corridors. It was late and they were empty. Had Floyd known? Had Floyd set him up? He was becoming as suspicious as Frank McCormick. Gerri had been right to put him on Haldol. One hundred and fifty grand. Would that make him less angry? Or would it just confirm his suspicions, feed his paranoia?

Chris was gone. He tried to call Gerri at her office, but got no answer. He looked at the proofs and tore them in half. He wrote out a brief letter longhand. They could do one of three things with his chapter: publish it as he had written it; publish their version complete with "posits," but without his name; or they could publish the book without his chapter. There was a fourth choice, but he left that out.

He put his letter in an envelope and dug into his drawer to find the address.

He pulled out the file labeled "Contracts." There was another file stuck to the back of it. A file labeled "Consents."

"Consents."

He opened it and found what he wanted. The signed consent form. It was too late, but there it was. Frank had signed it. His father had signed it. That SOB must have remembered that all the time. He must have been behind it all. Not Frank. He wasn't that clever. That made it cold, calculated, premeditated murder. Jackie had witnessed it. She had signed her own death warrant.

He put it back, looked through the other file, found the address he wanted, addressed the envelope, and put the file back.

He found a stamp.

He called Gerri. Once again there was no answer. By now she must have left for the day. Was she coming to Highland Park? He called home and got an answer. It was Carolyn.

Had Gerri called? No.

That meant she was still coming to dinner.

With dessert and salad, Carolyn reminded him.

She must have left early to pick them up, he told her.

He called Gerri at home. He heard a click. "Gerri."

"Hello."

"Hi," he said happily.

"This is Gerri."

"Damn."

"I'm not available at the moment . . ."

"No kidding."

". . . to take your call. But if you wait for the signal and leave a message, I'll try to get back to you as soon as I can."

Uncharacteristically he waited and left his message with neither sarcasm nor bad language.

She had to be on her way to Highland Park.

Gerri was not on the way to Highland Park. She was on her way to Paul's office. She had to tell him about Frank. She had to tell him about Rotblatt. She had to hold him. She had left her process notes in her office. She had meant to bring them. She hoped he had not left yet. His phone had been busy when she called. She was hurrying as fast as she could. She took the shortcut he had taught her to use. It was just like the tunnel Frank had described in his dream. The thought did not please her. As she got to the top of the second landing of the internalized fire escape, she reached for the doorknob. It was almost pitch dark. The one small bulb which hung over the narrow landing was out. The landing itself was clothed in darkness.

Paul was right. The shortcut saved time. She wasn't sure it was worth it. She could imagine Frank at the other end of the tunnel shooting at her. Filling her with his bullets.

The knob was slippery.

And tight. It didn't want to open.

The entire place was dark, gray, and damp. There was no color at all. It could well be a scene from one of Frank's dreams.

The knob wouldn't turn.

She tried both hands.

It began to budge.

There, it was opening.

The light hit her face.

Bang.

Her head.

It was like a hammer blow.

And another.

And another.

She started to slip.

A succession of blows.

One after the other.

She staggered.

She held on to the doorknob with both hands. Her legs buckled and her knees cracked against the concrete.

The doorknob was in front of her face like some obscene tool.

She held on as tightly as she could.

Another smash.

Another blow.

Her head was exploding.

She couldn't hold on anymore.

Another bang.

They came with a steady rhythm now. She was beginning to lose consciousness. The pounding hurt less. It was becoming less frightening. It reminded her of . . .

She couldn't remember.

Her head fell forward.

Her mouth hit the doorknob and slipped off.

She fell to the rough concrete.

Her head hit the top stair. She felt it hit.

The hammer blows continued.

She tried to get up. She grabbed at the doorknob. It was slippery and bloody.

What did the blood taste like? she wondered.

Her head weaved from side to side. The blows stopped.

The rhythmic banging was over.

Her head slumped backward as if she had no muscles left to hold it up. Her eyes rolled up in her head. Her mouth fell open. It was being forced open. She tried to get up. She had to.

She fell back as if someone had kicked her legs from under her. She didn't feel her shoulder hit the fourth step or the flesh of her thigh as it was torn open by a jagged edge. Or her pantyhose being torn apart, exposing her thighs. All she had left protecting her was a thin pair of panties.

She lay motionless. Her torso was on the landing. Her head was dangling onto the lower flight of stairs. Her legs were splayed apart and pointing obscenely up the upper stairway.

She tried to move. She couldn't. She tried to close her mouth but was unable to.

Her legs fell farther apart.

She was more open.

More inviting.

The only motion was of her chest wall. It continued to move in and out shallowly.

That and the blood collecting between her legs.

16

I t wasn't quite as easy to lie this time. Gerri was not at their house in Highland Park when he got there. She was not in her office or, if she was there, she did not answer the phone. Her phone at home was still attached to her idiotic answering machine. Of course that didn't prove that she wasn't at home: she simply may not have wanted to answer the phone. More specifically, she may not have wanted to talk to Paul. He left a message as he had done just before leaving his office.

There wasn't much reason to wait for her. After half an hour the three of them sat down to dinner without Gerri and without salad. No one missed the salad. Nor the dessert. Especially not Paul; he really had to lose a few pounds.

The conversation did not get serious until they started to clear the table.

"Do you think Gerri got sick again, Dad?" Joshua asked.

"No."

"Then why didn't she come over?"

It was a difficult question.

"I invited her and she told me she was going to come."

"It's not your fault, Josh. It's just that she is not very happy with me."

"Does that mean that we won't see her anymore?"

"I don't know. Maybe."

"I don't believe that," Carolyn said. "Something happened to her. She must not be feeling well. You'll see. She'll call. She'll call me."

"I hope you're right."

The table was cleared. "I'm going to Northwestern," Carolyn announced. "I'll have to live on campus since I can't drive for the whole year. I'll live in one of the dorms."

She had made her decision. "Are you sure?" Paul asked.

"Yes. It'll be easy to come home for weekends and things. I can just hop on a Northwestern. Sometimes you could even pick me up on your way home from the hospital. If I could still drive I could live at home and we could all still be together. But I can't."

It was the decision he had hoped she would reach. She had reached it on her own. He had not pressured her at all. He hoped that Joshua hadn't. "It'll be just fine with you in Evanston. Living away from home is part of going to college."

"That was what Gerri said you would say."

"When did you talk to Gerri?"

"Last night."

"When?" he asked slowly.

"While you were driving to her house. I called her. We talked about college. She helped me make up my mind. She said she would help me decide where to live."

For the first time, he began to sense that something might be wrong. Carolyn could be right—something might have happened to Gerri. She might not have called him, but she would have called Carolyn.

Had Gerri talked her into Northwestern? Had she done it knowing that she was about to walk out on him? That fit in with last night. She sure as hell had set him up. Had she planned it like this so that he wouldn't feel completely deserted? After all, Carolyn would still be virtually next door—a twenty-minute ride from home. That way Gerri could just disappear without a guilty conscience. Then why did she tell Carolyn that she would help her pick out a dorm? Maybe it was only him she was leaving. What right did she have to his kids? Every right. She was good for Carolyn. Carolyn was good for her. If he didn't fit, he didn't fit. It didn't have to be a package deal.

"Let's go out for dessert. To celebrate your decision."

"Where?" Carolyn asked.

"Your choice."

"Poppin Fresh."

"Okay."

"Right on," Joshua added.

That was where they went. Joshua and Carolyn each had a piece of French Silk. Paul had just plain old-fashioned cherry pie without ice cream. After all, he did have to lose some weight. The pie was good but it wasn't much of a celebration.

As soon as they got back home, Paul tried once again to call Gerri. Once again he got the same infernal machine. He left a different message. She should call Carolyn. That was a message she would probably answer.

He turned on the TV. The Sox were on from Seattle. Why was there a major-league team in Seattle?

There were so many questions he couldn't answer. Why now? When they had fit so well together physically?

So had he and Jackie the last time they had made love, and he had never wanted to touch her again. And she kept calling him. Just as he persisted in calling Gerri. He decided not to call anymore. Or at least not to leave any further messages.

As soon as he got downstairs in the morning, he tried again. This time he told her machine to call Joshua.

It was a perfect day. Spring was in full bloom. Chicago's mildest winter on record had become its coldest, wettest spring. But now it looked like that, too, had finally passed. It was truly a perfect day for a ballgame. And the Sox were on the road. In Seattle of all places. They might as well be in Timbuktu. And they had lost. The ignominy of it all.

It was time to leave. Paul drove Carolyn and Joshua to the synagogue. Carolyn assured him that she had arranged for a ride home if he was not done with rounds in time to pick them up.

There was only one show that he could listen to on a morning like this. The true American Rite of Spring. He had the tape in the car. Adler and Ross' second Broadway smash, *Damn Yankees*.

The Damn Yankees. The villains of his youth. If he had not been able to cheer his White Sox to victory over their eternal enemy, he could at least sing about the Washington Senators taking the pennant away from them.

Paul smiled as he listened to the chorus of baseball wives praise the fielding plays of Willie Mays.

That was a lyric that was right up there with the best of them. At least no one had written a great lyric about Mickey Mantle. That would have been too much. Jolting Joe was different. DiMag belonged to America, not just to the Yankees. Mantle was a Yankee, through and through. A hated pin-striper from the Big Apple. DiMaggio had made it in two different hit songs. That made the score DiMag 2, Willie 1. And Mantle a big fat zero.

Jerry Ross had not been so lucky. That memory jarred Paul.

He had been thrown out of life much too early—two shows, two hits—and that was it. *Pajama Game;* then *Damn Yankees;* and fini. A sudden rupture of an abnormal blood vessel sitting there inside his head, and his ballgame was all over.

Perhaps now that kind of disaster would not happen to Donna Kolloway.

But what about Gerri? He'd never even seen her angiogram. He wondered what it looked like. What advice would he have given her? Certainly not the advice that she got.

She had not bled in over ten years. That was a good sign. Not a guarantee, but a good sign nonetheless. It was probably better that he had never seen her angiogram.

It was a typical Saturday morning. The hospital parking lot was all but empty. The office was empty. It was 9:55. He'd take his usual weekend shortcut via the old fire escape and be on the ward in plenty of time for rounds. He'd have seconds to spare.

He put on his white coat and slammed his office door to be certain that it locked, checked the knob, and headed down the short hall to the left of his office. He went up half a flight of steps to the dust-covered door marked "Closed for Repairs" and "Do Not Enter." They were the same signs he had been ignoring for over a dozen years now. They were each signed "Richard J. Daley, Mayor." He had only been dead for eight years.

As always the door was stuck and he had to yank on the knob to get it open. He gave it a hard yank.

It opened.

It always did.

They couldn't lock it. It was still an official fire escape, his own private fire escape. No one else ever used it. Hardly anyone even knew that it existed. He was certain that the dean didn't. It dated back to the original 1872 structure and probably had not been repaired since then. They didn't make fire escapes like this one anymore.

The first step was loose. It had been loose for the last six years. One of these days he was going to report it, if he only knew to whom to report it. He jumped over the first step. The second step bent forward under his right foot. He was being thrown forward. His left foot was aiming for the third step.

There was no third step.

Nor any fourth step.

His foot hit nothing. The last four steps were not there. His right foot had slid back and become wedged between the first two iron stairs.

It was like a slow-motion movie. He could almost see himself falling and then being brought to an abrupt halt as the two remaining top steps like old friends grabbed hold of his right leg and broke his tumble.

Paul could see the cracked concrete three floors below him. It was that first step that was a killer.

He looked back up toward his right leg. His heel was caught under that rickety top stair. God, he should have made that report to someone. Anyone. His leg was wedged between the only two remaining stairs and he was hanging by that one overly thick leg. He tried frantically to grab the frame with his right hand. He attempted to grasp on to the sharp metallic edge, and it tore a deep gash in his palm.

He had to grab something.

But what?

And with what?

His right palm was macerated.

The other railing. That was it. The other railing with his left hand.

He had to try. It wasn't going to be easy. He swung his left arm up and back in a slow, agonizing arch. He had to hurry. He had to be careful. He didn't want to slice up his left hand too. The railing was almost within his reach.

Just an inch away.

Less than that.

He felt it with his fingertips.

It felt good.

He made it. His left hand seized the side of the stairway. The surface was sharp against his palm, but it had not broken through his skin this time.

He looked down again. It didn't look any closer. Or any more inviting. All that was between him and . . . He didn't want to think about that. His right leg stuck between two rusty old stairs dating back almost to the Great Chicago Fire and his left hand painfully grasping a sharp edge of steel were all that there was.

If only that first stair holds out. Come on, baby. This is no time to call it quits. His heart was pounding violently somewhere between his chest and his throat. His head was pounding just as viciously. His right leg was killing him. His own weight was crushing his shin against the rough and ungiving metal surface. He could feel it cutting into him further and further. He could sense his bone being dented. His right palm was throbbing. He could see the torn skin and the ripped muscles. The short adductor of the thumb was nearly severed. He'd never throw another curve.

The blood oozed out of the gaping gash and formed a thin rivulet down his forefinger and then a continuous series of drips into the seeming oblivion below him. He was not sure how much longer he could support himself. Not long. His left shoulder was sending out distress signals of its own. More than mere pain. It was about to burst out of its socket. His knee was being stretched beyond enduring. Now he understood all those Jews who had converted on the rack.

As long as his leg and that stair held out he would not fall. The concrete would remain three stories below him. He flexed the fingers of his right hand. They still worked. The thumb didn't, but the fingers did.

With his injured right hand Paul tried to reach the near side of the railing to which the stairs had so very recently been firmly attached. He was not sure how well he could grasp it with that torn hand. He had to try. Any small bit of relief that he could give his left hand and his left shoulder would be a blessing. As soon as he shifted his weight, he knew he had made a mistake. A terrible mistake. The first stair began to pull upward, and at the same instant, the second metal slat started to slip forward. The combination of movements decreased the pressure on his shin. That pressure had been holding him, saving him. He was yanked abruptly forward by his own weight. That was it. It was all over. And he knew it. He could feel the concrete getting closer. He could see himself hurtling forward. Forward and downward.

The journey would be a short one.

It was. Shorter than he had expected. No more than a brief eternity. The gash in his shin ripped down toward his ankle. It stopped. Paul stopped. His heel once again became lodged in between the two slats of steel. He had traveled no more than an inch and a half. That was enough. The deep gouge in his leg was now an inch and a half longer and deeper. The rusty black iron was digging right into his naked bone.

He was glad he couldn't see what was happening to his leg. The inch-and-a-half journey had done more than destroy his shin. The strain on his left shoulder was now overwhelming. His shoulder was being pulled further and further out of its overextended joint. His balance was more precarious than it had been before. Much more precarious. He was forced to twist his back more sharply to try to relieve the pressure on his shoulder and his left hand.

He tried not to look down into the abyss below him, but it was more difficult to try to hold his head up than it was to let it drop. It took too much effort. He let his head fall. And it was impossible to close his eyes.

In that position it was ever so easy to watch his blood as it dripped out of his right palm.

From his right thenar eminence.

From the short adductor of his thumb.

He could see each individual drop as it fell off his hand.

He could not see the drops as they struck the floor three floors below him. He imagined that he could. What he could see were the dark spots formed by his own blood there below him, slowly enlarging.

The sensation from his right leg was now much more intense than any pain he had ever heard any patient describe to him. It seared into his brain. It felt as if someone had his leg in a great metal vise and was trying to forge a new knee joint halfway between his old one and his ankle. The pain was threatening his consciousness. The pain and the never-ending pounding in his ears.

He wondered if that was the kind of noise that Donna Kolloway had had in her head all of her life.

A constant, unrelenting blasting.

Did Gerri's head pound like that?

It was enough to drive you crazy.

He had to do something.

Anything.

But what?

There was one thing he could do.

If he was careful.

Ever so slowly he began to move his left leg. So far it had been dangling freely in the void, pulling him downward. Just so much deadweight. Now he was going to put it to good use. He had to.

Inch after agonizing inch, with the same terrible slowness that characterized the movements of the slowest parkinsonian he had ever treated, Paul raised his left leg.

He was succeeding.

His left foot was touching his right knee.

He could not see it happening.

His left foot could feel it.

His right knee could not. Its ability to feel anything was aborted by the pain coming from his shin as it was being crushed against the rough steel of the lower stair. The pain it generated was making him forget the tom-tom beating inside his skull.

Keep it slow, he told himself.

Inch by inch.

His left foot slid along his right calf until his toe reached his right ankle. Slow motion merged into a series of individual frozen frames. His toe had reached his instep. He prayed that his movements would not further weaken that top stair. He tried to remember if he had noticed any deterioration over the last few years. He couldn't remember. The pain and the pounding had erased his memory.

It seemed to be working. It was working. Both of his heels were now caught in the same vise. The pressure on his right shin decreased. It was now merely unbearable. The pain was now shooting through both of his legs, but it was less intense, less consuming. He could once again feel the pounding of his heart. It was a welcome sensation. His consciousness was no longer threatened by the terrible pain. He would be able to hold out longer. And think better.

Was it worth it to make another try? His right hand was getting numb and it was further away from the support than it had been when he had torn it. The numbness scared him. His hand felt like a senseless hunk of wood, like something dead. Still, it was worth one more try. It had to work.

He tried.

He didn't succeed.

He was just too damn heavy. He never should have had that Entenmann's doughnut. Nor a hundred others.

He had to think. He looked at the frame where he had ripped his right palm open. He had sliced his hand on the sharp edge of a support rod. On the very recently cut sharp edge. The marks of the saw blade were not as fresh as the piece of his skin and muscle that were stuck to it, but damn near. It reminded him of an image. The bloody strands of hair on the fireplace in the Rue Morgue. The Rue Morgue of Frank McCormick's twisted mind.

Then he remembered—that stair had not been getting any looser. Not a bit. Not in the last half-dozen years. He could remember that much clearly.

When had he last used that staircase? Two days ago. It had been fine then. Had someone been following him? Someone who knew that he was the only one who ever used this fire escape? Someone who wanted to kill him and make it look like an accident? Who, he wondered, knew his habits? Anyone who knew the medical center and had bothered to tail him for a few days.

A new message was beginning to bombard his brain. It was from his left hand. It too was now bleeding. There was a constant trickle of blood rolling down his wrist, past his watchband. But it was not the blood that his brain registered; it was the pain. The thick skin of the palm of his hand was being sliced open by the sharp knifelike edge that he was holding as tightly as he could.

He looked at his watch.

It was only three minutes after ten.

That was one hell of a time to die.

And he would make one hell of a splatter when he fell.

What would the force be?

$E = MC$ squared. Wrong formula.

$F = M$ times A.

Mass times acceleration.

Too damn much mass.

His legs were becoming numb. There was pain from both of them now. And it was killing him.

Anybody who knew him knew that he had always taken these stairs when he made rounds on Saturday. Hell, the only other shortcut was locked on weekends. His head was full of pain and pounding. He could hardly think straight.

Who knew he was making rounds today?

Bud. It had been his idea in the first place.

The whole department. Everyone on the research team.

Gerri.

Frank. He could have found out from Gerri if he had done anything to her.

That was getting him nowhere. It was insane. He wasn't even certain that anything had happened to Gerri.

Once again he tried to grab onto something with his right hand. He didn't even come close.

His left hand was slipping.

He tried not to think about Carolyn and Joshua. It didn't help. They filled what little was left of his consciousness. They and Gerri. Maybe she would help take care of them. Unless something had happened to her too. Unless one by one someone was knocking them off.

It must have been a trap. No one else ever came this way. It was his private fire escape. A trap. Set by whom?

Paul's hand was getting weaker. The pain that was centered there was being replaced by a worse feeling: complete numbness. It would not hold on much longer.

And the first step seemed to be shifting.

He could just barely make out his watch. It was becoming covered with blood.

Seven after ten.

He had been hanging there for only nine minutes. He could hardly feel either of his feet.

Nine minutes.

How much longer?

Not another nine minutes.

All he had going for him was one numb hand.

Who?

Bud. It had been his idea. He knew about Jackie's letter. How? From Chris? That's what he had claimed. Paul had meant to ask Chris but he never had. It was too late now. Had he killed her to keep her from writing that letter? And how had he set this up?

Not Bud.

Frank?

Would he have known enough about his shortcuts?

Who else could it have been?

John?

Herb?

Don? Shaky Don Lenhardt?

He heard a noise.

He immediately knew what it was.

The door above him was being yanked open.

He heard it creak.

It was his stairway.

His fire escape.

No one used it but him.

And the killer.

Who?

He'd find out soon enough.

The door sprang open.

17

"**P**aul!"
It was a voice he had heard before. A voice he knew. It was shouting his name. But whose voice was it?

He couldn't place it. All the pounding and pain inside his head prevented any recognition.

"Paul!"

The voice was louder now and shriller. Almost violent. But it wasn't threatening. It was familiar. His head was pounding too furiously. He couldn't remember the voice.

"Paul!"

Bud. It was Bud's voice.

Bud Chiari.

Not Bud. Of all people. Anyone else.

"Bud. I can't hold out much longer."

"How . . . ?" Bud realized this was not the time to ask any questions.

"Not any longer."

Bud held on to the hand railing and slowly edged his way toward Paul's hand. It only took forever until he got there. He reached down and grabbed Paul's left wrist with his right hand. Paul saw Bud's hand circle his wrist. He knew Bud was holding him but he felt nothing. He saw Bud start to pull his hand away from the edge. Was this how it was going to end? Paul tried to clench his fist more tightly to the metal railing. He couldn't. He saw the fingers begin to slip. "Paul, let go of the railing and hold on to my wrist."

Paul did not have much choice. His left hand was so numb it had become frozen into a claw. He would do whatever Bud told him to do. If only Bud could stop his pain. And the pounding.

Bud.

It couldn't be Bud who had set this trap and now had come to finish him off. Not Bud. No. Not that.

It didn't matter. Paul could resist no longer. He had to do whatever Bud said. There was no other option.

Paul told his left hand to open.

It did. Ever so slowly. His hand was no longer a claw. It was free of the railing. The numbness was still there and Bud was now holding him up by the wrist.

"I'm going to pull you up. Help shift your weight. You should end up kneeling on that stair. Here goes."

Bud pulled on Paul's wrist. Paul could only barely feel the pressure of his grip. He tried to help.

It was hard. His left hand was still numb. His legs felt dead. His head was heavy with blood and throbbing. His left shoulder felt half out of its socket. He threw his head and shoulders back. His knees were bending. The first stair was giving way. He could feel it moving. He could hear the metal creaking.

It wasn't going to work. He knew it wouldn't. He could see his blood splattered three floors below him. And it was still dripping—drop after drop.

Paul felt as if his shoulder was going to pop out completely. If he could only arch his back . . . The vertebrae ached but they moved.

Bud yanked again. Paul could feel the pressure.

Bud yanked a third time. Again Paul tried to arch his back. It was such a slow process. No parkinsonian patient had ever moved so slowly and survived. He had to do it. They had to succeed. Dammit. They had to.

They did.

Paul was up. He was on his knees on the second stair.

Bud stayed on the railing.

"Can you stand up?"

"I don't know. I don't think so."

"Try."

"I don't know. I'm just happy to be here. What a relief not

to be staring down." He looked at his right palm. The wound was still bleeding and the mutilated muscles bulged out at him. Gingerly he rotated his left shoulder. It moved, first slowly, then easily. The pounding was decreasing. The pain from his shins was not as all-consuming. He could almost think.

"Bud, what are you doing here?"

"I was in the lab checking something out and I decided to make rounds and let you go home. I looked for you at the office and then I called the floor. You weren't there yet so I came this way to catch up with you."

His left hand was no longer dead. He started to palpate his shins with it. First the right one. "Thank God you did."

"Let's get you up into the hall. Then to the ER."

"That sounds good to me."

Bud edged up the railing to the doorway and pushed the door open. "Can you make it?" he asked.

"To the hall, yes. To the ER, I don't know."

"You get to the hall and I'll get you to the ER in a wheelchair."

"Fair enough."

"Let's go." With that Bud took hold of Paul's wrists and half-lifted him into the building.

The X rays were all negative. Nothing was broken. Nothing was even dislocated. They dressed his legs and sutured his right hand. His left hand required nothing more than a couple of Band-Aids. All told, it took about an hour. Most of the time was spent in X Ray, waiting. By the time he was patched up, Bud had finished rounds.

"Next time you don't want to make rounds, you don't have to be this dramatic; just tell me. I'll be happy to cover for you. Even on a Saturday," Bud told him.

Paul was able to smile. "Thanks for the offer. I'll remember it."

"I'm sure you will."

Paul's mind was perfectly clear now. There was very little pounding. Only the pain remained, and that no longer completely occupied his entire brain. "Bud, I didn't think you were coming in today. I'm glad as hell you did, but weren't you going to take the weekend off?"

"I still am. I just came in to check one thing in the lab. You remember the second Metrazol test I did on Maurie Rath?"

"Yes."

"Well, I was thinking about it at breakfast this morning and it still didn't seem right. So I came in and got the Metrazol from EEG, the same vial, and tested it on some rats in the lab."

"And what happened?"

"Nothing."

"How much did you give them?"

"Four times the convulsant dose," Bud told him.

"That should have killed them."

"It didn't. In fact it didn't faze them at all."

"No seizures?"

"No nothing."

"Maybe it was too old."

"The expiration date is next December."

"It must have gotten oxidized or something," Paul said.

"The fluid is still clear and colorless."

"Did you taste it?" Paul asked.

"No."

"Do you still have it with you?"

"Yes."

Bud gave the vial to Paul. Paul had the nurses bring him a syringe. He punctured the rubber top of the multiple-injection bottle, removed a small amount of fluid from it, and squirted it on his finger. He then raised his finger to his mouth and tested it gingerly.

"Metrazol is bitter. This isn't. It's not bitter at all. There was no Metrazol in that vial."

"No wonder Mr. Rath didn't have any change on his EEG. The bottle must have been mislabled."

"Hi, Doc."

"Tom, what are you doing here?"

"I came to see a friend in the ER."

"Who?"

"You."

"How did—?" Paul interrupted his own question. It was obvious. The hospital security people had been told about his accident and they must have notified the police or maybe even Tom directly.

"I took a look at the fire escape. You took a nasty tumble. You were damned lucky not to have gotten yourself killed."

"I know. Thank God Bud came by."

"The rungs were cut very recently," the detective said.

"I took that fire escape on Wednesday and it was fine," Paul told him.

"There was no official work order to repair it, but we still haven't located the maintenance crew in charge of such things. They're all out fishing someplace in Wisconsin. Do many other people use that shortcut?"

"No. Nobody but me and Bud once in a while."

"That's what the security guys told me."

"Did somebody do that intentionally?" Bud asked.

"Perhaps," Tom responded noncommittally.

"Frank McCormick!" Paul said.

"What?" Bud asked. He seemed surprised. Tom didn't.

"It has to be him," Paul said. "There is no other explanation." He went on ignoring the obvious fact that Bud would have trouble following him. "Gerri Scala is missing. I've been trying to get hold of her since early last night. I've left a dozen messages. She's gone. And then I have this accident. She told me about Frank's dreams and I told you. You picked him up and let him go. He's smart enough to know what happened. It must be him."

"Slow down, Paul," Tom said.

Paul had also gone too fast for him. Paul took his time and explained it all. They both understood.

"You could be right," Tom agreed. "We'll pick him up again. But just because Dr. Scala didn't return your phone calls doesn't mean she's missing. You can't jump to that conclusion."

"You may be right about that," Paul conceded. "Still, I'd feel better if you checked out her apartment."

"I will, Doc."

"And call me."

"Where will you be?" Tom asked.

"At home."

"They want to admit you overnight," Bud said, interrupting their dialogue.

"Nope, I'm going home."

"I was sure you would. They wanted to put you in the same room with Rotblatt."

"Is he in for more chemotherapy?"

"Yes."

"The poor guy."

Bud just nodded.

"I'm going home. First I'm going to go by Gerri's office."

"Why?"

"Maybe she came in this morning. I don't know. Then I'm going home."

"By the way, I brought you a get-well-soon present," Tom informed him.

"You did?"

"Yes. A book to read."

Paul understood. Jackie's diary. Tom gave Paul a plain brown envelope. It was the perfect wrapping.

It hurt to walk but he wasn't going to stay at the hospital. Not with the kids at home by themselves. Bud walked with him. They took the long way. No more shortcuts. Not today.

Gerri was not in her office. Paul let himself in and found her appointment book. She had canceled all the patients who had been scheduled for that morning. Her process notes were on her desk. He took them. It would give him something else to read.

Paul didn't realize how much he hurt and in how many different places until he sat down in his car. And then there was nothing to do until he got home. The drive took thirty-one agonizing minutes. It was an average Saturday afternoon with virtually no traffic. Twenty-four miles and one stoplight in thirty-one long minutes.

He tried putting on WFMT but nothing sounded good. His head had completely stopped pounding by the time he hit North Avenue. So that was how Donna Kolloway had gone through life, with a constant sensation in her head. Now she could listen to music. No wonder the Exploding Plastic Zeppelin sounded good to her. He tried again. Vivaldi. So ordered. So controlled. He could hear each note. No cacophony but enough forward motion and variation to sustain interest.

Thank God for an automatic shift. His legs were so sore he knew he could not have used a clutch. Cruise control was a

further blessing. Gerri also had a noise in her head. Not all
the time, but sometimes. A gentle swishing sound she had
told him. Where was she? She could have gone away for the
weekend. She had done that the last time they had had an
argument. She had canceled her patients and disappeared.
And he had turned to Jackie.

He was at the junction. Vivaldi was over. He hoped they
would play some more. Or some Bach. An early Haydn
symphony began. Close enough. This was not the time for a
Strauss tone poem and certainly not Mahler or Shostakovich.
Heaven forbid.

His head was beginning to ache. It was the only pain that
was steady. The others all beat like kettledrums, like the giant
bass drum of the Purdue marching band. That drum had once
belonged to the University of Chicago when they still played
football and Jay Berwanger had won the first Heisman trophy.

Highland Park. The one traffic light. It was red. He waited.
He pulled off the highway, executed a couple of turns, and he
was home.

Carolyn and Joshua were on the front lawn playing catch
and waiting for him.

He eased the car into the driveway and turned off the
ignition. He opened the door and struggled to pivot his body
out of the seat. His legs seemed frozen in place. As he got out
of the car, he saw Carolyn's smile fade. Her eyes opened
wide, her mouth began to move.

She screamed.

Joshua screamed.

What the hell was happening?

They were frozen in place with screams of terror on their
lips. Both of them. It couldn't be the beginning of another
seizure. Both of them were screaming. They couldn't both be
having seizures. Why were they standing there like that? And
those looks. Why?

It was Joshua who ran toward his father and fractured the
tableau. "Dad. What happened? Are you okay?"

Paul looked at himself. His pants were torn and covered
with blood. His left shirt sleeve was also blood-splattered.
His right hand was heavily bandaged.

"I'm fine. I really am. I just . . . fell down a couple of
steps. I'm fine. Like my grandfather's brother." It was a very

old family joke, one of his favorites. No one laughed. But the three of them were as one, hugging each other.

"Help me into the house. I'm stiff. My legs don't want to move."

He put one arm around each of them and let them guide him toward the door.

"You remember my grandfather's story. He was one of four brothers. All of them were named Susskolnick except one, who was named Fine. At Ellis Island when he got off the boat, they asked who he was. He thought they were asking him how he was. So he said, "Fine," and they put it down. So his name became Fine."

They had remembered the story; it was no more successful for the retelling. They didn't laugh.

Paul virtually collapsed as soon as he got into the house, sprawling on the couch in the family room. Joshua brought him a glass of water and he took two of the Percodans they had given him in the ER. There was a baseball game on TV. It was the Cubs, but they decided to watch it. It was the third inning. The Cubs were down 4–2. Buckner was up with a man on second. Buckner singled to right. The runner rounded third and headed for home. That was the last thing Paul rememered. Good old Billy Buck.

"Dad."

Paul heard Joshua calling him.

"Dad."

Paul also felt Joshua shaking his shoulder. At first he had a hard time remembering where he was. Now he knew what his patients felt like right after a seizure. What Carolyn . . .

"Dad."

The TV was off. Paul looked at it and remembered. "Was Bowa safe?"

"What?"

"At home. Did he score on Buckner's single?"

"I don't remember. That was a couple of hours ago. You've been sleeping. We let you sleep. We've been checking on you every fifteen minutes. There's a phone call for you."

"From Gerri?"

"No. A Mr. Ward."

Paul jumped up to get the phone. His knees buckled and he fell back on the couch. He felt as if he had been hit by a sledgehammer and it was still bouncing repeatedly off his legs and the back of his head. The pain and pounding became one.

Joshua brought him the phone. The cord just reached the couch.

"How are you, Doc?"

"I've felt better. A lot better. What did you find out about Gerri?"

"She didn't have any patients this morning. She canceled them all."

"That I knew. I checked her appointment book."

"She usually did see a couple of patients every Saturday unless she had special plans or something."

That Paul also knew.

"I went to her apartment. She never picked up yesterday's mail or this morning's newspaper. If she slept in the bed, she changed the sheets and took the dirty ones with her."

"She's missing," Paul said. "Something happened to her. I knew it. Somebody is out to get us all." He was acting as paranoid as Frank McCormick.

"Wait a minute, Doc. Nobody was out to get you."

"I suppose someone cut through those rungs by accident."

"No, that was done on purpose. We talked to the work crew about an hour ago. It seems the fire inspector had suggested that something be done with that stairway, and the sooner the better, so they started to work on it yesterday. They knew that nobody used the passageway except you and they knew you never came in on weekends anymore. The new stairs would be in first thing on Monday. And besides, the old warning signs were still up."

"And they couldn't lock the door because of the fire code."

"Right again, Doc."

"What a hell of a way to run a hospital."

"One other thing. Dr. Scala may be in Wisconsin. We found the numbers of some motels in Door County scribbled on a pad near her bed."

"Did you call them?"

"We did. No Scalas registered but there were a lot of Chicagoans named Smith. John Smiths and Jane Smiths. In varying combinations."

"What about Frank McCormick?"

"He wasn't home or at the halfway house last night. According to his father, his behavior hasn't been any different in the last couple of days."

"I don't trust either that kid or his father," Paul reminded him.

"I know that."

"And I know he did something to Gerri. I'm sure of it. I can taste it."

"I've got to get back to work. Take care of yourself."

Paul lowered himself back onto the couch. He wanted some more Percodan. It had only been two hours. He knew that he should wait at least another hour. Tom was probably correct. Nothing had happened to Gerri. She had merely rescheduled her patients and gone off somewhere by herself. He began to doze off again. The phone rang in his ear. Its ring felt like a dagger piercing his eardrum. It magnified both his pounding and his pain. He felt for the phone. It was just beyond his reach. Each ring seemed louder, more painful. Paul bent and picked up the receiver.

"Hello," he gasped.

"Paul, is that you?"

"Yes."

"It's Bud."

"Bud," Paul realized.

"Are you okay?"

"Yes."

That was all Bud wanted to know. They both hung up. Paul could not wait any longer. He didn't want to get up. Where were the kids? He listened. They were upstairs. Joshua said they came down once every fifteen minutes. He couldn't take it for another fifteen minutes.

He tried to figure out which was worse, the knife in his ear or the sledgehammer. The sledgehammer, he decided. The continuing boom of the hammer.

He picked up the phone and dialed their other number.

One ring.

Two.

Answer it.

Three.

The sound bounced around his head.

"Hello."

"Carolyn."

"Dad! Where are you?"

"On the couch."

"Are you okay?"

"I need something to drink so I can take some pills."

"I'll be right there."

Click.

She brought him some orange juice. He took two more Percodans. "Who called just now?" she asked.

"Your doctor."

"Dr. Chiari. I like him."

"He's a good doctor and a better friend." Carolyn sat down next to him and he told her what Tom had learned about Gerri. There was no reason to make her a victim of his paranoia. Gerri was probably somewhere in Wisconsin taking a weekend off. Carolyn didn't seem entirely convinced. He also told her a little bit about his accident and how Bud had saved his life.

"It's a good thing he was there," she said.

He smiled and finished his orange juice.

"Would you like some more? It's really good. The last bottle we had was spoiled and bitter but this is fresh."

"Yes, I would."

It certainly was a good thing that Bud had been there. A good thing that the Metrazol had been mislabeled, that Bud had been so compulsive. That . . . that . . . He remembered the orange juice dripping off the table. Bitter orange juice. Bitter . . . Like Metrazol. It couldn't be.

She had had a single seizure.

Who could have put something into that orange juice? Anyone who had been in their house at that meeting. Anyone but Frank McCormick.

"Carolyn!" Where was she?

She was back. "Here I am."

"When was the orange juice bitter?"

"On Monday, before I had my seizure."

"Right before."

"Yes."

"Did Joshua drink any?"

"No. He doesn't like orange juice. You know that, Dad. You and I are the only orange-juice drinkers."

"I know."

"Is everything all right?"

"Yes, I'm just going to rest."

"Call me if you need anything."

"I will."

Bitter orange juice. That eliminated Frank McCormick. Bitter orange juice. Bitter from Metrazol. Metrazol aimed at him. They all knew he liked orange juice. He drank it at every research meeting.

Why? That he didn't know.

Who? Someone who was here for that meeting. Who was here? He had a little trouble remembering who had been to his house that night. His mind was still working slowly.

He went over the list. One by one.

Dean Willis.

Don Lenhardt.

Floyd Baker.

John Corrigan.

Herb Adams.

The lawyers Connors and Terwilliger. He tried to recall if he'd had orange juice that night. He hadn't. Carolyn had served coffee.

And Gerri.

The lawyers didn't count. That left six suspects. No five. Not Gerri.

But why?

Was he getting too close to something? But what?

The Percodan wasn't helping. He lay back. The *1812 Overture* was playing in his head. With the University of Michigan Marching Band prancing on his shins, playing "Hail to the Victors."

He closed his eyes.

Was Lenhardt that afraid Paul would find out about his relapse into drugs?

Could Herb have done it to hide some lab error?

Herb and John screwing up in the lab.

Or John just plain screwing, taking advantage of his open marriage.

But was it really that open?

Paul just had John's word for it.

Was it all tied together? The Percodan seemed to be having

more effect on his mind than on the pain. His thoughts moved in slow motion. It must be part of the murder. Whoever killed Jackie must have poisoned that orange juice to distract him. He had to be getting too close to something. But what?

They each had a motive to kill Jackie. She knew about Don Lenhardt's excursions into drugs, about Bud and Bill and John and the missing charts, about Herb's lab error, and about Gerri and Jackie. And then there was always Floyd. Floyd. Floyd and Edie. Two separate eternal triangles which converged on Jackie. Edie had not been here. Nor had Bill Goodman. Nor Bud Chiari.

The music was getting softer. There was less bass, less percussion. It didn't sound like marching music anymore. Just two orchestras playing different Rossini overtures. One was the *William Tell*. The other was not one he recognized.

It was amazing what he had learned from that bitter taste. A taste without an odor.

Frank McCormick. Hadn't he smelled things? And not just in his dreams. What had Gerri told him? He should have paid more attention. Seizures sometimes began with an unpleasant odor or a bad taste. He did have her process notes. They were in the car.

He called Carolyn. He told her about the notes that he wanted from the car. She brought them to him.

He was beginning to feel better. The Percodan was working now. He started at the back and worked his way toward the front, until he reached the day of Jackie's death. It was hard to believe that it had happened only a little over two weeks ago. He turned to the next page. It was headed F.M. He began to read. It was that first dream. The one from *Murders in the Rue Morgue*. Then came another dream. Then the complaint that his brain was rotting, that he could smell it. He read on. It was all perfectly clear. Frank was right: the surgery had made him worse, but not in the way he thought. He wasn't crazier than he had been two years ago. If he were he couldn't have carried out such a grand scheme. No, his schizophrenia had not been made worse. That was not the problem at all. His schizophrenia was probably better, but in its place he had a new problem: temporal-lobe seizures. A peculiar smell followed by interruption of consciousness. Epileptic attacks beginning in the temporal lobe where they had put the implant. Why? Paul was not sure. A surgical error? Perhaps. Growth of the implant? Maybe. An unavoidable surgical scar? Or a surgical injury caused by the trembling hand of a surgeon in the late stages of some addiction? They would have to reexamine Frank. EEG's. CAT scans, the whole works. He needed to be on anticonvulsants.

That changed everything.

Or did it? Frank had lied about his dreams, and about signing the informed consent. Perhaps the seizures had frightened him. Had driven him to act out and kill Jackie. No. That sort of thing didn't happen.

Perhaps he should call Tom and tell him that Frank's problem was no longer schizophrenia, that he hadn't killed Jackie in some insane rage.

After Paul read the process notes for Gerri's last session with Frank, he was glad he had not called Tom. He hated changing his mind. Maybe McCormick's dreams were made up of things he had read, but they were all adapted and his adaptations were all tinged with violence, lust, insanity, and just plain old-fashioned craziness. It was all there in the last session. Hatred, violence, paranoia. Maybe he hadn't killed Jackie, but he sure as hell could have done something to Gerri. And Paul cared a hell of a lot more about that.

Paul picked up the phone and dialed the hospital.

"Austin Flint Medical Center."

"This is Dr. Richardson. Can I have Dr. Rotblatt's room?"

"One moment, please."

He waited. The phone began to ring. "Hello."

"Mel."

"Yes."

"Paul Richardson."

"Hello, Paul."

"I have to talk to you about Gerri."

"Paul, she's my patient. I can't talk to you about our sessions. You know that."

"This is important. I have to find out something that might have been said yesterday."

"Paul, I can't. It's not ethical."

"I don't give a damn about ethics. This is no theoretical issue. This may be a matter of life and death."

"I can't," the psychiatrist said.

"You must."

"We seem to have reached an impasse," Mel said, and then continued, "Paul, I know you wouldn't have asked this if you didn't think it was very important. I'd like to help you out if I could without violating her confidence or privacy, but I don't see how—"

Paul interrupted him. "Can I just ask you one question?"

"Perhaps," the psychiatrist said.

"All you have to do is answer it yes or no if you possibly can."

"I can't promise I can answer it. But I'll try."

"That's all I can ask." Paul wasn't sure where to start. Mel needed to understand the issue. It was such a simple question. He told him about McCormick and then about Gerri's behavior on Thursday and her subsequent disappearance. He asked his one question. "Do you think Gerri would have left town this weekend without calling me?"

There was no answer.

"Can't you answer that question?"

Again the psychiatrist hesitated.

"Mel, for God's sake."

"I can answer your question, Paul, and I will. But I don't want to be too hasty. Our last session was not a straightforward one."

"Wouldn't she have at least called me or the kids?"

"No."

"No!" Paul hadn't wanted that answer.

"No. Not your kids. Once she might have, but not yesterday."

"And me."

"She would have called you. In fact I'm fairly sure she would have wanted to spend the whole weekend with you, if she'd had the choice. The way our session went, I'm sure of it."

"Thanks, Mel."

"Thank you, Paul."

"For what?"

"At least a dozen of our colleagues have stopped by to see me or called me. You're the only one who made me feel that I could still be useful. Thanks."

"You're welcome."

She would have called him. But she didn't. If Rotblatt was right—and he ought to know his own patient—she might well have canceled her patients. But it would have been done to be with him, not to avoid him. Where was she? Where had she gone when she left the hospital. Had she even left the hospital? Was she still at the hospital? There was no evidence she had gone home. He had to go back to the hospital to look for himself. It was easier than lying there and worrying.

He checked. He had plenty of Percodan. He got up. It was easier than he thought it would be. He would take two more, change clothes, and drive back to the hospital. He hoped the traffic would still be light.

─── 18 ───

He made it. He had gotten as far as the parking lot. Now that he was there, Paul was no longer confident that it had been such a good idea. It was not the pain that was forcing him to rethink his decision. That, much to his surprise, was under fairly good control. Nor was it the throbbing. The pounding sensation of his own exaggerated pulse moving throughout his body had returned once again, but only as a constant low-level background beat. Nor had he rethought the issue. He still wanted to look for Gerri. The problem was that he had no idea at all where he should start his search. As he sat there in the lot, Paul could not remember a single detail of his half-hour-long drive into the medical center. Thirty minutes of his life were missing without a trace. He could not even recall what music he had heard, though he had a vague notion that he had been humming along with it. How could a man who could not clearly reconstruct the last half-hour even hope to find someone who'd been missing more than twenty-four hours?

He'd already made one error—he had parked his car in the wrong place. His usual parking space near the old Herrick Building that housed the Neurology Department was not where he should be. He drove his car through the nearly empty lot to a spot near the somewhat less ancient psychiatry facility. Gerri had been there on Friday afternoon. In her own office and in Rotblatt's. This was the best starting place. She had actually been there. When he got out of the car, he staggered. His instability startled him. It had been easy to forget what he had been through while sitting in his car and humming his way along the Kennedy Expressway. His legs were stiff and wobbly. His knees ached. His shins were sending out intermittent flashes of pain. He wasn't twenty-five anymore, he reminded himself. Hell, at twenty-five he had not been in shape to tolerate what he had been through. He staggered for a few more steps; then it became easier, and he was able to walk without resembling a rejected derelict from West Madison admitted to Austin Flint for alcoholic degeneration of the brain. Some fresh blood appeared on the left leg of his slacks, staining the fabric a couple of inches below his knee. The gash in his leg had silently begun to bleed again. It didn't hurt any more than it had before he got out of the car; it was merely bleeding.

Fortunately the door to Psychiatry was not locked. Paul pushed it open. There was a security guard at the desk reading a magazine. He never even broke his concentration as Paul hobbled past.

Penthouse or *Hustler*? Paul wondered.

Gerri's office was locked. He had left it that way. It was also dark. Paul automatically reached into his pocket. Had he remembered to take his key ring with the key to her office? He had. He let himself into her office and turned on the light. It was very still in the office and extremely empty. Her desk was in its usual place. So were her plants. And the chairs. And the couch. He was glad to see her couch. He suddenly felt exhausted and half-fell, half-collapsed onto it. That was as good a place as any.

Where should he start?

Where should he look?

Where would he be if he were a thirty-four-year-old blond, sexy, female psychiatrist who was afraid that a patient might try to rape her? Or murder her? Or both?

What would he do? It didn't take him very long to answer that question. He knew precisely what he would do. He wouldn't have fled to the hinterlands of Wisconsin, to some secluded place which was only a refuge in the mind of the pursued. He wouldn't have tried to avoid himself. Just the opposite. He would have talked to that one person in the medical center who knew the most about that patient's problem. The one who really understood the experimental surgery that had been performed on Frank McCormick. That was Paul Richardson. He'd have gone to talk to himself. When? As soon as he could have. Gerri had seen Frank in the morning. She had tried to call him after that but they had kept missing each other all day long. Then she had had that long appointment with Rotblatt. Had she had any appointments after that? Where was her appointment book? It was on her desk. He could see it from the couch.

It was only four steps away. He hesitated.

It was worth it. He got up and walked over to her desk. It was easier that time. The book was still open to Saturday. He turned back one page. M.R. was written in from 2:30 to 4:30 and after that there were no entries. If he was right, Gerri should have started out for his office at about 4:30. But did she? There were other issues between them. Maybe Rotblatt was wrong. It wouldn't be the first time a shrink had been wrong. Gerri could have gone to Wisconsin. She had done that before when they had had an argument. Maybe she had fled more from him than from her patient. That way she might feel that she would be safely away from both Frank and him.

No. She might well have run away from him. That was possible. But not from her patient. She was too damn good a doctor to do that.

She would have done the same thing he would have done.

And he would have run, not walked. After all, it was Friday, and on Friday he tried to leave as early as he could. Gerri knew that. Paul would have gotten his ass over to Neurology as fast as he could. He would have taken that old passageway and then gone through the tunnel. That was by far the fastest way from Rotblatt's office to his. That's how he would have done it. But would Gerri? She knew about that passage. He had shown her through it himself. More than once. Security never checked it. They were too busy reading *Hustler*. To them it was just another of the hospital's unused byways dating back to some unknown time in the dim past.

That was the place to start. He knew it. He looked at his leg. The bleeding had stopped. He hoped that she was in Wisconsin fishing or doing anything. With the whole damn repair crew that had gone fishing. All of them. Even that would be better than what he was afraid he would find.

Before he could find her, Paul had to make another choice.

There were two ways to get from Gerri's office to Rotblatt's. Both were well-traveled. Normally Paul took the stairs. Not this time. He took the elevator. He had to save whatever little strength and stamina he had left. Once he reached Rotblatt's closed office his pace quickened. His left shin was bleeding once more. He could feel the blood trickling down his leg. His head banged away in time with his throbbing legs and pounding heart. He went down the narrow corridor to the left. The emergency door was closed, as it should be. The "Do Not Enter" and "Use Only in an Emergency" signs were both in place. As always he ignored them. For once it might actually be an emergency. There were no new signs. Hopefully there had been no one cutting rungs off these stairs.

The door opened easily. That was a good sign. He started down the stairs. Each time either leg hit a metal step, a sharp pain shot up his leg, jolting him. They were worse on the left than on the right. The irregular blasts of pain added a syncopation to the steady kettledrum beat in his head. Bands were playing two separate symphonies in his brain. Shostakovich and Mahler. And they were both being played quadruple fortissimo. He stopped in his tracks. He could feel the blood collecting inside his left sock. There had to be a better way. There was. He turned sideways on the narrow staircase. He'd do it one step at a time. Paul stood with both feet on the same stair. Then slowly he lowered his right foot to the next black iron stair, taking care to put it down as cautiously as he could. Once his right foot was stable, he brought his left foot down to meet it with a motion that made his first move seem fast by comparison.

Each step was negotiated in the same manner.

One at a time.

The throb of the Mahler was fading.

The first flight was above him.

Only the Shostakovich was left—a slow movement.

One down. Three to go.

It hadn't been such a brilliant idea. He hadn't found her.

The second flight was easier. He had enough sense this time to start sideways.

The entire flight took him only a couple of minutes.

Two down. Two to go.

Paul stood on the rusty landing and peered down the next

flight of stairs. The next landing was virtually lost in dim shadows. The light was out. But there was something down there. A form. A shape. He could hardly make it out. His eyes were adjusting to the darkness.

Feet.

Legs.

Thighs.

Blood.

Gerri.

Gerri's legs. Pointed up the stairs and covered with blood.

Paul was locked in place. He could see her clearly now. That bastard. It was like a scene from one of his damn nightmares. Borrowed this time from the Marquis de Sade and acted out on Gerri. Her head and shoulders were on the landing. Her legs were splayed lewdly up the stairs. Her left thigh was covered with blood from her knee to her . . .

That SOB. Paul took the stairs two at a time. He felt nothing. The music had stopped.

He had raped her. Blood and sex were the same thing to him.

Paul stared at Gerri.

She was nearly bare.

Her pantyhose had been torn out of the way.

He could see her blond hairs though her thin bikini panties and her own blood.

"She was a real blond."

The sentence ricocheted across his brain. "You bastard," he screamed.

Two more steps and he was on the landing bending over her. He touched her cheek gingerly. It was warm. She was still alive. It was hot. He could see her chest wall move. Paul knew precisely what he had to do next. It was a built-in set of reflexes.

He watched. Her respirations were regular. The soft sound of air moving in and out of her lungs sounded as wonderful as the last movement of Beethoven's Ninth, and more meaningful.

He yelled her name. The sound echoed in the stairwell, bouncing from wall to wall and then reverberating through his head. There was no other response. Gerri said nothing. No response to verbal stimuli.

Her pulse was regular.

Over a hundred, but regluar.

He felt her forehead.

She had a fever. About one-oh-one, he guessed.

He opened her eyes.

Her eyes stared straight ahead, unseeing. They were in the midline where they belonged. The pupils were equal.

He felt in his pockets.

There was no flashlight.

No matches either.

Paul looked into her eyes. They looked more green than gray-blue. They were midline and conjugate.

He moved her head. Doll's-head eye movements were present. Her brain stem was intact.

With his left thumb he felt along the ridge of bone just above her right eye. He found the small notch there where the nerve came out, and he pressed directly down on that small nerve. He pressed as hard as he could. The tip of his thumb blanched. He could feel the pain. So could she. So could she! She groaned. She lifted her right arm.

Coma. Light coma with a wonderfully appropriate response to pain.

Paul tested her other side. Once again his thumb blanched. Once again he felt the pain. And once again Gerri did too. Her left arm went up toward her face and the source of the pain.

It was such a sweet pain.

Normal response to pain bilaterally. There was no evidence of permanent brain damage.

He had to get her to the ER. He didn't want to leave her alone. He was more than just her doctor.

Paul stood up and looked down upon her. Her lower lip was swollen. There was a small amount of blood caked at the corner of her mouth. Had he violated her there too? There was no other blood around her face or her head. Only down there.

Why did he have to rape her?

Paul could not leave her like that.

He took off his sport coat. It was the brown one she had liked so much.

He began to cover up her near-nakedness.

He saw the blood that had collected on her loins. And her blond hairs.

"She was a real blond."

He saw her torn pantyhose. And her bikini panties. Bikini panties. Just like those in Frank's last dream. But something was wrong—she was still wearing her panties. They were still on her, covering her.

McCormick had not raped her. Her pantyhose had not been torn off her in a mad attempt to get at her vagina. The rip started just above her left knee. That was where most of the blood had come from. A gash on her left thigh.

He had not raped her.

Thank God, she had at least been spared that. She wouldn't have to spend the rest of her life reliving that.

But what else had he done to her? What would she have to live with? If she lived.

He had to get help.

He covered her with his jacket. He had to call the ER and then he had to call Tom Ward. Let Tom get that SOB. The murdering bastard.

— 19 —

aul dragged himself to the nearest phone as quickly as he could and dailed the page operator. There was an emergency in the old fire escape outside of two Altrock.

"Where?"

He knew it would be too hard to explain.

"Two Altrock," he said.

"What—?" she started to ask.

"It's one of our doctors."

That was all he had to say. One of the family was in trouble.

He heard the emergency page within seconds.

"Doctor red. Two Altrock.

"Doctor red. Two Altrock.

"Doctor red. Two Altrock."

Three times. That made it a genuine emergency. And three more to be on the safe side. Then: "Anesthesia on call. Two Altrock." Repeated twice more.

"Doctor red," another shrill triplet followed by a call to Cardiology. By the time the operator got back to "Anesthesiology," the troops were arriving in full force. No group of overworked interns and residents had ever looked so good.

"It's Dr. Scala. She's on the fire escape. She's been beaten. She's unconscious. But not raped." Paul knew he wasn't making sense. "Head trauma. Severe. She's in coma, but her brain stem's intact. She's febrile."

"Where?" one of the residents asked.

"Through there," Paul said, and pointed.

"Get a stretcher," the senior resident ordered as he headed through the door.

Paul shuffled after them but waited at the top of the stairs. He was glad he had covered her nakedness with his coat. The scene was bad enough the way it was.

Why hadn't he raped her?

Maybe his gun didn't work. Maybe it only worked in his nightmares.

Two orderlies tore by him with a portable stretcher.

Six men carefully lifted her to the stretcher and then they carried her by Paul to get to the ER. Paul's sport coat was still covering her hips and thighs. Some of her blood had stained it.

No one stopped to say "She'll be all right." This was family. He was one of them, a physician. He knew the score. There was no need for reassuring platitudes. Like hell there wasn't!

Paul tried to keep up with them but couldn't. His legs were too wobbly, his head too full, his shoulder too tender. By the time he got to the ER everyone was busily crowded around her. His coat was no longer draped over her hips. It lay on the floor covered by her torn pantyhose and bloodstained skirt and panties as well as her blouse and bra. A clean hospital gown had been hastily thrown over her and now just barely covered her right hip and thigh. Unclothed and all but uncovered, she was less naked than she had been on that stairwell. The internal-medicine resident was listening to her heart and chest. The general-surgery resident was examining the wound on her thigh. It would need cleaning and a number of stitches. The nurse had hooked her up to an EKG machine and started an IV. "We need blood gases," one of them shouted.

One resident was already drawing some venous samples of blood.

A second resident exposed her groin area and cleaned it, located the femoral artery, and plunged in an arterial needle. Bright red blood filled the tube. "I've got the blood-gas sample," she said. A nurse took them from her.

Paul stood at the foot of the cart and watched the activity. The doctors reported each conclusion and observation to all the others. He was not sure they even knew he was there monitoring their actions.

The Percodan was wearing off. His shins were searing, his head exploding.

"BP one-ten over seventy."

"Pulse ninety-six and regular."

"Her chest sounds bad. She may be infected."

A female voice reported her temperature: "One-oh-one-point-six."

"The leg wound isn't that bad. I'll just clean it and dress it." That was the surgeon. "I can stitch it later."

"We'll have to get a chest X ray and see those blood gases."

"Where the hell is Neurosurgery?"

"The EKG is ready."

"Let me have it." The nurse handed it to him so he could read it. It took him barely twenty seconds. "Nothing here."

"Her abdomen is benign."

"With those bruises we ought to get a skull film as well as a CAT scan."

"Should we catheterize her?"

"Yes."

"Straight stick or indwelling?"

"Indwelling."

"Do we need Gyne to do a pelvic?"

"No."

"He said something about rape."

"She wasn't raped. Her pants were intact."

"Okay."

They were right. He had seen that for himself. Her pantyhose had been ripped in half and virtually torn off her legs but her brief, thin panties had been left untouched.

"Let's put her on a monitor, just to be on the safe side."

"Where's Rickert?"

"Page says he's in the OR."

"Page Neurology."

"Richardson's right here."

Someone had noticed him.

"X Ray will be ready for her in ten."

"We'll send her with a monitor, an ambu, and be ready to intubate her if we have to."

"How about some O_2?"

"Let's start a mask at forty percent."

Paul heard every word. Each report slammed his consciousness. He watched as they hooked her up. She looked like Mrs. Wright. A younger, more beautiful version of Tammy Wright. Tubes. IV's. Monitors. Everything but a respirator of her own. He prayed that it wouldn't come to that.

"Respiration twenty-six and regular."

"Pressure one-twelve over sixty-five."

"The catheter is in."

"X Ray is calling for her."

"Which room?"

"E-3. They'll do the chest X ray and skull films there and then the CAT scan next door in F-3."

"Do you want to examine her again?"

Paul said nothing.

"Dr. Richardson!"

They were talking to him. Examine her . . . ?

Yes. "Yes." He did. Quickly and efficiently. "She's the same."

"Can we move her?"

"Yes."

"BP one-ten over sixty-eight."

"Pulse one-oh-four."

"X Ray's waiting."

"Christ! Let 'em wait. We always have to wait for them."

"Hook up that portable monitor."

"It's almost done."

"Rickert will be closing in ten minutes. He can't break scrub."

"Tell him that's okay."

"The monitor's hooked up."

"Let's go."

"Put the IV on the bedpole."

"Watch that catheter."

"Somebody get the O_2."

"Got it."

"X Ray's on the phone again."

"Tell 'em we're on the way."

"Get those blood-gas results."

Paul stood back and watched the procession leave the ER and make its way down the hall to X Ray.

"How are you doing, Dr. Richardson? You look terrible."

It was the surgery resident who had been looking at Gerri's torn thigh. He had examined Paul that morning. Paul didn't know his name or didn't remember it through the web of sounds reverberating inside his skull. He was not surprised that he looked terrible. He felt even worse than that.

"Not so good," he said. "Not so good."

"You should have let us admit you."

"No. I did the right thing." Paul sat down. His legs could no longer support him. He needed something. "Can I have some Demerol?"

"You going to stay around here?"

"Yes."

"Sure. You look like you could use it. How about a hundred milligrams IM?"

It sounded good to Paul.

He didn't even feel the injection. It would take another ten to fifteen minutes for them to start the CAT scan. It was just a two-minute walk down the hall. He could rest another five minutes. By then the Demerol would start to work and he would be able to support his weight and walk again. He would sit for just a couple of minutes. Gerri was in good hands.

Hands. Paul looked at his torn and bandaged hands. If he ever got them on that McCormick kid, he'd break his neck. Had anyone called Tom Ward this time? He asked the security guard. No, no one had. He told them to do so immediately. He got no argument.

Five minutes had passed. His mind was clearer. He felt stronger. He would wait two more minutes. He peered at his watch like Mr. Kreevich had, remembering each part and its correct name and its function.

Two more minutes passed. It was time to stand up. Nothing momentous, just stand up.

His legs were shaky but they held. The two-minute walk took closer to five minutes. That was less time than he had figured on.

Gerri was already in F-3. The only one with her was one of the ER nurses.

"Her signs are still good," she informed him.

Paul nodded.

"One-oh-eight over seventy. Pulse one-ten. Respiration twenty-eight."

He opened Gerri's eyes. Midline. Pupils equal. Doll's-head movements were present. Pain reaction. He pressed as hard as he could. She withdrew. Unchanged. No worse. No better, but at least no worse.

The residents came in. "No skull fracture," one of them said. "The chest film shows some scattered infiltrates. If the gases aren't good we'll probably have to intubate her."

"Damn that bastard."

"What?"

"Nothing." He hadn't realized he had said it out loud. "Her neuro exam is unchanged," he told them. They said nothing in reply. Not that he had expected any answer. It was their turn to receive information without saying anything at all out loud. All they had to do was understand it and incorporate it into their thinking.

Once Gerri's head was supported and in place they all went into the control room, leaving her alone with her face covered by an oxygen mask and her head half inside the giant horse-shoe of the CAT scanner. Her monitor was turned so that they could see it from the observation area.

"She has an AV malformation," Paul said, surprising himself with the calm, steady tone of his voice.

"I've never seen it on CAT scan or angio. I'm not sure she's ever had a CAT scan before. It was diagnosed over ten years ago by an angiogram. It's supposed to be a big one."

"Which hemisphere?"

"I . . . I don't know." How could he not know? "Wait." He knew. She had a mild right facial. "Left hemisphere. She has a mild, old supranuclear seventh on the right."

What was taking so damn long? Paul wondered.

How many CAT scans had he seen? Hundreds? Thousands? One. Only one that he could remember now. And that had been earlier this week.

The routine was always the same. All CAT scans followed the exact same routine. They all had to be done one cut at a time.

All CAT scans are equal, he thought, just like people.

But Orwell was right. Some were more equal than others.

And they took ever so much longer to do. The ones you cared about always took longer.

To Paul it was like a slow-motion replay of Carolyn's CAT scan being recreated one dot at a time on the computer screen.

He heard the whir and knew that the radiation had been emitted, had passed through Gerri's head, been deflected and detected and digested and transformed. During an interminable silent delay, each quantum of radiation was translated into a dot of specific density. Even Neils Bohr had not envisioned this.

The first picture came out. It was almost all skull, with only a small area of the top of her brain. That part was normal. Just like Carolyn's had been. And Donna Kolloway's, he reminded himself. Whir.

The process repeated itself one and a half centimeters deeper into Gerri's skull.

Whir and wait.

Again it was normal. Maybe her malformation wasn't as big as she had told him. Or as big as they had told her. As Don Lenhardt had told her. Lenhardt, who didn't even remember her, to whom she was just another patient, just another young girl he had sterilized. That drug-popping son of a . . . Maybe he'd been wrong. It was a worthwhile hope. Maybe her AVM was small. Maybe she didn't have one. Maybe they blew the diagnosis. He could hope, couldn't he?

No, he couldn't.

The third cut showed it. The first traces of her malformation were there. A bright cluster of abnormal dilated vessels full of blood. It was inside her left hemisphere. Exactly where he knew it had to be from the clinical observation he had never made. A right-facial-nerve injury like hers always meant disease of her left hemisphere.

It was another of Murphy's unpublished laws.

They were always on the left hemisphere. Whenever it mattered, they were always on the wrong side, the left side, the side where the ability to speak is controlled. It was more toward the back than the front and more deep than superficial. And large. Very large. Lenhardt had not been wrong.

"It's huge," one of the residents said.

Paul nodded.

"I've never seen one that big before," said another of the residents.

Whir.

"It must involve half of her left side."

"Did it bleed?"

The next cut appeared on the screen.

Paul studied it.

Whir.

Wait.

Study.

Another cut.

"Yes, it did," Paul said. "Look here. There's a thin layer of blood over the brain and some blood at the base of the brain. Not much. Not enough to cause any real problem." Not yet anyway. "There's no evidence of bleeding into the brain itself and no swelling." He wasn't sure if he was talking to them or himself. "No indication for any surgical intervention. That blood should start to reabsorb . . . and with any luck, she should start waking up."

"Should we start steroids?"

"No."

"Mannitol?"

"No!"

"No measures for edema?"

"No! There is no edema! Look for yourselves." Wait. Calm down. Stop shouting at them. They aren't neurologists. They only want to help her.

Why the hell was he making all the decisions? Who else was there to do it?

"Should we hyperventilate her?"

"No."

The telephone rang. The blood gases were back. The pO_2 was down. pCO_2 was up. Paul knew what that meant. Intubation. And a respirator.

"We're going to take her straight up to the ICU."

No answer was required. Paul gave none.

He stood at the monitor playing with the dials. He went through the entire scan again. Cut by cut. Top to bottom. Side to side. With each different instruction he gave it, the computer constructed a new image for him.

He was satisfied. There was no edema and only a small amount of bleeding. She should do all right.

He looked over to the CAT scanner. Gerri was gone. The room was empty. Everyone else was gone.

Paul's legs were holding up. He was amazed. They felt strong. That Demerol certainly did a hell of a lot more than the Percodan. It was easy for him to walk. He decided not to go straight to the ICU. They could intubate her without him.

Paul walked back to his own office, taking care to avoid any shortcuts. Once there, he called home. Carolyn answered. Where was he? He was at the hospital. He told her that Gerri had had an accident. Would she be okay? Yes, he thought she would. He was going to stay at the hospital and keep an eye on her. Would they be all right without him? What a question. She wasn't a baby. She'd be in college in a few months. He laughed at himself and apologized. She accepted his apology. "Take good care of Gerri."

"I will."

"Give her our love."

"I'll be sure to do that."

He rolled up the bloodstained leg of his slacks. The bleeding was from the wound in his shin where the metal stair had scraped off much of the skin. The dressing they had put on that morning in the ER was soaked with blood. He pulled it off. The tissue under it was raw. It would have to be covered again. He found some gauze and some adhesive tape and redressed his own wound. When he was done, the bandage looked pretty good. Almost professional.

He would wait another few minutes and then he would put on his white coat and go up to the ICU.

How long would it take them?

Ten minutes to get to the ICU. Ten more to intubate her. Maybe fifteen. He still had a couple of minutes to wait. Should he make some coffee? Yes, he decided, but he was interrupted.

"Hi, Doc."

"Tom."

"You don't look so good."

"I don't feel so good."

"Tell me what happened to Dr. Scala."

Paul told the detective every detail. He described exactly

how she had looked when he found her. The image was permanently locked in his head. He didn't even have to flick a switch to see it. Her legs spread apart, pointed up the stairs. Her pantyhose torn and covered with blood. But her bikini panties were still there. When he had finished, Tom made his first comment. ''You figure McCormick did it.''

''Yes.''

''Why didn't he rape her?''

''How the hell . . .'' There was no reason to be angry. It was his job. It was a clinical question. Like something a doctor had to know. ''Gerri said he had never had sex. He was asexual. Impotent maybe. Get the SOB. He killed Jackie and he tried to kill Gerri.''

''It sounds that way. I'll put out a bulletin on him. We'll pull him in and see what he has to say.''

''Don't pay too much attention to any alibi his old man supplies.''

''We won't.''

It was time to get to the ICU.

''He may have . . .'' Paul could not say it. ''He . . .'' Paul shook his head. One more try. ''Her lips were bruised. He . . .''

''Christ.'' Tom understood.

Paul had to see her. He got up. His legs felt spongy.

''Why didn't he kill her, Paul?''

''What?''

''He killed Jackie. But he didn't kill Dr. Scala. Why not?''

''Ask him.''

''I intend to.''

Paul knew exactly what to expect. He had been in ICU's countless times in his medical career. He must have seen several thousand patients plugged into respirators and monitors, with IV's and catheters. Intubated. And with central venous lines and God knows what else. He had seen them in Chicago and Los Angeles. In London and Amsterdam. And Israel. They all looked identical. Yet this was different. He felt a distant chill as he watched the succession of blips on the screen of the monitor. He had seen his father on a monitor once. So long ago. Well over a dozen years earlier. In an entirely different lifetime. It hadn't helped his father any.

Blip . . . blip . . . blip . . . A regular succession of electronic noises and sharp wave forms. The blips sounded the same all over the world. All the waves looked the same.

Whoosh . . . *whoosh* . . . The respirator was going at about twenty-four per minute. She was triggering it herself. Each time she started to inhale, a light went on on top of the respirator and it pumped oxygen into her lungs. Its sound acted as a hushed counterpoint to the pizzicato rhythm of the cardiac monitor. He realized there was no throb at all in his head. He hadn't missed it.

The dripping of the IV added a third all-but-audible rhythm. The multiplicity of rhythms was like a Stravinsky ballet. But there was no Fokine to choreograph it. No Balanchine. No Nijinski. Just Paul Richardson. He watched at the bedside. Gerri no longer attracted a crowd. She was now just one of a collection of critically ill patients, part of an unmatched set of tragedies being watched by a group of nurses and physicians. Yesterday she could have been one of them. That was the way it went.

Blip . . . blip . . . blip . . . blip . . .

He did love her.

He knew that as he listened to the rhythms of her life.

Whoosh . . . *whoosh* . . .

Blip . . . blip . . . blip . . . blip . . .

She was going to wake up.

She was going to live.

She was going to be all right. He had told Carolyn that she would.

There was a hospital identification band on her wrist: "Geraldine Scala. 223-306. Dr. Paul Richardson."

She was not really his patient. She couldn't be. He couldn't make any decision that might mean life or death. It wasn't fair to him. Or to her. In his next existence, he was going to do it differently. He'd be reincarnated into an occupation where he didn't have to make decisions about people's lives. He'd be an actuary. Or an astronomer. And a Yankee fan. It would be so nice to win a few.

Whom else could he trust?

He examined her again.

Pupils: equal.

Eyes: midline.

Doll's-head eye movements: intact.

Response to pain: still appropriate but less vigorous.

He wrote his findings in the chart, and one order. Neurosurgery to see in emergency consultation. Stat.

The nearly silent noises of her life were now ricocheting through his skull. It sounded like two marching bands playing different tunes had come together in his midbrain, like a scene from the New England remembrances of Charles Ives. He had to turn them off. Standing there in the ICU was not helping either Gerri or him.

He wasn't sure at first why he went to his lab or even how he got there. Once he was there he knew what he wanted to do. He looked at his watch. There was still some caked blood on the wrist band.

It showed the time as 9:15. It had to be later than that. More time must have passed. The clock on the wall agreed with his watch. He looked up a number in the phone directory and dialed.

The phone began to ring. It was Saturday night. Most people were out somewhere. He hoped that Herb wasn't one of those people.

Someone picked up the phone.

"Hello."

"Hello, Herb."

"Boss?"

"Yes."

"It's Saturday night."

"I know."

"Where are you?" Herb asked.

"I'm at the hospital."

"Why?"

"I'm . . . seeing a patient."

"Is everything okay?"

"Yes, but I have some time to kill."

"Oh."

"I'm in the lab now," Paul began to explain. "I wanted to look at that last group of rats we gave JNF-2 to."

"The ones who died?"

"Those are the ones."

"I only finished about half of the brains," Herb told him. "Half are still in formalin."

"That's fine. In fact, that's perfect. Just tell me where to find them."

Herb told him and asked another question. "Is anything wrong?"

"No. No. See you Monday."

Why was Herb so suspicious? Was he fearful that Paul would find something? Did he know something that Paul didn't know?

Herb's instructions were easy to follow and Paul had no difficulty finding exactly what he needed. Suddenly this simple study done routinely after a few minutes of thought was no longer a mere academic exercise. There was blood inside Gerri's head, pressing on her brain. Most likely one of the blows to her head had torn a small hole or two in her AVM. He wasn't sure whether the blood had spilled out of her malformation when McCormick had hit her or when she had fallen and hit her head on the fire escape. It didn't make any difference. She had not bled a great deal. That blood collected insider her skull was not a threat to her. But if she bled anymore, it could threaten her life or her speech. They might have to operate on her and if it came to that, JNF-2 might be their best bet. Her vascular abnormality was enormous and it was located in the worst of all possible places. They couldn't possibly cut it out. Surgery like that even in the best of hands would leave her aphasic. And Don's shaky hands were not the best.

JNF-2 had certainly helped Donna Kollaway. It might end up as Gerri's only hope.

JNF-2 had not helped Sam Rogovin. Paul tried not to remember that clinical observation. Rogovin had bled from an abnormal blood vessel with a thin, fragile wall. And he had bled spontaneously. No crazy patient had pounded his head in. He died on his own. That probably didn't make any difference. He had had blood in his head pushing on his brain. So did Gerri. And the JNF-2 hadn't saved him.

Hopefully Gerri would not get any worse. Her coma was light. There wasn't that much blood squeezing in on her brain. But if she did get worse and they did have to do something, he had to know as much as he could about JNF-2. Hadn't Corrigan himself invented it? Yes. It was a real advance. No question about it.

Strange that if you worked in a university and developed a new drug, you got a Nobel Prize and fame and fortune. If you worked for a drug company, there was no Nobel Prize. No fame. Maybe a bonus. Or the boss's daughter. Medicine was so indebted to the unknown John Corrigans of this world working in the basements of drug companies and coming up with new molecules for old diseases.

Paul started with the brains that were still floating in formaldehyde, one in each small bottle. In these he would examine the entire uncut brains. Unlike Herb and John, he had been trained in neuropathology; both gross pathology as seen by the naked eye and microscopic sections.

Each bottle was labeled with the number of the experiment and keyed to the number of the animal. It was experiment 83-14.

There were three brains from the experimental group that were still in formaldehyde. Three rat brains in which they had produced fresh bleeding and then injected JNF-2. There were two others treated with JNF-2 in which there had been no fresh bleeding. Those were the two he looked at first. He took the two brains out of the small vials and examined them one at a time. Rat brains were so much easier to work with than the rats themselves. They looked normal. The linings over the brain were thin and glistening. The brains themselves were firm and smooth. No swelling, no bleeding, no discoloration, no softening. No evidence of brain damage. In each, one vein was distended and hard.

Then came the three experimental brains. This was what counted. He took the three brains out and again examined them one by one. These brains were far from normal. In each of them the lining covering the brain was thickened, dull, and stuck to the brain itself like a piece of adhesive tape. Even underneath the disfigured covering it was easy to tell where the JNF-2 had been injected. Each brain was swollen on the side of the injection, distended, soft, discolored. All three brains looked the same. There was no fluke here. Just major chemical injury. Fatal brain destruction.

So much for the gross pathology. Next came the microscopic sections. He located the slide box labeled 83-14 and after looking at the notebook pulled out the slide he wanted to see.

83-14 #27.
83-14 #28.
83-14 #29.
Three experimental animals.
83-14 #35.
One control brain.

He started first with the control brain. It was even easier to work with the slides than the whole brains. Only his knowledge of anatomy reminded him that these thin slices of pink tissues were from rats. God, how he hated rats. Just like . . . Winston Smith. That was his name. Orwell's hero. He finished the first set of slides. The brain was normal.

The three experimental brains came next. He knew that they could not be normal, and they weren't. Each of them had a large necrotic area centered around the sclerosed vein and destroying much of that side of the brain.

He studied the first one, #27, very carefully. It looked like a massive toxic reaction. The other two he only glanced at. They looked exactly like the first one.

The conclusion was obvious. JNF-2 plus fresh blood equals a disaster. A total disaster. A wipeout of half the brain. They couldn't use it in Gerri. Her brain might become battered by her own blood. But her blood wouldn't do this to her. It took JNF-2 plus blood to do this. How the hell had Corrigan ever said it was safe? It wasn't safe. Not in a patient who had just bled. It might leave her talking like Mike Kreevich did right after his surgery. Except what he saw in the rat brain would never go away. It would be permanent. They couldn't rob Gerri of her speech. It would be better to do nothing.

Above all, do no harm. Medicine's first law.

The FDA was right to pull JNF-2 and limit its use. The junk was not at all safe.

Or were they right?

He closed his eyes and reconstructed the brain of Sam Rogovin. First the brain cutting. Cut by cut. It was like reconstructing a CAT scan. He could remember each of the individual cuts.

The meninges covering his brain had not looked like soiled adhesive tape. They had not been glued to his brain. They had looked pretty damn good. They still glistened some. They were partially dulled by the bleeding but they were still thin and were easily separated from the brain itself. The brain had also looked much different from those rat brains. It had not been swollen. Nor soft.

There had been no necrosis when the brain had been cut. All they had found was a big red hemorrhage. JNF-2 had not caused any damage. In Rogovin JNF-2 plus blood meant nothing. In these rats, everything.

Different effects in different species? That was what they always fell back on. Such differences had been recorded before, but relying on that explanation was almost always a cop-out. Species just weren't that different. Poisons worked the same in most animals. If you looked long enough and hard enough, there was usually some other explanation. Unfortunately, Gerri might not have time enough for him to look that hard.

They had done those other studies of JNF-2 two years ago. He looked through the notebooks. He found the right one: 81-29. Forty-eight guinea pigs. Guinea pigs, not rats. Another species. The next step was not so simple. He was tempted to call Herb again. It was after eleven. It was too late. He searched on his own and managed to find the slide box. He skimmed the slides to see if he could find any brains with evidence of accidental bleeding. He remembered how difficult Herb had said the injections had been. Some of the animals must have bled at least a little. He held each slide up to the light. Training in pathology came in useful every once in a while. He found two sets of slides in which he could see blood collected outside the brain: #18 and #23. In these two animals, blood vessels had torn during the experiment and they had accidentally carried out the same experiment they had just finished. Two animals were not much of a sample. You could never do any statistics, but it was a start. Back to the microscope. He systematically pored over each slide. He found no evidence at all of any injury to either brain.

They still had the old caveat of species specificity to fall back on.

Gertrude Stein was probably right. Pigs is pigs. They ain't people. Guinea pigs were rodents. So were rats. Yet in guinea pigs JNF-2 didn't seem to interact with fresh blood.

Hadn't Herb said that all the animals had died?

Why had the control animals died?

Some animals died in every experiment. From pneumonia or sepsis or diarrhea.

He went back to the newest lab notebook and went through the daily notes on 83-14.

Five experiment animals had died and only one control rat. And that rat was sick. It wasn't all the animals, just those that had bled and had massive brain injuries.

Herb had sacrificed the others.

Herb?

Was this just a lab error?

Had he made the same error with the Dillinger #307?

Did Frank McCormick have a lesion like this in his temporal lobe?

Was that why he had killed Jackie? And beaten up Gerri? Gerri!

He looked at his watch.

It was midnight. Time to make rounds again.

His shins were beginning to throb once again. He would stop in the ER on his way and get another shot of Demerol.

It was good stuff.

—20———————————

Gerri was still intubated. The flexible tube which entered her trachea and extended from her mouth was attached to another tube connecting it and her to the respirator.

Blip . . . blip . . . blip . . . blip . . . blip . . .

Whoosh . . . *whoosh* . . . whoosh . . .

The litany of rhythms and sounds had not changed.

Nor had the crowded, impersonal, chilled bustle of the ICU.

There were two physicians at her bedside. Paul silently watched them examine her.

"Sorry I took so long to get here, Paul," Don Lenhardt said as he peered into Gerri Scala's right eye with an ophthalmoscope. "I was at the Symphony when I got the page. I called here and talked to some resident. He told me that you were in charge. He said that you'd examined her and seen her CAT scan and that you'd decided that she was stable. I figured that there was no acute need for me, so after the concert was over I drove my wife home and changed clothes before I came in."

Paul knew there and then that he would have to be Gerri's treating physician, even if he didn't want to. No one else wanted to make decisions on a colleague. No one else could be trusted with her life. Certainly not Don Lenhardt.

"I understand she's had a known AVM for many years," Don went on as he continued his exam.

"Don't you remember her?" Paul asked.

"Did I ever see her as a patient? I don't recall it."

387

"Back in Boston."

"When?"

"Twelve, maybe fifteen years ago."

"No wonder I don't remember. You know how many of these I've seen in the last fifteen years? A couple of hundred at least. I can't be expected to remember them all. Especially not the ones I couldn't even operate on."

Paul could hear the rhythms again. He himself was still hurting. The second shot of Demerol had not taken over yet. Much as he didn't want to, Paul could understand how Don had forgotten her. What was one AVM more or less to him? An offhand judgment. An everyday occurrence. No more meaningful to him than slapping a mosquito. What difference could it possibly have made to him? None. To her? Everything. It had damn near destroyed her entire life and now he didn't even remember her.

The neurosurgeon had finished his examination and was writing his note on the chart. "She's beginning to show some evidence of increased pressure," he said as he put down the chart. "Otherwise she's pretty much as your note described her at nine . . . except I couldn't get any pain response."

"I couldn't either," Marv Rickert added. "I examined her about an hour ago."

"Let me try," Paul said. They both stepped back to give Paul room. He did exactly what he had done several times earlier in the night. He pushed until the tip of his thumb turned almost pure white. "She's not responding." There had been no necessity to say it. They were both watching each move he made. They had seen the same lack of response that he had observed. He said it again, "No response." He then pulled the sheet out of the foot of the bed, exposing her legs and the freshly bandaged wound on her thigh, and rubbed his knuckles up and down her shins as forcefully as he could. Once again bone scrapped against bone, catching the small unprotected nerve fibers in between. Nothing. He pulled the top of her sheet down and yanked her gown up, exposing her chest and breasts to full view. Using his bare knuckles and pushing down as hard as he could, he moved his fist up and down her sternum. Up and down. Bone against bone. Again. She didn't move. Damn. "No movement . . . No response . . . No . . . nothing." There was one other trick to cause pain. They used to do it when he was a resident. Twisting a patient's nipples. His hand started reflexively to reach for her right nipple. His fingers touched it and he pulled his hand back as if it had been touching a live flame. He'd let that one pass undone.

"Her coma's deeper," Don said.

"Not much," Paul argued.

"No, but some."

Paul didn't want to think about it. If he did, then he would have to consider what it meant, and that he did not want to do.

"She may still be bleeding. If she gets any deeper, we may have to operate."

The blips sounded softer now.

The whooshes were hardly audible.

They, like his own pain, had become part of the background of the ICU.

He had to think about it. Lenhardt was right. Gerri was probably still bleeding. Once one of those vessels was torn apart, it could bleed for weeks. The vessels had no way to repair themselves if the hole was very big. The brain had almost no way to defend itself.

That murdering son of a . . . Maybe the cops had found him. Better yet, maybe he resisted arrest and they shot him. That was a comforting fantasy. One that made Paul feel better. Justice would be served, and besides, it would save the state a lot of money. Hell, if he ever came to trial, he'd just cop a plea of insanity.

God, how it hurt to think. His head was once again aching.

Blip . . . blip . . . blip . . .

The blip had returned, louder than before.

So had the respirator.

Whoosh . . . *whoosh* . . .

Whoosh . . . *whoosh* . . .

It seemed to be shouting at him. He focused on the respirator. There was a volume switch. If only he could turn it down. He could, but it wouldn't help any. That switch controlled the flow of oxygen into Gerri's lungs, not the loudness.

The familiarity of the sounds made him feel no better.

He looked around at the array of electronic gadgetry. It was easy to believe that *1984* was just around the corner.

A 1984 without Big Brother. There was no one watching your every move. No one watched any of Frank McCormick's moves. Someone should have been watching him. They shouldn't have implanted any adrenal cells in his brain. They should have put some sort of electronic homing device in his brain so they could have traced each and every one of his movements. Then he wouldn't have killed Jackie Baumer. He wouldn't have tried to kill Gerri.

There were so many different facts that didn't add up.

The missing Metrazol.

The missing consent form.

The missing Frank McCormick.

Why did he attack Gerri now, after the case had been settled?

Thank God he hadn't raped her. Or had he? Paul forced himself to look at her bruised lips with that tube coming out between them. Was that symbolic of what he had done to her? Had they checked? He looked through her chart frantically, as if time made some difference. They had. There had been no traces of sperm in her oral cavity. He had not raped her in any fashion.

If only he hadn't beaten her head. Then maybe the vessels wouldn't have ruptured. She might have been better off to have been raped. The thought made him shiver. It was much too cold in the ICU at night. McCormick was as bad as that Verban jerk. Verban had hit Emily on the face, and Edie too. He remembered Emily's swollen lips and black eye. Frank had done the same thing to Gerri.

Paul looked at Gerri's face. He reached out and touched it. It was warm. She was still running a fever.

He let his hand rub across her forehead and cheeks tenderly.

She made no response. The neurologist in him knew that she could not feel what he was doing to her. Paul was not so positive. Had she still been able to feel things when she was on that landing and he pulled her legs apart and ripped her pantyhose off? Was that what she would remember? The prelude to an afternoon of anticipated rape.

He continued to massage her face ever so lightly.

She had a swollen lip.

No black eye.

No swollen jaw.

Just a single tube passing obscenely between her full lips.

Her face was still so damn pretty. Nose and all. He loved that nose. He loved that entire face. It was okay if she didn't love him and didn't want to be with him anymore. He could live with that. As long as she was alive and well and had made that decision on her own. But he could not accept her being torn out of his life by fate—or what passed for it. It was fortunate that her face had not been harmed. When she recovered, there would not be any physical reminders for her to see in her mirror every morning. Her features were unblemished.

Where had he hit her?

Had he?

The question startled him. He was not prepared to consider it. What evidence was there? Couldn't she have gotten that one big bruise by falling down those stairs?

He examined her head very carefully. Aside from her lip, there were only two significant bruises. One, hidden by her hair, was above her right ear, and then there was the ugly one at the back of her skull. He reconstructed the scene. That one was where her head had been resting on the landing. It must be where her head had struck the landing. Paul shook his head as if that were the only way to shut the picture off and get it out of his mind.

That scene left only one bruise and her swollen lip that were unaccounted for.

She could have been walking down that isolated stairway all alone when that damn vessel gave out. It could have just happened. It had ruptured once before. She could have been running down those stairs and it could have burst open, spewing her own blood out over her brain. Suddenly her head would have felt as if it were exploding. She might have fallen to her knees, hitting her lip against the doorknob, and then collapsed down the stairs, banging her scalp, tearing her hose and her thigh, and crashing onto the landing.

Paul knew that that made more sense. McCormick hadn't tried to rape Gerri because he hadn't been there. He probably would have if he had been there, but he wasn't there. There was no reason to implicate that malignant bastard in this one. Just some malignant God.

She had fallen on her own. No one had helped her.

That made more sense.

Terrifyingly more sense. It was a leap of logic that frightened Paul more than the fantasized attack by some out-of-control schizophrenic. If that vessel bled this much on its own, there was absolutely no reason for it to stop bleeding. None at all.

Like Sam Rogovin all over again. No one had bashed Sam's head in. A simple cough had triggered his death. A cough caused by the tube they had put in his throat during surgery. And now Gerri had that same type of tube carrying oxygen into her lungs. She would cough from it, too. Everyone did.

He had to get out of there. Suddenly he was hungry. It was one o'clock in the morning and he was hungry. He wanted a milk shake or something else cold and fattening. Some childish proclamation of his own immortality.

He walked out to his car and started it and pushed a button to turn on the radio. Jackie's diary was there on the front seat. He turned off the radio.

Maybe he wasn't so immortal after all. It was a simple syllogism. Freddie Sanford made love to Jackie Baumer. Paul made love to Jackie Baumer. Sanford had AIDS. Paul could get AIDS. Sixty percent fatal in two years. And probably uniformly fatal in five. One hundred percent. Quite a penalty for a couple of lousy screws. It was enough to make anyone believe in a vindictive God.

Suddenly he wasn't hungry anymore. A milk shake didn't seem like such a good idea. He turned off the motor and picked up the diary and walked back toward his office. He settled for a diet cola from the machine in the basement and then took the elevator up to Neurology.

He did switch on WFMT. The all-night program was on. The Midnight Special was over. He was glad. He was in no mood for a series of folk songs that confused illiteracy with charm. They were playing some late-Romantic fiddle concerto or other. It was perfect. Just boring enough to read by. He didn't recognize which concerto it was.

He started the diary in 1980 and read it page by page.

It was like reading Schnitzler's merry-go-round. Schnitzler had been a physician. From Vienna. The Vienna of Freud and Mahler and Kaposi. Not of Graham Greene and Harry Lime. Had Schnitzler's *La Ronde* really been nothing more than a metaphor for the social life of his own hospital? *General Hospital* set in turn-of-the-century Vienna. With each scene describing a different liaison.

The Hooker and the Soldier.

The Soldier and the Young Maid.

The Young Maid and the Rich Young Man. There was one big difference between that play and the diary that he was reading. The diary was a vehicle for one single actress. Jackie was in all of the scenes.

The nurse and the attending physician.

The nurse and the business executive.

The nurse and the nurse.

There was another difference. Schnitzler wrote much better. Jackie's prose was stodgy. There is nothing worse than stodgy pornography. D. H. Lawrence had the right idea. It was perfectly permissible to write smut if you wrote it well.

The nurse and the resident.

The nurse and the young psychiatrist.

The young female psychiatrist.

Gerri. The seduction of Gerri. What right did he have? Was it any of his business? Tom had been right not to show this to him before.

He read on. The scene was over almost before it started. Schnitzler had not included any such totally aborted seduction attempts. Maybe Jackie had succeeded in bedding her later. He couldn't get himself to use any other verb. He flipped through the next few months. She had tried again and failed again. That wasn't what Gerri had told him.

They had never been lovers. Jackie had tried. More than once. But she had failed. Gerri had rejected her. Why had she lied to him? Why had she wanted to make him angry? To drive him away. It was both a question and an answer.

That eliminated Gerri as a suspect. She had no reason to kill Jackie. Jackie had nothing on her.

He continued forward. Acronyms came and went. He learned about the sexual proclivities of people whose names he didn't know and didn't want to know. And much more than just their sexual habits was recorded. Jackie was a collector of all the local gossip and rumors. A twentieth-century Samuel Pepys.

Nineteen-eighty was over. It was 1981. F.B. entered the

picture. Just as a rumor. B.C. was there, a piece of irrelevant gossip. J.C. Was that John Corrigan? Yes, something about Dillinger, Inc. A sarcastic remark, nothing more.

Other initials came and went.

E.R. It was obvious who that was. Jackie had been more successful with E.R. than she had been with G.S. Much more. The details were more graphic than he needed them to be. Or had Edie been the one who had been successful? It was hard to tell. He would never know. Did it make any difference?

D.L. came in for the first time. It was a brief entry about Lenhardt's arrival as the new head of Neurosurgery and his taking drugs immediately prior to surgery. He checked the date. March 7, 1981. The week they had operated on McCormick. She had confirmed it with two other witnesses. She didn't list their initials.

D.L. had a motive. If he knew that she knew about his habit. But did he?

Occasional references to others in Neurology were sprinkled across the months, but there was little if any apparent significance. At least none that was obvious to Paul.

There was a mention of H.A. Herb Adams. Not as a lover, but as a friend, a fellow gossip. Someone who helped keep her up-to-date on those little delicious tidbits she so loved to collect.

J.C. again. He was still with R.W. John and his lover, Red Wilson. Jackie knew about it, as he had supposed. Tom Ward had already confirmed that.

Had she ever confronted Corrigan? He read on. Probably not. It wouldn't have been worth it. R.W. told her that Mrs. Corrigan knew all about their little arrangement. They'd even met each other at a party at the Dillinger mansion.

This was one bit of gossip that Jackie could not have used as a threat. John could not have killed her to save his marriage and his career. Paul still had the same number of suspects, but John Corrigan had one less motive.

In November, she made another pass at G.S. The attempt was well-described. There was no question as to which of them was the seducer and which the seducee. Paul had missed this one the first time through. Jackie had struck out again.

And it had cost her. E.R. blew up at her. They had a real to-do over it as far as he could tell.

That left E.R. in.

D.L. and E.R.

In December she recorded Bobbie's death with a cryptic note: "Give him six to nine months." That bitch. That calculating bitch. It had been her idea as soon as Bobbie had died. That's just about what had happened. They had become lovers nine months later. And he had thought it was his idea. She was smoother than he had ever realized.

Nineteen-eighty-one was over. So was the violin concerto, replaced by an Elgar symphony. Number Two. The longer one. He was too absorbed to pay any attention to it.

Nineteen-eighty-two began.

New pairs of letters came and went. Others stayed. D.L. Another drug charge. There was less documentation this time and no other known witnesses. H.A. told her about his problems with the adrenal-culture lines. "Now I have him" was all she added. Was this Herb's motive? What did she do with all of these collected tidbits?

B.G. and some charts in the ceiling came in. "Told B.C." So Bud knew about those charts over a year ago. "B.G. could be in a lot of trouble, and J.C." She knew the charts were all tied to Corrigan. Two more suspects. If they knew. Bud knew, and knew that Jackie knew. Had he told B.G.? Of course, and Goodman must have told Corrigan.

And yet it still went on.

Corrigan knew that Jackie knew all about the hidden charts.

Corrigan and Goodman.

Two more motives.

No. Just one. He could fire Goodman. But—and that was a big but—there was not a thing he could do to Corrigan. The only motive that left Corrigan with was a possible lab error. The same as Herb. Not the greatest of motives.

He was finding out more that might help Tom Ward than he was about AIDS. No Fred Sanford yet.

Spring came. More of the same.

Summer. The Elgar was finally over. He half-wanted to hear some Vivaldi. Instead, a Beethoven trio came on.

She recorded the fact that Paul had left for his sabbatical in Israel. "When he gets back . . ." What a sucker he'd been.

More charts. Goodman, Chiari, and Corrigan: "Finally have something over B.C. Ditto B.G. and J.C." Was it Bud's failure to carry out his policy that she meant? He was acting chairman of the department while Paul was out of the country. It was his responsibility to carry out departmental policy.

Fall. He was back home. D.L. was said to be on the wagon, so to speak. P.R. as lover. He appeared for the first time. He got poor grades. So did she. There were no new pairs of letters. No new pairings.

Nineteen-eighty-two was over.

Nineteen-eighty-three began.

The *New England Journal of Medicine* article was mentioned, and just as Bud had told him, F.B. entered the diary as a lover. He got good grades. Much better than Paul.

A fight with D.L. "Told him that I knew and to lay off or else. He won't bother me again." She might have been very right or very wrong.

D.L. knew. There was no longer any question about that. She could have cost him his career. That would have been a second time he was charged with drug abuse. There was never a third chance for neurosurgeons. She had threatened him.

Had he killed her in return?

Winter. Still Beethoven.

No more G.S. It had been over a year. Overall there were fewer initials dotting the pages. His were there once again.

The last return of P.R. as a lover. He closed to better reviews than he had opened to. He always knew that he had improved with age. That was what Bobbie had said. "Got even with G.S. at last." Had she been thinking of G.S. while they made love that last time? Why not? He'd been thinking about her. Wishing it was her. Pretending it was her beneath him. Imagining that it was her body he was entering. Why couldn't Jackie have done the same thing?

The Phyllis Masi story was on the same page. In explicit

detail. Jackie had made a threat of exposure to B.G. There was no longer any reason to speculate as to what Bill Goodman knew, or John Corrigan or Bud Chiari. They all had been threatened by her. But why? Her activity was as erratic as it was erotic.

All three of them had motives to kill her. Bill, John, and yes, even Bud.

It was more of a motive for Goodman than for Bud. Bud wasn't a resident whose entire career could be jeopardized by being canned. Bud was a tenured faculty member. Paul couldn't just fire him. Paul wouldn't fire him even if he could. And Bud knew that. At least he knew that now. Did he then, when Jackie had been murdered?

John was a different matter. Why the hell was he being so damned overprotective about those charts? Sure, an ounce of prevention was worth a pound of cure, but he was being downright paranoid.

Why? Paul wished he knew.

Jackie had known, and she had been sure of it. "John could be the big loser. I have him."

So John had a motive too.

It might be easier to find out who didn't have a motive.

The trio was over. Prokofiev's First Violin Concerto. With Heifetz. Paul recognized the tone of his playing. That was easy.

E.R. and F.B. seemed to alternate.

F.S.

For the first time.

Fred Sanford.

His first appearance came after Paul's last one-night stand.

F.S. came after him.

He was not at risk for AIDS. He breathed an audible sigh of relief. The sixty-percent mortality in two years could not include him. Edie and Floyd were at risk. They had been exposed, but he hadn't. He had no worries. No worries at all!

There were no other new partners. She had reformed a bit. Three were enough. Floyd and Edie with an occasional visit from Freddie Sanford.

It went on like that for six weeks or more. The most boring six weeks of the entire diary. Then it all changed. Her handwriting changed, became more messy. Larger, more tremulous. So did her style. The sentences were shorter and less often complete. Paul didn't think it was a conscious literary effort. She hadn't been studying Hemingway.

There were more grammatical errors.

More spelling mistakes.

The syntax deteriorated.

She was more short-tempered. She recorded more arguments. Arguments and threats. More and more of her words were misspelled.

She threatened D.L. again.

She threatened B.G. again.

She threatened C.J. That must be J.C. with the letters transposed.

She threatened H.A.

She fought with E.R. and F.B. All in the last week before her death.

She started going back to singles' bars and picking up men.

It ended abruptly. An unfinished script. One scene had been omitted, to spare the reader.

The nurse and the schizophrenic.

For the first time. That made no sense at all to him. The others did, but Frank didn't.

Frank couldn't have taken the informed consent. That was one fact of which they were sure. Arft had sworn to it. If Frank didn't take that form as part of his father's scheme, then he wouldn't have killed her as part of the same plot. And he wasn't a crazed killer. If he was a killer at all, he was a cold, calculating, premeditated murderer. And now that didn't make sense anymore. His dreams were full of women with long blond hair, but they weren't Jackie. They were all Gerri. He had done that just to frighten her, to convince her he was getting worse. The first dream was only after Jackie was dead. It must have been Jackie's death that gave him the idea. Not the other way around. Paul was sure of it. Prokofiev was over. It was a Bruckner symphony. A short one. The unfinished Ninth. They were already playing the last movement.

Jackie's life had been a revolving sexual odyssey much like Schnitzler's play. Life imitating art. Or vice versa. It was easy to see why Schnitzler gave up medicine to become a playwright. One simple truth. The theater has intermissions.

Real life doesn't offer such respites. Not for him. Not for Gerri.

Gerri!

Who was checking on her?

It was almost four A.M.

He got up. His legs were sore. He would need more Demerol soon.

— 21 ——————————

Once again Paul's brain registered each blip and every whoosh. Those blips meant everything—they were Gerri's life. They also meant nothing. Both the blips and the whooshes were devoid of meaning. They didn't reflect the real story. They told him nothing at all about what was going on inside her head. That beautiful face and head that he did love. All the costly monitoring devices of the whole damn expensive care unit couldn't answer the real questions. Was more blood seeping out of Gerri's brain and beginning to press more and more forcefully back in on it? Squeezing it? Was she going to end up like Rogovin had? Would some other vessel deep inside her brain blow up and send bright red blood ripping across her gray matter, destroying those little gray cells and with them her life? They couldn't let that happen, not to her. She meant too damn much to him.

Objectivity. He had to maintain his own objectivity. He was lost somewhere between the audience and the stage, half-observer, half-participant. It was so damn difficult.

The blips kept blipping and the whooshes kept whooshing. The drummers of two separate bands maintaining their own measured beat.

We measure the wrong things. He recalled a play he had seen right after he and Bobbie got married. What the hell was the title? Something about . . . dancing. *I Was Dancing*. That was it. It had been the first turkey that Thanksgiving. There was an Irish doctor in the play, an out-and-out quack. He never examined his patients, never took their blood pressures,

401

never counted their pulse or respiration. Instead he merely took a yearly photograph and compared them serially to estimate the annual rate of deterioration.

That bastard had been right. We do measure the wrong things. The numbers hadn't changed. Gerri's blood pressure was stable. So was her pulse rate. In fact, her temperature was down. And the blood gases. Just think, the blood gases were back in normal range. And the serum electrolytes were also normal. All the numbers were fine. The only problem was that Gerri wasn't fine. Far from it. All Paul had to do was look at her face. Her mouth was more slack than it had been. The muscle tone of her face was washed out, especially on the right side. She was less Gerri now and more just anyone, another anonymous patient with the same featureless face of someone whose brain was sending out too few impulses.

A gomer.

His own subconscious use of that horrid term nauseated him. Worse than that it frightened him. That word had sprung into his consciousness for a reason. She must look like one.

Gomer. He understood all too well where that word had come from and what it really meant. G-O-M-E-R. It wasn't an acronym. It was a borrowed word derived from the three-letter Hebrew root meaning "finished."

Finished. He must have recognized that Gerri was . . . No. She wasn't. She couldn't be.

She had to be examined. By him. He had no other choice. Once he got started, it didn't take him very long.

The pupils were no longer equal. The one on the left was larger than the one on the right. It was the classic sign of increasing pressure on the brain, of impending disaster. It was the last of the ninth. The pupil just barely reacted when he shone a light into her eye. That disaster was getting closer. There were two out. There was no response at all to pain. No arm movement. No grimace of her featureless face. Two runs down. He moved her head. No doll's-head eye movement. No one on base. And no Casey to put up to bat.

What a terrible analogy.

Casey had fanned.

He paged Don Lenhardt. Don answered in less than thirty seconds.

Paul told him what he had found.

"We've got big trouble," Don said. "She must still be bleeding. And now there's a big clot compressing her brain." None of this was news to Paul. He had understood the implications of what he had found on his exam. That was why he had called Don in the first place. "You arrange for another CAT scan. We might as well make sure exactly where all that blood is."

"That'll cost her some time."

"We can afford a few minutes, Paul. It'll make the surgery both easier and safer."

"You're right."

"You do that and I'll get the OR ready. Unless things deteriorate too quickly, I'll plan on cracking her skull at seven-thirty."

It was the one word, "cracking," that did it. How could he have said that? "Cracking her skull," as if she were just another patient. Just . . . The reality hit him. She *was* just another patient. She had to be. She had that right. So did he. His game was over. He was through. He called Bud at home. It took Paul only three minutes to give Bud all the details. No resident had ever summarized a patient more concisely. Not a single pertinent fact was left out. Not a single extraneous one was included. Paul told Bud everything he needed to know to manage Gerri. No more. No less. More he didn't need to know. Less could be a disaster.

Bud understood the situation completely. "I'll take charge," he said.

"Thanks."

"I'll be there by six."

Another hour.

Six thousand more blips to sit through. Paul arranged for the CAT scan and called the admitting office. Geraldine Scala, a patient in the ICU, he told them, was no longer his patient.

She belonged to Dr. Chiari now.

Chiari and Lenhardt.

"What is her hospital number?" the voice asked.

He didn't have to look at her wrist. "Two-two-three, three-oh-five."

"How do you spell that name?"

Spell.

They didn't even know her.

She was just another patient. She was . . .

"S-c-a-l-a," he said.

He collapsed into a chair by the bed, his hands folded in his lap, his eyes focused on the flashing light of the respirator. He sat and waited. The sounds lost their reality. All that he saw was that one light going on twenty-four times each minute. Once with each breath she initiated.

The orange flashes traveled from his eyes to the back of his brain, where they sparked other permanently etched images.

Carolyn on the kitchen floor. With the orange juice dripping down.

Gerri on that landing with her legs reaching up so lewdly.

In with the oxygen.

Jackie tied on her bed with a kitchen knife in her breast.

Out with the carbon dioxide.

Bobbie dead.

Gerri.

It kept on flashing.

In.

Out.

Its hypnotic spell pervaded his consciousness.

In.

Out.

He could think of nothing else.

Bud got there before six. X Ray had not yet called for her.

"How are you, Paul?"

Paul just shook his head.

"Anything change?"

He raised his hands in a useless gesture.

"Paul!"

Paul shrugged his shoulders.

"What time is the CAT scan?"

"Six."

"I'll take her down myself."

A nod.

"Did you get any sleep?"

A shake.

"I brought you a razor and shaving cream. They're in my office. Go clean up. You look terrible."

Paul did as he was told. He didn't even wait to watch Bud

examine her, but merely took one glance at her face. Her lip was still swollen. Her eyes were closed. It was even less her face. The tone was less. Her cheeks had less form, less shape. They were being blown passively outward each time the respirator forced oxygen into her chest. He was sure her numbers were all fine. God forbid she should die in the ICU with her numbers out of balance. One last long look at the orange light flashing on and off and he turned and left.

He shuffled his way to Bud's office and then to the bathroom. The sight in the mirror gave him a jolt. Was that him? The face was of someone nearer sixty than forty-five.

When he had finished shaving and combing his hair, he looked better. Fifty-five, not sixty.

It was 6:30. Zero minus one.

He sat in his office and waited in silence.

Murphy was right. Whatever can go wrong, will. Especially if the patient's a physician. Or someone you love. Or worse, both.

Murphy was probably an optimist. He'd been a West Point cadet. What did he know about blood vessels exploding inside people's heads? What did he know about violent paranoid schizophrenics? Paul stopped his own train of thought. Frank hadn't attacked Gerri. He knew that now. She had attacked herself. One of those abnormal vessels had broken open because that's what they do. It had happened before. It happened again. And now the blood was building up outside her brain, increasing in pressure, pushing on her brain, squeezing it, crushing it.

He saw Bud's face in the doorway and then his entire body.

"You were right, Paul."

Bud didn't wait for an answer. "She has a large clot over the left side of her brain displacing the hemisphere to the right. She'll be in OR in less than an hour. Don is a good surgeon. There's no evidence of any real permanent—"

"Talk about something else. Anything else."

"The Sox won. Hoyt pitched a good game. They're only two games out. Fisk got the big hit. We listened."

"I didn't know you had become a Sox fan."

"I haven't. I don't like baseball. You know that I never have. But my son does. He's the one who's a Sox fan."

"How old is he now?"

"Nine."

"I did that to my dad too. He hadn't been a fan since the 1919 series. I got him rekindled." It was hard to keep it light. There was no reason for it. But Paul had to talk about something other than Gerri. Anything. He started with Fred Sanford. Bud probably didn't care, but Paul did. He had to tell someone, and Bud was the best one to tell. He didn't have to repeat anything. Bud grasped it all the first time around.

"So Floyd is at risk for getting AIDS."

"Yes."

"Serves him right."

"Bud!"

"Don't, Paul. I refuse to be that nice. He's a real ass. He has been out to knife me for the last year. Well, he hasn't. I've learned how to protect my backside. That was something I couldn't learn from you, but I did learn it."

"Why would . . . ?"

"Why? He wants my job. He wants to be number-two man in this department. Someday he'll be out for your job. Hell, he probably put Jackie up to writing that damn letter."

"It's worse than that."

"Worse?"

"Jackie couldn't have written that letter. The spelling was perfect. So was the sentence structure. In her diary her spelling and use of language had been deteriorating for two or three weeks before her death. My guess is that she had an early encephalitis, causing some mild degree of aphasia."

"Why would . . . ?" Bud figured it out without much effort. "From her AIDS."

"Yes."

"But we didn't see anything at brain cutting."

"We never looked at the speech area when we did the microscopics. We had no history, so we just did routine sections. Remember Abe Baker's law?" Paul asked.

Bud did. "If you don't look in the right place, you won't find the pathology."

"Whoever killed her may have done her a favor in a strange way. AIDS is a hell of a way to die."

"Some favor! Look at how she died."

It was all too easy for Paul to conjure up that image, but for once it didn't disturb him. There were too many other competing images that made this one less intense, more remote.

"Jackie didn't write that letter," Bud reiterated, returning to the issue that concerned him.

"No. Someone else did."

"Floyd. It must have been Floyd."

For a moment Paul wondered if that were just Bud's own paranoia surfacing. No, he was undoubtedly right.

"Most likely," he agreed. "The key fact is that Jackie actually signed the letter. It had to be someone she knew and trusted who wrote it and got her to sign it. Either Floyd or Edie."

"Why would Edie do something like that?"

"She wouldn't. She had no reason to write that letter. And she didn't know what was in it. She was worried that it might be about her." There was one other fact. "It's possible that the letter could have been mailed after she died. I originally attributed its late arrival to our screwed-up hospital mail system, but it could have been mailed after she died. It was postmarked Wednesday morning. There is no mail pickup here after six P.M. It could have been mailed anytime between seven that night and six in the morning."

"That makes Floyd the killer."

"Perhaps," Paul responded.

"Perhaps?"

"Yes. It doesn't prove he did it. It does make him a likely suspect. That I accept. But not necessarily the killer."

"Sure. He gets me. And he's not even implicated. If she was still around, you might ask her why she sent the letter and she might have told you!"

"She would have told me, if I asked her."

"How can you say that?" Bud demanded.

"She was always honest with me."

"Paul, how can you still believe that?"

"I . . . I don't know," Paul admitted.

"You sure as hell don't. Listen to me for once. They were a well-matched pair. Neither of them could be trusted. After he had gotten rid of me, he'd probably be after your neck."

"He may have already started."

Paul told Bud about his meeting on Friday with the dean.

"I told you so. I tried to warn you."

"He made one mistake."

"Attacking you?" Bud asked.

"No," Paul said. "Attacking you. There was no way I was going to fire you and no way you wouldn't tell me . . . eventually."

"I'm going to check Gerri once more and then I'm going to the OR. Are you going to scrub in?"

"No."

Bud was not surprised. "It's probably better that way. I'll call as soon as we know something. Anything."

The silence that returned with Bud's departure was no longer welcome. It made it too easy to worry.

The morning show was on. It was just after seven. WFMT would be the only classical show in town for another hour. Some soprano was singing in German.

A lied by Schubert? No. Too lush. Too orchestral.

A song by Mahler? No.

Strauss. It was Richard Strauss. One of his *Four Last Songs.* "Autumn." How could it have taken him so long to recognize it? And it was Schwarzkopf who was singing. He'd recognize that voice anywhere. He had owned that record for twenty years. The realization came quickly. Kiri Te Kanawa was better. Her vocal line soared more easily. His memory had not served him well. Or at least his nostalgia had not.

He concentrated his energy on hearing each note. Strauss. Barber. Berwald. Whatever they played, he listened to it as intensely as he could. Music. Weather reports. The traffic. The time. It was 7:30. Gerri was in the OR. Don would be shaving her head. With any luck at all he could remove the clot and stop the bleeding.

And if he couldn't . . . He looked through the hospital staff directory and then dialed a number.

"John?"

"Yes."

"It's Paul. I need some JNF-2 for a patient."

"Is there any evidence of recent bleeding?"

"Yes."

"Then I can't release it, Paul. You know that the FDA has limited its use."

"I've got to have some, just in case," Paul pleaded.

"There is nothing I can do. Paul, my hands are tied."

"That's nonsense. You saw Rogovin's brain. There was no problem."

"The rats died."

"Rats are one thing. People are something else. It did kill the rats, but not the guinea pigs and not any patients. No humans. It's just some damn species difference."

"The FDA won't let me."

"But she might . . . keep bleeding . . . and . . ."

"Paul, I have no choice. You know that. I have to follow the rules. It's not just an individual thing. This is a corporate matter and we cannot afford to take a chance and stretch the rules like that. The FDA could really make things tough for us. There are no exceptions, Paul, and that's final."

"Not even for—?"

"Not even for you."

Paul knew he had lost the argument so he just hung up. Part of him knew that John was correct. From the corporate viewpoint, it was the right decision. If they stretched the rules and something went wrong, the FDA might suspend the entire project. There was no reason to quit, not yet. He still had one other option. He dailed another number. "Herb, it's Paul."

"How are you? I heard about your accident."

"I'm fine. Look, do we have any JNF-2?"

"We used up the new batch. But I'm pretty certain we still have some of the old stuff."

"What was the shelf life?"

"It's supposed to be good until next year."

"Can you get here as fast as you can and bring it up to the neurosurgery OR? I'll meet you there in—"

Herb interrupted him. "It'll take me at least twenty minutes."

"Twenty minutes is fine. I'll meet you in the OR in twenty."

Twenty minutes. She had to be shaved and prepped by now. And her scalp was probably already opened up. The bone was probably being drilled right now. "Cracked."

He decided he would wait in his office a little longer. They played something by Britten sung by Peter Pears. It was lovely. He hardly heard it.

The phone rang. Paul grabbed it in the middle of the first ring. "Bud!"

"Hi, Doc."

"Tom."

"Sounds like you were expecting someone else."

"I was."

"I won't keep you long."

"It's okay."

"Frank McCormick didn't attack Dr. Scala."

"I know."

"How do you know? I just found out myself. He flew to Amsterdam on Friday. On KLM. Checked in at O'Hare at three-thirty in the afternoon. She was in with Dr. Rotblatt until four-thirty. He still could have killed Jackie Baumer. We will probably ask the Dutch police to pick him up."

Somehow it didn't seem to matter.

"Have you learned anything more?" Tom asked.

"No. Not really."

"How is Dr. Scala?"

"I have to go and see. Now."

Herb Adams was already waiting outside the OR suite. He gave the vial to Paul and started to tell him about it.

"I've got to get in there."

"Boss, listen. There's something I have to tell you."

"Okay, but make it quick."

"Use a wide-bore syringe. This stuff is very viscous."

"I thought you used number-twenty-five needles in that last experiment. We used thin needles in the OR."

"I did."

"So?"

"This stuff is different. They changed the adjuvant or something."

"I've got to go."

Paul started taking off his clothes as soon as he was through the door. There was no time to find a locker. He stuffed his wallet and keys in the one pocket of the scrub shirt and left his own shirt and slacks where they had fallen.

He burst into the washroom and scrubbed in as quickly as he could. He could feel the vial of JNF-2 in the back pocket of his scrub pants as he dried his hands.

He made sure his mask and cap were in place and then he remembered to back into the OR with his hands in front of him.

The OR was cold. His legs started to hurt.

Her skull had been opened.

Cracked.

So had her dura. There in front of him was her brain.

Did he have the right to be here, to see her this way? Did he have a choice?

He stood there transfixed as other images came out of the depths of his brain.

Gerri on that landing, indecently exposed.

Jackie naked, covered with blood and tied in her bed. He and Jackie had made love on that same bed.

Gerri was strapped down and exposed.

He forced himself to look at her brain.

It was a brain.

It wasn't Gerri.

Just a brain.

He had to remember that.

The abnormal vessels were right there on the surface of the brain. You couldn't miss them. Some were reddish blue, others were almost violet. The blood clot was gone. Don had already sucked that away, exposing the brain and those damn fragile vessels.

Paul had his gown on now, and his gloves, so he went right up to Gerri's head. He could see better standing between Don and Bud. Two of the vessels were still bleeding. Maybe more. Blood was beginning to collect once again outside her brain. It was as if his own blood was once again dripping down and . . .

"It's not going well, Paul," Don Lenhardt said without looking up. "I can't stop the bleeding. Those veins are too damn thin to hold a suture. If I touch them they start bleeding again. And they go right into the brain. I can't tie them off. They're too big to burn. God only knows what they supply."

Murphy was a cockeyed optimist.

"The second unit is in," the anesthesiologist announced.

"Start the third," Don told him. "She has lost a lot of blood. I don't know what I can do. Nothing I've tried so far has worked."

"We tried lowering her pressure," Bud told him.

"How far?" Paul asked.

"Eighty over forty."

"That usually doesn't help in venous bleeding, and those look like veins to me," Paul complained.

"It didn't help. Nor have any of the clotting devices," Don added.

Paul watched. The two veins were not just dribbling a few drops each minute. Gerri's blood was flowing out of each at a rapid pace. Four or five cc's a minute. Maybe more.

"They're bleeding faster," Paul whined.

"I can see that."

"Then do something."

"I don't know what to do. Dammit."

Don's hands were shaking. Jackie must have been right. Paul had noticed that tremor only once before. That was during the operation on Friday. It was worse today. Every time the surgeon reached for something, his shaking increased.

"I do," Paul said. "I know what to do." His voice was surprisingly calm.

"What?"

"Use the JNF-2."

"We can't do that, Paul," Bud said.

"What other choice do we have?"

"Paul," Bud said. "The rats all died."

"So what! Rogovin didn't."

"The FDA," Don said firmly.

"Nuts to the FDA. We have it and we are going to use it."

"Don't, Paul," Bud pleaded.

"We have to."

"I won't," Don said.

"I don't care whether you will or not."

"This is my OR."

"This is the hospital OR," Paul corrected him.

"You are not a surgeon."

"No. I'm not, but I have clearance to give injections of JNF-2 in the OR as chief investigator on the project."

"I will not stay here and participate."

"So go. I don't need you. I can do it myself."

"I don't think the anesthesiologist will stay if there is no surgeon in the OR."

"Don't put me in the middle."

"He'll stay," Paul said. "He can't leave his patient and he knows it."

"You're right. I'll be here. I have no choice."

"The only choice is yours, Don. If you want to leave, leave. If you want to stay, stay. I'd rather you helped me. But I will do it myself if I have to."

"I . . . I . . . can't."

Don's hands were shaking more visibly than ever. The neurologist in Paul observed every detail. The tremor was bilateral. And symmetrical. Four or five cycles per second. No rotary component. Was it fear? Or anger? Or something else? Was he on something? Did he need a fix of some sort? Was this fight merely an excuse to get out of the OR and to his drug supply?

The tremor could easily be due to drug withdrawal. It could be so many things. What it was made no difference. Lenhardt was in no shape to go on. Paul had to do it himself.

"Get out, Don. I don't want anyone in here who doesn't feel he wants to be here."

"I—"

"Get out of here." Paul was now totally in command, and Lenhardt knew it. He left without any further argument.

"Bud."

"Yes."

"You in or out?"

"What do you think? I think you're wrong. You're taking too big a risk. But I'm still with you. You know that."

"Marv?"

"Lenhardt's my boss. I work for him. I . . . don't know."

"Make up your mind."

"I'll stay and close up. You'll need help putting the bone back. One of us should do that."

Rickert was right. Paul had no idea how to do that. Paul thanked him and scanned the room. The scrub nurse was still behind the instrument table, but he needed one more person.

"Where the hell is that damn circulating nurse?"

It was the anesthesiologist who answered him. "She left just before Lenhardt did."

"Bud, break scrub and act as circulator."

Bud did as he was told.

"The JNF-2 is in my pocket. My back pocket. Get it."

He felt the fingers take the vial out of his pocket.

"Got it."

"Good."

There was no reason to panic. His legs were beginning to throb. He had to be calm and ignore the pain.

Paul turned to the scrub nurse. "Thank you for staying."

"I come with the room," she said.

It was a voice he recognized.

She had been a nurse in the OR for years. He didn't remember her name. He wasn't sure he'd ever known it. Might as well start off right. "I'm Dr. Paul Richardson," he said.

"That I know," she laughed. "I'm Patricia Kelly. Everyone just calls me Kelly."

"Okay. Kelly, it is. Tell me, Kelly, what size needles do we have?"

"Everything from seventeen to twenty-nine."

"Let's try a seventeen. This stuff is supposed to be very thick. Dr. Chiari, the new circulating nurse, is going to open a vial for you, Kelly. Use a number-seventeen needle and draw up some of that goop. Make it one cc."

Bud opened the vial and held it as the nurse drew up one cc.

Marv had stepped back from the operating field. He was more an observer now than a participant. He watched as Paul took the suction and cleaned off the dark blood that had built up over the abnormal vessels.

"How's she doing?" Paul asked.

"BP one-ten over seventy," the anesthesiologist said. "And her pulse is ninety. Down from one-ten. The third unit is running."

"How many more do we have?"

"Two."

"It flows fairly easily in a seventeen," the nurse said.

"Let's see."

She handed him the syringe. He withdrew the barrel farther and then squeezed a drop out. "Sure does. Give me a smaller needle. It'll be safer. I'll have better control."

"What size?"

"A nineteen."

She handed it to him and he changed needles.

"Marv, can you handle the suction for me?"

Marv hesitated.

"For God's sake. This is your business. You're the pro."

Marv grabbed the suction and a small piece of gauze and went to work.

Paul squeezed a drop of the fluid through the number-nineteen needle. It was a tight fit. He could see why Herb had had so much difficulty pushing it through a thin-gauge needle in those guinea-pig experiments.

"It looks like three of them are bleeding," Paul said as he looked down at the brain.

"Four," Marv told him.

Paul looked again. "You're right! That one at two o'clock is leaking. Not that much, but still . . . I'm going to start with the one at seven o'clock. The large purple one."

He plunged the nineteen-gauge needle into the vein. Blood spurted out. He injected. The syringe emptied easily. More blood spurted out. He held the needle in place.

"The third unit is in."

"Suction."

Marv applied suction.

"Ten seconds," Bud said.

"Should I start number four?"

"Yes."

"We only have one left."

"Keep it clear!"

"I'm trying."

"I know. I'm sorry." Then, "Order two more units.

"Time."

"Twenty-five seconds," Bud said.

"Ninety percent in forty-five seconds," Paul said, reminding them of a fact that each of them already knew. "Ninety-eight percent in a minute. Come on. Work."

"Suction."

"Thirty five seconds.

"Forty."

The blood was still spurting out. The damn needle had made too big a hole. It was like a river of blood.

"Forty-five."

"Suction." Work, dammit.

"Fifty."

It slowed. The river became a stream, then a small creek, and finally a dry creekbed. He pulled out the syringe. It started to bleed again. Had he left the damn syringe in too long and now dislodged something by pulling it out? Maybe they were right. He should not be doing this.

"One minute."

He said nothing. He just stood there and watched as drop after drop of Gerri's blood dribbled out through the hole he had himself created.

"Seventy seconds."

More blood rushed out of the torn vessel.

"Eighty seconds."

Another unneeded reminder. They could all tell that time was passing.

It stopped. Just like that it stopped. Marv took a small piece of gauze and wiped off the area.

They all watched.

There was no more bleeding.

He hadn't hurt her. It probably wouldn't happen if he used a smaller needle.

"Draw up another cc."

Paul surveyed the brain.

"Make it a cc and a half. We're going after that big one up front."

Bud opened the vial again.

"How much do we have?"

"Ten cc's," Bud replied.

"Good."

"You shouldn't use more than seven and a half."

"I'll use whatever I have to."

"What size needle, Dr. Richardson?"

Paul looked at the vessels. "Signs?"

"BP one-ten over eighty. Pulse ninety-six."

The walls of this vessel appeared to be even thinner than the first one. He didn't want to put another big hole in it.

"Let's try a twenty-one, Kelly."

She handed him the syringe.

"Vital signs?"

"No change."

"Blood?"

"Number four is running. I have number five here."

"Suction around that big one."

Paul took a deep breath. "Here goes. That wall looks so damn thin." Like Rogovin's. The thought made him shudder.

He stuck the needle in.

The vein collapsed. There was a rush of dark blood. His hand jerked involuntarily. He went too deep. He had struck another vessel. An artery. Its stream of bright red blood leapt out of her brain. Dammit, there had been an artery hidden deep inside the vein. He hadn't seen that on the CAT scan. He steadied his hand and pushed the needle ever so slightly deeper inside the tangle of twisted veins and arteries.

"Hundred over sixty-four."

It was now or never. The spurts of bright red blood continued their repeated eruptions. All you had to do to tell her pulse rate was to count them. That was a fact of which none of them needed reminding. Arterial blood was pumping into the air in front of them. What had merely been an emergency was rapidly becoming a state of panic. Ninety-six spurts per minute. One and a half jets of bright red blood each second. He started injecting.

"More suction. I can't see a damn thing."

"Ten seconds."

He kept pushing on the barrel of the syringe. It was almost impossible to force the JNF-2 out through the thinner needle. He should have stayed with the nineteen. Nothing more came out. The damned needle was clogged.

"It's stuck."

"Twenty seconds."

He pushed harder. The bright red spurts continued. One right after another. He pushed again. The barrel moved. It moved.

"Thirty seconds."

He was done. The syringe was empty. He held it tightly in place, afraid to move it even one millimeter. "It's all in."

"Forty."

The artery was still spitting its bright red blood into the air. A steady flow of darker blue-red blood was still running out of the vein. It was all Gerri's blood. Her brain looked like a scene from her process notes, from one of McCormick's purloined dreams.

Her brain was not going to rot. Not if he could do anything about it.

"Get me another cc."

"Fifty seconds."

"More suction."

More dark red blood. The vein was pouring out more of its blood, at an even faster rate. The arterial spurting continued unabated.

"Pulse one-ten."

"Hang number five just in case."

"Here's the syringe."

"Seventy seconds."

"Start the count again."

"Paul, what are you doing?"

"It was John's voice. He wasn't in the OR. He was above them in the observation suite. Paul recognized the distinctive echolike timbre the intercom gave to his voice.

"Paul," he repeated, "what are you doing?"

"Injecting a little bit of JNF-2."

"Ten seconds," Bud announced.

"More suction."

"Pulse one-twenty."

"Speed up the blood. We're losing. We can't lose."

"Twenty seconds."

The outpouring just wouldn't stop.

"Paul."

The two separate streams of red continued to fuse outside her brain.

"I'm saving a life. Dammit."

"Thirty seconds."

Marv was now applying the suction continuously, sucking up both streams of blood as quickly as he could. He seemed to be fighting a losing battle. There was more and more blood there. It was getting harder and harder to see her brain.

More spurts.

"Forty seconds."

They were closer together now as her heart quickened to make up for the lost blood.

"Her pulse is one-thirty. No, its closer to one-forty."

It had to stop. It just had to.

"Fifty." Stop. Slow down!

It did. The tide was turning. She wasn't bleeding as quickly. They could see her brain again.

The blue blood was all gone. The collapsed vein had stopped bleeding. The artery was still erupting into the air, but that was all.

"One minute."

"Pulse one-thirty."

Her heart might be slowing down. Maybe they were now adding blood at least as quickly as she was losing it.

"Seventy seconds."

He watched the succession of red spurts, counting them half-consciously.

"One two three.

"One two three.

"One two three.

"One. Two. Three.

"One . . . two . . . three.

"One. . . . Two . . ." And then there were no more red streams of blood shooting up at his face.

"It's stopped!" Paul shouted. "It's stopped!"

Marv continued to suction until he had cleaned off all the blood.

The brain looked pink and healthy. It still glistened. It still pulsated like a normal brain. No brain had ever looked so good.

"One-ten over seventy. Number four is in. Should I start number five?"

"Hold off."

There was no more red fountain coming out of her brain.

"Paul, you have to stop." It was John again from on high. He sounded just like Charlton Heston receiving the Ten Commandments—or giving them, or both.

"Not on your life."

"You have no right."

No one was paying any attention to him.

"It's not approved. The FDA will send an inspector down here."

Marv had put the suction down. Paul inspected the entire brain. Everything looked good. There were two areas of oozing left. But no spots with any major amount of bleeding. Panic had returned to mere emergency. "We should be able to finish up with three, maybe four more small injections. Half a cc each. Let me have half a cc."

"What size needle?" Kelly asked.

After looking at the vessels, Paul answered, "Let's use a nineteen."

"Nineteen it is."

John was still there. "Paul, what about the FDA?"

"Let 'em come and inspect us. I've had my hands slapped before," Paul said.

When he heard no reply, Paul looked up at the observation deck. No one was there.

"John?"

No one answered.

The rest of it was mere child's play.

The larger of the two vessels that was still bleeding took two injections of half a cc each. The smaller one required only one. After those Paul stopped again to take stock of where they were.

"Pulse eighty-eight."

"BP one-fifteen over seventy."

"Unit four is in," the voice reminded him. "Number five is hanging. Should I start it?"

"No."

There were two more vessels that looked too fragile to trust.

"Let's do them both. One half cc each."

"That'll make six cc's," Bud said.

"A nice safe amount," Paul responded.

"Paul." It was John again. Paul looked up. John wasn't alone. Dean Willis was with him.

"Hi, guys."

"What have you done?" Willis asked.

"I hope I saved Gerri's life and her brain."

"You broke an FDA rule," the dean reminded him.

"Did I?"

"Yes!" John replied.

"I never received anything in writing."

"I told you."

"Yes. You told me. But I'm the chief investigator. When the FDA pulls a drug, they send the chief investigator a telegram, or at least a registered letter. But I never heard from them. Not so much as a penny postcard.

"I should have figured that out before. Holmes was right,

of course. It's always easier to figure out the clue that is there. It's the one that isn't there but should be that causes trouble. Syringe, please."

Kelly handed him the syringe. He palpated the chosen target. It was becoming routine. There was nothing to it. Anyone could be a neurosurgeon. The vessel was not bleeding. There was no hurry. No need for controlled pandemonium. Not even any need for suction.

He began his injection. Bud began timing it.

"I should have figured out what had happened long ago. The FDA didn't issue any injunction. All they did was say they would investigate all further use of JNF-2 in the presence of fresh bleeding. For that they don't send a telegram. It's not a recall. They send out a form letter. It takes three months for that kind of notification."

"Twenty seconds."

"You issued the recall. You. Dillinger. Not the FDA."

"One-fifteen over seventy-eight."

"Now, why would you do that? The answer is simple. Look at our lab results. The difference between the rats and the guinea pigs we did two years ago. That wasn't any species difference. It was a product difference. It was something that Dillinger was doing in the manufacturing process. Poor quality control. Lousy manufacturing techniques. It was there all the time. One batch is viscous. One flows well. One works. One kills. It wasn't just the adjuvant. I know what adjuvants you could have used. I'm not some damn neophyte. I've been in this business for a long time. I've used them all. They might change the rate of flow by ten percent. But no more. No, the difference between batches of JNF-2 is a hell of a lot more than that."

"Sixty seconds."

He withdrew the syringe and gave it back to Kelly. "One more, please, Kelly."

"Coming right up."

"Pulse seventy-eight and regular."

"BP one-twelve over sixty-eight. That's just about where we started."

The surface of the brain was shining brightly. The once dark ugly collection of abnormal vessels was now a pale blue-gray that complemented its pink color. What had been a vibrant Matisse less than an hour earlier had become a soft pastel by Monet. A pleasant water lily. In the Orangerie. In Paris.

"Here's the last one, Dr. Richardson."

Paul took it, felt the last purple vein, and pushed the needle into it. He began compressing the barrel.

"Ten seconds."

"You couldn't tolerate an investigation, John, so you pulled it yourself. You. Not the FDA."

"John, is that true?" Dean Willis asked.

John Corrigan said nothing.

"Thirty seconds."

"I'm sorry we bothered you, Paul."

"It's okay, T.B."

"Sixty seconds." He removed the syringe and started to hand it to Patricia Kelly, but changed his mind.

"We're done," Paul said. "Marv, will you close up?"

"Sure thing."

"I'll take her to the ICU, personally," Bud said.

"Thanks, Bud."

"What are you going to do with the syringe?"

"Keep it. Or give it to Gerri as a souvenir."

22

One more nightmare was over. At least for a while. It had been the second one for Paul in less than twenty-four hours and the third in less than a week, but they were all behind him now. As soon as he got back to his office he took his last two Percodans. They were sufficient to dull his various pains and throbs and yet leave his mind clear enough to concentrate on what he at last knew was the truth. It had not been Frank McCormick who had killed Jackie Baumer. True—he had not-so-innocently triggered the process which resulted in her death, yet he was not even an accomplice. The solution was obvious. How to prove it was much more complicated.

Sprawled on the couch in his office, he could just barely reach his phone. He called home. Joshua answered. "Dad, you okay?"

"Sure. Perfect in fact."

"Really?"

"Yes."

"How is Gerri?" It was Carolyn. She was on one of the other extensions.

"She'll be fine."

"Are you sure?"

"Yes. We had to operate on her but she'll be just fine."

"Operate? What for?"

"Don't worry about her. It wasn't any big deal. I'll tell you all about it when I get home."

"When will that be?" she asked.

"I want to see her once in Recovery," he said, thinking out loud. "Two, maybe three hours."

"Shall I make dinner?"

"No, we'll go out."

Dinner. When had he last eaten? Months ago, as best as he could remember. He wondered if Chris had left any of the doughnuts in the office. Unlikely on a weekend.

"You look beat, Doc."

Paul recognized the voice coming from his doorway. "I am, Tom."

"Too beat for something to eat?"

"No, not at all. What have you got?"

"I ordered chicken salad on rye toast and a couple of Cokes."

It sounded great to Paul. Tom put the food on the low coffee table and sat down in the chair next to the couch. Paul sat up and attacked one of the sandwiches.

"It's tuna. You said it was chicken."

"No, I said I ordered chicken. All they had was tuna."

"It's not Tuesday already, is it?"

"No," Tom reassured him. "It's still Sunday. They said they ran out of chicken salad."

"It's pretty good," Paul said, "for tuna." They ate in silence. Neither one of them was sure where to start or how much to say. Gerri had to be in the ICU by now. Bud was with her. He ought to be calling soon. His not calling was most likely a good sign. Most likely did not mean absolutely.

"Doc?"

"Yes."

"You read the diary?"

"Yes."

"Did you learn anything?"

"Yes."

"Anything I need to know?"

Had he? Of course he had. At the end. Where else but at the end.

"I know who killed Jackie," Paul announced.

"The McCormick kid. You've already told me that a dozen times."

"No, not him." He started on the second half of his sandwich. It was, he decided, rather good tuna salad. Neither too dry nor drowned in mayonnaise. And the lettuce was crisp.

"You gonna tell me or do you want to keep it a secret?"

"No," Paul said.

Tom was not sure exactly what the answer meant, so he asked another question. "Now or later?"

"Yes."

Tom started to say something else. He would learn just as much by not asking any more questions.

Paul finished his sandwich and his Coke. Except it wasn't a Coke; it was a Tab. He had stalled long enough. "You read the diary before I did. It pretty much listed the suspects by revealing their motives, at least to someone who understands the workings of this medical center and the sorts of things that regulate our lives. You know them all. Floyd, Edie, Don Lenhardt, Herb Adams, and John Corrigan." He reconsidered. "Me, Gerri, Bill Goodman, and even Bud.

"Some of them, or rather some of us, were easy to eliminate. Others were not. Gerri was never really a suspect. Despite her lies, she had only one possible motive."

"Lies?"

Paul chose not to answer that question. It wasn't any of Tom's business. Gerri's lies to him were part of their personal life, not of some dammed official investigation. It was just between them. The method she used to get him to leave her was not anyone else's concern.

"She could have killed Jackie that last time I . . . made it with her. That was three months ago. I had just asked her to marry me. Or at least to think about it. Then . . ." Saying it all out loud triggered something. "You eliminated that possibility when you told her about Jackie and me. Gerri was truly surprised. She had never known until you spilled the beans."

"She could have been acting," Tom said.

"She wasn't. Believe me. Not with me. I paid the price so that you could rule her out. She was enraged." Why hadn't Bud called? Paul began to reach for the phone and then stopped. Bud would call if anything important happened.

"One down."

"Bud," he half-whispered.

"What?"

"Bud Chiari."

"Oh."

"He was the next one who was easy to eliminate."

"How?"

"I know him." Paul recognized the look on Tom's face. "Don't act so damned convinced. What do we know about the killer?"

"Very little."

"No. We know he was at my house and put some poison in some orange juice in my refrigerator."

"What?"

Paul forgot. Tom didn't know about the Metrazol. So many things had happened in the last couple of days that he had not had time to tell anyone, not even Carolyn. She was still taking her Dilantin and not driving. He had no choice but to take the time now and put all the facts in order. Paul told Tom how Carolyn's seizure had been caused by Metrazol, a chemical that is used for that specific purpose. The drug, needless to say, had been stolen from the hospital and put into their orange juice.

"Why orange juice?"

"That's how we give it sometimes. In orange juice with a lot of extra sugar. That pretty much hides the flavor. The orange juice just tastes a little bitter. Besides, everyone here knows I drink a lot of orange juice."

"Then why does that eliminate Dr. Chiari?"

"He wasn't there that night. He wasn't being sued. Besides, he's the one who reported the missing Metrazol to me."

"Two down."

"Yes." Why hadn't Bud called yet?

"Why?" Tom asked.

"Why?" Paul repeated. He had to think about their conversation, not about the phone that wasn't ringing.

"Why would someone try to poison your orange juice?"

"To distract me. It probably wouldn't have killed me, although I usually drink twice as much orange juice as Carolyn does. I always get up first. Funny, I got delayed listening to a singer who had just died. Cathy Ber . . ." He stopped his own reverie. "I'm sure it was aimed at me."

"Why?"

"So that I couldn't help you. Everyone knows you like to

work with me, and your visits to my office were certainly no secret. I can help you understand what really goes on here. That meant that the motive had to be something medical. Some twist that I would understand but that you wouldn't pick up on your own. If I was right about that, then the whole business had nothing to do with Jackie's sex life. As sordid and complex as it was, who she was sleeping with was irrelevant. If someone could get me out of the way for a few weeks, that might make it less likely that you would find the killer.''

"That's probably true."

"How long would you have stayed on the case?" Paul asked.

"Not long. There's already pressure to drop it. Willis never likes to have us around here. Nor does your Board, and there are some very influential people on that board of yours. Just another nurse killed by some disgruntled lover or other. No big deal.''

"So he was right. Make sure it's not solved in two, three weeks at the outside, and it'll just go away."

"He?"

"Yes, he."

The phone rang. Less than one full ring.

"Bud! How is she?"

"Her pressure is—''

"Not her pressure. Her. How is she?"

"There's no paralysis."

There was something he wasn't saying. Paul knew what it was. He couldn't say the word. He had to know. "Can she name objects?"

"Yes . . ."

"But not all of them."

"No."

"What did she miss?"

"Hands. Watchband. She got stem."

"Spelling?"

There was no response.

"Could she spell 'world'?"

"W. That was all. She didn't get any further."

"Can she stick her tongue out on command?"

"Yes."

"I'm coming up."

"Wait."

"I—"

"Wait. She's beginning to improve. Don't torture yourself. I'll call in half an hour. I'll be here."

"Call me if—"

"I will."

He put the phone back.

"Don Lenhardt," Paul began. His voice was flat, almost as if he were reading from a name picked out at random from some telephone directory.

"What?"

"Lenhardt. The neurosurgeon. I didn't eliminate him until just a couple of hours ago, and I didn't even realize it at the time. You remember what Jackie said she had on him?"

"Yeah, drugs."

"And how she had warned him that she was going to expose him someday and end his career?"

"Sure."

"Well, her story doesn't hang together."

"Why not?"

"First of all because of when his tremor appears."

"When he's excited or under stress."

"That's right."

"What's wrong with that?" Tom asked.

"It's okay for a cheap novel to have a drug-releated tremor be precipitated by stress, but that's not the way it happens. Drug-related tremors come out during periods of drug withdrawal. It would be a most peculiar circumstance if he always underwent withdrawal at times of stress, when most drug users increase their intake. His shaking happened at the wrong times. Tonight he rushed here to operate on Gerri and his tremor was terrible."

"Maybe he didn't have time to get his fix."

"That is undoubtedly what happened," Paul explained.

"Huh?"

"And the witnesses prove it."

"What are you talking about?"

"Jackie's corroborating witnesses. No junkie would let three people witness him taking something. But if he were on some medication and he needed it, he'd go ahead and take it.''

"So it was medicine?''

"Sure. Inderal, most likely. He must have a familial tremor. That kind of shakiness is always increased by stress and excitement. He probably forgot his medicine this morning in all the excitement. We just had a crazy argument today that may have been nothing but an excuse for him to get out of the OR. He was shaking like a leaf.''

"So Jackie had nothing on him,'' Tom concluded.

"Nothing at all. Her threat was meaningless.''

"Another suspect down the drain. By the way, you said it had to be a male. Why not Edie?''

"She wasn't at my place that Friday night. And besides, their romance had been cooling down and that was at least as much Edie's choice as it was Jackie's. And remember what I said about the Metrazol. That was done just to prevent me from working with you. You don't need my help to understand a sex murder.''

"Who else was at your place?''

"The dean,'' Paul replied.

"You don't suspect him?''

"T.B.? Of course not. You asked me who else was there, not who else was still a suspect.''

"Be serious.''

"Floyd Baker.''

"One.''

"John Corrigan.''

"Two.''

"Herb Adams.''

"Three.'' Tom pulled out his notebook and checked some of his notes. "They were all at the hospital the night Jackie was killed, so they all had opportunities.''

"And motives. Herb had one. So did John. And Floyd had more than one.''

"He did?''

"Yes. Jealousy and ambition. He loved her and he wanted Bud's job.''

"That's a potent combination.''

"I eliminated Herb first. All he would have lost was his job, and that might not have been permanent. He could probably have caught on somewhere else. That seemed to be a fairly flimsy motive.''

"People have killed for less."

"True, but he admitted his error to me. He didn't cover it up. And more than that, he isn't sophisticated enough to have taken the consent form to block the investigation.''

"We're back to that form of yours."

"Yes. It's the key. You had to be an M.D. or someone who really knew something about malpractice to realize that getting rid of that lousy piece of paper left us so vulnerable that we would settle and abort any investigation that would be part of the lawsuit.''

"There is only one M.D. left," Tom realized. "Floyd Baker. As a lover of hers he might have killed like that, out of jealousy.''

"I considered that possibility. But there's one big problem."

"Namely?"

"He needed her alive in order to confront Bud Chiari. Floyd was smart enough to know that a letter like the one they sent to me wouldn't by itself be enough to get rid of Bud. He typed it for her and made certain that she signed it and then he put it in the mail himself. He didn't want her to change her mind. But I'm sure she was alive when he left. Alive and kicking. Or whatever else she was into.''

"But why not McCormick?"

"You don't kill someone just to win a malpractice suit."

"Then why do you?" Tom asked.

"Not to lose."

"John Corrigan."

"Give that man all sixty-four dollars."

The phone rang. Paul got it during the first ring.

"How is she?" Paul burst out, aborting any greeting.

"Better."

"How much?"

" 'Word' for 'world.' She got 'stem' and 'crystal.' She'll be fine.''

"I'll be up in a few minutes."

"Okay. She can have visitors, but don't stay too long."

"Visitor!"

"Paul."

"You're right. I won't stay long."

"She's in 703."

"A or B?"

"She's the only patient."

"See you soon, and . . . thanks." He hung up.

"John Corrigan," Tom repeated.

"What?"

"We were discussing John Corrigan."

"Yes. He killed Jackie."

"How do you know?"

"I've eliminated everyone else, and on top of that he had the best motive. And it probably was their fault in the first place. I mean, if anything had gone wrong, it would most likely have been their screw-up, and he knew it."

He was going too quickly. "We put some cells into McCormick's head along with a chemical. That chemical was made by Corrigan's company. The first things that any lawyer worth his salt would have looked into were the preparation of those cells in my lab and the production of the chemical by them. John couldn't let that investigation take place. He had to avoid the whole legal discovery process at all cost." Paul told Tom all about JNF-2, about the rats and guinea pigs and Sam Rogovin and how John Corrigan and Dillinger Chemicals, not the FDA, had made the decision to limit the use of JNF-2. Though Paul couldn't pinpoint the exact problem, his best guess was that something was not controlled well enough in the last step of the synthesis. The final product was obviously not pure, and one of the impurities could injure cells. Just a few hours earlier, Paul had finally realized that that was what had happened in his lab with another of their chemicals, JNF-2. Well, the same thing had gone wrong with Dillinger 307. The present batch worked well in his lab. The previous one had not. It was the same kind of problem. Herb had assumed that it was his fault that all of the adrenal-cell lines now looked better than the ones they had put into Frank McCormick. He was wrong. It had been a problem with one of Corrigan's chemicals. If that stuff could louse up cells growing in Paul's lab, it might do the same thing inside a patient's brain.

"Corrigan couldn't tolerate an investigation of JNF-2 or Dillinger 307 either. So he killed Jackie."

"How can you prove it?"

"We could get all the suspects together in a big room."

"Paul, that won't work."

"True. Besides, we would have to rent an English manor house." Paul got himself back on track. "He took the form. Corrigan's the only one who could have taken it. They've known about the case for over a year. He was the only one of us who knew long enough ago to take it before a copy of the chart was sent to Henry Arft. Don't forget one other thing. He's a Ph.D., not an M.D. Once he heard about the McCormick's lawsuit, he had to shift the blame, so he took the consent form. That way, he thought, we had no defense. In the drug company he might be able to avoid any investigation, and we'd pay off the settlement. But he made a mistake no M.D. would have made—he only took the consent form and not the operative checklist."

"We're back to that operative checklist. I had never even heard of that before."

"Of course not—only a physician would have known about it. It's a system at Austin Flint—one of the nurses reads through the chart and fills out the checklist. If everything is kosher, she says nothing and the surgery goes on. No one else even knows it's being done. When Corrigan learned about the checklist, it meant that despite the murder, discovery was still possible. He had to do something. So he got together with the dean. That explained the rush on the consortium and the need to settle the suit immediately to spare us bad publicity and save the consortium grant."

"How did he know?"

"That you'll have to find out. But I can make a good guess. When a patient's records are requested by a lawyer, Medical Records must notify our lawyers, who then tell the dean. From there it is just a phone call away from John. As soon as he knew trouble was brewing, he took the form, and when the suit was finally filed and the papers served, he killed Jackie. That way he thought he could save his company. And he did. We settled out of court. I have to go see Gerri."

"Thanks."

"You're welcome."

"I hope Dr. Scala's all right."

"She is," Paul said. "I'll walk you to the elevator."

They were halfway there when he heard the page: "Paul Richardson . . . Paul Richardson . . ."

It was an emergency. He didn't want to hear his name a third time. Gerri. Something had gone wrong, very wrong. He should have been there. There might have been something he could have done.

What could he do that Bud couldn't?

Inject JNF-2.

Had that been what had gone wrong?

So soon?

Up the stairs. Which room had Bud said? Room 703.

Fifth floor.

Why had he done it?

What choice had he had?

And now she had gone sour. Why had he had to play God?

Gerri.

It was his fault.

His and Corrigan's and those screwed-up chemicals.

Sixth floor.

His knees were buckling.

His shins screaming.

Blood was again collecting in his shoe.

Seventh floor.

Right or left?

Right.

He burst through the doors into the ICU. It was quiet. He missed the sound of organized chaos. It should be there.

707 . . . 705 . . . 703.

That was it.

703.

There she was.

There was no one at the bedside.

He stopped.

There was no respirator.

No tube coming out of her mouth.

No oxygen being sent into her lungs.

No reassuring whooshing sounds.

Her tube had been pulled.

They gave up. So quickly.

How could they have just let her die without a fight?

How?

Why?

"Gerri!"

"D-l-r-o-w," she said. "I can name the presidents back-
wards, and the parts of your watch I can name in my sleep."

"Gerri. I . . ."

"My throat's sore from that damned tube."

"Gerri."

"Are you perseverating, Paul?"

"Gerri, you're okay."

"I think so."

"Gerri, I . . ."

"Yes?"

"I was worried. I . . ."

"Yes."

"Nothing."

They looked at each other, searching for the right words.

"I thought that triple page was you. I better check."

He called the page operator. It was Mrs. Kell. She was
threatening to kill herself. No one had told her anything. She
had somehow gotten lost in the shuffle.

Paul called her room. She was crying. Would he come see
her? He wanted to stay with Gerri but he had no real choice.
Mrs. Kell was his patient and she at least said that she needed
him. And furthermore, he could say something that would
help her.

──Epilogue──

The summer went by more quickly than Paul had any right to expect. One reason was the White Sox, who inexplicably put it all together right after the All-Star Game, stormed into first place, and waltzed away with the Western Division pennant.

Despite the unexpected glory of rooting for a winner, Paul's summer did not glide by painlessly. Austin Flint Medical Center adjusted to the solution of Jackie Baumer's killing as easily as it had to the murder itself. Perhaps more easily. After all, when she was murdered, they'd had to hire a new nurse.

The hospital itself continued to function as though nothing had happened. New patients were admitted every day. The bed-occupancy rate remained the highest in town. This of course kept Dean Willis and the board of trustees very happy. Big Brother, or at least good fortune, continued to look out for them. Some patients did well and went home improved, others got worse, still others went home unchanged. Some even died. No one knew what the exact breakdown was. Except for recording the number of deaths, no one even bothered to compile statistics like that.

It took the Department of Neurology longer to return to normal, but by the end of the summer it too was back in full swing. Patients came and went, as did medical students. Paul continued to run the research team, and in August and September he also took over the consultation service from Bud

Chiari. This double duty kept him on rounds six hours a day and left him with precious little time to ruminate.

Gerri Scala had remained in the hospital two and a half weeks. Though she was well enough to leave the ICU by the third postoperative day, they elected to keep her there for an entire week. If the same thing happened to her that had happened to Sam Rogovin, they wanted to be ready. Marv Rickert and Bud Chiari virtually lived in the hospital that week, sleeping little and waiting in fear for an event that never happened. For an awake, alert patient, being in ICU is a combination of solitary confinement and Chinese water torture, and by the third day, Gerri was going stir-crazy. Day and night she was bombarded by continuing barrages of electronic blips, mechanical whooshes, persistent warning wails, and impersonal interruptions. What few visitors braved its hostile atmosphere could stay only briefly, standing awkwardly in a much-too-public place filled with other patients, noisy machines, overworked nurses, and half-exhausted doctors, all seemingly striving to make anyone not actively involved in saving at least one life want to flee at once.

Paul did stop by to see her every day. His visits varied from awkward to uncomfortable for both of them. Paul told her what they had done, what decisions he had made, and how he had injected the JNF-2 himself. He made it sound as undramatic as he could and, of course, played down his role. He felt uneasy when he started to talk about anything else, not being sure how she felt or what she wanted. And she said very little, waiting for something to go wrong inside her head. It was not a time for her to consider her future—if she had any.

Nothing went wrong.

On the seventh day, she begged Bud and Marv to let her be transferred out of the ICU so that she could get some sleep and have a TV to watch. After all, even God had had to rest on the seventh day. But Bud told her that God didn't turn on the TV to watch *General Hospital*.

On the eighth day, Bud finally felt secure enough to let her leave the ICU. A week later she went home. The last time Paul watched her in the hospital, he was fully aware that her facial weakness was significantly more pronounced than it had been when she had first drawn his attention to it at lunch, just three weeks earlier, in Chinatown. He was not trying to be her physician. That was the last thing he wanted to be. All his years of training and experience made it impossible for him to ignore what he saw. He also realized that Gerri still had some speech deficit. Not much, but some. He noted it first as he sat in her room watching a Sox game with her and she kept referring to cleanup hitter Greg Luzinski as the mop-up hitter. She also made other word substitutions, but Paul never said anything about it. He was not her doctor, just an old friend.

It was only when she got home that Gerri knew that her brain was not back to normal. Some words she had known quite well before were now suddenly foreign to her. They made no sense at all. The only known treatment for that was time. She stayed home for four weeks, and by the time she returned to work, she made few if any errors.

Carolyn of course was thrilled when Paul told her that she didn't have epilepsy and that she didn't have any reason to worry that she might have another convulsion. No more seizures. No more Dilantin. No more EEG's, but most important of all, she could drive. She had been unable to drive for only one week, but she felt as if Moses had just led her out of her own personal bondage.

Freedom. She didn't have to depend on someone else to go out to visit a friend or a store. She could drive herself. She could take Joshua wherever he had to go. She was free. She could not understand why Paul hadn't told her sooner. It had skipped his mind, what with the operation on Gerri and all. It had only been a little over a week. Would she forgive him? She did.

The first trip she made was a visit to Gerri in the hospital. She went there almost every day, and when the time came for Gerri to be discharged, Carolyn drove her home.

Paul didn't see Gerri again until after she came back to work. It was the middle of August and she called him and asked him out to lunch. He accepted her invitation. He was never one to miss a free meal.

She picked him up in her car and drove. She didn't ask him where he wanted to go but took him to the Chinese Deli.

He was puzzled at her choice.

She ordered the same meal they had had much earlier in the baseball season.

While they waited, nervously exchanging small talk, she removed her glasses. He stared at her face.

She smiled broadly.

She wrinkled her forehead.

She closed her eyes as tightly as she could.

"You're better."

"I know."

"Not as good as you were before you . . ."

"Say it," she said.

"Bled," he said. "But much better than you were post-op."

"Bud is pleased with my recovery."

"So am I."

"I'm a little aphasic. I choose the wrong word sometimes, especially when I try to use words I don't use all the time."

"I know."

"You do?"

"Yes."

"How?"

"What does Greg Luzinski do?"

"I know," she answered proudly. "He bats mop-up."

"Cleanup, not mop-up."

"They're the same thing," she complained.

"Close, but no cigar. That's part of aphasia: substituting a related but incorrect phrase."

"I know his nickname," she proclaimed with a nearly normal smile.

"Tell me."

"The Tank."

"Wrong again."

"What is it?"

"The Bull."

"Those aren't much different."

"I didn't say they were. It's a word substitution using a closely related word."

"Paul, those mistakes aren't due to aphasia," Gerri said, shaking her head.

"They aren't?"

"No."

"Then what are they due to?"

"A lifelong history of dedicated indifference to baseball."

"I'd rather you were aphasic."

"Thanks." She reached out and put her hand on top of his. "Bud says you saved my life."

"What?"

"He told me exactly what happened in the OR. The way you told it to me, it sounded as if using the JNF-2 were a natural decision that anyone would have made. Bud told me that without you I might very well have died on the table."

"He shouldn't have told you that."

"Why not? Don't I have the same rights as other patients?"

"Of course you do."

"Then why not?" she persisted.

"You're not just a patient. We used to be lovers. It's not that simple."

She let it pass for a moment. The waitress brought the chow fun. The pan-fried noodles would be ready in a minute or two. Did they want chopsticks? They did.

"I'm glad he told me."

"I'm not sure I am."

"I had to know whose decision it was."

"I told you that while you were in the ICU."

"I was so confused then, I'm not sure I understood exactly what you were telling me."

"Did he also . . . ?" Paul stopped.

"Yes, he told me all the details."

The fried noodles arrived.

"What would you have done if it hadn't worked?" she asked.

"How do I know?"

"Could you have lived with that?"

"Hell. No." He shook his head slowly. "Do you really want to know the truth?"

"Yes."

"The truth is, I blew it. You were in bad shape. I mean it. You were either going to . . ."

"Die," she said.

"Yes, or have your brain messed up. There was nothing at all we could do, so I played hero and did something. I couldn't stand watching helplessly. I had already lost the only other woman I ever loved. I didn't want to lose you. Not that way. I had no right to do what I did, but I had to.''

"I'm glad you did.''

"So am I. Now. Could I have lived with it? Yes. I would have had no other choice. I have my two kids.'' He stopped. The noodles were getting cold.

They began to eat.

"Did you mean what you said before?'' she asked.

"What was that?''

"That we used to be lovers?''

"I guess so.''

They continued eating and finished both dishes. Dessert came. It consisted of a pair of fortune cookies. Gerri's told her that she would soon go on a trip. Paul's said that a modest man never talks of himself. He was sure she had planted it. She asked for the check. Paul started to argue, but didn't. Lunch had been her idea, not his.

"Would you live with me?'' she asked.

"Is that a proposal?''

"If marriage is the only way, yes.''

"Why?''

"Because I like the way you make coffee at the office.''

"Chris makes the coffee.''

"Doesn't she come with you?''

"Gerri, why did you ask me that?''

"Because I want to be with you, always. I knew that before, but it was all so complicated. Was it you I wanted, or Carolyn and Joshua? The answer is both. I was worried that something might happen to me, that I might bleed again. Would that be fair to you? Yes, it would. I finally realized that. I'm good for you. I know it. Every day we get to spend together will be a plus for both of us. If something goes wrong, that's too bad. We both need those good days.'' She hesitated. She had to say it all. "Then I worried that maybe you were the father I never had. Maybe. Who cares? I love you.''

"I love you too.''

"I don't have any patients this afternoon,'' she said.

"Neither do I,'' he said.''Just brain cutting. I can skip that.''

"We'll have to hurry,'' she said.

"Why?"

"Carolyn is coming over after school."

"Good. She can be the first to know."

"She already knows."

"What?"

"I told her I was going to ask you. I wanted her permission."

"Oh."

They drove quickly to her apartment, and as they drove, she told him that she had been rereading her process notes on Frank McCormick. One thing bothered her.

"What's that?"

"His fourth dream."

He remembered. *"The Third Man."*

"Yes. It started strangely. He said he had been born without a nose. That's not from Graham Greene."

"No."

"I'm sure I've read that somewhere. Some book we've both read started that way. Right in the opening sentence. I know it. I just can't think of it."

"Nothing I ever read started like that. How could you open a book with a sentence like that? You couldn't."

"Maybe I'm wrong."

"You are."

It was after two when they arrived at her place. They made love quickly. It was not the best lovemaking they had ever shared. They were too hurried for that, but it was something they would not forget. Especially Gerri.

"That was fantastic, Paul."

"It was good."

"It was wonderful."

"We've done it better."

"Sure, but this was different."

"Different?"

"Yes, for the first time ever, I had an orgasm without getting a headache. I always got a throbbing pain on the left side of my head, a sharp, throbbing pain. It was from my . . . malformation. And now it's gone."

"Maybe it was just a second-rate orgasm."

"Not on your life, buster. I'm cured."

She hugged him and began to kiss him, but it was time to get dressed.

*   *   *

In early September, Fred Sanford was readmitted to the hospital. He was admitted on the infectious-disease service with pneumonia. Paul saw him in consultation. He had no neurologic problems at all. His cryptococcal meningitis had been cured. There were no signs of an abscess. His CAT scan was normal. He died in five days and became recorded as the fourteenth death from AIDS in Chicago. Paul and the internist both noted that he had developed Kaposi sarcomas on his legs before he died.

Donna Kolloway continued to do well. Her weakness was improved. She had no headaches. She was feeling wonderful. Paul wanted to ask her if sex had ever caused her to have headaches but he was too embarrassed or too old-fashioned or both.

Mike Kreevich was doing brilliantly. He had been seizure-free since the operation and his speech was entirely normal.

Maurie Rath was not doing that well but the surgery had helped him a great deal. He had had only two seizures in four months.

Mrs. Nicholson, the lady with spasmodic torticollis, was some fifty percent improved. Paul was fairly happy. She was better. Her disease had not progressed, which it would have done without treatment, and she was finally convinced that she didn't have a terminal cancer.

Edie Robinson kept him up-to-date on Emily Verban. Mother and newborn son, named Emil after her grandfather and namesake, were doing well. Her husband had been released on his own recognizance and had left the state. It was unlikely he would ever return. Emily had decided to go into nursing when the baby was old enough to be left with someone during the days. Edie continued to impress Paul, and vice versa. In August she told him she wanted to go into Neurology instead of neurosurgery and, true to his word, he told her he had a place for her in his residency program.

Mrs. Kell had had a small benign tumor behind her ear. Don Lenhardt removed it and she went home ten days later looking ten years younger.

Oscar Felsch, the Parkinson patient who had received the implant of adrenal tissue, was clinically unchanged. He was neither better nor worse. It was still too early to tell whether his implant would make any difference.

It was not too early, on the other hand, to evaluate the efficacy of Frank McCormick's implant. He was better. He was not cured by any means, but his schizophrenia was better. He had lied to Dr. Scala because he wanted her to think he was worse. He was sorry. He liked Dr. Scala. It had all been his father's idea. Besides, he was frightened by those smells. The smells turned out to be seizures due to a small scar from the surgery. He was started on Dilantin and phenobarb and his spells stopped. He continued to be Gerri Scala's patient and was soon doing better than he had in years.

There was nothing the hospital and its lawyers could do about their settlement with the McCormicks. They had made the offer freely and they had no recourse. Next time, Paul suggested, they might check with him before settling any case involving him. They told him they might. As Paul realized, it was also possible that the world might just be flat.

John Corrigan of course was arrested and charged with the murder of Jackie Baumer. The story didn't get very much publicity. In part this was due to the far-reaching influence of the board of trustees. In part it was a matter of timing. On the day of his arrest, a Soviet-built rocket fired by Druse tribesmen just missed Secretary of State Schultz, who was on a fact-finding mission in Lebanon. That story got the headlines. Israel blamed the PLO, who had given the rocket to the Druse. Lebanon blamed the Syrians, who had gotten the rocket from the Russians and given it to the PLO. Paul was not sure that the hospital might not have been somehow involved. It saved them a lot of publicity, and one of the trustees was a big shot in a major oil firm.

The trial, such as it was, got even less play in the newspapers and on TV. Corrigan pleaded guilty to a reduced charge of manslaughter and got three to seven years. It was Willis who convinced him to plead guilty and avoid a messy trial. The trial was brief. It opened and closed on the day the Russians shot an unarmed Korean Air passenger plane carrying two hundred and sixty-nine people out of the Soviet sky, killing all aboard. What was the plane doing over Russia? Paul refused to speculate. After all, coincidences do happen.

Tom Ward was able to find out how John Corrigan had

learned about the suit one year before the other defendants. Paul had guessed right: it had been the result of one of the little-known routines of Medical Records. Whenever a lawyer requested a record, they notified the legal office. That office reviewed the record and reported to the dean. That's what happened when Henry Arft requested the McCormick record, with one addition: the report didn't stop with Dean Willis. He discussed it with Corrigan. Only then was Medical Records given a clearance to send out the record. Right after Corrigan had reviewed the record and removed the form.

Corrigan knew all about Jackie's sexual proclivities. Not from any firsthand information. But anyone who listened to the hospital grapevine would have learned enough. He had been observing her off and on for weeks. As her behavior got more erratic, he decided what he would do. On the night of the murder, he watched her apartment from the neurology lab. From there you could see into her bedroom. Not the entire room, but enough. She rarely pulled her shades. John stayed there late that night, after urging Herb to call it a day. He had some calculations to finish on a new idea of his and would stay late, as he often did. When he saw Jackie's second visitor leave, he called her and invited himself over. She made no objection.

The building was quiet. No one saw him enter. She was wearing a thin robe which showed more than it hid. It was easy to get her to take it off and lead him into her bedroom. The rope marks that were already on her wrists completed his plan. First he stopped in her kitchen. He told her he was thirsty. When he got to her bedroom, she was on her bed, naked, waiting for him. He killed her with her own knife. The first two stabs were enough but he didn't stop with two. Then he tied her up again, using the ropes he knew he would find in her bedroom, and added a few more bruises to her body in various locations. The lab experts had found only minimal evidence of any struggle, but if she was into that sort of thing they wouldn't have expected to find much. And no pathologist could tell the difference between a bruise made one moment after death and one made just minutes earlier.

Paul and T. B. Willis reached an acceptable compromise on the consortium plan. Eighty percent of the money given to the medical center would go to goal-directed research that might result in patentable products. The remaining twenty percent would go into general research funds. The selection of investigators to be supported would be left to the medical center and would be administered "according to previously established guidelines." The dean announced it as if it had been his plan. Paul didn't care.

Floyd had been wrong about the bylaws. At first Paul thought that Floyd had set him up, but when he confronted Floyd, the younger neurologist told him he had gotten the doctored bylaws from Herb, who in turn had gotten them from John Corrigan. Paul should have figured that out himself.

Floyd did admit to typing the letter about the charts in the ceiling. But Jackie had signed it. It had been his idea. Why? He never said, but Paul knew. All was fair in love, war, and academic medicine. Especially academic medicine.

Floyd was offered a job in Texas and took it. When he left in September, he was in good health. He had no sign of AIDS. No Kaposi sarcoma for him. At least, not yet.

Carolyn started school at Northwestern and life away from home in a dorm in Evanston.

Joshua began his second year in high school. He had done a great deal of reading over the summer. He had liked *Knock on Any Door*, but he had fallen in love with Petrakis. He read every one of his books and couldn't wait to get his own copy of his new book, *Days of Vengeance*, when it was published in September.

With October, the cool weather returned, accompanied by the playoffs between the White Sox and the Baltimore Orioles. Paul was one of a small minority of Sox fans who appreciated full well that the Orioles had, in a previous incarnation, been the St. Louis Browns. The White Sox lost the playoffs. Paul and Joshua were at the last game. All in all, it had been a good year. As Paul drove home, he put on his tape of Berio's *Folk Songs*. Cathy Berberian's voice sounded as sweet to him as it ever had. The world was not such a bad place to be.

Paul and Gerri got married on a Sunday afternoon in the rabbi's study during the fifth game of the World Series. Paul's old college roommate, Jonathan Weiss, came in from Jerusalem to be the best man. George Bruyn came in from Amsterdam for the occasion, following two weeks of lecturing and touring in the U.S. On the Friday before the wedding, Paul received a letter from George with a chess move. The letter was postmarked Amsterdam and had been mailed just five days earlier. When Paul asked his old friend about this, George admitted that for the last year a computer had been playing against Paul. Paul was aghast. How could George have ever even contemplated such a despicable form of deception? The very idea was deplorable. George apologized.

About the Author

Harold L. Klawans, M.D., is a senior attending physician and professor of Neurology and Pharmacology at Rush Medical College in Chicago. He also holds the distinction of being the only American editor of the *Handbook of Clinical Neurology*, a seventy volume neurology encyclopedia. Dr. Klawans is the author of over 300 scientific articles and an author/editor of over 30 scientific books, and has written the novel *Sins of Commission*, also featuring Dr. Paul Richardson.